DADDY'S STL_ _

GIANNI HOLMES

Editor: Tanja Ongkiehong

Proofreader: Partners in Crime Books

Cover Designer: Cate Ashwood

Warning

This story consists of content that may prove triggering for readers. Please see the detailed trigger warnings in the author's note.

CONTENTS

DEAR READER,

Thanks for taking a new and exciting journey with me into the Daddy's Little Deviants world. Each book in this series will be of different and unrelated couples, so feel free to read out of order or to skip a book if the contents may cause you distress. Daddy's Stepstalker is heavy with content warning that you might find triggering. Much of what you will encounter, however, involves villains in the story. The relationship between the two main characters is sweet, and conflicts expressed are, for the most part, external in nature.

If you are absolutely sure you have no need for trigger warnings, you can skip this portion and jump right into the prologue. For those who need to prepare themselves before going in, here's a detailed list of trigger warnings and kinks. I have no desire to surprise you with anything you would not like to read in a book, and hence the full disclosure in this note.

First, let me just say that as is customary with my books, the kinks explored are merely one aspect to these character's identities and only make up a small portion of these books. They are woven into the main plot of the story but they aren't THE focus of the plot. Now that's out of the way, let's look at the nitty gritty details.

The following are content warning for events that occur off the page and are just mentioned: physical abuse, rape, forced prostitution, murder, suicide of a close friend, the death of a family pet, bullying in high school.

And the on page content warning include but are not limited to: stalking, attempted rape, non-consensual drugging, murder, manslaughter under self defense, wounding with intent, false accusation of sexual assault, torture and arson. These events occur on page and may be mild to graphic.

The kinks that you will find in this book are daddy kink with age play and mild ABDL, golden shower, spanking, cock warming, and suckling. If after reading that you're still forging ahead, once again, welcome to Daddy's Little Deviants, where the boys are rotten and only their Daddies can tame them.

Gianni Holmes

Prologue

Ari

DRESSED UP IN MY mother's lingerie, clattering around the house in her heels, was definitely not the way I wanted my parents to see me after their night out. Mom's giggles faded, and my stepdad stared at me with a combination of bewilderment and shock on his face.

My heart pounded in my chest as I glanced from him to Mom, whose features radiated disgust and dislike. She would have looked at me that way anyway, even if I hadn't been wearing the silk lingerie my stepdad bought her specially for tonight.

Mom took one look at the open bottle of wine and the half-eaten box of expensive chocolate Daddy gave her this Valentine's Day, and she advanced at me.

"You bitch!" she screeched, her hand raised. Before she could slap me, Daddy pulled me back, out of her reach. Once he had me out of harm's way, he stood between us, stopping Mom from touching me. The little shit that I was,

I held on to the back of his jacket like I was scared of the crazy woman he was trying to protect me from.

"Anne, calm down," he said. He removed my hand and turned to me. "Help me out here, buddy." His low and husky voice went straight to my dick.

"What do you need help with, Shaw?" Mom yelled. "He's a fucking deviant. I told you. Something's not right with him, but you won't listen to me. You still keep him around."

"Anne, get a hold of yourself."

Daddy's voice was calm, and I was grateful for it. She acted like I'd wanted them to catch me dressed this way. I didn't want Daddy to have a reason to believe her venomous words about me. Her solution to fixing any problem was threatening to send me off to live with my biological father, whom I didn't know from Adam.

"I'm sorry, Daddy," I whispered.

"Don't fucking call him that." Mom took a step forward, but Daddy shifted, blocking her. She peered at me around him, practically foaming at the mouth. "He's not your Daddy. He's not your anything, so stop with the sick, twisted nonsense."

"Anne, get me a glass of water, please," Daddy asked.

"No." She crossed her arms over her chest. "The minute I get out of this room, it starts all over again. He manipulates you into believing every lie that comes out of his mouth. He can't be trusted, Shaw."

"Anne, that's enough." Daddy's voice boomed in the living room, and a delicious shiver ran down my spine. It made me want to be bad, to admit that Mom wasn't wrong and I was just as wicked as she claimed. Just to have him yell at me like that. I could come so hard by him yelling. But…I couldn't.

Even though Daddy thought I was a perfect angel, I wasn't. The evidence was staring him in the face: me clad in the red lingerie he'd bought for Mom to wear when they got home from their dinner. I stood before him, decked out in her finery with her strappy heels on and makeup, and he still denied it.

I could almost see the thought turning in his mind. *Sweet little Ari could never do any wrong.* I hadn't decided yet if I ever wanted him to find out how wrong he was.

Maybe that was why I was so into him. Because he saw the best in me, even when everyone else thought differently.

Daddy steered me to a chair and gestured for me to sit. He stopped before me, which brought his crotch on eye level. He was provoking me and he didn't even notice. For him, it mattered what was going on in my head. He believed there was a reasonable explanation for me wearing Mom's sexy lingerie.

"Ari," he said calmly. "Hey, look at me. What's going on with you? What's all this about? There's gotta be an explanation, right?"

Behind him, Mom scoffed, but Daddy didn't pay her any mind. I liked that more than I should. His whole attention was on me and not her. She'd ignored me so much for all my life that I liked taking his attention away from her.

"I'm sorry." I let my bottom lip tremble. "I-I just wanted to feel pr-pretty like Mom. I ha-hate my own clothes. Hate that it's always so masculine. Why can't I have a bit of girly stuff too? I'm sorry."

Right on cue, tears spilled down my cheeks. They were mostly fake, but I was upset I wasn't allowed to wear what I wanted. Mom always made snide remarks about me looking too much like a girl. About me being too pretty for a boy and if I wore girlish clothes, people would mistake me for a girl. How did that even matter?

"It's okay. Don't cry," Daddy said. "You can buy your own."

"No, he can't!" Mom screeched. "He's a boy, Shaw. He needs to act like one."

Daddy's hand on my knee tightened. "Anne, I can't believe you right now. He's your biological son. You'll love him regardless."

"It's hard to love someone who'd do something like this. He's sick, and you need to wake up and see it already."

"I'm sorry, Mom." I met her gaze head on, but inside, I just wanted to giggle at the way she flipped out.

"Oh, save it. You're so full of shit."

"Anne!" Daddy jerked to his feet. "We need to talk in private."

"No, Shaw. I'm done with this. He's a pathological liar. I've known him longer than you, and as your wife, I need you to trust me on this. I'm not comfortable coming home to this…deviant."

"Anne —"

"Don't *Anne* me. I'm pretty sure he stole those diamond earrings you bought me."

I gasped, clutching my hand to my chest. "Why'd you say that? I'd never steal from you. You're my mother, and I love you."

"Anne, you need to cut that boy some slack." Daddy shook his head when she opened her mouth to speak. "We all need to sleep on this. We're tired and we need a break from each other before we make any more accusations and say things we don't mean. Ari, go to your room and stay there for the rest of the night unless you need to use the bathroom."

"Yes, Daddy."

My mom gritted her teeth, but this was one thing I'd never give up. I intended to call Shaw *Daddy* until they all admitted he *was* my Daddy. She stole him from me. I saw him first when I tried to win a stuffie from a carnival game. My attempts had been in vain, but we'd started talking, and I would take that as a win.

"For god's sake, take my shoes off!"

I ignored Mom and hurried out of the room. Would they see how well I walked in those heels? This wasn't the first time I wore them. I'd been practicing every chance I got. Heels were sexy, and when I paired them with the lingerie, I looked hot. Daddy was so busy trying to calm down Mom, though, I doubted he noticed.

"Bitch," I cursed under my breath.

In my bedroom, I kicked off the shoes and lined them up in my closet next to my high tops. I dropped down onto my bed and waited. It didn't take too long before they came up the stairs, Daddy reassuring Mom that it would all be fine.

Almost an hour passed when a knock sounded on the bedroom door. I was lying across my bed with my head dangling over the edge, enjoying the rush of blood flowing the wrong way. The last time Mom and I had a confrontation, she slapped me silly. I swore my ears rang for a week. I wasn't in the mood to talk to her right now.

"Ari, may I come in?"

Daddy.

"Yes, Daddy."

He'd changed into gray sweatpants, the ones that showed off his ass so well. And when he wasn't wearing any underwear? I'd use the image as spank bank material for days.

"What are you doing?" He stopped at the foot of the bed.

"Thinking."

He sat beside me. "Sit up for a minute, will you?"

He was being so serious that I didn't argue. I slowly pulled myself upright and crossed my legs, spreading the fabric of the lingerie around me.

"Are you going to send me away?" My stomach clenched at the idea. "Please don't let her send me away. Not to him. Please don't."

Daddy slung his arm around me and pulled me into his side. "Shh, I'm not going to send you away."

"Swear it," I begged. "Swear on your life that no matter what she says, you'll never send me away."

"Ari, I—"

"Please, you have to."

He kept silent, and I jerked out of his arms. What a fool I was to believe he would go against my mom. Without a word, I shuffled off the bed and walked over to the window that overlooked the quiet suburban street we lived on. I was badly in need of a smoke, but I couldn't take out my pack of cigarettes with him here. I couldn't let him see that side of me.

I'm his sweet little Ari. Always will be.

"Ari, I'm not going to let her send you away," he said from behind me. "You're a part of this family. I know everything's not good for you right now, but if I'm going to get your mother to lighten up on you, you're going to have to work harder at being nicer to her. She's your mom."

"One who tells me she regrets having me," I replied stiffly. That sort of remark would fuck with your mind when you were only eight the first time you heard it.

"I'm sure she didn't mean it. Your mom had a tough time raising a child on her own. You understand, don't you?"

No, I didn't. I never would. Not when the image of her screaming into my eight-year-old face that she wished she never had me was stuck in my mind forever. I hated her. I hated my mom, but for him, maybe I could pretend.

I was good at pretending. Like right then. He didn't know how much I wanted to back him up against the bed and climb on top of him.

"Okay, I'll try."

I saw his reflection behind me as he got up from the bed and approached me. I held my breath. If only he would slip his arms around my waist and kiss my neck. Instead, his hand came down on my head, and he stroked my hair. It was almost better than the kiss I wanted, and I melted into his touch.

"That's a good boy," he said softly. "Just a bit confused, but you're a good son."

It took everything out of me not to go down on my knees for him, but it wasn't the time. If I did it now when I was still in school, he would only start believing what Mom said about me. So I kept my mouth shut and took pleasure in him stroking me like the good boy he thought I was.

ONE

SHAW

"THIS IS YOUR LAST warning," I said sternly to the two boys sitting before me in my office. "One more strike and you're both out."

"But I didn't even do anything, man." Jonas, the eighteen-year-old who hadn't been a kid for a long time, scrunched up his face. "That fucker started it."

"Yeah, that's right. Your mom thinks I'm a good fucker."

Just like that, the two boys, whom I'd separated, launched at each other again. That was how much regard they had for me as their principal. The man who could get them kicked out of this school faster than they could say they were sorry. Again. Without meaning it.

"Hey, hey, break it up," I snapped, and when they didn't do as I said, I stepped between them, which got me a fist to the chin. My head snapped back, and I bit down hard on my tongue, the coppery tang of blood filling my mouth.

"Fuck, it was you!" Jonas cried. "You're the one who hit him."

I walked over to the wastepaper bin and spat the blood out. Damn, it was a lot more than I'd expected. The two teens were still arguing. That was it.

"You've left me with no other choice," I said calmly. "You're both suspended for ten days. Ms. Shakes will call your parents in to talk about the next step. If you don't comply with school rules, then I'll recommend the district superintendent to expel you."

"I can't be expelled," Jonas said.

"Too bad you don't show it. Now go."

When they were gone, I rocked back in my office chair and sighed. I used to find so much joy in my job, but now it was one mundane task after another. Apart from all the paperwork, I spent most of the day disciplining students. The issues were getting worse, from bullying to suicide attempts. I didn't know how many years of this I had left in me. In a couple of years, I'd be hitting fifty, and I couldn't see myself still sitting in this chair, but if not this, then what?

The bell to signal the end of school didn't come a moment too soon. At least most of the students would go home, minimizing the risks of further incidents that required my attention.

I was stuck at the office for three more hours before I got to leave. A few teachers were still in the teacher's lounge, but the last thing I wanted was company. My big, empty house was exactly what I was looking forward to. Add a bottle of Budweiser and some Sinatra while I cooked dinner, and I'd be in the right frame of mind again.

I hurried to my car, then stopped, cursing under my breath. Dammit, that wasn't what I wanted to see right now. I turned in a slow circle, but the culprit was more than likely long gone. A tall, gangly teen with a gray hoodie over their head crossed the parking lot.

"Hey!" I called out to them. "You saw who did this to my car?"

They bolted, and I wasn't crazy enough to think I could go after them and catch up. They were young and energetic, while my extra pounds would hold me back.

"Fuck!" I stared at the offensive words sprayed in white. *Cunt. Dickhead. Cocksucker.*

"Stupid kids," I muttered, mentally calculating how much it was going to cost me to get a new paint job done. The district didn't pay me enough for all this craziness. I jerked the car door open, threw my briefcase onto the seat, got in, and slammed the door shut for good measure.

On my way home, I stopped at a gas station and picked up a six-pack of beer. I parked in the garage and unlocked the side door that led inside just off the washroom. I made a beeline for the kitchen, my phone to my ear as I waited for my mechanic to pick up.

What the hell? I dropped my hand and stared. I never thought I'd see him again, but here he was, prancing around my kitchen, wearing a dress with ruffles on the hem and an apron that reminded me of the women in *I Love Lucy*.

The boy did always love his dresses, and that hadn't changed. I didn't know why, but elation filled me.

"Ari." His name fell from my lips.

He turned from the pot he was stirring on the stove and bestowed the sweetest smile on me. That face. I'd missed him. He looked the same. His bottom lip was pierced twice at the left corner, but that was all. It was almost like the day I came home and discovered he was gone. Four years ago.

"Daddy."

My ex-wife always found it weird he called me that, but I liked it. I didn't know how to explain it, but the way he said it made the title sound important. Plus, it reminded me how much I enjoyed taking care of him, having him around me.

"Jesus, Ari, where have you been?"

"Did you miss me?" he asked with a cheeky grin.

Did I miss him? A lump filled my throat. I had been devastated when I came home and discovered he was gone. Forever. My ex-wife stubbornly never told me where he was. It'd been the end of our marriage. Nothing we did could bring us back from that place of betrayal. Of her kicking him out of our home without my consent.

What consent? According to her, I had no rights whatsoever when it came to Ari.

"Yes, of course. Where have you been?"

He pulled a face and shrugged. "That hardly matters now. Are you hungry? I made your favorite stew just the way Mom always made it."

I was still too stunned to move. To think clearly. Hell, I wasn't even breathing properly. This was so unexpected. Was my mind playing tricks on me? I'd resigned myself to the fact that I'd never see him again, but here he was, in the flesh.

"Ari, I—"

"Don't you want to freshen up?" he asked me with a cheery smile. "Go! I'll be done by the time you get back."

I needed time. Time to think. To process everything that was happening. I nodded and walked out of the kitchen.

You can't trust him. He's not the sweet little angel he pretends to be around you.

My ex-wife's words stopped me in my tracks, and I turned back to Ari. She couldn't be right. He was so small, so delicate, his brown eyes so piercingly honest.

"How did you get in?" I asked.

I'd locked the door this morning, hadn't I? It was a part of my routine to double-check since a year and a half ago, when the police found my neighbor stabbed to death with a knife in his bed. They never did find his killer when the only suspect, a.k.a. me, because of the contentious nature of our relationship, had an alibi.

"Silly, Daddy. I know where you keep your spare key, remember?" His smile faded, his full bottom lip drooping.

"Why? Did I do something wrong by letting myself in? You don't want me here."

"No, Ari, that's—"

"She got through to you, didn't she?" He ripped off the apron and tossed it onto the table. "She's somehow made you believe every vile thing she used to say about me. I'm sorry. I thought you'd be happy to see me. I'll let myself out."

His eyes were full of tears when he walked by me.

If you try to hold on to him, Shaw, you're going to regret it.

I held on to him, enclosing my hand over one slender bicep. Wow, when did he get all those muscles?

"Ari, please stay." The plea fell from my lips. "I'm just a bit caught off guard, is all. It's been four years."

"Four years of me trying to find my way back to you."

Our eyes met, and I believed him. His gaze reflected nothing but honesty. He was the same sweet boy I'd known since he was fifteen.

"I'm going to change, and then we'll eat together. You can tell me everything. How does that sound?"

He nodded, a smile peeking at the corners of his lips. "Are you sure? I don't want to be any trouble. I just wanted to see you again, you know. You've always been so good to me. Better than my deadbeat dad."

"I'm sure. " And for good measure, I chucked him under his chin. His head barely reached my shoulders. He was still so incredibly small and vulnerable. The instinct to protect him reared its head again.

Some things never changed. I wasn't sure I wanted them to.

"Welcome home, Ari."

Two

Ari

"WHAT'S ALL THIS?"

A bittersweet ache filled my chest as Daddy entered the dining room, where I'd set the table for us. He'd changed into one of those sweatpants that always fucked with my brain cells, and that hadn't changed, even though he'd aged considerably in the last four years. I didn't recall the lines bracketing the corners of his mouth being that deep. His hair was more silver now too at the sides, and the six-pack he always joked he would have one day seemed nothing but a distant memory.

I liked it. He reminded me of home and how much I missed it when my mother had kicked me out.

"I set the table the way I remember you liked it." I placed the last utensil on the table and stepped back to admire my handiwork. Just like old times. Almost. I cocked my ears. Nothing but the refreshing silence of my mother's absence.

"You didn't have to go through all this trouble, Ari," Daddy said. He stared at me constantly as if he had trouble believing I was here. "We could have eaten in the kitchen. Less fuss that way."

"But you like when we eat as a family, remember?" He always insisted on it. It didn't matter that my mother and I didn't get along. When it came to mealtimes, he didn't want to hear any excuses. He would give in for breakfast but never dinner.

"That was a long time ago."

"Too long," I agreed, unable to fully keep the bitter edge out of my voice. "But I'm here now. Sit. I'll get everything from the kitchen."

I breezed by him and grabbed the salad and gravy bowls. Instead of taking a seat, he followed me into the kitchen.

"The least I can do is help."

I opened my mouth to argue, but at the gentle smile on his face, I nodded. That smile was the reason I'd stayed, even though I'd known better. I should have left before he came home from work, but I needed to see him and catch more than a glimpse this time.

Together we brought out everything to the dining room, then took our seats across from each other. I'd deliberately set a place for myself where Mom usually sat. This was my place now. For as long as I was here. When Shaw didn't comment on it, I knew I was right, even if it would take him a while to catch on.

"Are we expecting company?" Shaw chuckled. "This is enough to feed a small army."

"I might have gone a bit overboard," I said sheepishly. "If your neighbor wasn't such an asshole to you all the time, you could share the leftovers with him."

Silence fell over the table, and I glanced up from piling food on my plate.

"What? He still giving you a hard time?"

"Murray died a little over a year ago," he replied, and I could have kicked myself for bringing up the man. This wasn't exactly the atmosphere I wanted for our first dinner with me being back.

Are you really back, though?

I ignored my conscience. I had done it my entire life, so it wasn't so hard to do, especially given the past four years.

"I thought you'd be happy he's finally not making trouble for you."

The man had done everything to get to Shaw. From dumping his garbage into ours to killing our family pet, who'd crossed over into his yard. I had no remorse for him after what he'd done to poor Lilac. Our dog hadn't just died. He'd suffered.

"But the way he died…"

"How'd it happen?" I asked.

"It's too gory."

"Please. I'm not the same little boy you knew. I'm all grown up, and trust me, I have seen *too gory*."

Too much.

Again I'd said way too much.

He stared right at me with a deep frown. Had he figured out the truth yet?

"I'm sure it's a coincidence," he said. "Remember how we found Lilac before we had to put her down?"

Yeah, the fucker had slit our dog's throat but done such a piss poor job at it, Lilac had suffered. We'd gotten her to the vet in time to save her life, but still the vet had advised to put her down because of other disturbing wounds he had found on her.

"So he was tortured with the instrument of his own making?"

He nodded. "Yeah, but enough of that. What do you mean by you've seen gory? Where have you been?"

I forked a piece of beef into my mouth and chewed to give myself some time to think. When I decided to stay for a little while, I'd never thought it through fully. Like how much I should reveal to him.

"Just the world happening." I shrugged off the rest of my explanation and changed the topic. "Are you still working at the high school?"

"Yeah, I'm the principal now."

I beamed a smile at him. "They finally got rid of Mr. Polk?"

"Actually, he abandoned his work. Just didn't show up, which I thought was weird, but it seemed his house was cleared out and his car gone."

"Hmm, maybe one of the kids he used to mess with was finally going to squeal on him."

His fork clattered to the plate. "What?"

"He used to feel up the girls. Everyone knew it."

He shook his head. "No, not everyone."

That wasn't surprising. Daddy was way too good. He was oblivious to a whole lot of things that happened around him.

"That was just hearsay, Ari. Nobody proved anything."

Oh, I proved it all right, but I just shrugged.

"So do you like it? The new position?"

"It's a lot of work, but the kids are getting worse. You want to help them, but it's hard to do when they don't want to accept our help."

"Yeah?"

"Yup, just today one of them spray-painted my car."

"You know who?" I clenched the fork tighter as I thought about those punk-ass kids giving him a hard time. Shaw was a good man with a good heart. They should behave for him just like I did. Even when I was bad news in everyone else's eyes, the kindness of this man made me want to be good for him.

"One of the two boys I had to suspend today." He shrugged. "But I'm just assuming. It can be any of the kids I'd had to discipline this year or someone new entirely."

"I'm sorry."

The worry line that furrowed his brows evened out as he smiled at me. He relaxed his shoulders and took a sip of his drink.

"You have nothing to be sorry for. In fact, you being here right now is the best surprise I've had in a long time. You're everything that's good in this world, Ari."

Warmth pooled in my belly and stoked the low flame that always burned when I was around him. His kindness always turned me on more than anything else. How did a man reach this ripe old age of forty-eight and not be corrupt at all? I wanted to know, but more than ever, I wanted to preserve it. Even from me.

"What do you think about the food?" I asked.

"You're a great cook, but you always liked being in the kitchen."

"You used to joke that I'd make some man a good housewife." Fun times. I never got to spend as much time as I wanted in the kitchen, though. Mom never let me forget that was her domain and I didn't belong there.

"You remember how you used to buy me the ingredients to bake stuff, so Mom didn't know what we were up to?"

A light blush crept over his cheeks, and he shuffled in his seat. "Yeah, maybe I shouldn't have done that. She—"

"—was a horrible mom."

"Still, I went against her wishes."

"Because you realized how unfair she was being to me." Why did he still make excuses for her? "She was a bitch."

"Ari, this isn't like you."

It was exactly like me.

"Why are you still defending her?" I asked. "You saw everything she did to me, the way she treated me. Why did you even marry her?"

Shaw gaped at me, his eyes bulging. This wasn't what I wanted at all. This wasn't supposed to be about her. We were supposed to move past the fact that he ever married her and go right to the part where we wound up together.

"I'm sorry." I pushed away from the table, the chair legs scraping on the floor. "I made apple pie for dessert, with vanilla ice cream." His favorite. His taste was so much like him. Plain and dull, yet that turned me on more than all the excitement of the past four years.

"Ari, wait!"

I darted to the kitchen, needing the moment to get myself back under control. My hands shook as I took the tub of ice cream out of the freezer and placed it on the counter.

"You're right. Your mother was never truly kind to you," Shaw said, entering the kitchen.

"Bowls," I said, forcing cheer in my voice as I opened the lower cabinets and peered inside. "I know I spotted them somewhere earlier."

Please get the point. I don't want to talk about this.

"Ari, please stop. I'm trying to talk to you."

If only I could ignore the plea in his voice, continue pretending that nothing was out of the ordinary. That me wearing my favorite fifties' swing dress and heels, cooking meals for him, and being the perfect "housewife" would get him to see me differently. The way he'd seen *her* differently.

My mom.

Otherwise, it didn't make sense that a man so good would end up with a woman so wrong for him. Maybe if I became what she'd been to him, he would keep me for one minute longer than he should. Because if she was wrong for him, I'd be the death of him.

"Can't we just eat ice cream and forget everything?" I made one last effort to give him my best smile. The one that brought out the dimples in my cheeks.

"No, we can't. We have to talk about it."

"Why?" I dropped my smile and faced him. "What do you want me to say? That you promised me you'd not let her send me away, and you broke that promise? That for so long I felt betrayed and hurt that you never got her to bring me back?"

"Ari." My name was a torn cry from his throat. "I know I let you down and I'm so sorry, but you have to understand I didn't know what she was up to. I never agreed to have her take you away. In fact, she told me you wanted to visit your dad for a while but you would be back."

"And you believed her?"

"I didn't know what else to think." He made a step toward me, and I took one back. "She'd been feeding me information for a while that your biological father wasn't doing well. I thought…I thought you wanted to see him before things got worse. It would only be for one week of summer, she said. Then she kept telling me you liked it there."

"Why didn't you call me if you were worried?"

"Because I told myself if you were really in trouble, *you* would know to call me. When you didn't, I assumed she was right and you preferred to stay there."

Was he lying? As one who'd mastered the art, I knew to look for another person's tell, but I saw none. He was pale, his eyes tortured as if he'd been as upset as me when my mother sent me away.

"I was hurt that you left without a good-bye," he added.

I retracted that one step I'd taken back and crossed the distance between us. I grabbed the hem of his T-shirt and tugged on it. "I didn't want to leave. I swear I didn't, but she made me. She-she…" I shook my head. No, I couldn't tell him the truth.

Frustrated tears filled my eyes, and my shoulders shook with the effort not to break down fully. I didn't cry anymore. I had toughened up. Silly pranks turned into deadly games. Half truths turned into deception and traps. Yet the tears came faster, and a sob tore from my throat.

I'd missed him so much. He was the only man in my life who'd shown me any kindness, and my mother had taken that away from me out of jealousy. Because she'd feared he paid me too much attention, and one day, he would leave her.

"Oh god, Ari, I'm so sorry." He wrapped his arms around me, and his warmth engulfed me. This was why I came back. I'd forgotten what it felt like to have someone care about me and not just because of what I could do for them. I'd forgotten how to feel. The blood running through my veins turned to ice and cut off my emotions for every wrong deed I committed.

"You promised." I sniffed hard. "You were supposed to stop her."

"Jesus, Ari, you're killing me every time I think about what you went through." He rubbed my back comfortingly. "Tell me he was at least good to you."

He was worse. He made a monster seem like an imaginary friend. What he'd done to me...I could never forget. And thankfully, I didn't need to forgive a dead man.

"He wasn't a good father like you." The understatement of the year. "But he wasn't so bad."

"I don't get why you didn't call me. Why did you stay if you wanted to come back?"

Because dear Mom had been smart and ensured I had no choice in the matter.

"I thought it was best."

He scoffed. "A whole lot of good that did. Only when she walked out did she admit you didn't have a choice in leaving. She seemed positive I'd see you again. Told me to ask you why you had to leave when I did."

"I didn't want to be responsible for your marriage falling apart." I pulled back from his chest so I could see his face. I had to know if he believed the words coming out of my mouth. "I knew she'd been acting crazy about us, accusing you of sleeping with me. I was afraid she would do something stupid like make an untrue report to the police."

His body stiffened against mine. He dropped his arms and stepped back.

"Your mother had issues."

If he thought she had issues boy, was he in for a shock.

"Yeah, she did."

He walked over to the counter, ripped off a couple of paper towels, and returned to me. He raised his hand, then paused and handed me the towel.

"Your mascara's running a little," he said.

I giggled. "I missed this. Having someone around who doesn't disapprove every time I wear makeup and a dress."

"Whatever makes you happy, Ari."

What if I tell you that being with you would make me happy?

"I should probably go upstairs and clean this makeup off." I felt better now that I was a hundred percent sure he hadn't been in on my mother's crazy plot to send me away. It had weighed heavier on me than I'd thought.

I would have forgiven him for it, but this was so much better.

"You do that, and I'll get the ice cream and pie for us," he said.

"Sounds good."

I shuffled past him, but he stepped neatly in my way.

"I came to find you, you know."

My breath caught in my throat. This I hadn't expected.

"You did?"

"Yes, but I was too late. The neighbors told me you already moved on with your dad, and I wasn't sure where else to look."

THREE

SHAW

I WOKE UP WITH a start. Ari was standing over me as if his singular purpose in life was to watch me sleep. As I straightened up, he stepped back. A pair of black skin-tight jeans hugged his slender waist. They were ripped and showed off the fishnets he wore beneath. The long-sleeved cherry-red top alluded to being modest if not for his bare, toned stomach peeking through in the loose cropped style.

A bit of jewelry glittered from his navel, and since when had he gotten a tattoo? Ink climbed up from his jeans at the side and snaked to his back.

My cock twitched. Way more than that. I was getting hard from looking at my stepson, something that never happened before. But then I never saw this grown-up version of Ari before now. Sultry yet sweet. Innocent yet tempting. So damn fuckable.

A conversation I had with Anne played in my mind.

"Don't you want me anymore?"

In the darkness, I shifted on my side to face Anne, even though I couldn't see her. I was still able to make out the stiff, unyielding lump in bed beside me.

"What are you talking about, Anne?"

"I'm talking about the fact that we haven't had sex in two months."

That long? I searched my mind to prove her wrong, but it was futile. With doing more than my share of work as the vice principal of a public school and having to act as a referee between her and Ari, it was draining coming into a household where the atmosphere was rife with tension.

"We'll make some time tomorrow," I said.

"You make it sound so clinical. Like I need an appointment to fuck my husband."

"I'm just tired, Anne." Even if I was willing, I doubted I could get hard.

"I'll be on top." She ran a hand over my chest. "You can enjoy the ride, baby."

"I don't know. Ari's still up."

She laughed softly. "Ari's not a baby. He knows we're fucking."

"Don't say that. It makes me feel uncomfortable. You can be loud sometimes."

"Shaw, that boy's getting dick more than I am. He's not a prude."

I rolled over and turned on the bedside lamp. "I'm sure that's not true. Why do you always have to put him down?"

"Why do you always defend him? Maybe it'll do him some good to hear us fucking. Then he'd know you're my husband. Not his. That you'll never have sex with him."

"Now you're being ridiculous."

She sat up as I rolled out of bed. My stomach clenched in tied knots. All I could see was Ari's innocent, shy smile. Why would she even think that of the boy? Besides, there was no way she knew I was also into men. I hadn't shared that side of myself with her after seeing the way she was with Ari because he was flamboyantly gay.

"You keep denying it, Shaw, and I'm going to start believing you actually want to fuck him."

What? I gaped at her. She had insinuated more than once that I was sleeping with her son behind her back, but this was the first time she'd ever been so bold as to spill it out.

"Don't look at me like that. You think you're the first grown-ass man who's fallen for his little innocent act? Why do you think your neighbor does his best to get to you?"

I eyed her warily. "What are you talking about?"

"I've seen Ari flirting with Murray. The man's clearly jealous because he thinks you're fucking the boy he wants."

I pinned her with a glare. "And what do you think, Anne? Do you really believe I'd sleep with your son?"

Anne hadn't answered me that night, and as I stared at Ari now, a deep sense of shame washed over me. How could I even look at him that way? How could I validate what Anne had been obsessed with almost our entire marriage?

"You don't want me to go out," Ari said, even though I hadn't spoken.

I quickly tried to disguise the truth with a smile. "You're old enough to do what you want, Ari."

"But if you'd rather I stick around and keep you company, I can stay."

Bad idea. Bad, bad idea. I needed to fix what the hell was broken with me that I thought this way about him, but I couldn't do this with him around.

"No, no, go have fun." I waved at him. "You have friends I'm sure you're dying to catch up with while you're here. By the way, you never said how long you're staying."

He exaggerated a gasp. "You're already tired of having me here?"

"Of course not, brat." It was supposed to come out as a joke or teasing manner. We'd always had that easygoing banter between us, and I'd never thought twice about it before. But after my crazy chemical reaction to him, it sounded different. Sexual. Like something I would say to a lover.

His face stretched into a charming smile. "You've never called me *brat* before."

"Yeah, well." I cleared my throat. "Where are you heading off to anyway?"

He shrugged. "I'm meeting a couple of guys at a bar for a drink."

"There better not be a bar that'll sell drinks to a minor."

Ari chuckled. "I turned twenty-one two months ago, Daddy."

A shiver ran down my spine. He always called me that, and I'd never thought much of it, though it had annoyed the hell out of my ex-wife. Now all the blood rushed to my cock. His soft purr and sweet innocence pulled me in like a moth drawn to a flame. Goddammit. The very idea of getting singed excited me. And there was no mistake that I would burn if I touched him.

"That's right." I swallowed away the lump in my throat. "I've missed four birthdays."

"Yeah, you did."

Had they been happy birthdays or sad ones? I'd taken this boy in, sworn to protect him, and failed so miserably.

"Go have fun," I said sincerely. "You deserve it, and thanks for dinner."

"You're welcome, Daddy."

I shifted on the couch, grabbed one of the cushions, and discreetly placed it on my lap. Damn, damn, damn.

"Do you want to borrow my car?" I asked. "It's covered in spray-paint, but—"

"Actually, I called a cab. Just waiting for it to get here."

And right on time too. A car drove up to the house. Then a horn blasted.

"Your ride's here."

"Yeah, I'll be back soon, but don't wait up. Four years is a long time to catch up."

Don't I know it?

What had he been doing for the past four years? I would wait to ask him. Dinner had already been overwhelming for both of us. I could get more answers tomorrow.

"If you need anything, a ride home, call me."

He nodded, then leaned in and kissed my cheek. "Thank you. It's been a while since someone really cared."

My heart broke for him. I wanted to know what he'd been through, but I just watched him go, stifling my groan. Ari had grown and filled out his jeans in a way I didn't recall at all. I couldn't stop staring.

Never in a million years would I have thought Ari would get tattoos or pierce his belly button and lip. Butterflies, intertwined with delicate petals and vines, snaked up from the waistband of his jeans and disappeared under his top. Did his tattoos extend all over his back?

It suited Ari more than I wanted to admit.

"Later, Daddy."

I couldn't answer him through the lump in my throat. The front door closed with a thud, and I collapsed against the back of the sofa and exhaled.

"Jesus, you're disgusting," I muttered, passing a hand over my face. The urge to go upstairs and rub one out was strong. It'd been so long since anyone turned me on the way he did. My cock was so hard it felt like I would burst if I didn't get it all out, but I couldn't. How could I jerk off knowing Ari had prompted this arousal?

I couldn't prove Anne right.

I pressed a hand down hard on my cock to adjust it so it didn't hurt so much.

"Damn."

It felt so good. Disgust and shame roiled into pleasure. I wouldn't do it to get off. Just to fuck. Ari's sweet face and plump lips flashed through my mind. Eyes so expressive, body just begging to be touched.

A choked cry startled out of me. My body stiffened as I came in my pants. A blissful calm washed over me as I fell back against the sofa, panting.

"Daddy, you okay?"

I snapped my head up. Ari was standing in the doorway, his eyes wide. How much had he seen? Had he heard me come?

My face flamed. I was pathetic, sitting there with pants full of cum from my almost incestuous thoughts of my stepson.

"I, uhm, I'm fine." Better to pretend nothing happened in case he didn't actually see anything. "Did you change your mind about going out?"

He brandished his phone. "I came back for this. I'm going now."

"'Kay. Have fun."

And stay away from the twisted son of a bitch that I am. He didn't need me adding this to his plate.

I waited until the car engine faded away before I ran up the stairs to hide the evidence of my sick perversion. In the bathroom, I changed out of my clothes and took a shower.

I felt dirty. Even dirtier when my cock got hard again. Something that never happened so fast after I'd come.

What the hell's wrong with me?

I stumbled out of the shower, hastily dried off, and changed into a pair of pajamas. On my way downstairs, I passed Ari's old bedroom. I really shouldn't invade his privacy, but just a peek would be all right, wouldn't it? I pushed the door open farther.

On the bed was one bag. He didn't plan to stay for long, then. The stuffed sloth I'd won him at the carnival six years ago lay on the bed beside his bag. The open closet door revealed two dresses similar to the one he'd worn for dinner tonight. In the corner where his computer desk had sat empty for so long, an electric-blue laptop was plugged in. Nothing that couldn't be packed up and moved out again in no time.

I closed the door soundly and returned downstairs to catch the nightly news. Little good did it do me, though. I kept watching the clock. What was Ari doing now? He reminded me he was no longer a kid. He had the legal right to drink if he wanted to. To do things I didn't even want to contemplate.

It was none of my business. Then why did thinking about Ari with some other man made me feel all tight and bothered?

If it wasn't a school night, I would have drunk the disturbing thoughts away, but no such luck. Not even sleep was a reprieve. I dreamed of Ari, naked in bed with a man who turned out to be my next-door neighbor, Murray.

Disoriented, I woke up. The room was dark, the television timed out. My heart beat steady and hard inside my chest. What had woken me up? Was Ari home?

A thump sounded outside the house. What was that? I heaved myself out of the cushion and stood, still groggy and unsteady on my feet. The thumps continued, getting louder as I stumbled to the hall.

"Goddamn it, Ari. Your body's made for fucking."

I froze. The nightmare of a few seconds ago turned into reality. The voice wasn't Murray's. It couldn't be, since he was dead, but Murray or someone else, did it make a difference? Envy burned in my stomach, but instead of giving in to it, I took a step back.

"Please stop." I halted at Ari's soft-spoken plea. "Please. I told you no. I don't want this."

"You're so fucking good." The gruff words were followed by a laugh. "Keep that up. Tell me how much you don't want this."

"I don't. Get off me! Don't touch me!"

I'd heard enough. I yanked the door open and stepped onto the porch, where Ari was being pushed back against the wall. A young man, taller than him, caged him in; his hands—what I could make of them—groped Ari's backside while a much more slender Ari tried in vain to push him off.

"Please don't. I just wanted you to take me home, that's all."

I rushed forward, grabbed the man's shirt, and dragged him away from Ari. He stumbled back, arms flailing as he tried to keep his balance.

"What the fuck?" he cried out.

I didn't wait for him to regain his equilibrium. I punched him in the face and pushed him down the steps.

"Get the fuck away from him!" I growled, my chest heaving. It took everything inside me not to beat him to a bloody pulp. His bloody nose wasn't nearly damage enough.

"You broke my nose," the guy yelled. "I was just doing what he asked me to do. Tell him, Ari."

"I told you to stop," Ari sniffled. "I didn't mean to lead you on. I just wanted a drive home. That's all."

"You lying bitch, tell him the truth! That you begged for this. You didn't want me to stop."

"Get in the house, Ari," I said through clenched teeth. He shuffled away from the wall and rushed through the doorway.

"Ari, you tell him the truth right now, you fucking tease!"

I clambered down the steps, and he ran toward the car parked in the driveway.

"Get off my property!"

"He's a liar. A fucking liar. You keep him away from me, or I'm gonna fuck him up for what he did."

He dove into his car and backed out of the driveway. I watched until he rounded the corner, then made my way back inside, slamming the door shut behind me. Ari yelped. He was huddled against the wall, his arms wrapped around his body.

"I'm sorry," he said, his head bowed. "It's all my fault."

"No, no, you're not going to blame yourself for him putting his hands all over you." I slowly approached him, meaning to give him just comforting words, but this was Ari. The sweetest boy I knew. I couldn't let him suffer like this alone. I held out my hand, and with a sob, he scrambled up and dove right into my arms.

"I shouldn't have gone with him," he sniffed, face pressed to my shirt front. "I just didn't want to disturb you. I know you have to work tomorrow."

"I'm not going to blame you for what that asshole tried to do to you." I tucked his head under my chin, my heart pounding. What if I hadn't woken up when I did? He was so small. He wouldn't have stood a chance against that other guy.

"I did kiss him," he whispered. "But it was only supposed to be one kiss."

"It doesn't matter if you gave him a kiss. The moment you said stop, he should have backed off."

"You're not mad at me?"

I groaned. If only I had that asshole before me again so I could deliver another punch. This time I'd knock him out and call the cops to deal with him. He'd touched Ari. *My* Ari.

"You need to file a complaint against him at the police station."

He shook his head. "Please don't make me. I just want to forget it happened."

"If he tries anything—"

"I won't give him the chance. I was being stupid when he offered me that ride and I accepted."

I tipped his head so I could see his face. "You know him?"

"Yeah, he was a year ahead of me in high school."

Which meant I should know him as well, but I never got a good look at his face. I'd been too enraged to see straight.

"Did he hurt you?"

His head fell forward. "No, I'm fine. He just felt me up."

A shiver ran through him, and I rubbed his back. "It's okay. You're fine now. I've got you. No one can hurt you anymore."

Not his mother. Not his dad, and not that asshole who tried to take something he wasn't interested in giving.

"I should go up to bed," he said.

I slowly loosened my hold on him, reluctant to let him go. "Yes, do that. I'll go to bed as well. If you need anything, let me know."

When I didn't move, he eyed me. "Are you coming?"

"I just have to check the locks before we turn in. Murray's killer was never found, and I don't want to take any chances. Go on up."

"Good night, Daddy."

"'Night, Ari. Sweet dreams."

He climbed the stairs, and I checked the front door. I didn't just check the doors, but I also tested the windows. Although I supposed anyone determined enough would be able to bust through the glass and make their way inside.

I trudged up the stairs, the day taking a mental toll on me. At my bedroom door, I stopped and stared at Ari's. I wanted to check up on him to make sure he was still fine. No, I'd better not. God, these feelings were so confusing. I shouldn't go anywhere near him.

I dragged my feet over to the bed and stripped the bed covers down. I sighed as I sank into the softness of the mattress. Falling asleep on the couch hadn't been the smartest move, but at least everything was the way it should be now. I was in bed, and Ari was home, safe and sound.

In the early morning, my bladder woke me up. I shuffled to the bathroom, not bothering to turn on the lights, and relieved myself. I returned to my bed, plumped up my pillow, and slid under the covers. My feet bumped against something hard.

I clicked on the bedside lamp. Ari was curled up at the foot of my bed, with his arms wrapped around his body. He was fast asleep, his face relaxed and so precious. I watched him sleep, protective instincts filling my chest. He must have been so scared that he hadn't been able to sleep in his own bed.

I tucked the end of the sheet around him securely. He sighed, his eyelids fluttering open. I froze. Would he wake up fully and panic at the sight of me hovering over him?

"Daddy," he whispered. Then his eyelids drifted back to a close. "Love you."

It wasn't the first time he told me he loved me. Why I suddenly felt lightheaded was beyond me.

"I love you too, Ari." Not the first time I'd told him this either, so why did it feel different this time? Why did it feel like so much more?

Four

Four

I LOST TRACK OF how much time passed as I lay in bed watching Daddy sleep. I had no idea if he'd woken up in the night and seen me in his bed. Common sense dictated I leave before he woke up, but I couldn't make myself get up just yet. For as long as I could remember, this had been my dream. To go to sleep lying next to him and waking up with him still there.

In sleep, he seemed younger. He was sprawled on his back, the sheet tangled around his legs. Snores were always considered annoying, but his were sexy—soft puffs through his slightly parted lips.

I moved slowly so I didn't wake him as I positioned myself next to him. Much better. With my head on the pillow next to his, I almost wished Mom was here seeing me now.

Look at me taking your place. Didn't think that would happen, did ya, Mom?

My eyes roved his face and down his body. His shirt flattened over his torso, and the hem rode up high on his soft, hairy stomach. I wanted to rub my face all over that pudgy belly like a kitten, and my cock was on board with the idea. If only I was certain of how he would react.

I dared to do a lot of things in my life, but none with a greater risk than the one I was about to take. If he woke up and discovered what I was doing, there was no telling what he would do. Would he be disgusted or intrigued? Sometimes the way he looked at me made me feel we were on the same page, but he was—always had been—the perfect father figure. I couldn't bear for him to wake up and find repulsion in his eyes.

But I could no sooner stop my actions than I could stop loving this man. Obsessing over him. I shifted onto my back and slid one leg forward. I snaked my hand down my belly and into the waistband of my shorts and wrapped it around my erection. A soft moan spilled from my throat, my heart thumping hard in my chest at the risk of being discovered.

My hand was dry, which made it more difficult. I brought my hand to my mouth and spat, then rubbed the saliva over my shaft. So fucking good. For a hand job. It would have to do until he finally caved in, spread my legs, and took what I wanted to give him. I wanted his hands pressing my knees into my chest as he fucked me.

Would I be able to act innocent then, or would the dirty words fall from my lips as I begged him to pound my hole harder? He would treat me like glass in bed. His precious china. Would it be safe to show him who I truly was? Or would he be disgusted in his beloved Ari?

His dirty little boy, who made himself feel so good while watching him sleep. Oh, if only he would wake up. Be surprised at the sight of me but not repulsed. Never repulsed. I wanted him to brush my hand away and take over, his mouth mastering my cock to the point of its submission.

My back tingled, tightened, bowed under the onslaught. I bit into my bottom lip to stem the cry that threatened to come.

There was no stopping it.

My body trembled from the full force of my climax. I lay on the bed, catching my breath, and still he slept, oblivious to the pleasure he'd brought me.

If not for the soiled shorts, I would have remained in bed with him and damn the consequences. Facing him with cum stuck to my skin wasn't the way I wanted to have this discussion, though, so I rolled out of bed and tiptoed back to my bedroom. I wanted to take a shot of his sleeping form to add to my collection, but my phone was in my room, and I didn't dare to double back and wake him.

I took a shower, then sat at my desk, sketching dresses inspired by a 1950s swing style. The design program I used helped me to draw much faster, but sometimes I preferred to sketch in my notepad. My phone ringing startled me.

I ignored the call—I had a good idea who was calling—and when it rang again, I turned off the sound and headed for the kitchen to get started on breakfast. Being here in Coleyville was safe. No one knew where I was, so it was the perfect spot to lie low for a while.

I finished preparing breakfast, which came out perfectly. I rewarded myself with a cup of hot chocolate. Leaning against the counter, I stared out the window at the fresh morning unfolding. I hadn't felt this peaceful and settled in a long time. Since never, really. Even when I lived here before, tension had been thick and heavy. Mostly because of my mother, who had delighted in ruffling my feathers.

Now my heart threatened to burst as hope welled up inside. Maybe this was the chance to start over. I could be good and be everything Daddy wanted. I'd take care of him and the house, and he would continue to adore me.

"Good morning, Ari."

I jerked around. Still dressed in his jammies, Shaw looked rumpled and sexy. He didn't even know it, which made him even more appealing.

"Good morning, Daddy."

A blush rose in his stubbly cheeks, and he took a quick intake of breath. Interesting. That hadn't happened before when I called him Daddy.

"You didn't have to go through all this trouble." He gestured at the table. "I don't expect you to wait on me hand and foot."

I shrugged. "I don't mind. It keeps me busy."

"I usually just have a fruit in the morning and make up for it at lunch." He rubbed at his pudgy stomach. "Although my body's not about to thank me."

"Silly, Daddy," I said with a smile.

"Are you mocking me?"

I shook my head and placed the mug on the counter. "Nope. I just think you look good the way you are." I fussed with the coffeemaker. "Sit. Let me get you coffee."

I'd already gotten out his favorite mug, and I poured his coffee the way he liked it. No creamer, just a bit of sugar.

"Did you...sleep okay?" he asked, not looking at me.

So he did know I slept at the foot of his bed last night.

"I should have asked before I snuck into your room." I placed the mug in front of him. "I'm sorry. I just couldn't sleep after what happened."

He caught my hand and squeezed. "Are you sure you don't want to take my advice and report it?"

"No. It'll only be embarrassing to talk about. But I never thanked you for intervening. If you hadn't been there..."

A class act. That was what I was, choking on a manufactured sob. In a split second, Shaw was up and pulled me into his arms. I hid my face into his chest and smiled at the comfort I found there. This was home. Always. Not even a twinge of remorse rippled through me for what happened last night. Rich deserved it for past unforgotten wrongs. I wasn't done with him yet.

"Do you want me to stay home with you today to ensure you're okay?" he asked. "I can take a personal day."

As much as I'd love that, I had errands to run. "I'll be fine. I just need a minute."

"Take all the time you need. You're safe now."

Eventually, he had to release me, and I sighed when he did.

"Better?" he asked.

"Everything's always better with a hug. Your hug."

I busied myself with preparing him a plate but sent surreptitious glances his way. He watched me, and a shiver ran down my spine. I liked his eyes fine where they were. Firmly placed on me. Was he feeling it yet? How right we were for each other?

"This is great, Ari," Shaw said as I set down his plate laden with lightly browned waffles and hash browns with a slice of raisin bread and apple butter.

"I like taking care of you," I said softly. "You've always been good to me."

"You're too good for this world."

I giggled. "Not when you're in it."

Too much too soon? He didn't speak, a frown marring his forehead like he was struggling to decide what to say. I knew that well enough, always measuring my words so I didn't push too far.

"Sit with me," he said. "Did you eat already?"

"I'm not really hungry in the morning."

"If I'm eating breakfast, so are you. You could do with a little fattening up."

I ran a hand down my body. "Is that your way of telling me I'm too skinny?"

His mouth bobbed open as he watched my slowly wandering hands down my sides and hips. If only they weren't so narrow, but I couldn't do anything about it that didn't involve going under the knife.

"Um, you're perfect the way you are." He cocked his head to one side. "Isn't that your mother's?"

He gestured at me. I'd found a shirt of my mother's in their closet. It was too big for me, but with a woven belt wrapped around my waist, it fitted me perfectly as a dress.

"I hope you don't mind. I didn't bring many clothes with me."

He nodded. "Does that mean you're not staying long?"

He'd asked me that question last night, which I'd ignored, teasing him with one of my own instead.

"It depends." I bit my bottom lip and peeked at him through my eyelashes. *Take the hint, Daddy. You're the reason I'll stay, even though I'm not supposed to.*

"On what?"

"If I feel comfortable here."

Alarm flashed over his face. "You're not? Did I do anything to make you feel that way?"

"No, no, don't worry about it. You're the only person I trust in this world never to hurt me."

"Ari."

I stared into his eyes, and I could swear the want was inside, but he would never act on it himself.

"Yes, Daddy?"

"Maybe it's time you stop calling me that."

Not exactly what I'd expected him to say. "Why? I like it. I don't think I could stop now." And I meant more than calling him Daddy. I couldn't stop stalking him, couldn't stop needing him, couldn't stop killing for him.

"It's a bit awkward now that your mom and I are divorced."

"You think I call you Daddy because you married her?" I scoffed. Silly, silly Daddy. So clueless. If I didn't love him so much, I'd toy with him.

Maybe I still would, just a little.

"You don't?"

"Me calling you Daddy has nothing to do with Mom." I joined him at the table with only a slice of bread and apple butter. "I do that because of what you've been to me."

"Like a father, you mean?"

My response was a grunt. If that made him feel better.

After Shaw went off for work, I got some more sketches done. When I was satisfied with the designs, I took out Mom's old sewing machine from the attic and dusted it off. Just another symbol of her unfair treatment and unwilling acceptance of who I was.

Shaw bought her the machine, but she admitted she had no patience to learn how to use it. When I expressed interest in learning, she agreed. Until she saw my first creation—a beautiful dress in my size, not hers. She'd confiscated the machine and placed it in the attic. Not even Daddy had been able to persuade her to allow me to use it.

Before he left for work, Shaw had asked me to drop off his car for him at the garage. It was a perfect opportunity to get the fabric I needed. I changed into jeans and a cutoff T-shirt and slipped my pocket knife into the waistband and the other inside my left boot.

After all, I heard a killer was loose on the street.

Giggling, I backed out of the garage. Damn, I'd left my phone again. I hated the thing and often forgot it, but I'd given Daddy my phone number, and if he called, I didn't want to miss it.

I parked the car in the driveway and ran back inside. As I hurried down the stairs, I swiped away the missed calls from the same number as earlier. I shut the front door behind me and rushed to the car.

Hands grabbed me from behind and slammed me into the vehicle. My phone fell to the pavement, the glass shattering.

"You think you were gonna get away with what you did last night?" a raspy voice growled into my ear. "You practically accused me of rape."

I relaxed. Rich. For a minute, I'd thought someone from my past found me. I had a habit of pissing men off, but I could handle Rich.

"Relax, Rich. It was a joke inspired by what you did to me in the locker room five years ago. Remember when I begged you back then not to, but you didn't listen?"

"That's beside the point." He was so close his hot breath warmed my cheek while his hard dick poked me in the lower back. Even though he was angry about last night, he still wanted to fuck me. "You set me up for your old man to attack me."

"I don't know what you're talking about."

"Don't fucking lie to me." He yanked at my hair. Ouch, that hurt. He pressed his crotch against my ass, humping me through our clothes. "You told me it was a game. That I should touch you anyway I wanted, and if you said no, that it just meant I should do it harder. That's what you said."

"Except you can't prove it."

"I can't, but I can fucking take what you promised me, you cocktease."

"So you're gonna do what? Rape me right here in plain sight?"

He yanked me back by the hair. Tears pricked my eyes. He flung the back door open and shoved me inside. I went along with it, twisting at the last minute to fall on my back. I tugged my knife from my waistband just as he tumbled in after me, sprawling on top of me.

"Now that's much better." He leered down at me, wedging himself between my legs. "You were begging for it back then in the locker room too. Anyone ever told you your mouth's made for sucking dick? That's still the best head anyone has ever given me, and it was your first time, wasn't it? So you must suck dick like a pro now, huh?"

"I'm pretty good at it," I said truthfully. "There have been many over the years."

"Slut. Are you good at spreading your legs too?" He laughed, his breaths shallow and quick in his excitement. "No, don't answer that. I'll know for myself 'cause I want in this time. In that tight little ass." He roughly pushed his hands under my shirt, more aggressive than last night. He pinched my nipples, and I gasped at the sting.

"Get off me, Rich." I gave him the opportunity to do the right thing. "I don't want to hurt you."

"Still playing your little game, huh? Well, guess your stepdaddy ain't here to protect you this time. I'll get off you when your ass is dripping wet from me coming so hard inside you. You like the sound of that?"

"The fuck, Rich! For the last time, get off me."

"Don't worry. I promise it'll feel better than when your stepdad sticks it inside you. Bet he can't get it up for long." His hand wandered to the front of my jeans. "What do you see in him anyway? He's old, fat, and ugly while you're so fucking pretty. Can have any man you want. Straight ones too. You're pretty enough."

I plunged the knife into his stomach. He stilled on top of me, his eyes bulging, his mouth forming a big O.

"You stabbed me."

"No, don't stop." I loved the look of fear on his face. I even licked his jaw. "Tell me everything you're gonna do to me. But I especially love the part where you talk shit about my Daddy." I twisted the knife and pushed deeper. "Do you know why he'll have me in his bed and you won't? Because he's a good man, Rich. Everything you're not. I tried to give you a chance, but you just wouldn't listen."

"Fucking bitch," he grated out, grabbing my hand. "Stop, please. What the fuck did you do?"

He tried to pull back, but I wrapped my legs around his waist, trapping him in the back seat with me. Blood dripped on my skin, but I held on tight as we grappled.

"Stop it!" He only managed a hoarse cry. "Call the ambulance. Please call the fucking ambulance."

"It's too late for you, Rich." I chuckled, stroking my bloody hand along his jaw, leaving a red streak. "Now why don't we play another favorite game of mine? It's called 'let's see how long it takes before you bleed out.' But do try not to bleed too much on Daddy's car seat. Blood never truly comes out, you know. I bet you're wondering how I know that."

"Please, Ari—"

"Shh." I kept my legs locked around him, twisting the knife so deep he screamed. "You want to keep holding that knife as long as possible. I wouldn't want your guts spilling out on the floor. That's just fucking gross."

Rich's pained eyes met mine. "You're a psycho."

"Hey, no need for name-calling. If you want to get into my good graces, you might want to apologize. Start with what happened in the locker room five years ago and make your way to all the mean things you just said about my Daddy."

"I'm sorry…"

I adopted a sincere expression on my face, while inside, I was laughing. There was nothing better than giving them false hope, only to take it away.

FIVE

SHAW

FOR THE THIRD TIME that day, I punched in my ex-wife's number but deleted it without letting it ring. I placed the phone on my desk and rocked back in my comfortable chair. The one thing in the office I splurged on. Since I was on my ass for most of the day, I'd figured it was a worthwhile investment.

I took up the file about the new student, an Army kid who would likely not be around for long.

The phone buzzing on my desk interrupted my work. That must be Anne. I shook my head. Of course it couldn't be her. I never made those calls to her. Besides, it was the landline ringing: my secretary.

"Yes, Julieta?"

"I have a parent requesting to speak with you, sir. Do you want to set up an appointment, or do you happen to be free and can take him now?"

She knew damn well I had no pressing matters to deal with. I'd immersed myself in work all morning to stop myself from checking up on Ari every minute. From calling an Uber to take me home to make sure he was still there and wouldn't disappear on me again.

"Who is it?" Hopefully, I'd know the student enough to mentally prepare before the parent walked through the door.

"Judd O'Connor."

Shit, I almost asked her to make up an excuse, but there was never a good time to deal with Judd. We both grew up in Coleyville, and I knew too much about his history. Always got in trouble in school until he was finally kicked out. His wife moved out on him, leaving behind their only son. She should have taken the kid too, but the boy was already so much like the dad.

"You can send him in, in five."

"Will do."

I hung up and used the five minutes to take deep breaths, knowing full well what the conversation would be about. It wasn't the first time he'd shown up or called. The last time he was here, he accused the system of failing his son and threatened to pull his kid out of school. He never once assessed the role he was playing in raising a juvenile delinquent.

The door swung open, banging against the wall, and in barged Judd as if he owned the place. Pompous ass. He must have come straight from work. He still wore his hard yellow hat and a safety vest. His boots were dusty and beaten up, but somehow women always found that appealing. It didn't hurt that he was built like a tank and had a crude charm about him.

"Shaw, what's this I hear about my kid being suspended again?" He made no effort to mince words as he slammed the door closed behind him.

"He got into another fight, Mr. O'Connor. You—"

"Why don't you cut the *Mr. O'Connor* bullshit. We went to school together, man. You're not seriously recommending the board remove my son from the school, are you? Because that's some kind of fucking stunt you're pulling right there."

"Your son is out of control," I said calmly. "During his last altercation, another student had to be taken to the hospital and needed a couple of stitches."

"They got a little rough, so what? Boys will be boys."

"I'm sorry, but it can't be ignored anymore."

He stalked up to my desk, glaring at me. "You have a responsibility to my son."

"And I also have a responsibility to all the other students in my care that they can attend school in a safe environment. Your son harms that safe environment, Judd. He has for a while now. Have you thought about getting him into therapy like I suggested the last time?"

"He doesn't need some fucking therapist messing around in his mind. You gotta get him back into school."

"It's out of my hands now."

"Then take it back into your fucking hands." He placed both hands on top of my desk and leaned forward. "I don't care what you have to do, who you have to call, who you have to fuck. Just get it done, or else."

I raised an eyebrow, prickles skittering down my spine. "Are you threatening me?"

His nostrils flared. "You sleep with men too, I hear. Ain't the superintendent gay? Why don't you make him really happy and have him overlook that recommendation you sent to him? You don't want to fight me on this, Shaw. You wouldn't want to have to relocate when you're in the prime of your life, would you?"

"Get out of my office," I said quietly.

"You have two fucking days to call me to let me know that my son is welcome back in school."

I shook my head. He must be delusional. "Instead of threatening me, have you thought about changes *you* need to make so your son has a better role model in his life?"

"I don't want your advice, Shaw. All I need from this shithole of a school is for my kid to graduate with his high school diploma. Now make that happen. Or else."

Bullies like Judd never truly changed. His son was a danger to the school, and as much as I would like to have him in the system so he would get the chance to grow up into a responsible adult, I couldn't take that risk with the other students I was responsible for.

I made a note of Judd's visit, jotting down a brief summary of his threats. In my job, written records were all that mattered if I wanted to get things done, and even an informal log of the meeting was good enough in case the situation got ugly. I didn't trust Judd any farther than I could throw him, but I wouldn't let his threats get to me. Bullies rarely acted on them, especially when someone stood their ground.

After the end-of-day bell rang, I forced myself to stay put in my chair and not take off like the kids, overjoyed the day was over. I had too many calls to make and documents that needed my signature before I could leave.

When the last item on my to-do list had been ticked off, I grabbed my cell phone and punched in my ex-wife's number, but this time, I let it ring. I swallowed past the nerves gathered in a bundle in my throat. Our divorce hadn't been peaceful. We'd fought. I'd accused. She blamed. Nothing remained of the affection we felt for each other when we got married.

"Hello?" She sounded groggy like she was just waking up.

I cleared my throat. "Anne, it's me, Shaw."

"I know. I recognize the number. What do you want?"

My mind went blank. I hadn't thought this through properly. What to say to her when she answered the phone?

"Shaw, what do you want?" she snapped.

"Sorry, I shouldn't have called."

"But you did, so tell me what this call is about. You haven't talked to me since the divorce."

"You didn't call me either."

"Because I was pissed at you for ruining our marriage because of my son," she grunted. Then the line went quiet.

"Anne?"

"It's him, isn't it? You're calling me because of Aristotle. He's the only one you ever cared about."

Here we go again.

"That's not true. I cared about you."

"Never as much as you cared about that boy. Just tell me something, Shaw. Was that the reason you asked me to marry you? To get close to my son?"

My stomach roiled at the thought of *that* Ari, a timid boy who came out of his shell whenever I bestowed some kindness on him. I liked the effect I'd been able to have on his life. Even now that I discovered my attraction to Ari, the young man, I still couldn't think of the teen Ari with anything else but tenderness in a completely nonsexual way.

"No, Anne," I said simply. Elaborate answers never seemed to work. "I liked being with you, plus we were both single. I wanted to settle down and get married."

"Did you ever love me?"

The lie wouldn't come. "I cared for you." Even to my ears, the words sounded like a cop-out. I pinched the bridge of my nose. This wasn't exactly what I had in mind when I called her.

"Did you call me to tell me Ari's dead?" she asked. "I'm not paying for the funeral."

"What?" How could she be so callous? Her own son. Anger boiled inside me. "Why would you even think that?"

She gave a loud sigh. "He's alive, then. Or don't you know?"

"Ari's fine. He's back here with me."

She laughed, but it ended in a coughing fit. "I told you he'd come back, didn't I? Maybe now you'll start to believe everything else I told you. Did he say why he left willingly and never called to tell you how much he hated his home?"

She knew Ari hadn't been in a good place? That conniving bitch.

"You convinced him he would ruin our marriage," I said.

"And you believe him?"

"Well, you brainwashed me into believing he was okay. You kept feeding me lie after lie. So what else could I do but believe he did indeed go away willingly?"

"The important part isn't that he left but that he left without a fuss, and that's not all."

"I'm not playing this game with you again, Anne. What are you speculating at?"

"Not speculating." She scoffed. "He fought me at first, refused to leave his precious 'Daddy.' But then I turned his own manipulative games against him. I told him if he didn't go, I would expose all the photographs and videos he has of you."

"What? Which photographs?"

"He'd been spying on you, Shaw. He had photos of you sleeping. Of us fucking. But you know what he did? He used Photoshop and replaced my head with his. There are all sorts of pictures."

The idea of someone watching me without my knowledge and permission made my skin crawl. Even if it was Ari. No, Ari would never do such a thing. She had to be making this up.

"I shouldn't have called you," I said.

"You did the right thing. Listen to me, Shaw. You and I have our differences, but you've always been a good man. If I wasn't good enough for you, there's no way Ari will be. He's not like us. He does bad things to people."

"What bad things?"

"You can't tell anyone what I'm about to tell you."

"What?" She was right. I wouldn't tell anyone, especially if I didn't believe her words.

"He and his dad couldn't get along. They fought constantly. Ari would call me, begging to take him away from there. Sometimes when he called, he had a black eye. Another time, he had a broken arm. Turned out his father was beating him. Then one day, both Ari and his father left the state. At least that's what the message his father sent me shortly before they disappeared said. Sometime later, Ari resurfaced without a trace of his dad. I'm pretty sure he killed him."

"What?"

"I'm pretty sure my son killed his father, Shaw."

No. No, that can't be true.

"Not that I don't think the guy deserves it if that did happen, but Ari would never do something like that. I saw the pic of his dad you kept in your purse. That guy is like twice the size of Ari."

"And that's going to be your downfall. You look at his stature and beauty, but you're blind to the monster inside. I hope you never come face-to-face with that other side of him."

Six

Shaw

WHEN I ARRIVED HOME, my car was in the garage. And those hateful slurs still flashed mockingly at me. I frowned, running my hand over the hood. Ari promised he would get this taken care of today. Why hadn't he? He'd always been good on his promise.

I walked through the side door that led to the mudroom. From there, I stepped into the hall. If my breath quickened and my pulse fluttered in my neck, I chose to ignore the signs. Just as I'd done all day, I suppressed thoughts of me jerking my cock with the beautiful boy on my mind.

Nothing good could come of this. The boy obviously thought of me as a safe haven, and the more I dwelled on this, the more I was likely to break his trust.

He needed a father figure, not an old man perving on him.

I inhaled deeply. And again. Nothing wafted from the kitchen, no fragrance of spicy soup, no delicious aroma of freshly baked cookies. All day I'd been looking forward to a home-cooked meal. It was one of the things I missed about Anne. She always took care of the house, and maybe I was old fashioned, but I liked that. Liked the thought of coming home to a clean house and a warm, nutritious meal.

"Ari?" I called softly.

What if he left again? A gut-wrenching ache filled my chest, and I gasped for air. He couldn't be gone. Not again. In the past four years, I'd been so worried about him. Finally, I'd been thinking of him less, and now he was back. How was I supposed to return to forgetting about this boy who did things to me I didn't understand?

"Ari?"

The kitchen was empty. The counters gleamed. He'd washed and put away everything we'd used for breakfast. I hurried up the stairs. His bedroom door was ajar, and I pushed it open farther, then let out a long, shaky breath. His bag was on the bed. Alongside a pack of adult-sized diapers that seemed to have been ripped open hastily.

"What the hell's going on?" Had he gone out? Why on earth did he need diapers?

A part of me wanted to go digging for answers in his bag or the computer on his desk, but I refrained from violating his privacy. There had to be a perfectly good explanation, and I wasn't going to believe all that madness Anne spewed at me earlier.

It didn't stop my mind from going a million places, though, as I changed out of my suit. Where was he? Why would he need diapers?

Anne's voice from the distant past popped in my head.

"It's bad enough that you wear those sweatpants around the house. Don't you see how he watches you? At least put on some underwear and stop giving him a show."

I stopped with my fingers hooked in the waistband of my boxers and stared down. I found it freeing to go commando at home, and I never put much stock into Anne's words before, so why now? One call and she made me doubt Ari.

When I descended the stairs, I was dressed in my usual sweatpants, my balls and cock swinging freely. I turned on the television in the living room. Even though the people weren't real, they would keep me company, make the house feel less empty.

I stopped in my tracks, and my heart pounded loudly. Ari. He hadn't left but sat on the floor, his back to me. He only wore a small sleeveless shirt and a diaper. Of all the scenarios I'd run through in my head to explain the diaper, this wasn't one of the versions. Not of Ari looking so comfortable sitting on the floor, wearing a diaper. It fit snugly between his legs, swaddling his ass perfectly, and something flickered to life in my belly.

Even with his back to me, his head bowed, he exuded vulnerability. He must have heard me calling his name. Once he knew I was home, he could have hidden, but he chose to share something that must have been difficult. I didn't understand it, but warmth spread through me that he allowed me to see him like this.

If Anne ever saw him this way, she would have ridiculed him.

"Ari, I'm home," I said softly.

He lifted his head a fraction but then lowered it again and went back to whatever he was doing. I caught a whimpering sound, but it was so faint I might have been mistaken. I stepped closer to him, then did a double take. A stuffed sloth was sitting next to him, ratty and one ear tacked on with big stitches.

The same sloth that started all this.

He'd been at the carnival with his mother when I saw him desperately trying to win the stuffy. I thought it was sweet seeing a boy his age being so innocent after all the crap I had to put up with from teenagers. When I'd handed him the stuffie, he'd hugged the sloth and thanked me prettily.

His mother pulled my attention away from him then. I'd been lonely. She was pretty. I knew I was no prize. I'd taken them both to dinner, and the relationship progressed fast. A year later, we were married, and it had been nice having Ari in my life, the smile he provoked every time he cried, "Hey, Daddy!"

Ari's focus was on the coloring book on the floor before him. Jumbo crayons spilled out of a thirty-six pack. The little sounds I'd heard was him sucking hard on the binky in his mouth, as if his life depended on it.

"Ari, what are you doing?" Why did I even ask that question? A fool could see it, and I was no fool. He was lost in his own little world, coloring his heart out. He was almost finished with the horse in an open field. The coloring looked haphazard, with big strikes and a riot of colors, nothing a grown man would have produced.

"Help me out here, Ari," I said quietly. "I don't understand what you're trying to tell me."

He gave his head a tiny shake. One I would have missed if I hadn't been watching him so intently.

"No, but why?"

He ignored me and went back to drawing bold lines where the flowers were. He didn't even color within the lines.

"Do you want me to go?"

Another small shake.

"Then what do you want me to do?"

He pointed at the sofa across from him. "You want me to stay?"

He nodded and flipped the coloring book to reveal two horses this time. He didn't hesitate but went back to coloring.

"Okay, I'll stay." I crossed over to the sofa and sat, watching him. Dinner was inconsequential to what was happening. I lost track of how long I sat there before he glanced up at me. He shifted his gaze shyly, then grabbed

the sloth, tucked it under his arm, and returned to his
artwork.

I had no idea what this was or what I was doing, but he
wanted me there, so I sat and watched over him while he
colored. He no longer sucked as hard on the binky as when
I'd walked into the room. In fact, he seemed more relaxed
doing his activity. He took his time now, trying to color
between the lines. And all I did was wait for him to
explain.

It was quite the wait, though, and I was getting restless.
He scrambled to his feet. His whole demeanor was so
timid I made an extra effort to relax so I wouldn't spook
him. Hopefully he would tell me exactly what this all
meant.

Ari shuffled over to me, practically naked, and climbed
onto my thighs. His legs were smooth and bare, with only
the diaper guarding his nakedness below the waist. He
looked so small, so vulnerable, I didn't have the heart to
boost him out of my lap. He wiggled around until he was
comfortable, then leaned sideways and rested his head on
my chest.

Whatever this was, I knew it would never change the
way I treated him. The level of trust he placed in me as he
snuggled against me tightened my throat. I wrapped my
arms around him and pulled him into my chest. The binky
fell from his lips. He wailed like a wounded animal and
tucked his face into my chest. He grabbed a handful of my
shirt front, his shoulders shaking violently as he burst into

tears, and all I could do was hold this broken boy so I could help him to put himself back together.

Anger and confusion welled up inside me. I wanted to find whoever hurt him and made him so timid. That cry could only come from someone who'd suffered, and I wanted the person responsible to suffer just as badly.

"Shh, it's okay." I bounced him on my knees just like I would a baby, and then I said something I'd never called myself before, although he constantly did. "Daddy's here."

He let out a tiny gasp and raised his head. His face was so beautiful, even with tears streaming down his cheeks, his eyes red and droplets clinging to his long lashes. I couldn't stop staring at him, that perfect bow of his mouth, the delicateness of his features. I should look away. I needed to look away, and yet I couldn't.

His small hand brushed against my jaw, and his breathing deepened. Mine hitched, the room lacking air, my chest tightening.

"Daddy, please." Ari leaned forward and kissed me, lips feathering lightly over mine. Groaning, he straddled my lap and deepened the kiss. His sweet, hot tongue hit mine, and a shiver ran down my spine. My hands cupped his face of their own accord. I thrust my tongue into his mouth, seeking more, the trembling in his body heightening my senses.

"Ari." I broke off the kiss and stared at him, torn between wanting to lay him down onto the sofa and protect him from the intensity of the desire growling inside me to take him.

Shit, had Anne been right all this time?

"Kiss me," he whined.

"I can't, Ari." I evaded his lips. "This isn't right."

He wouldn't listen, tugging at my shirt, but I didn't help him get it off me. He rocked back onto my lap and ripped the tapes from the sides of the diaper.

Don't look. Don't look.

"Don't you want to see, Daddy?" he whispered.

"No, Ari. God, Ari, this can't happen."

"But it feels so good." I closed my eyes, but it didn't block out his excited breaths. "It's all pink and hard. Look, Daddy. It got hard for you."

"Ari, please."

"Why won't you look? You don't think I'm beautiful anymore?" His voice cracked.

As did my heart, and I looked, inhaling sharply. Ari was a vision, slipping his hand up and down his cock, which was perfectly proportionate to the rest of his body, the head slick from precum.

"Yes, Daddy." His breaths came in short, excited pants. "Feels so good."

I couldn't tear my eyes away from Ari's hand working his cock. His still diapered ass rubbed against my thighs restlessly. He threw his head back, his cheeks feverish, neck flushed, and mouth parted. So beautiful. So hot and tempting. I hated being on the periphery watching him orgasm. I wanted to own his climax. To be the one to make him come apart at the seams.

Ari cried out, his eyes closed, body jerking backward. I caught those slender hips so he wouldn't fall off my thighs. His eyes flew open, and he watched me, riding the waves of his climax. Ropes of cum shot onto my shirt, staining more than just the fabric. Staining the relationship I thought we had. But after this, how could I go back to pretending he was just the son of my ex-wife? That he hadn't ridden my lap and begged me to watch him get off?

He collapsed against me, his face pressed to my neck while he gulped air into his lungs. A giggle escaped him, then a sigh. "That was so good. Now it's your turn. I want to play with you, Daddy."

What the hell just happened? And what was he doing? Ari slid off my lap, dropped his diaper to the floor, wedged himself between my knees, and yanked down the front of my sweatpants. The waistband was already loose enough that my cock sprang free, unencumbered. And proudly reporting for duty.

He didn't seem to mind being bare-assed before me as he played with my cock.

Ari glanced up at me with the naughtiest smile. He licked his lips, and my cock twitched.

"This is going to be so much fun." He caught my cock in his mouth.

Holy   shit,   Ari's—mouth—was—on—my—cock. Anne's I-told-you-so smirk flashed before me, and I pulled away when he released me. I jerked to my feet so quickly I knocked him over. I would have offered him a hand, but I couldn't. I needed space. Needed some time to think. I did the only thing that still made sense.

I bolted.

SEVEN

ARI

SHAW HAD A GOOD head start on me when he left the house, the car squealing out of the garage. It was the sound of the vehicle that had me jumping to my feet. I sprinted to the front door, not caring I was naked. I was too upset at the way he'd left, leaving me behind and confused as to what had just happened.

Had I pushed too far, too soon? I hadn't wanted this to happen, but given the latest development, I had no choice. I needed little space, and then I lost track of time, and Daddy walked in on me. I could have hidden, but I was tired of hiding this side of me. If anyone would know and accept me, it was him. At least, I'd hoped so. I thought he didn't care until he ran.

"Daddy, come back!" I yelled, running down the porch steps. "Please stop."

But of course he couldn't hear me.

"Shit."

I went back inside. He had to come back. If he discovered... He had to return so I could explain everything to him, but I had no car and no idea where he even was.

Left with no option but to wait for him to return, I trudged up the stairs to my bedroom. I took a quick shower to wash away the cum. Then I dressed and headed back downstairs to get started on dinner.

What else was I supposed to do? Eventually, he would come home, and we would talk. The topic of conversation would depend on whether he opened his trunk, which realistically, he wouldn't need to do unless he had a flat or something.

"Fuck."

I dropped the knife I was using to cut onions and braced my hands on the counter as I worked on my breathing. Damn Rich. This was supposed to be a new beginning for me. I was supposed to gently ease Shaw into accepting that we always belonged together. That there was no use fighting the attraction between us, and he *was* attracted to me.

I'd ground my ass against that evidence. I'd seen the way he watched me hungrily as I fisted my cock and nutted all over his shirt. I'd tasted his desire on my tongue when we kissed.

Shaw wanted me, but if I wasn't careful, I would ruin it.

An hour later, I had dinner finished, and still there was no sign of Shaw. I tidied the living room, then flipped through the coloring book I'd bought earlier today after all my hard work. I'd needed the time to unwind, and the book helped. I had no desire to return to my coloring, though. Where was he, and what was going through his mind?

What if I'd been mistaken about the whole situation? Shaw had always defended me against my mother, but what I'd done was a far cry from me wearing dresses.

The clock struck eight, and I was sitting at the table eating my cold dinner alone. I'd figured out where he more than likely was. Shaw didn't live an exciting life. Granted, it'd been four years since I lived with him, but he was a creature of habit, and I doubted much changed. Mom always argued that he never took her anywhere because he preferred being at home. He went to work and returned at the end of the day.

I called an Uber and cleaned up the kitchen while I waited. When the car pulled into the driveway, I streaked up the stairs, pulled on a black hoodie, pushed my wallet into my pocket, and with my phone in hand, raced back down again. The driver barely looked at me as I shut the door.

"You wanting to get to the high school you said?" he asked, adjusting his rearview mirror.

"Yeah, you can drop me off a block away."

"Suit yourself. You've already paid me for the full trip."

I didn't respond. Other times I might have wanted to leave a lasting impression, but not this time. I kept my hoodie pulled over my face and leaned against the door. He didn't make any attempt at conversation, which was fine by me.

Twenty minutes later, he pulled up at the curb just as I instructed. I mumbled my thanks and got out, plunging my hands into the pockets of the thick hoodie. I'd put it on as a form of disguise for what I was about to do, but it also took away some of the February chill.

"Don't do anything stupid," the guy said through the window. "You know what they'd do to a pretty guy like you in prison?"

He was watching me more intensely than I liked. The familiar urge to get rid of anyone who threatened my well-being surged, but I smiled.

"I'm just waiting for someone here. He's married and in the closet."

He nodded. "I can see that. I'm straight, and I'd do you."

I fluttered my eyelashes at him. "I don't think you can afford me."

He flashed me a grin and honked his car horn. "That's what I was afraid of. See ya!"

He drove away, and I let the smile fade. I walked until the school grounds came into sight, then took the shortcut that led to the playing field. I located the lowest side of the fence, which they still hadn't fixed in all this time, and I easily scaled it. I dropped down on the other side and landed on my feet.

Now to avoid the guards. That shouldn't be too difficult. They stayed at the guard post and only made a few walkabouts around the campus to ensure everything was fine. I cut across the field to the boys' locker room. It was way too easy to pick the lock. I slipped inside and breathed a sigh of relief.

Please be here. Please be here.

I switched on my phone light and shined it down. I would have checked the parking lot first for his car, but I couldn't risk the guards seeing me. I went with my gut and hurried along corridors until I arrived at the administrative block. The door leading inside to where the secretary usually sat was half-opened, and light spilled out.

I hesitated. I didn't have to do this. I could pack all my shit and hoof it out of town. No one would be able to find me. I could get lost like I had before, but the thought of leaving him again hurt. Maybe I wouldn't stay forever, but I needed more time before I was going to say good-bye.

The door creaked as my shoulder hit it as I sidled my way inside. Shaw's office door was closed. I bypassed the secretary's desk and grabbed the doorknob. The hardest thing was to turn the doorknob and push the door open.

Just as I predicted, Shaw sat at his desk, staring at the wall, his hair disheveled as if he had run his hands through it. I closed the door behind me with a soft thud, and he jerked his head in my direction. He straightened in his chair, flushing a bright red, then plastered on his principal look.

Damn, if only it didn't affect me so much. How many times had I dreamed of entering his office and having him spank my bottom with a ruler while I lay draped over his desk? Right before he'd take me hard and punish me for not being the perfect angel he thought me to be.

I wanted him to be dirty with me, just like the way I felt most times.

"Ari, how'd you find me?" he asked, his voice low.

I linked my hands behind my back and stopped before his desk. "I couldn't think of anywhere else to look."

We stared at each other until he looked away, speechless.

"I made you dinner," I said softly. "Chicken pot pie, which you like so much. Will you come home? Please?"

"You shouldn't have come, Ari." He dropped his gaze to his desk.

"I had to." I wrapped my arms around myself. "I was worried."

"You should have thought twice before you did that."

I bit off the apology before it tumbled in an unceremonious lie from my lips. "I'm not sorry about anything."

He snapped his head up, and my heart thumped hard in my chest. If he rejected me, what was even the point in trying to be good?

"Do you know how much I worked on convincing your mother nothing sexual was going on between us?"

"And nothing was, but I'm older now."

"You were—are—like a son to me, Ari."

"*Like* a son," I cried. "You are *not* my father." Never that asshole who'd—I shook my head to get rid of the disturbing mental images.

"Then why do you call me Daddy?" He gave a hoarse laugh and turned the computer monitor to me. "This is what I've been doing here, Ari. Trying to understand what all this means 'cause I don't know what I walked into."

The article's byline was catchy about a twenty-four-year-old adult who wears diapers and uses pacifiers. A young woman with her hair in two pigtails, wearing a pink onesie with the word "Baby" on the front and sucking on a half-filled bottle, took up the side of the screen.

"It's not as unpopular as you think." I tried to gauge his reaction. Did he find it repulsive? "There are many people into that kink."

"So this is the reason you call me Daddy?" he whispered. "You want me to-to do all this with you?"

"Yeah." I dropped my gaze. "You've always taken care of me since you came into my life. It made sense you would be the one."

"Is it sexual for you too?" he asked, his tone hopeful. "What I've read said it doesn't have to be sexual."

I could tell the answer he wanted to hear, but I couldn't lie to him. Not with this. It meant way too much.

"Yes," I replied. "I do like sex in little space. I like Daddy treating me like a little baby while he fucks me." I inhaled deeply, just the thought of it turning me on. "I like to suck on my binky while Daddy drills me, like to-to-to use his cock as a pacifier."

"My god, Ari." The color drained from his face; his eyes were wide in shock.

"But I also love the nonsexual parts." I stepped around his desk. When I stood next to him, I went down on my knees and stared up at him. "I love it when Daddy gives me bubble baths and makes me baby food. I love cuddles and naps during the day. I like silly cartoons and coloring, theme parks, and playing outside. I don't always need it, but sometimes I do when life gets extremely difficult." Like today.

Shaw shook his head and swallowed hard. "Jesus, Ari. This is—"

"Something beautiful when shared between people who respect and trust each other," I told him. "The way we respect and trust each other. There's no one else I trust as much as you with this."

"But can I trust you, Ari? My whole perception of you seems like a lie. Your mother warned me about this for years, and I didn't listen. How could you expose yourself like that to me?"

"You liked it," I said simply.

His cheeks returned to a delightful pink. "That was wrong of me. I should have put a stop to it."

"Why? We're both adults."

"I was married to your mother."

"Was," I argued.

"You're so young."

"But not underage."

"People will think I was sleeping with you while I was married."

"Don't they already think that?"

He frowned, and the intense look smoldered my insides. "You have an answer for everything, don't you?"

I smiled, feeling more confident than on my way here. "Not for everything, but for this, I do. We belong together."

He was lost in thought for a few seconds. Then he was back to shaking his head. He was doing a lot of that tonight, as if rejecting the ideas he was thinking about.

If only I could get him to see that this was okay. That *we* were okay. That someone who loved him as much as I did deserved to be with him. I would do anything for him. I did do unspeakable things for him. Things that if he knew, perhaps he would look at me differently, so he could never know.

Eight

Shaw

THE WORDS COMING OUT of Ari's mouth and the innocent picture he made as he kneeled by my legs didn't go well together at all. I couldn't believe the crudity with which he'd blurted out what he wanted from me. I'd never heard him speak that way before, and I was struggling. Struggling to reconcile this image with the boy I'd known since he was sixteen. Anne's words kept resurfacing in my mind. If she was right about this, had she also been right about everything else?

He waited patiently for my answer, his windswept hair a bit overgrown and hanging into his eyes. My hands itched to brush the locks to the side, but I fisted them in my lap instead. All the better not to reach out for him when I wasn't sure what was going on here.

His eyes in his small, upturned face gleamed with hope. Ever since I came here in my office, I'd been reading up on what could have caused Ari to behave the way he had.

I'd started with what I could find about something called little behavior and ABDL. There seemed to be a whole community of people into the lifestyle, which shocked me. Twitter accounts were dedicated to sharing the lifestyle with users.

"How long?" I asked Ari, and at his confused look, I added, "Since you realized you were a little?"

"I guess a part of me always had the inclination, but I didn't truly understand it until I was forced to live with my dad."

"Tell me. What happened with your dad?"

He bit his bottom lip. "Do I have to talk about it? It was so long ago."

"Four years isn't that long, Ari. Before I can decide anything, I need you to be honest with me."

He shuffled closer to me, rose onto his knees, and placed his head in my lap. I stiffened at first, then realized he was only seeking comfort. This was the side of Ari I was used to, always needing to be touched, to be reassured, to be loved. Was it really any different from what he wanted from me now? The same result, just another way to get there.

"I told you my dad was a deadbeat," he said. "He-he didn't really care about me. I took care of myself."

"He used to hit you."

"Yes, but most times, it wasn't bad."

"How did you get away?"

"I met someone." He took one of my hands and placed it on top of his head. "I love to be petted. For my hair to be played with."

As if they had a will of their own, my fingers combed through his hair, and he relaxed against me with a sigh.

"So good."

"What happened next?" I asked. I was only doing this so I would get answers.

"He wanted to take care of me, so I let him—ouch."

Damn, I'd been petting him too hard. "Sorry." Even though I'd seen him in action earlier, a part of me wanted to believe Ari was untouched by anyone else. What the hell did that make me?

"I had to. It was the only way I could think of surviving. You know I didn't have good grades in school."

"You did okay."

"But not good enough to get into any decent colleges and have a future."

"That's not true."

His lips curved in a smile against my thigh. "Why can't you see how perfect you are for me? You're the only one who cares about me."

"What about the-the other Daddy?"

"I never called him Daddy. That's reserved for you only."

I stopped petting him, my hand falling to the side. He scrambled off the floor and climbed onto my lap. I let him. I knew where this might lead, and somehow I hoped for it.

"There's only one Daddy for me," he said. "And that's you, Shaw. Don't you get it? I've wanted you forever." Just like earlier, he pressed his lips against mine in a hard kiss. "Tell me you don't feel it too. Tell me you don't want this with me. That you don't want to take care of me, because I think you kind of have to, and I need you to."

I should have avoided his kiss, but the déjà vu happened. His lips were so sweet. They were to me what a popsicle was to a parched kid on a sunny summer day.

"Please, Daddy, let me."

He kissed across my jaw and down my neck. His hands slid under my T-shirt. They stroked my hairy belly, and I was tempted to suck in my gut.

"I love touching you so much," he said. No way would I make myself thinner than I was now.

Ari slipped off my thighs and pushed his way between them. Just as before, he pulled down the waistband of my sweatpants and exposed me. I should have been more prepared this time, but the hungry look on his face as he held me in his slender hand had my heart racing with anticipation.

"I wish I had all night to play with you." He stroked me from the base to the swollen head. "I'm going to be naughty for you, Daddy, and suck on it so hard that I make you come. Then baby's going to swallow your load, clean you with his tongue, and take you home for dinner."

If only that were as half as good as it sounded, I would have no complaints. It was even better. Ari's blond head dipped as he took the crown of my cock into his mouth. He massaged the glans with those succulent lips, kissing and sucking on the head while stroking my shaft.

He swooped down and took me deep to the back of his throat.

"Holy fuck!" I cried out, a shiver spearing through my body. "Ariiiiii."

He didn't let up, taking his task quite seriously. Lips massaged, tongue stroked, and jaw sucked while teeth gently scraped in sensitive places. I gripped the arms of the chair as I lifted my ass off the seat, thrusting my hips, seeking more.

Ari, sweet Ari with the bright smiles and beautiful dresses. My movements faltered, and I stopped. Until his eyes flew open and found mine. The carnal knowledge in their depths was the final straw. I rose from the chair, and he moved along with me, clinging on to my cock with his mouth as though afraid I was going to pull out and leave again.

No such luck. I was too far gone. Too lost. I braced my arms against the desk, trapping Ari between me and the hard wood. I thrust, fucking his mouth the way his eyes begged me to. Sounds I interpreted as pleasure and encouragement slipped out of his mouth along with the gurgles of having my cock hit the back of his throat. He didn't even flinch, took it like a pro, deepthroating all of me.

Jealousy and anger surged through me. Jealousy that someone else taught him this. Someone else placed their cock between those beautiful lips and tainted his insides with bits of them. I wanted to wipe out every memory that wasn't me.

I cupped his slender neck, holding him by the throat as I fucked his mouth in a way I'd never done any of my lovers. Anger that someone else had had him, even before I knew I wanted him. Never had I been so furious with a lover. It was a burn that refused to be quenched. Until it did.

I cried out as I climaxed. Through half-lowered lids, I watched Ari's head bob up and down as he wrung every drop out of me.

"Shit." Breathing hard, I stumbled back into my chair. He used his index finger to wipe a streak of cum from his bottom lip and popped the finger into his mouth. I groaned at the provocative gesture while he looked at me with big, not-so-innocent eyes.

Ari knew how to please a man. I was way too exposed, and I snapped the waistband of my sweats back into place, covering my dick.

"Are we doing this?" Ari asked me.

"I don't want to disappoint you."

His smile turned megawatt on me. "You could never. You're a born caregiver, and you listen. Should we go home for dinner?"

"Sounds good."

I was doing this, then? I followed Ari from the office and closed the door behind me. We were silent as we walked side by side, but he kept giving me glances, then grabbed my hand. My instinct was to pull away in case anyone saw us and got the wrong impression. But there was no one else around, and I agreed to this.

"Could we keep this quiet just between the two of us for now?" I asked.

"You mean not tell Mom?"

"Yeah. You know how she gets."

"I don't care about her. As long as I got you, I'm okay."

As we approached my car, a thought hit me. "By the way, how did you get past security?"

"I jumped the fence."

"What?" I spun to him. "Please tell me you're joking."

"I had to talk to you. I was desperate."

I stroked his chin. "Don't do anything so reckless again."

"I'll try."

He slid into the car, and I climbed in as well and pulled out of the parking lot. As we approached the gate, the security guard admitted us through without even glancing at the car. About five minutes later, Ari inched closer to me and placed his head on my shoulder. I had to slow down and drive with one hand while I wrapped the other around him.

"I'm so happy," he said.

"Me too." And I was. I found myself smiling until a police car behind us flashed its lights. Just great. I really needed to get the hurtful words off my car. Ari straightened and looked over his shoulder.

"What are you doing?" Ari asked when I put on my indicator.

"I'm stopping so we can talk to the officer. It'll be fine."

"No, no, it won't. Don't stop."

The flashing lights were getting closer. "What? I have to pull over."

I made to turn over, but Ari yanked at the steering wheel.

"What the hell, Ari!" I pushed him gently back into his seat. "What's wrong with you?"

"Please trust me. You can't stop."

"Why not? You're not making any sense."

Ari took a sharp intake of breath. He gripped the sides of the seat and craned his neck to check out the police car.

"You just can't."

"If I don't get a good explanation... Hell, I'm still pulling over."

Ari grasped my thigh, his grip so hard it hurt. "You can't stop because there's a dead body in your trunk."

"Jesus, Ari, I'm being serious here."

"I swear it's true, Daddy. I'll explain it later to you, but you can't stop."

I watched Ari and found no trace of deception on his face. He was telling the truth. I didn't know how or why, but I had a dead body in the trunk of my car with the police flagging us down.

What the hell was I going to do?

NINE

ARI

SHIT.

I wasn't positive what terrified me more: the look of abject horror on Shaw's face or the flashing lights and the siren of the car gaining on us. This was the first time I'd ever seen him look at me this way. Was it fear, disgust, or something else?

"Please whatever you do, just don't stop," I begged him, hoping he would listen to me despite whatever was going through his mind.

Even before he eased his foot off the gas pedal, I could see from Shaw's features that he wasn't going to disobey the law. Wasn't that one of the things I loved about him? How innocent and good he was? Why did I expect him to do differently because I asked him to? Still, disappointment and terror filled my insides like maggots eating out the remains of a decomposing body.

"What are you doing?" On instinct, I reached for my knife, but when Shaw glared at me, I dropped my hand. What was I going to do? Attack him? He was the one person in the world I could never hurt. But I couldn't sit here either and allow myself to be thrown in jail for someone like Rich, who'd only gotten what was coming to him.

"I don't know what the hell you've done, Ari," he said quietly, "but we're not going to run from the police. I'm sure it'll be fine."

Unless they asked him to pop the trunk.

Shaw pulled off to the side of the road, and all I could do was sit and wait for my fate. Or was that the only thing? I leaned sideways and fondled the switchblade in my shoe. I'd die before I let them take me to prison and away from Shaw. Not after just getting the chance to be with him. I needed more time.

The squad car parked behind ours, and a tall, lean man stepped out. He seemed to be alone.

"Now's our chance to get away," I urged him.

"I said we're not running from the police."

The police officer stopped at the driver's window and tapped on it. Shaw lowered the window, and the man peered inside with a flashlight. It would be so easy to reach across Shaw and plunge the knife in his neck. But was that the way I wanted Shaw to remember me? If he couldn't manage to do something as simple as to run from the police, how could I expect him to understand me?

"Good evening, Officer. Is there a problem?" Shaw sounded calmer than I thought he would be. A part of me had expected him to point the police officer toward his trunk. It wouldn't be out of his character.

"Vice Principal Wheeler, that you?" The man poked his head even more inside the car with a big grin on his face. He looked quite young, a few years older than me.

"Nathan Graham," Shaw said. "Yes, it's Principal Wheeler now. Isn't this a nice surprise? You made it through the police academy."

"Passed with flying colors." He beamed, patting his badge. "What's with the colorful decorations on the car?"

"Some kid at the high school. I'm sure you can understand that. Didn't you snatch the librarian's wig and hoist it up on the flagpole outside the school?"

"There's still no proof I did that." But from the way he laughed, he sure as hell had. "You're not going to get me to admit to anything." His gaze landed on me, and his laugh fell away. "And who's this?"

"You remember my stepson, Ari?"

A thrill ran through me. That dirty little secret of how he'd come down my throat just a few minutes ago, plus the heightened adrenaline from this close encounter, turned me on.

"Wow, you're all grown up now, huh?" Nathan said. His gaze wandered over my frame. I brushed at my hair and smiled demurely at him.

"Just a bit." I bit my bottom lip, and sure enough, his eyes remained on me. Straight guys who weren't interested would have looked away already.

"I'd say a whole lot. The principal ever give you a chance to go out? Or is he just as strict at home?"

Oh, how I would love for Shaw to get all strict and domineering on me, but Shaw was my sweet teddy bear of a Daddy.

"He's as strict as he needs to be," I replied.

"You wouldn't mind going out with me, would you?"

"Depends on where you're taking me," I murmured.

Shaw shifted. "Didn't they teach you it's unprofessional to pick up men while wearing your uniform?"

He groaned. "Always so proper, Principal Wheeler. All right, how about I come over when I'm off and take him out. That all right by you?"

"Of course, it is." I winked at him. "I'd like that very much."

"Great." He patted the side of the car. "You wouldn't mind popping the trunk for me, would you?"

All the breath left my lungs, leaving me painfully breathless. Beside me, Shaw sat just as frozen.

"Say what?" he asked.

Nathan chuckled. "That's for all the detention you gave me." He stepped back from the car. "You may go, and try to get that cleaned off the car."

"Have a good night," Shaw said, his voice strained.

"Good night, Mr. Police Officer."

Nathan's grin was lascivious as he took his last fill of me. The car engine started, and we peeled off the shoulder of the road. Shaw drove faster than he had before, white-knuckling the steering wheel. His jaw was clenched tight, and he didn't even look at me when we stopped at a traffic light. I tried to find the words to apologize for putting him in this situation. But they wouldn't come.

The only time I'd seen Shaw this silent was when he'd been upset at my mother for taking away the sewing machine from me.

We arrived at his house, and he drove straight into the garage. He jerked his door open and got out. I quickly tumbled out as well, then grabbed my knife from the floor of the car where it had fallen.

"What's that in your hand?"

Shaw grasped my hand and took the switchblade from me. "What the hell's wrong with you?" he demanded, not a trace of a smile to be found on his face. "Why on earth did you do that?"

He didn't raise his voice, and he didn't need to. It still sent shivers down my spine.

"I'm sorry. I didn't mean to, I swear. He—"

"He's still an asshole, and a badge doesn't change that!" Shaw snapped.

Huh?

Oh. He was mad at me for flirting with Nathan.

"I did what I had to for him to leave us alone," I answered.

"Don't do that." He cupped the side of my face tight. "Don't tell me you want me and then five minutes later plan a date with some other guy right in front of my face."

I gaped at him until he released my jaw. I rubbed a hand over my skin. He'd held me so tightly I wouldn't be surprised if I had a bruise there tomorrow.

"I didn't mean it," I whispered. Wow, Shaw was jealous. To the best of my knowledge, he'd never shown jealousy where my mother was concerned, and she'd been a flirt too.

While others might not think it was a good thing, jealousy was a language I understood well. I'd been perpetually in that state as I watched him with my mother. As I hid in their closet and listened to her moans while Shaw grunted from fucking her. And in all those stolen moments of getting close to him, I'd thought about him being on top of me instead.

"You flirted with him, and that's unacceptable," he said, blowing hard. This was something new for him. Something he was struggling to get out. "If you're mine, you're only mine, Ari. No one else gets to have you."

For sure, I'd thought he would be ready to dump me and carry me into the police after I'd confessed what was in his trunk. Did he even remember that? He seemed so hell-bent on getting me to understand that he wouldn't share me.

"I'm sorry, Daddy," I said softly. "I was just trying to protect us."

"Don't do it again."

"I won't." But even as I said the words, I knew I was lying. If Shaw was in trouble and I needed to fuck someone to get him out, I'd do it, no questions asked. He was worth so much more than some random guy getting off on my body.

"Fuck." Shaw expelled a deep breath and staggered back as if it was just hitting him what had happened. His face pale, he swallowed hard and glanced from the car to me. "Let's get inside."

I hesitated. "But, Daddy, what about—"

"What about what, Ari?"

"The body in the trunk."

He ran a hand over his face. "Why would there be a body in the trunk of my car? How would it have gotten there?"

I wrung my hands in front of me. "I put it there."

"And where did you get this body from?"

I licked my bottom lip and concentrated on the cracks in the tiles under my feet.

"Ari, please tell me you were joking."

"It was self-defense," I said. "I had no choice. I swear I had no choice, Daddy."

Without another word to me, Shaw stalked over to his car. He unlocked the trunk and raised the lid. I didn't move from where I was. I knew what was inside—a man wrapped up in clear plastic and conveniently tied up in a bag.

"Oh my god, you're telling the truth." Shaw stumbled back, his face turning green. "You killed him, Ari? Why would you do that?"

I shrugged. "Does it matter why? He's dead, and I need to get rid of his body."

"Get rid of his body? Are you insane?"

I stiffened at his words. My dad called me insane and regretted it. But Shaw was different. I loved Shaw. He just didn't get me yet.

"What else am I supposed to do with it?"

"We call the police, and they'll take care of it."

"So you want to send me to prison?" He didn't mean that, did he?

"I'm sure they'll be able to work something out if you tell them what happened."

"Except this body has been in your trunk all day. If I'd called it in then, I would have stood a chance, but now they'll never buy that it wasn't something I planned."

"We don't have any other choice."

"We can bury the body somewhere no one will ever think to look."

"You want us to bury the body?" His mouth moved up and down like a puppet's. "What are you thinking?"

"I'm thinking that I just found you again and don't want to lose you because the justice system sucks. I promise you, Daddy, he deserved it."

Shaw shook his head. "I-I can't think. I need some time to think."

"We don't have time. The longer the body stays in your car, the higher the risk of us being found with it."

Shaw had gone silent, his shoulders stooped. Hopefully, he'd make the right choice. I didn't want to have to hurt someone I loved as much as I loved him.

"Just don't say anything, please," I said. "Don't get the police involved. I'll take care of the body. You don't even have to help."

"You expect me to keep this quiet, Ari?"

I nodded, cupping my hands and holding them up to my chest in a plea.

"You don't have to do anything. It's my mess, and I'll take care of it."

TEN

SHAW

STANDING IN THE SHOWER, I watched the water wash away the mud on my hands. Hands I'd used to dig a hole to bury a body. I shouldn't have interfered. Shouldn't have driven far up into the woods on the other side of town on someone else's property. Ari had given me the out when he told me to leave everything up to him. He would take care of the body, but like the fool my ex-wife called me so many times, I volunteered to drive the car.

I vowed to myself to let him get the job done by himself, but seeing him struggling with the shovel to dig a hole big enough to sufficiently bury the corpse had been more than I could handle. Despite what he did, I couldn't get it out of my head that this was my sweet little Ari who made me breakfast in the morning, had the smile of a thousand suns and the kindness of a saint.

There had to be a good reason why he killed Rich. Maybe Rich had come back to harass him and it had been self-defense like Ari said, but doubt niggled at my brain. If it was self-defense, why hadn't he called the police once he committed the crime? Why had he taken this path? Had he done this before?

I didn't even want to contemplate what Anne told me. That Ari possibly killed his father. But no matter how much I tried, I couldn't stop thinking about Anne's words.

Even when the water ran clean, assuring me that all the dirt had been washed off my hands, I couldn't stop scrubbing. The dirt on my conscience couldn't be so easily cleansed. I didn't owe so much as a parking ticket. I lived my life within the law. I didn't break the rules, and now I was getting involved in all sorts of questionable activities since Ari's return. Was this karma screwing me over for being intimate with my stepson? Someone I helped raise?

The shower door slid back, and I turned, wiping the water from my eyes. A naked Ari stepped in with me. He'd been just as filthy as me when we got home, but here he was completely naked, tattoos covering the back of his slender limbs and lower back. I'd never found tattoos attractive before. In fact, I dissuaded teens from getting them, but the black ink on Ari's body was arousing. Flower petals cupped his bouncy ass cheeks.

But then he turned to me, and I couldn't get the sight of him rolling the body into the hole without so much as a wince out of my mind. My hard cock shriveled up.

"What are you doing here, Ari?" I asked.

His bottom lip trembled. "I thought you may need some help with washing up."

"I'm fine. You should go and wait for me so we can talk."

He pouted at me. "But I don't want to talk. I have other things I want to do to you."

With a playful smile on his lips, he curled his hand around my soft cock. He stroked it, squeezing with just the right amount of pressure. "I want to make it hard for me. Do you want me to make you hard, Daddy?"

"That's enough, Ari." I pried his hand away from my dick. How could he be so easily aroused after everything we'd just been through? I was still trying to come to terms with what I did.

"I know you're thinking about what happened," he said softly, making no attempt to touch me this time. Instead, he dropped his hand between his legs and cupped his small, erect dick. It was pink and pretty, tucked up to his belly. He was already soaked since slipping into my shower, but he didn't even seem to notice. He just kept stroking away. As I watched him, he brushed his other hand over his flat stomach and up and rubbed his nipples.

"Of course I'm thinking about what happened. I don't understand how you can simply shrug it off."

"It's easy," he replied. "I can show you how if you let me. Do you want me on my knees for you, Daddy? I'll make you hard with my hands, and then I'll suck you into my mouth and make you come down my throat." He half turned to me, showing me his delectable round ass. A finger disappeared between his cheeks. "Or if you want, you can put your cock into my tiny little hole. I got it all lubed and ready for you."

Speechless, I watched him slip a finger into his hole, a soft moan spilling from his plump lips. He stroked his cock as that finger fucked his hole hard.

"Stop it, Ari." But the words came out hoarse, and I wasn't even sure if he heard me over the pounding shower.

"Feels so good, Daddy," he whimpered, then removed his finger and slipped it into his mouth, licking it while he eyed me from heavy-lidded eyelids. The same finger slid back into his hole, his hand moving with excited vigor, his breaths coming out huffed and needy.

"Would feel so much better with your cock inside me," he murmured. "I'd come so hard riding your big cock. Don't you want that, Daddy?"

He gave a soft cry, and ropes of cum shot onto the bathroom tiles. He slowly removed his finger and slumped against the wall, his chest heaving.

Without a word, I slid back the shower door and stepped out. I couldn't be in the same room with him right now. How could he be thinking about sex after everything? Anne had been right. Something wasn't quite right with him. And I helped him bury a corpse when I knew what I should have done.

I was so fucked.

My stomach roiled and dipped. I swallowed down the bile that rose into my mouth — ignoring Ari's soft "Daddy" — snagged the towel, and made my way to my bedroom. I scrubbed at my hair and body, disappearing into my closet to find some clothes. I blindly chose a pair of cotton shorts and a T-shirt, then turned. Ari was sitting on the bed, the bed sheet pulled up to his neck.

As he sat there, staring up at me with hurt eyes, guilt gnawed at me. Like I was the one in the wrong when I knew he was. He dragged me into this madness with him.

"You should go to bed, Ari," I said. "Tomorrow, when I'm in a better frame of mind, we'll talk."

"We don't have to talk now," he argued. "If you're too tired, I don't mind being on top. I *love* being on top."

Jealousy and irritation mixed inside me. I didn't want to hear about him riding any other man. And I hated the way I got so irrationally jealous when he inadvertently mentioned someone else. This wasn't like me. I didn't get jealous. I didn't get possessive. Ever.

What the hell was he doing to me?

I scowled. "Didn't you just come in the bathroom?"

He shrugged. "I can go all night."

But I couldn't. What was I thinking? Why did I believe I could satisfy him? He would be gone soon enough, just like he'd left years ago.

I shook my head. "You see, this is what I don't understand, Ari. I don't get it. How can you sit there so nonchalantly after what we did?"

"I said a prayer for him," he said matter-of-factly. "It's more than the son of a bitch deserved."

I yanked on my shorts. No way was I going to have this conversation with him naked. "Would it kill you to have a little remorse?" I lowered my voice. As if the walls would hear our conversation and report it to the police. "You took somebody's life, Ari. Doesn't that bother you in the least?"

"Not if he deserves it."

"And you were made the judge, jury, and executioner of whether or not he deserved to die?"

He shrugged, and the sheet fell down one creamy — naked — shoulder. He rubbed that shoulder while looking up at me from beneath his lashes. The minx was toying with me, trying to have his way when I already made it clear I wouldn't sleep with him tonight. Maybe not ever after all this.

Such a fucking pity. His body was made for pleasure.

"I gave him a chance to live, but he blew it."

"You better start talking, Ari. What the hell happened?" If he wasn't going to let it rest for the night, then he owed me trying to make me understand.

He dropped his gaze but remained silent.

"What happened last night?" I said as the incident popped into my head. "Rich insisted you were lying, that you invited him to-to have his way with you. Then you tried to make it look like an assault. Is that true?" He glanced up at me, his eyes too dark to read. "And for what you've gotten me engaged in, Ari, don't you dare think about lying to me!"

His cheeks turned red. "Will you do that again?"

"Do what?"

"Use your shouty voice at me. It makes me feel good."

What the...? I blinked at him several times. Sweet Jesus, he was getting aroused at me shouting at him.

"Did you lie about what happened last night? That's the last time I'm asking you, Ari."

He heaved a sigh as if I was bothering him with my questions. "Yes, I did, but only for payback."

"Payback? What's that supposed to mean?"

"Rich doesn't like to take no for an answer. I lured him home with the promise of sex. He wanted to fuck me so hard, tried to get me to do it with him in the back seat of his car, but I wanted you to hear us."

"You set him up?"

He nodded. "Don't look so repulsed by the idea. He deserved it."

"You keep saying that, but I have no idea what it means."

"It means that I wanted you to hear him not taking no for an answer so you could beat the shit out of him for touching me back in high school."

I lost a bit of steam. "Rich touched you in high school? What'd he do?"

He hung his head, pulling his knees up to his chin. "It was after PE class. I hated being in the locker room with the others, so I always waited until they left before I changed and freshened up. When I walked out of the shower, Rich was there, his zipper down. He told me to suck his cock. He took a picture of me doing it and used it to blackmail me. PE class became torture. He would always be lingering after, demanding a blow job, and there was nothing I could do about it."

The son of a bitch. Ambivalence weighed like lead in my stomach. What Rich did to him was despicable. No one deserved to be violated like that. And sure as hell not my little angel.

"I didn't tell anyone." He wiped tears from his eyes. "And when I went out last night, I saw him, and he acted like I should be grateful he let me suck his cock during high school. He hadn't changed one bit, so I decided to teach him a lesson."

"You intended to kill him? Ari, baby, that's going too far."

"I didn't plan to kill him. He didn't give me a choice."

I sat at the edge of the bed beside him. "You always have a choice, Ari."

He shook his head stubbornly. "No, not for this one."

"Ari, if we're going to be together, you have to show to me that you're capable of making informed choices. Otherwise, this relationship will never work."

Ari threw the sheet from his body and rushed to his feet. He was a small ball of fire and energy, his eyes flashing in anger.

"He cornered me, and I gave him a choice. I told him to let me go, but he wouldn't. He insisted he needed to fuck me in the back seat of *your* car, and he made it clear it was going to happen with or without my consent. I did not consent! Harlan didn't consent."

I frowned. "What does Harlan have to do with this? He died years ago." The boy had been Ari's friend back in high school until he committed suicide and shocked everyone who knew him.

"And do you know why he died?" His eyes flashed with unshed tears. "He died because Rich decided years ago that he no longer wanted just a BJ from me. He wanted more. I avoided him as much as I could. I was supposed to be there at Harlan's house when it happened. It was me he wanted when he stopped by, but I'd been cooking for you that night, so I was late. Rich decided that he didn't care after all which one of us he got. So he didn't give Harlan a choice. Rich forced him.

"You didn't see him the way I did after it happened. He didn't want to report it, didn't want to go to the hospital because he was ashamed. I thought I handled it. I thought I helped him to clean up and feel better. I should never have left him. I should have stayed with him. But I left, and he killed himself. Because of Rich, he killed himself, and Rich didn't deserve to live for what he did. Harlan was my friend, and I disappointed him, and he would still be alive if not for Rich!"

Ari burst into tears, his shoulders shaking. At first, the thought occurred to me that he was faking it, but there was no way he could have turned on those gut-wrenching sobs on a whim. This pain came from his soul. A pain he'd bottled up for a very long time.

I wanted to be angry with him. I wanted to send him to his room and even ask him to stay the hell away from me. But this was Ari. *My* Ari. No one got him the way I did. No one else accepted him the way I did.

How could I see his pain and ignore it? I couldn't. I pulled his slender body into my arms and hugged him to me, patting his naked back.

"I-I f-found him," he said, choked up. "I'd left m-m-my sketchbook and I turned back for it. And I f-f-found him. He was already dead, so I r-ran back home, and I-I didn't tell anyone ever why he killed himself. I should have told someone."

ELEVEN

ARI

I WAS LOSING DADDY Shaw, and it scared me. I hadn't been this afraid since Mom packed my bags and drove me to the airport, basically telling me to get lost or she would tell Shaw about all my misdeeds. We slept in the same bed every night, but you could hardly tell. He spooned me when we were in bed, but every morning I woke up alone, so I wasn't even sure how long he stayed with me. One night, I woke up and found him sleeping in the living room on the sofa.

Each day, the gap between us widened, and I was running out of ideas to get his attention back.

Stupid, stupid. I should never have told him about Rich, but I hadn't had much of a choice with the body in the trunk and the police officer stopping us.

I missed cooking for Daddy. He was usually gone before I made breakfast, and when he came home, it was so late he didn't bother to eat dinner.

And today it had to stop. I needed my Daddy back. I put my plans into motion by getting a used car. Since I was sticking around town, it made sense to get my own set of wheels. Then I didn't have to call a cab every time Daddy wasn't available.

Satisfied with the small hybrid I bought — wheedling a pretty good deal out of the salesman by batting my eyelashes and making promises that would never happen — I took my new old car grocery shopping. I tried to reach a can of coconut milk on a high shelf, but someone stretched above me and took it down.

"Thank you." I turned to the person who helped me. The police officer from the other night who flirted with me in front of Shaw. Shaw got angry, and that intrigued me.

"Just doing my civic duty." He grinned at me. "Have you given thought to our date and where you want to go?"

I shrugged. "You said you would hit me up without the uniform." I eyed his fit body. "Although I would dig the uniform."

He braced a hand on the shelf, leaning forward and caging me in. "Yeah?" He bit his bottom lip. "Want to show me how much you like it later? We can go out for dinner."

I tapped my finger against my mouth as I pretended to think about it. "I don't know, Mr. Police Officer. I've been a good boy and I don't think I need police custody."

"Good boy, huh?" His gaze swept over me from my head to my shoes. "You're telling me you haven't been naughty, just a bit?"

"Maybe." I placed a hand in the center of his chest, the muscles hard under my palm. He would have been a good toy to play with, but that wasn't my life anymore.

"See, I bet you can be a whole lot of naughty," he said. "Look at you, pretty much begging for it right here."

"Begging for what?" I opened my eyes wide.

"You know. Don't toy with me."

"Why? Am I going to get into trouble?" I dragged out the last word.

"You're in so much right now, baby, and you don't even know it."

I pushed at his chest a little. "Tell you what. I am kind of old-fashioned. Come up to the house around eight tonight and ask Daddy if I can go out with you. If he says yes, then we've got a deal."

"What?" He laughed. "Are you serious right now?"

Nodding, I shifted away from him and placed the can of coconut milk into my shopping car. I glanced over my shoulder and winked as I pushed the cart.

"If you get Daddy's permission, you can have me."

"You know it really sounds weird when you call him Daddy like that," he called after me.

I shrugged. "Shaw will always be my Daddy. There's nothing weird about that."

Nothing at all.

Nathan was persistent; I had to give him that. He didn't leave me alone but followed me around the grocery store, trying to persuade me to go out with him without making him face Shaw. What a waste of taxpayers' money.

"The guy low-key hates me," he said when I was at the cashier. "He'll never say yes, but you're grown." He took his time to give me an appreciative stare. "So grown, and I just want to get to know you a little. How can that be wrong?"

I gave him the same response. "Ask my Daddy."

He walked me to my car and helped me unload the bags. His persistence was commendable. Too bad my heart belonged to Daddy, or he might have been someone I could have fun with.

"Mr. Police Officer, shouldn't you be out there saving the world?" I asked when I closed the trunk.

He sighed. "You're a tough cookie. You're going to be sweet when I finally get a bite out of you."

I laughed and slid into the driver's seat. "Be careful. This cookie is fresh out of the oven. You don't want to get burned."

"Burn me, baby. I can take it."

I blew him a kiss just to mess with him, not feeling the slightest bit of remorse at leading him on. There never could be a relationship between us. I couldn't wait to see Shaw lose his shit when Nathan came to the door. But what if he didn't? What if he no longer cared?

No, I refused to believe that. On my way home, I picked up some scented candles and bath salts. I would remind Daddy why he should be with me. That I was the same Ari he always took care of, and none of that changed because we hid one body together.

If anything, it should bring us closer. We shared a secret no one else could ever know about. We had something that belonged to just us. Couldn't he see the beauty in that? I hadn't asked him. He'd volunteered to drive me and helped me dig the grave and push that corpse into the hole. He'd done it all by himself, so why did he act like I'd been the one to persuade him?

I spent the evening cleaning because I liked taking care of Shaw's house. I liked him entering with a smile in the evening. That the haggard look after a rough day at school changed the moment he smelled whatever I had cooking or the scent of pine from the cleaning supplies. And when he smiled at me, I felt like his whole world.

I *wanted* to be his whole world.

Just like the past few days, I expected Shaw to show up home late, which was the reason I'd given Nathan that time. I just hoped he didn't stay later than usual.

With the tracking app on his phone I'd installed and hidden in a secret folder, I knew the exact moment he left work. I put away the materials I was using for sewing a new project and turned the oven on a low setting to warm up the food. Right on time, his car pulled up in the driveway. I wore my favorite dress and took extra care with my hair.

"Hey, Daddy," I greeted him as I opened the door before he could.

"Hey, sorry I'm late. Work stuff." He walked past me, not even noticing the extra mile I'd gone getting dressed up for him. Had I lost his interest for good?

"That's okay. I made you dinner." I forced a smile, ready to give tonight my all. If that didn't work, I would go to phase two.

"I'm not hungry." He loosened his tie and headed for the stairs. "I ordered something while I was working."

"But I prepared duck," I protested. "I spent all evening cooking for you."

He turned at the foot of the stairs and looked at me then. His gaze scanned me from my hair to my feet, and when his eyes met mine, they were blazing. I instantly felt better.

"New dress?" he asked.

I spun in a circle, my skirt swishing against my legs. "Yes, you like?"

"You always look stunning," he said. He shook his head, as if realizing what he said, and climbed the stairs.

"I ran you a warm bath," I called after him. "I knew you'd be tired after work, so I hope it helps you relax."

"Thanks, Ari. You didn't have to."

"I know. I just want to make you happy, Daddy. To be the best boy I can be."

I needed him to remember that instead of how I'd taken someone's life. He didn't respond, and the door slammed shut. The back of my eyes burned, but I held it together until I was in the kitchen. I opened the oven, took out the roast spiced duck with plums I'd prepared for us, and dropped the dish onto the counter. I grabbed the thick butcher knife and went to town, hacking it to pieces, tears stinging my eyes. I was losing him.

Footsteps padded behind me, and I turned, holding the knife in front of me. Shaw stared at the massacred duck on the table, then at the knife in my hand. As calmly as I could, I set down the knife on the counter and gave him my best smile.

"Did you forget something?"

"Thank you," he said softly. "For the bath. Everything looks great."

I could have cried with relief for him acknowledging the lengths I'd gone for him. I loved him so much it hurt, and all I wanted was for him to love me back. Even half as much. I'd take that.

"I love taking care of you. Did you want something else? I can scrub your back for you."

"I, uh, I think I can manage." His eyes dropped to the knife on the table. Dear god, he'd seen my little meltdown and was now wary of me. Did he think I would hurt him? How could he even think that? I'd done everything for him and to get back to him.

"I can get you a glass of wine," I said.

"I shouldn't."

"Oh, you must," I insisted. "Tomorrow's the weekend, so you don't have to worry about going to the school, and it's only one glass. I've got your favorite bottle of Grignolino."

He narrowed his eyes. "You remember my favorite brand of wine?"

I beamed a smile at him. "If I want to make Daddy happy, I have to remember what Daddy likes."

He hesitated, then nodded. "I suppose one glass can't hurt."

"And are you sure I can't help you in the bath?" I lowered my eyelashes seductively, so he knew exactly what I was offering. The same thing he rejected a few nights ago.

The doorbell rang, and I straightened. I glanced at the clock on the microwave. Fucking perfect. Mr. Police Officer was here, right on time.

"Hmm, I wonder who that is."

I shrugged, and he walked out of the kitchen to get the door. I shuffled closer so I could hear what was being said while staying out of the way. Daddy couldn't know that I'd set this up. I had to be the innocent one in all this. I needed Daddy's anger to be generated at Nathan, not me.

"Nathan?" Daddy said, his voice frosty. "What are you doing here?"

"I'm here to see Ari. I mean, you did say I can't pick him up in my uniform, so I took a shower and changed."

"What do you want with Ari?"

"Just to hang out."

"Where are you taking him?"

"I don't know. I was thinking maybe that diner on Main Street and after we could go back to my place."

"Yeah? You think you're going to get lucky tonight, Graham?"

"I can hope. So what do you think?" Nathan didn't seem to notice the hostility in Shaw's voice. "Do I have a chance with Ari?"

"He's seeing someone else."

"What?"

"I don't know what's so hard to understand. He's with someone else."

"But he didn't say that."

"You talked to him?" Shaw asked.

Shit. Fuck. Shit. It was all coming out.

"Yeah, when I ran into him at the supermarket earlier today. He said if I got your approval, we could date. So come on. Don't block me here. I'm really interested in him."

"Like I said, Graham. He's not interested. Ari's a flirt. You can't take what he says seriously."

Was that truly how he felt about me?

"I don't know. With all due respect, he was really feeling me today. I think—"

The door slammed shut, and I jumped. Heart pounding in my chest, I backed away into the kitchen.

"You saw Nathan today?"

I slowly turned to Daddy, who stood in the doorway, his face flushed, and his eyes blazing.

I dropped my gaze to the floor. "I ran into him today at the grocery store. He wouldn't take no for an answer."

"Interesting how all these guys just supposedly can't take no for an answer, Ari."

I shrugged. "It's not my fault they like what they see."

"You want them to like what they see?" His chest rose and fell rapidly, and the color in his face spread to his neck. Was he flushed all over? "Answer me!"

I jumped. He never spoke to me in such an angry tone before, and it frightened me as much as it aroused me. He was being all tough Daddy on me, and I loved it.

"I don't know," I replied honestly. "It makes me feel good that they want me, but I only want you."

He was too silent. For way too long. He was studying me. If I could get a peek into his mind to know what he was thinking... Was he repulsed? Did he find me a psychopath? Mom called me that once.

"Be careful of the games you play with me, little one," he said softly, then turned on his heels and strode out of the kitchen.

Was it a good or a bad thing that just happened? One thing was clear: Shaw didn't like the idea of me being with another man. In fact, the whole idea of me being with someone seemed to drive him insane with jealousy and possessiveness. Those emotions I could handle. The silent treatment I'd gotten over the past days was not.

Giving him some space to cool down, I cleaned the mess I'd made, then grabbed the bottle of wine I'd set aside to chill. I poured myself a glass and downed it, then made my way up the stairs to his bedroom with his promised wine in hand. His aloofness was the worst.

I knocked on the door and opened it. One sweeping gaze revealed he wasn't inside. I went to his bathroom and rapped once.

"Daddy, it's me. I have your glass of wine. May I come in?"

Silence. Was he ignoring me?

"Please. I'm sorry."

Another few seconds passed before he replied. "Come on in."

It was time for phase two. I didn't have the patience to wait for Shaw to make his move anymore. If we were ever going to advance in our relationship, I would have to take the reins.

I pushed the door open and stepped into the bathroom. Daddy sat in the bathtub, lying back with his head in the rest. His eyes were closed, which gave me all the time to study him. If I was going based on looks and gorgeous body, I would have picked Nathan, but he didn't hold a candle to Daddy. Shaw owned me in a way he didn't yet understand.

My gaze traveled back to Shaw's face, right in his piercing eyes.

"You can put the wine down and go."

I didn't argue with him. Without a word, I placed the glass of wine on the edge of the tub and backed out of the bathroom.

"If you need help, call me. I'll be in the other room."

TWELVE

SHAW

ANGER BURNED INSIDE ME when Ari came into the bathroom. Even though I had my eyes closed, I sensed him and the way he disturbed my thoughts. He'd set this up. I knew he had. Insisting Nathan come up to the house to ask him out when he knew damn well I was his Daddy. Did he really expect me to say yes and share him with Nathan?

A part of me wanted to believe he'd done it only to make me jealous, but people found men like Nathan exciting and dangerous. I was a boring high school principal who looked nothing like the young cop. Nathan was the cool, handsome jerk whose sex appeal didn't need additional points by being in law enforcement. What if Ari really wanted a date with Nathan? I should have said yes just to see what he would have done.

But the thought of another man lusting after Ari fired up every protective instinct inside me. It wasn't just protective, though. The idea of someone wanting to touch him. Nathan practically salivated when I opened the door and he asked for Ari... No fucking way. Over my dead body.

And it scared the shit out of me. This new wave of possessiveness. The urge to keep him inside and away from the rest of the world. Locked in a tower. My own little Rapunzel.

He was mine.

I opened my eyes. He was so beautiful, all dolled up like that in one of those dresses he loved so much. He even had on stockings and heels. No one else got to see this side of him. Only me.

Here in my house, I could wade in the deluge of my filthy thoughts. Because it didn't matter that he made me angry, something few people accomplished. Or maybe because of that anger, I wanted to place his hands on the marble countertop, like the naughty boy he was, and lift his skirt. To make my way to what was beneath and take it because it belonged to me.

He was driving me insane, and these past days I'd been avoiding my home to get my sanity back. It was as if he'd been seeping under my skin all these years and he was finally wedged in so good there was no pulling him out. I might not even want to pull him out. Some sick, twisted part of me liked that he paid me so much attention. That he wanted to cook and clean and serve me in every way.

But the duck. I couldn't forget the way he'd hacked into that bird with the butcher knife. Was that the same way he'd laid it into Rich?

My stomach turned.

I met his gaze, filled with such eagerness to please. I knew if I told him to strip and suck me off, as hard as I was, he would do it in a heartbeat. I was finally beginning to understand what Anne had seen all those years. She hadn't been wrong that this boy wanted more from me than a father should give his son.

"You can put the wine down and go," I said.

I expected him to argue, to pout, for those long lashes to drip tears. Instead, he accepted my dismissal, nodding politely, and placed the glass of wine on the edge of the tub. I watched him walk out, the bow at the back of his dress so pretty and delicate. Just like him.

At the door, Ari paused and looked over his shoulder at me. He was up to something, but what? Was he off to meet Nathan now? I clenched my teeth.

"If you need help, call me," he said, giving me a small smile. "I'll be in the other room."

He slipped away before I could do something stupid and call him back. Just as well. The door closed behind his slender back, and I sank farther in the tub. He'd lit candles around it just for me, and the temperature of the water had been just right. How had he known I would be home soon?

With a sigh, I picked up the glass and took a drink. I was supposed to be relaxing, to make decisions about Ari, but instead, thoughts of how he'd entered my shower and rubbed his dick furiously played in my mind. Memories of how much I'd wanted to take his cock into my mouth and suck all that cum down. Or how I'd been on the verge of shoving him against the wall and fucking him senseless.

The volatility of my thoughts had frightened me out of the shower. I'd always been a gentle lover, someone who took my time to learn and please my partner. But at that moment, I hadn't cared if he came or not. All I'd been able to think about was stuffing him full of my cock and staining his insides with my cum. I'd wanted to have him stand there until I could see myself dripping out of his hole, which I'd just used.

And it scared me. A hysterical laugh bubbled out of my throat, and I gulped some more of the wine to chase it away. I'd buried a dead body, and now that made me what? Who was this man I was becoming?

I drowned my mood into the wine, wishing there was more but not wanting to call Ari for a refill. I wanted him as far away from me as possible. Maybe it was time to let him go. To shun the excitement his being here brought and return to my staid life.

When I tried to get up, my limbs felt like rubber. I frowned as my vision blurred. I hadn't drunk a lot. One glass of wine wasn't supposed to make me feel this way.

Ari.

What did you do?

He had to have added something to the wine. No wonder he'd left without a fuss. That butcher knife crowded my mind, but instead of that duck, it was me on the table before Ari, that innocent smile on his face, even as he hacked me to bits. Was that what this was all about? Did he plan to get rid of me now that I knew he killed Rich?

I cried out his name, but it didn't come out as strong as it should have. I'd trusted him. I'd invited him back into my home and protected him all these years from his mother. Would he really do this to me?

Whether he heard me or he'd been timing this whole thing, the bathroom door opened, and Ari entered with that same innocent look on his face, as if he hadn't drugged me.

"What'd you do?" I whispered.

"Nothing to hurt you, Daddy." He walked over to the bathtub and sat beside me. "It'll just make you relax and sleep a little. You haven't been sleeping well lately."

Even my heartbeat seemed to be slowing down with one giant thump after another. It was as if I could hear it in my ears.

"I trusted you," I murmured.

He shook his head and stroked my damp hair. "You don't trust me anymore. Not since Rich. I see the way you look at me, and it breaks my heart."

"You killed somebody."

"And we buried the body together." He caressed my face with the back of his hand. "Do you know how intimate that is? How exciting it is to share that little secret with you? It's our dirty secret, Daddy, and no one else will ever know. That secret should have brought us closer, but you don't trust me anymore. I'll make you trust me again, though. You'll see. I'll do anything for you. Anything."

"Ari, what are you going to do?"

"I'm going to make you see that you and I belong together. That men like Nathan and Rich can never come between us."

With the last bout of strength I could muster, I lunged at him and grabbed him by the neck. Water splashed out of the tub onto the front of his dress. He gasped, glancing down at the wet marks, but he didn't seem perturbed by my hand around his slender neck. I was sure if I tried hard enough, I could crush his windpipe. He was so small and helpless.

"You ruined my dress, Daddy," he pouted, brushing at the damp spots. "Now I'm going to have to throw it into the dryer."

Didn't he feel my hand around his neck? How could he so casually talk about wetness on his dress? I could snap his neck.

"You're insane," I said.

Hurt filled those pretty brown eyes. "Why'd you say that?"

"You don't even flinch."

He looked down at my arm and smiled. "Silly, Daddy. You'd never hurt me. I know that."

I wanted to prove him wrong. To show him how crazy he was driving me. He deserved it for drugging me, but my arm fell away. I was screwed.

"Now that's over with, let's get you into bed." He rose to his feet. "You'll see that you will feel much better in the morning. Well rested."

Was that all this was to him? Just to get me to sleep?

He released the drain and grabbed a huge, fluffy yellow towel I didn't recall being one I owned. He threw the towel over his shoulder and placed his hands under my armpits.

"Come on, Daddy. You're going to have to help me out here."

"You drugged me." And I was losing energy fast. I wobbled on my feet. He propped my naked body up and wrapped the towel around me.

"I'll do what I need to do for us."

Unable to respond, I dragged on heavy legs after him. He wrapped his arms around my waist to support me, and I leaned heavily into him. Even drugged up as I was, I felt how small he was, how addictingly fun-sized. His mother had been just as petite, and it'd been a treat feeling so much bigger than her. I pushed the thought out of my head, my stomach churning at comparing the two.

Ari was nothing like Anne. Anne would never have drugged me. Would never have killed someone and gotten me involved.

Eventually, we reached my bedroom, and Ari laid me on my back. I stared at him, losing lucidity by the minute. He was a beautiful haze as he reached for the zipper at the back of his dress and shimmied the material down his hips. Left clad in only the stockings and red lace, Ari slid into bed beside me. He cuddled up against my side, one hand around my body.

"Go to sleep, Daddy," he murmured.

Thirteen

Shaw

WHAT'S WRONG WITH ME?

I woke up foggy, without the slightest idea of where I was or what had happened. With a groan, I tried to rub at my face, but my hand wouldn't cooperate. I tugged again. My eyes flew open. What the hell? My heart galloped in my chest, and I came around fully. I was stretched out on my back on my bed, both my hands tied at the wrists to the headboard. My feet were secured with ropes that circled my ankles.

I yanked both my arms and then my legs, but the ropes didn't give. No way was I getting out of these bonds unless someone untied me.

Ari.

I jerked my head around. Ari was snuggled up in bed beside me. His chest rose and fell with his even breathing. So he'd tied me to the bed when I was knocked out and then got into bed with me?

"Ari," I called his name, my voice coming out as a croak. "Ari, wake up and untie me."

He shifted, one stocking-clad leg running smoothly up mine. "Daddy?" He stretched languorously, a soft, sexy purr escaping his lips that jolted my dick. How could he do these despicable things and still manage to arouse me?

"Untie me."

He sat up in the bed, the light from the bedside lamp swathing his skin in a light glow. He was still wearing the lace thong and gartered stockings.

"Not yet." He placed a finger in the center of my naked chest and ran it down the hair on my stomach. "I need something from you first. Something you've been denying both of us."

I frowned, jerking at my right hand. "Ari, you need help."

He smiled, leaned over, and licked my left nipple. "I know. And that's why you're going to help me feel so good tonight, Daddy. So, so good."

The bed dipped as he rolled off and stretched. His ass tightened, and as he relaxed, he reached a hand behind him to fix the thong that had slipped between his cheeks. He righted the waistband of the lacy underwear, then blew me a kiss.

"I won't be long."

"Ari, don't—"

He disappeared into the bathroom. I stared up at the ceiling. What the hell had I gotten myself into? I was trussed up so well there was no way I was getting out of the restraints until he was good and ready to release me. Still, I yanked at the ropes, only to have a sharp pain stabbing my wrists.

Ari returned to the bedroom with a dildo in hand. While not as long as my dick, it was almost the same thickness. He hopped up onto the bed on his knees and brandished the dildo. "You're so big, Daddy. I'm not sure I can take all of you without prepping real good."

"I'm not going to have sex with you, Ari."

"Of course, you are." He licked the dildo indecently. "Everyone wants to have sex with me."

"I don't."

"You're lying." He used his free hand to cup my cock. "You're already getting hard."

"I won't have sex with you, Ari. What are you going to do? Force me?"

"I know you want it," he said. "And you're going to love it. My other Daddy loved filling my ass. He used to call me his good little boy, but I didn't like it. I only want to be *your* good little boy."

I tried another tactic. "If you do this, you're not a good boy, Ari. Good boys don't force their Daddies to do something they don't want to do."

"But this is different. When Daddies don't know what they want, good boys remind Daddies."

He leaned over me and planted his lips firmly against mine. I closed my mouth, but he didn't seem to care. He kissed me just the same, his tongue running over my bottom lip. Thank god he moved on to my jaw because I'd have given in and kissed him back. His lips were so soft and sweet against mine. Holy hell, how was I supposed to keep up the façade that I didn't like what he was doing? Lying with him in bed at night was torture. He thought I couldn't sleep at night because of what he'd done to Rich? I couldn't because I was too busy trying not to touch him.

"Ari," I gasped his name when he rained kisses down my neck. His lips left hot trails all the way to my tingling left nipple.

"I love your nipples so much." His eyes were heavy with desire. "They're thick and hairy. Makes me want to suck on them like a little baby. Can I suck on them, Daddy?"

Oh god, I couldn't speak. The wrong thing might come out, like telling him yes when I meant to say no.

"Of course you want me to. It'll make you feel so good."

He lay on his side beside me and captured my left nipple between his teeth. My body jolted at the sensation that slammed into my gut and robbed my breath. He didn't just lick my nipple. No, he latched onto it and sucked on the nub, his other hand sliding through the hair on my front and down and taking my cock into his hand. He stroked me, and what little reserve my body had broke.

"Ari, god!" I grunted as his teeth skimmed the sensitive peak of my nipple.

"So good, Daddy," he moaned around the peak. His tongue flicked the nub, fluttering over the hard point. My chest heaved as if I'd taken part in a five-thousand-meter race.

When he shifted over me and treated himself to the other nipple, I gave up all pretense of not enjoying that. I'd never had my nipples sucked quite like that before. Maybe licked a little, but not completely suckled like Ari did. It was definitely one of those acts I would never forget, no matter how much I wasn't into what he was doing to me.

And I wasn't.

Holy shit, I couldn't be. He'd drugged me, for fuck's sake.

He licked, and I moaned, tugging at the ropes. I wanted to touch him.

Ari finally released my nipple, the hair around the area damp from his saliva. He kissed my belly and gave me a sweet smile. "Oh, I love your body so much, Daddy. We're so different."

He touched his hand to my round, hairy belly. Then, in one smooth movement, he straddled my chest with his back to me. He leaned forward, tilting his hips up, and the string of the thong slipped back between his cheeks, the material resting snugly against the slightly darker pink hue of his butthole.

"Enjoy the view, Daddy," he said. He took hold of my cock by the base and lavished the tip with his lips. He kissed the head of my cock, moaning loudly as he took me in deeper, inch by inch. I couldn't see his face, but I could feel the heat his tongue unleashed.

"God, Ari, please don't." But even as I begged him not to, the words came out in a moan of pleasure. The way his tongue wrapped around my cock was glorious. I sucked in a deep breath and let it out slowly to control the urge to buck up into his mouth.

Without warning, Ari rocked back, covering my face with his ass. He giggled as he rubbed himself over me, reached back to grab his cheeks, and spread them.

"Please, Daddy," he begged me. "Please fuck me with your tongue."

I wanted to. I wanted so badly to bury my tongue into his pink hole, but I resisted the urge. He obviously wasn't satisfied I wouldn't play his little game. He eased up and stared over his shoulder down at me, disappointment in his eyes, his bottom lip pushed out in a pout.

"I cooked for you," he said softly. "I kept your home clean, and twice I made you come. Would have made you come more if you'd let me. I think it's only fair you give me something back."

When I kept my jaw clenched tight, he narrowed his eyes. "Suit yourself, Daddy. You can suffocate on my ass or give us both what we want."

He sat on my face again, this time not giving me the space to breathe. It was oddly arousing, having the air deprived of my lungs while his lush ass rubbed over my face. God, how could I be so fucking turned on by this game we were playing? He jerked his hips up, and I gasped at the sudden air I was allowed. He snagged the lacy string of the thong and pulled it to one side.

"Fuck me with your tongue, Daddy. Do it now!"

He sounded like a demanding, petulant child, but when he rocked his hips back, I stuck out my tongue and delved into his hole, giving us both what we needed. He gasped and moaned, his elated cries of joy filling the room.

"Yes, Daddy. Yes, yes, fuck, yes."

He bounced on my face with his perky ass, giving me moments of air to drag into my lungs before he was back to sitting on my face. He leaned backward, gripped my trapped hands for leverage, and rode my tongue.

My cock pulsed at being ignored. I was so hard it hurt, and precum leaked from my slit. I ate his ass until he couldn't take it anymore. Until he fell forward onto my legs, breathing hard, trembling.

"So good," he groaned, then gave a shaky laugh. "You almost made me come. But I can't come yet. I need to come with you inside me."

"Ari." I took a deep breath. "Untie me, and let's talk."

"If I untie you, will you fuck me?" He bent over to the bedside table and returned with lube in hand.

I groaned. "Don't you get it? We need to talk before we do this. Sex is an important step in a relationship."

"I know. That's why I want to take it with you."

He grabbed the dildo he had before and lubed it generously. I tried to turn my head, but he wasn't having any of it. He latched the straps of the dildo behind my head. I might have raised my head to accommodate him. I swore I didn't mean to, but it was hard to say no to Ari. The base of the dildo rested against my mouth, the thick silicone pointing to the ceiling.

"This is going to be so good," he murmured. "I'm giving you a real view here, Daddy."

Unable to say anything, I grunted, my eyes focused on his ass as he straddled my face, grabbed the end of the dildo, and nudged it against his hole. Slowly, he inched his ass down, and I couldn't look away from the sight of his hole stretching to take all that girth.

"Do you see my hole taking that cock, Daddy?" he gasped. "That's how I'm going to stretch around your cock. But you're so much bigger, and it's going to hurt so good."

Leaning forward to balance against my stomach, Ari rode that dildo with slow caution at first. If only I could say it didn't affect me. That I was indifferent to the sight of the dildo invading his body, but I was jealous. Boy, was I fucking jealous of that dildo. Nothing should be inside his gorgeous body unless I put it there.

Oblivious to my dark mood, Ari moved faster, one hand going back to press an ass cheek to one side so I had an even better view of the dildo sliding inside and out of him. When he backed completely off the toy, I got treated to his gaping hole. Then he swallowed the dildo back inside.

"I think that's enough." Ari pulled off the dildo, gripped both his cheeks, and spread them right before me. "What do you think, Daddy? Can you fit now?" He inched a hand between his cheeks and plunged two fingers into his hole. "I guess the only way to know for sure is to try, but let me get rid of this thing first. Feels good, but you'll be so much better."

He slipped the dildo from behind my head, but he didn't put it away. Instead, he pushed it against my lips. "Open up, Daddy."

When I didn't comply, he smacked my lips with the dildo. I opened up, and he shoved the black silicone into my mouth. I gagged as it hit the back of my throat, and he pulled out, placing a hand over his mouth with a giggle. "Oops."

He brought the dildo to his mouth and sucked it, all the time watching me. God, he was so decadent and sinful, and he was teaching me things about myself I never knew. I would never have thought to find something so dubious to be arousing, but my cock was so hard I was shy of telling him to ride me already.

Satisfied, he placed the dildo on the bed and picked up the lube again. He coated my dick with the gel. Oh my god, he was going to fuck me without a condom.

"Not without a condom," I grunted.

"We don't need a condom." He straddled me again and pressed his lips against mine. "You haven't fucked anyone since Mom, and I got tested just for this."

"How long have you been planning this?"

"You were slipping away from me. I had to do something, Daddy."

Before I could respond, the head of my cock entered him, and blinding white light shifted through me at the tightness of that hole sliding down my shaft. He had been right that the dildo could have prepared him only so much. He gasped, biting his bottom lip as he tried to take more of me.

"So big," he murmured. "Feel how tight I am around you?"

As if I could feel anything but that vise. When he couldn't take more of me, he braced a hand on my stomach and rode me slowly. Just the tip of my cock at first, but then he swung his ass lower, claiming more and more inches as he adjusted to my girth. He mewled and moaned, head thrown back, hands caressing my belly. He looked so pretty, so hot and tempting.

Ari slid a hand down his chest, rubbing over his nipples. His eyes closed, and his lips fell apart. His breathing increased as nothing else seemed to matter but the boy taking pleasure from me. I couldn't close my eyes, couldn't fail to watch his skin turn flushed, sweat popping up on his body, the way he bit into his bottom lip.

Smack, smack, smack. His ass hit my pelvis harder. *Smacksmack.* A cry tore from his lips. He grasped his dick and stroked himself, aiming the deposit of his cum at my stomach and effectively tearing down my walls.

Fourteen

Ari

HOLY FUCK, RIDING DADDY'S dick was good. He was hung, long and thick, just the way I liked 'em. It was a challenge at first getting all of him to fit, but it burned so good. The stretch left me open, destroyed by him, and I was sated. This was how it was supposed to be between us. Now all I needed was Daddy to finish inside my hole. To treat my ass like the place to dump his seed.

I came down from my high with a smile of satisfaction. Daddy's face was so stony. I couldn't read what was going through his mind. His hands clutched at the ropes that bound him to the headboard, and his body beneath me was taut. His cock still pulsed, heavy and thick, inside my hole. With great care, I rocked back and forth, which had him catching his breath.

Good, he tried to deny it and hide it, but his body didn't lie. He wanted me, but now *he* had to act on it if he wanted to come.

I leaned forward, still slowly moving my hips, and licked up my cum from his hairy stomach. When he was clean, I sat back, his cock embedded as far inside me as it could go. The tendons in his neck strained.

"There, a good boy cleans up his messes," I murmured, then widened my eyes. "Did you want me to make you come too, Daddy? 'Cause I think I'm a little tired and may need to go to sleep now."

From the line of his jaw, I bet he clenched his teeth. These new sides of Shaw were so exciting. He'd always been so soft and gentle with me, but the glare in his eyes was anything but. He looked like he wanted to choke me. The joke was on him. I wouldn't mind him choking me, his hand against my windpipe, keeping me on the verge of a blackout while he ruined my ass.

I moaned at the thought but eased off Daddy, instantly regretting the loss. My hole ached but wasn't fully satisfied. Not without his cum. I reached back and stroked the way my hole had slackened for him. So good.

"Don't worry, Daddy. I'm going to untie you now."

Shaw grunted but didn't respond. With a sigh, I worked on the ropes at his ankles first, untying the knot. When his feet were free, I massaged the red area from the tightness of the rope and him struggling against it.

"I'm sorry, Daddy," I murmured, planting kisses on his ankles. I climbed onto the bed and untied one wrist, then the other.

As soon as he was free, Shaw sprang up off the bed.

"This is all your fault," he ground out. He caught my legs and tugged. I fell onto my back with an *oof*, barely regaining my breath before he yanked me to the edge of the bed. Wow, I never expected Shaw to be so rough, but it was no less arousing when he lifted me off the bed and sat with me lying over his lap.

Shaw's hand came down hard on my ass, and I yelped both in surprise and pain. "Don't." *Crack.* "Drug." *Crack.* "Me." *Crack.* "Ever." *Crack.* "Again."

By the time he spoke the last word, I was sobbing, tears running down my face as I writhed on his lap. It hurt so good. My ass smarted from his heavy hand. He'd spared me nothing with each slap.

"Stop!" I bawled. "It hurts. Please stop."

His hand didn't land on my ass again, but I didn't really want him to stop. I wanted him to continue hurting me, punishing me for all the bad things I'd done. I wanted him to make me the good boy he wanted me to be.

I looked back at him. "Don't stop," I whispered, sniffling at the snot running from my nostrils. "Please don't stop. I deserve it. Please. I'll tell you red if it's unbearable."

Without a word, he pushed my head forward and slapped me hard. I clenched my cheeks and let out a wail.

"I hate this," he said, even as he rained blows down on my squirming ass. "Hate what you're turning me into." Fire burned my ass all over, but I bit into my bottom lip, drawing blood to refrain from using my safeword. "I used to be pretty confident in who I was, and now I don't know who I am anymore, thanks to you. You've turned my life upside down. I can't sleep, can't eat, and it's all because of you."

"Red! Red! Red!" I screamed, finally unable to take any more. My butt was so sore, but I'd done penance for my misdeeds. For tying him up and drugging him, then fucking myself on his cock.

Shaw got to his feet with me in his arms and fastened his lips against mine. I sobbed against his mouth, the saltiness of my tears mingling with the taste of his lips. He pressed me down onto the edge of the bed, thrusting his tongue into my mouth. And then his lips were gone, but I didn't have time to feel the disappointment. He edged himself between my legs and pushed them apart. With a grunt, Shaw held my hips down onto the bed and plunged inside me.

I cried out. He was too rough, impaling me on his cock. He owned me, unlike earlier when I took what I needed from him. This time it was him taking from me, claiming me, showing me how much he wanted me, how fucking much he was out of control.

This wasn't the Shaw I was used to, and that excited me. The Shaw of my past would have tenderly made love, not like the man who pounded his way inside my body, seeking his release. His blunt fingernails dug into my hips as he held me down, needing no encouragement or movement from me. This was all about taking what he wanted.

"Fuck, Ari," he grunted, running his hands up my stomach and chest. He gripped my shoulders, snapping his hips forward. "Is this what you wanted?"

"Yes!" I took his nipples between my fingers, squeezing and releasing. He snapped his hips faster, his face flushed, and I knew it wouldn't be long now.

Shaw fell forward on me, crushing my body beneath his bulky frame on the mattress. He tucked my head into his chest, holding me against him while he tried to bury his way as far inside me as he could go. He filled me so well, and I whimpered against his chest, gasping and hanging on for dear life, feeling like a beloved rag doll, while he finally took the pleasure I'd always wanted to offer him.

"So wrong," he groaned. "This is so wrong, but I can't help it. I want to fuck you forever. Mine, Ari. You're completely mine."

"Yours," I agreed, thrilled at his possessive claim. That was all I ever wanted from him. To acknowledge what he wanted from me.

Fucking finally.

I lowered my head and latched onto his nipple with my lips. I sucked the protruding flesh into my mouth, licking as I tightened my hole around his cock pounding me.

"You have no business feeling so good beneath me. Shouldn't feel so good, but I can't help it. Can't help it, Ari."

I didn't want him to help it. He thrust hard into me, then stilled. A shudder rippled through him. His whole body tensed. And a hoarse cry tore from his throat. I continued sucking on that nipple, swirling my tongue around the hard point. His climax seemed to go on forever until his body sagged.

Shaw pulled his cock out of me and fell to the side. I felt between my legs at the wetness of his cum at the entrance of my hole. A smug smile tugged at my lips, and I curled into his body as he breathed hard. I ran my hands over his barrel chest and stroked his fuzzy stomach.

When he turned his head to the side, I didn't flinch from his look. He stared right into my eyes as though searching for something. I didn't know what he found there, but he leaned forward and kissed me softly. It was a far difference from the way he'd fucked the hell out of me just now. I liked that. He could be calm, soothing Daddy one minute and hard, disciplinarian Daddy the next.

"How's your bottom?" he asked.

"Sore," I replied, beaming at him.

He frowned. "You're very… peculiar. You know that?"

I waited for him to explain, and when he didn't, I just had to ask. "Is that a bad thing?"

"It can be," he answered honestly. "Like if you keep flirting with all these men, Ari, I…"

"You what?"

He frowned at me. "You'll make me angry. Is that what you want? To drive me insane thinking about somebody else's hands all over you like this?"

"It's just harmless flirting."

He rolled off the bed, leaving me cold and alone. I wrapped my arms around my body, although I would have preferred his.

"I don't know how to explain it." He scowled. "This is not me. I don't get jealous or possessive, but when it comes to you...I can't help it. You've become a poison, and I don't know how to get rid of it."

"But I don't understand. That's not a bad thing. I don't want you to get rid of that feeling."

"You don't get it, Ari." He hung his head. "That first night we ran into Nathan, I wanted to drive the car over him when he flirted with you. And tonight...tonight, I wanted to strangle him for having the nerve to come here and ask for my permission to date you. None of those reactions made sense. I'm not a violent man. This isn't who I am. At least not who I was before you."

I bit my bottom lip. "Does it make you upset?"

"That's the damn thing. Having you here makes me the happiest I've been in years, but I can't help feeling this won't end well."

He walked out of the bedroom and into the bathroom, leaving me to my tortured thoughts. I wanted Shaw to be happy. I didn't want him to be miserable with me, but he seemed to be a mixture of the two.

After a few minutes, Shaw returned with a washcloth and a tube of cream. I didn't protest when he guided me to roll over onto my tummy. He pushed my legs apart and passed the washcloth between my ass cheeks, cleaning me up so tenderly I wanted to cry. When he was done, he tapped two fingers against my tightly clenched hole, but I shook my head. I would hold him inside me for as long as I could.

He dropped the washcloth in the bathroom, then squeezed the cream on my ass cheeks and rubbed it into the flesh. The cream soothed the throbbing of my ass. I'd never forget this night…the first time he ever spanked me. I hoped it wouldn't be the last.

I could be very naughty.

"How does that feel now?" he asked.

"Better," I replied softly, suddenly overcome with fear and a feeling of inadequacy. What if I wasn't good enough for him?

Shaw returned to the bathroom, where he took a piss. When he came back, he lifted me up and set me on my feet while he changed the sheets. He spread a new cover on the bed and turned it down, then placed me in the center of the bed. He switched off the lights and slid into place beside me.

I shuffled under the covers.

"What are you doing?" he asked.

Instead of answering, I tugged on his hip until he rolled to the side. I slipped his soft cock into my mouth and sucked on it. Much better.

"Ari," he whispered, his hand in my hair.

But I didn't respond. I was content like this, sleeping with my Daddy's cock in my mouth for comfort as the feelings of uncertainty settled in my gut.

FIFTEEN

SHAW

LAST NIGHT SEEMED SO impossible, like a figment of my imagination, but it had been real. I woke up with Ari's mouth still around my cock. Everything came crashing down at the same time. Trying to avoid Ari because I didn't know what to say to him or explain the way I still craved him despite the fucked-up thing he did, killing someone.

My whole aim had been to avoid him, but then Nathan showed up at the door, having the gall to ask Ari out on a date. I hadn't known whether I wanted to be as far away from Ari as possible or keep him glued by my side. It seemed every moment he wasn't with me, he attracted attention I didn't like.

To top it all off, he drugged me, then used me. And I'd liked it, not to mention what I'd done to him after. Spanking his ass and watching his pale skin turn red. I'd loved hearing his cries, seeing him squirm and tighten his glutes every time my hand came down on the fleshy globes.

My cock hardened, and I let out a soft groan when he instinctively suckled as if it were a thumb. The suction only made me grow thicker, and I had to stop myself from rolling him onto his back and fucking his mouth until I came down his throat. He needed to sleep after last night's rough sex, and he seemed so peaceful. Plus, I needed a moment away from him to harness my thoughts. I couldn't trust myself to think clearly when I was around him. Apparently, I wasn't a good judge of character where he was concerned. Even knowing this, I had no urge to send him away.

As carefully as I could, I eased my cock out of his mouth. He grunted in protest but curled up in a small ball under the sheet. My god, he'd slept like that all night just to warm my dick. How many times had he woken up to slip me back into his mouth? His jaw must be so tired now. My cock wasn't the size of a thumb.

I pulled the sheet down his body and checked that he was okay. Sweat pearled on his forehead, but otherwise he seemed all right, so I left the covers down, staring at him for a while. Curled up the way he was, he had a half smile on his lips, and his breathing was even and deep. He was still fast asleep, oblivious to my scrutiny. And this was the part that made everything about him difficult. This peacefully sleeping boy was nothing like the crazed, sex-hungry maniac who tied me to the bed and threatened to smother me with his ass if I didn't treat said ass like a buffet.

My face heated up. His ass stifling me shouldn't have been as hot as it had been. He'd sedated me to take advantage of me, but bound and helpless with him in control had turned me on in ways it shouldn't have. How was I supposed to teach him a lesson if I couldn't even hide my enjoyment of what he'd done?

Where had he learned to do shit like that?

I rolled out of bed and quietly made my way to my bathroom, where I took a shower, ignoring my hard-on. I wouldn't waste rubbing one out when Ari had proven quite capable of handling me. Anne might have thought herself better than me, but this was the one thing she never did give me any lip about. She'd enjoyed sex with me, and perhaps for a while, that was the only thing keeping our relationship intact.

Now I enjoyed spreading her son's ass and fucking him too.

When I entered the bedroom, Ari was still sleeping. I kept my eyes off his small frame, fighting down the protective instincts seeing him like that brought up inside me. I got dressed and slipped out of the room. This was usually the part where I escaped from the house by using work as an excuse so I didn't have to bump into him. But I couldn't do that today, since it was the weekend.

Coward.

That one word screaming in my head buoyed my reserve to stay home and have a heart-to-heart with Ari instead of escaping the house. Instead, I forced myself into the kitchen, where remnants of last night's dinner were left on the table. So unusual for Ari, who always made sure he cleaned up everything. Not that I asked him to do that, but years of living with Ari made me aware of that side of him. He wasn't chaotic but strove to keep his environment clean. Whenever he was having a bad day, he tidied like crazy, taking things out of place only to organize them again.

I cleaned up the kitchen, and when I was satisfied that everything would meet his expectations, I checked the fridge for ingredients to make breakfast for us. He was the chef in the family. It was the one thing Anne hadn't been able to refute, even when she would shoo him out of the kitchen because it was hers. We'd have had better dinners if she allowed Ari to help her cook.

And I would be able to prepare something better for us if I'd bothered to learn beyond heating the frozen meals and ordering takeout I survived on before my marriage and after my divorce. I couldn't get the eggs fluffy the way Ari liked them, and they didn't taste quite the same either. He must add something when he prepared his eggs, but there was no way I was going to figure out what.

I spent too much time with the toaster oven and only realized the eggs were burning when I smelled them.

"Shit." I grabbed the skillet and promptly dropped it on the counter. Damn, I forgot to put on the oven mitt. I rushed to the sink and held my hand under the cold water to soothe the burn.

"What's burning?"

I swiveled around. Ari came in, fresh out of the shower, the tips of his hair still wet. He hadn't bothered to put on his own clothes but wore one of my long-sleeved T-shirts that covered his fingertips and fell to mid-thigh. My clothes made him appear even smaller than he was, but he looked absolutely adorable and so completely mine.

He peered into the skillet at the burnt eggs. "You were hungry? Why didn't you wake me to make your breakfast?"

"I wanted to make you breakfast."

His face radiated his pleasure; his cheeks were flushed, his eyes beaming with happiness.

He threw himself at me, and I instinctively held him to me, lowering my lips to his when he raised his head and puckered his lips. He was so sweet and so carnal at the same time. And I was surprised by the effect he had on my libido. When was the last time I'd been this horny? Ready to fuck at the sight of his bare legs or the way he plunged his tongue into my mouth.

I cupped his bottom, and he moaned. I loosened my grip and gazed down at him. "Hurts?" I inched my hand under the hem of his shirt and met bare skin. He was buck naked beneath my shirt. It took everything out of me not to pull his cheeks apart and rub my fingers over his hole. Last night, I'd worked him so loose I'd been able to fuck him hard, but how open was he still?

He nodded and placed a hand in the center of my chest, dropping his eyes. "I wasn't sure what to think. Whether or not you would be angry at me."

"Why would I be angry?"

He lifted his head then, bright spots appearing in his cheeks. "You know why. I've been naughty."

"I want you to say it. How have you been naughty?"

"I slipped something into your drink."

"Before that."

"What comes before that?" At my narrowed gaze, his eyes widened. "Oh, Nathan. Yeah, that. I shouldn't have tried to make you jealous by inviting Nathan to the house. Shouldn't have drugged you, tied you up, and fucked myself on your cock."

"I don't believe you. You're not sorry for doing those things, and you'd probably do them again."

Instead of denying it, he smiled at me and squirmed out of my embrace. "Sit. I'll make us breakfast before you burn the kitchen down. Honestly, I don't know how you survived without me. It's time you admit how much you need me."

His teasing tone belied everything we'd gone through last night. I couldn't resist crowding Ari at the sink. My heart beat to one rhythm. The rhythm of *mine*. Even with just the two of us here together, I tried to ward off the rising panic at the idea of someone taking him away from me. I wouldn't let them. Wasn't that the reason I'd hidden that body with him? To keep the authorities from taking him away from me?

Ari giggled as I nuzzled his neck and wrapped my arms around his waist to hold him to me. I needed to feel him. So badly. Not in a sexual way. Just to feel he was here. I ran my hands up his stomach to his chest and then down his sides. His bones were so fragile. I could lose him so easily, especially if he continued playing these dangerous games.

"Daddy, that tickles." He swatted at my hand, massaging his ribcage.

"Promise me," I whispered in his ear. "Promise me you'll be more careful. You won't be reckless with what's mine."

He inhaled sharply and nodded. "I love when you call me yours. It makes me feel so wanted."

I pushed his shirt up to his waist, leaving his ass bare as I kissed his neck, the side of his face. "I want you. It's not good for me, but I still do."

I pulled down the front of my shorts and took out my hard cock, then pushed the head against his hole for him to feel just how much. My precum left a trail over his hole, and with a groan, I slid my cock up and down his crack. He gasped, clutching the edge of the counter and thrusting his ass back.

The ringing of the doorbell woke me out of the lust that almost had me fucking him dry, which would have been nothing shy of a disaster. I kissed his shoulder and lowered his shirt, then stepped away and rearranged my shorts. There was no hiding my erection, though.

"I'll get the door for you," Ari said.

Before he could even take a step, I was fisting his shirt and pulling him back to me.

"Not wearing that you won't."

He beamed up at me. Jesus, something was wrong with him if he enjoyed me being this controlling. Even a part of me was sickened by the way I acted toward him. He wasn't a toy for me to own.

Still mine, mine, mine.

"Okay, Daddy," he said.

I frowned, not trusting his wide-eyed innocent look. Once upon a time, I would have no questions asked. After last night, no chance. What Ari wanted, he went after. I'd need to do something about that. At the prospect of curbing his stubborn, manipulative behavior, my adrenaline spiked.

I opened the front door partially, hoping to shield my erection from whoever was calling. I didn't get many visitors, but from time to time, a colleague stopped by for no other reason than they were bored.

The door was pushed back with such force it smacked me in the face. I was thrown off-balance, unable to do anything about the punch that snapped my head back. My nose exploded from the pain. I stumbled backward, hitting the ground. Judd O'Connor hauled me to my feet, his face mottled.

"I warned you that you'd regret it, Shaw," he spat. "You having my boy to face the district despite our little chat?"

"Get your hands off me, Judd!" I tried to throw him off, but he was so much stronger than me, fueled by his anger.

"I'm not fucking done with you yet." He slammed me hard into the wall at my back.

"Get the fuck off him!" Ari screamed.

It distracted Judd enough for me to elbow him in the face and drive him back. Blood trickled into my mouth, and I swiped at it with my shirt sleeve. His attention was on Ari, who aimed a small gun directly at Judd.

"Ari, put the gun down," I said calmly. Before I knew what he'd done to Rich, I would have thought the gun was just a prop to get Judd to leave, but I could no longer tell. And from the anger gleaming in Ari's eyes, he had every intention of pulling the trigger.

"What's this?" Judd threw Ari a look of disgust, then me. He couldn't miss the way Ari was dressed or my hard-on, which hadn't died at all. The adrenaline was pumping through my body. "You fucking your own son, Shaw?" he asked. "I wonder what the district would have to say about that. Have you been touching the boys at the school? Because you know, I can get testimonies from students that will ruin you."

"I haven't touched any of my students," I said between clenched teeth. "No one will believe your lies."

"I don't hear any denial about the one you're fucking right under your roof. How long has this been going on?" He looked past me to Ari. "When did he start touching you, kid? He brainwashed you to defend him?"

"You need to get out of my house." A pounding pain started in my head. And what the fuck was he doing, eyeing what was mine?

"I'd listen to him if I were you," Ari said softly.

Whether it was the quiet of Ari's voice or my direct order, I didn't know, but Judd took a step back.

"You fix this, Shaw," he spat out. "Or else." He turned but stopped and glanced back at Ari with a look I wanted to slap from his face. "And I'd keep that boy close to you from now on. It's not safe for something that pretty to be left out alone."

Anger thrummed through my veins. "You fucking touch him, Judd, and you'll regret it."

"It's not a matter of *if*, Shaw. It's a matter of *when*."

He slammed the door shut. Only then did Ari move, his face unreadable.

"I'm going to follow him," he said, but I grabbed his arm and pulled him back to me.

"No, you won't."

"He hurt you."

"You think I've never been hit before?"

"Not when I'm around, you haven't." He touched my nose gently, and when he spoke, his voice was matter-of-fact. "I'm going to kill him, Shaw. I swear I'm gonna."

I tightened my hand around his arm. "No, listen to me. It's not worth it. I don't want to lose you."

"I'm careful. No one will know."

"I said no, Ari, and that's final." I gathered him to my chest. He was stiff as a board. "Come on, let it go. I don't want you anywhere near that asshole. He'll hurt you."

"Not if I hurt him first."

I growled in frustration and released him, only to shake him. "You will not go after Judd."

"Judd what? What's his last name."

"Ari—"

"Fine, don't tell me. I'll find out on my own. Let's get your nose cleaned up."

I captured the hand he placed on the side of my face, pleading with him to see how scared I was for him. For us.

"Promise me, Ari. Promise me you won't go after him."

He frowned. "He hurt you. Why wouldn't you want me to go after him? Why protect him? He doesn't deserve it."

"I'm not protecting him. I'm trying to protect you. I can't lose you."

He bit his bottom lip. Was he thinking about what to eat for breakfast or whether or not he should take a human life?

"What if he makes good on his threat and attacks you or me again?" he finally asked. "Can I kill him then?"

I gaped at him. "Ari—"

"You've got to give me something to work with, Shaw. I promise not to go after him unless he antagonizes you or me again. Is that okay?"

No, it wasn't fucking okay, but my head throbbed, and my nose was bleeding again.

"Fine, then you can k—" I couldn't get the word out.

His body relaxed as the tension eased from his shoulders. His smile was smug. "Good, 'cause assholes like Judd never know when to stop. I'm quite looking forward to him trying to hurt you again." His eyes met mine. "And don't even think about trying to stop me. It's bad enough you're making me wait."

Sixteen

Ari

I WAS FINISHED. FINISHED washing Shaw's car which now sat in the driveway, so clean you could eat off it. Following the new paint job, I'd wanted the inside to look as new as the outside. The interior had been vacuumed and air freshened. I'd washed the floor mats and the slip covers for the headrests.

But Shaw's car wasn't the only thing I was finished with. I finished cleaning the house from top to bottom, and I still felt restless. Like I had something to do. And I knew exactly what, but Shaw wouldn't let me, and now I was a ball of energy trying to fill my days cleaning so I didn't have to think about it. About how that asshole Judd forced his way into our happy home and threatened my Daddy. How did Shaw expect me to turn a blind eye when I had to sit across from him at meal times and see his swollen nose? Or when he grunted in pain from me kissing him because he accidentally bumped his nose against mine.

Hands placed on my hips in fists, I stared around the yard. I already mowed the lawn, so there was nothing left to do unless I wanted to individually inspect each blade of grass was the same height. And I was vengeful, not crazy, so not even I would go *that* far. Yesterday, I dug up and replanted his rosebush and repainted the gate while he was at work.

That's it.

I turned to the house. Painting it would be a good project to keep me busy for a few days, and if I really took my time to do it, it could even take weeks instead. Maybe by then, the bloodlust would have left me, and I would be satisfied just being Shaw's lover again.

I returned the hose I'd been using to wash the car to the garage, then ran inside. Did I deliberately track mud from my shoes inside just so I'd have something to clean up after? Yes, definitely. But first, I had to talk to Shaw.

"Daddy! Daddy!" I cried, rushing into the living room.

Shaw, who'd been napping on the couch, startled awake, his face full of concern. "What is it? Did Judd return?"

He was more worried about Judd than he wanted to admit to me. His mind immediately went down that road because he thought I was in trouble.

"No, I just finished washing your car." I rocked back on my heels, staring at the trail of mud I'd tracked onto the carpet. "Now I'll have to clean the floor and carpet, but I was thinking, before I do, can we go get paint?"

"Paint?" He stared at me, his face a picture of confusion. His nose was almost back to normal on day eight post-Judd's appearance. "What do you need paint for, Ari?"

"To paint the house." I beamed at him. "It's perfect."

"I just had the house painted six months ago."

"So? I could do it all over—"

"We're not painting the house, Ari."

"Why not?"

"Because it doesn't need painting. Why don't you come sit beside Daddy and rest? You've been going nonstop for a week, baby."

Shaw calling me baby was the best damn thing ever, but I fought the warmth and instinct to obey him because he was my Daddy. Didn't he realize I needed to keep busy?

"I don't want to sit and rest."

He patted the couch beside him. "But you'll do it anyway because Daddy asks you to."

"No, I want to paint the house!" I glared at him, my inner little being forced out. "I want to paint the house! I want to paint the house!" And for good measure, I stomped my feet. "I want to paint it now."

His expression turned thoughtful as he regarded me. *Please. Please understand what I need.*

"You're not going to do what Daddy says, Ari?"

"You're a meanie!" I threw at him. "I hate you. You never let me do anything I want."

I couldn't kill Judd. I couldn't paint the house. Daddy's stupid rules. I should just disobey him anyway, but I was so scared he wouldn't love me anymore. For now, all I could do was throw a tantrum and express how unfair and stupid everything was. Somebody hurt him; I took care of it. That was simple.

Why wouldn't he let me take care of Judd?

"You need to calm down right now, or you're going to end up right across my knees."

"I don't care if you spank me. I still want to paint. In fact, I'm going to get paint with or without you. Maybe I'll call Nathan. I think he'd love to give me a ride. Don't you think, Daddy?"

It was a low blow. I knew how much he hated the idea of me being around horny Nathan, but if something didn't give, I was scared of what I would actually do. And of course I now had my car and could drive myself, but little kids didn't drive, so my little wouldn't let me.

Without a word, Shaw rose to his feet and came after me. I screamed and ran, but I didn't get far. He plucked me off my feet while I kicked my legs.

"Let me go!" I yelled. "I don't like you anymore. I hate you. I hate you!"

"That's fine," he said through gritted teeth as he threw me over his shoulder and marched out of the living room with me hanging upside down. "Hate me all you want, but you're never going to see Nathan. You hear me, Ari?" His hand came down hard on my ass. The jeans I wore softened the impact a bit, but I still howled. "I told you I don't ever want to see you hanging around Nathan."

"Well, you can't stop me. I'm going to sneak out and find him. He'll get me paint. He'll get me anything I want, I bet."

Another hand cracked against my ass harder this time. My hard dick pressed into his shoulder, where I was folded up like a pretzel.

"Over my dead body, Ari."

It thrilled me that Daddy Shaw could speak this way after being such a nice, predictable guy all these years. He rushed me into my bedroom and threw me onto the bed.

Instead of coming after me to give me the spanking I so deserved, he stalked over to the door and threw me a furious look over his shoulder.

"You're going to stay here all by yourself and calm down," he told me.

"Can't you just spank me?" I wasn't below begging for it.

"No, because I'm not sure I'll be able to stop if you code red. Sit there and think about your careless words and how you're trying to provoke me."

He slammed the door shut. I threw myself down onto the bed and grabbed the pillows while I sulked and bawled. I threw things at the door. And when that didn't get his attention, I yelled that I was going out the window to find Nathan. He didn't respond. I didn't go out the window.

Oh, Daddy was good. He didn't give me any attention while I was in timeout. He completely ignored me, and it was the worst feeling in the world — being ignored by my

Daddy. I paced the room, I sat on the floor, I banged on the door, even though the actual door wasn't locked, but I didn't dare to leave the room without Daddy's permission.

I yelled lies about why I needed to leave the room. I'd cut my arm and needed to go to the hospital. I'd left the hose on in the yard and was probably flooding us out. I was hungry and needed something to eat.

Finally, I had an excellent reason. One that was very true.

"I need to pee, Daddy!" I cried. "Please let me go to the bathroom."

"Use your diaper! That's what they're there for."

"I don't know how to do up my diaper. I need adult help."

He went silent. Was he ignoring me again? I'd never leave that room without his permission.

The door opened, and Shaw came in. He surveyed the damage I'd done, all the missiles I'd launched across the room: the broken clock, a photo frame, fashion magazines, even a pair of scissors. I'd thrown anything I could get my hands on.

"I came up here to help you put on a diaper," he said softly. "Because you're grounded and not allowed to leave this room without my permission. But you don't deserve your diaper. You've been a very rotten boy, Ari."

"But I have to go."

"Then go."

"What? Without my diaper?" I sucked in a deep breath. Who would have thought Daddy Shaw had a streak for humiliation? Just what other dirty secrets did my Daddy have? Was I going to have to provoke them out of him one by one? First his possessiveness, now his apparent humiliation kick.

"Good boys get their precious little bottom diapered."

"But, Daddy, it's coming down."

"Then let it."

I searched Daddy's face. Was he naïvely asking me to do something, or did he truly wanted to see me wet myself? The tented front of his sweats gave me the answer I needed.

I closed my eyes and released my bladder. The warm pee gushed down my pant leg. I'd never done this with the one Daddy I had before, and it was strange, distressing, and disgusting to wet my pants in front of someone else, especially someone I'd looked up to for so long.

What's he thinking? Does he think I'm disgusting now?

"Open your eyes and look at the mess you've made on my floor."

I popped my eyelids open and stared down at the floor, where a small puddle had formed. Most of it had absorbed into my pants, leaving telltale wet marks at the front and soaking through to the back. The smell wasn't pleasant either, but it was that filthiness that also made my cock hard.

Daddy's hand was inside his sweats. He hesitated, but then he pulled out that big thick cock I loved so much. My ass clenched in anticipation. We'd had sex since the night I'd drugged him, but never penetrative. Now all I could think about was being stuffed full of him again.

But Daddy had other plans. When I went down on my knees without being told to and inched to him to take his dick into my mouth, he shook his head.

"Stop."

I whined. I wanted it so bad. My mouth was empty. Every night I slept at his hip just so I could suck on his cock for comfort and fall asleep. I would keep him in my mouth for the entire day if he didn't have to be at work and we didn't have things to do.

"Good boys get to suck their Daddy's cock," he said, his breathing shallow. His cock was so thick I couldn't take my eyes off it. "Bad apples get sprayed with Daddy's pee."

I sucked in a deep breath, and my cock jerked. *Thump. Thump.* My heart pounded in my chest.

"What's your code?" Daddy asked.

"Green." I was so green to be soaked in my Daddy's pee, even more so than my own. That mark of ownership, of Daddy's scent all over me. *Mine. Mine.* This had his stamp of possessiveness all over him, and I wanted it all.

SEVENTEEN

SHAW

I CAN'T DO THIS. I can't do this.

The thoughts reverberated in my head, even as I pointed my cock at Ari and splashed him with a stream of pee. It hit him in the chest, soaking his shirt with the rich ammonia that permeated the air, mingling with the scent of his own piss and forming one. I watched in fascinated horror as this boy challenged everything I knew about myself. The sadistic smile on his face, the way he arched into the stream, and as it dwindled, how he moved forward to catch every bit he could.

It was dirty, and it was sick. It was fascinating and arousing. I'd defiled him just like he'd walked into my life and defiled me. Now we were one and the same. I'd become what he wanted me to be, and it was terrifying and the most exhilarating I'd ever felt in my life.

It was freeing not to hold back.

Ari opened his eyes, and his smile grew. He unzipped his pants and took out his dick. His knees skidding on the floor from our piss, he waded in it like it was a cleansing stream and stopped before me, his hand on his cock, stroking and pumping. That boy who I'd thought needed protection from the big bad world captured my dick with those sinful lips. And then he moaned, eyes still holding mine, as he lapped up what dripped of my pee and sucked my cock deep into his mouth.

He didn't stop staring at me, even when he gagged. Just sucked my cock down his throat, his nostrils flaring. I was horrified at my arousal. He was rank and needed a bath. We were in a puddle of our own pee, yet it didn't seem to bother him. In fact, it was the opposite.

Had he done this before? Had he let some man pee all over him?

I let out a gasp as his tongue swirled over the soft glans of my cock, his eyelashes fluttering as he groaned. He was coming so hard his body twitched, eyes rolling back in his head.

"Fuck, Ari!" I wanted to apologize for humiliating him this way. Having him suck my dick while he was kneeling in my piss. He was made to be loved and cherished, to be pampered and treasured like a jewel. But each time I tried to treat him this way, he pushed and pushed until he broke something inside me and made me into someone new.

Ari gasped, his body shaking from his climax. My cock slipped out, and I grabbed it at the base and stroked my turgid flesh. I pumped hard, bracing my legs, groaning as cum spurted into his face. His tongue came out, his mouth opening wider. I tugged down on my flesh, squeezing and pumping every last bit I could onto him.

I stumbled back, my cock still clutched in my hand. He was a mess, cum splashed onto his cheek and in his hair. His release stained the floor. He'd wanted this, right? We'd never discussed if it was okay. Guilt washed over me. I would never have thought to discuss *this*, though. I didn't go around peeing on people. It had all been a spur-of-the-moment decision. A result of him antagonizing me about Nathan he knew damn well I didn't want anywhere near him. The rest, him peeing his pants, me peeing on him in return. I hadn't wanted this. Hadn't planned this.

"I wanted it," he whispered as if he could read my mind. "I love you treating me this way when I'm naughty."

And as if to prove his point, this beautiful, sweet, dangerous contradictory boy who evoked feelings inside me no one else ever had fell backward on the floor in the mess we'd made. He giggled, fanning out both his arms and legs as if making snow angels, with his dick soft hanging out of his pants.

"Stop that." I meant to say the words gruffly, still pissed off at him for using Nathan to get to me. But if I were honest, I was more upset with myself for letting it get to me, even though I'd known what he'd been doing. "You're dirty and filthy. You need to be cleaned up."

"Better dirty on the outside than in."

Would I ever understand this boy? I plucked him off the floor, and he cried out a protest at first, then curled up into me, wrapping his legs around my waist and getting me all dirty as well. Like he hadn't already placed his sullied handprints all over me. I took him to my bedroom and through to the bathroom, where I stripped him while he just stood there, not lifting a finger to help me.

"I'll burn these." I wrinkled my nose at the ruined clothes.

"No, I want them."

He stood before me, naked, shivering, arms wrapped around his body. I wanted to go to him and cuddle him, but I had to clean up the mess we'd made.

"What do you want with these?" I asked. "I'll buy you new clothes if that's what you're worried about."

"I don't need you to buy me new clothes. I want these."

"Why on earth would you want these? They are filthy."

"Because they are our filth, so please don't throw them away, Daddy."

Earlier he'd egged me on, but now the need flickered in his eyes. For some reason, these clothes meant something to him. He wanted to hold on to them while I just wanted to dump them so I didn't have to think about what I'd just done to him.

"Please, Daddy."

I sighed. "Can I at least wash them first?"

He nodded. I found a bag under the sink and shoved the clothes in. I'd wash them later, but first I needed to take care of Ari.

I prepared the bath and undressed as well.

"Wait," Ari said. "Can I get some toys to play with in the bath?"

"I'll get them. Where are they?"

"They're in my diaper bag in the closet."

I settled him into the warm bath and told him to stay put while I returned to his bedroom. God, what a stench. The floor would need a solid scrubbing. Penance for my perversion. What would Judd think if he knew what I'd just done? If anyone knew? The board would fire me for sure. I found the diaper bag in his closet and unzipped it. The sweet scent of baby powder wafted in my nose. He had all sorts of things: rattles, bottles, a blankie, and the plastic squeak toys of various animals. I unpacked a diaper and his blanket.

When I returned to the bathroom, Ari sat waiting for me. His eyes lit up when he saw the toys. I climbed into the tub behind him and pulled him backward to sit between my legs. He ignored me, his attention solely on the toys. I didn't mind and washed his hair and cleaned him up. He was squealing and chortling, the sound bringing me such happiness I gathered him to my chest and held him.

"Daddy," he protested.

"Shh, let me hold you."

He stopped struggling and sagged against me. We sat there until the water cooled, and he complained he getting wrinkled all over.

"All right, let's wash you off and get out." I rose, lifting him to his feet, and we abandoned the tub for the shower. I scrubbed his body. He was so small and adorable. Oh. My. God. He hadn't just wormed himself into my life and exposed parts of me I didn't know existed. I'd gone and fallen head over heels in love with this boy. And I liked making him filthy so I could clean him up again.

"Daddy, are you okay?" Ari peered up at me from behind his wet hair.

I forced a smile. "Everything is fine. Now let's get you dressed and give you some little time. Would you like that?"

"You'll play with me?" he asked in a small voice.

"Yes, just tell me what to do." I turned off the faucet and guided him out of the tub. I grabbed a towel and wrapped it around his body, indicating for him to sit while I used another to rub his hair.

"You've been driving me crazy over the past couple of days," I told him.

"Huh?"

"Yeah, with all the cleaning and dusting you've been doing, but I thought it was a good distraction from other things." Like going after Judd and taking the man's life.

Rich and Judd were two different men, though. Rich had been a spineless coward who preyed on those who were physically weaker. Judd was an asshole who could crush Ari.

"I didn't want to say anything. Just wait it out until you get it out of your system, but by god, Ari, you started talking about painting and then being a mouthy brat. I should have realized before that all you needed was some little time. I'll do better, okay?"

He nodded. "Okay, and I'll try not to be such a brat next time."

I chuckled, kissing his hair, which smelled clean and sweet of honeysuckle. "About what happened after, Ari. I —"

"Loved it," he finished quickly. "I was so turned on by it."

My hands in his hair stilled. I tugged his head back so I could see his face and look into his eyes. He'd better not lie to me.

"Have you ever let anyone else do that to you?"

"No, just you."

I nodded. "Good. Nobody else does that to you, understand?"

He rolled his eyes but then stopped. "Yes, Daddy. I'll be good."

"I know you will because you're Daddy's little angel."

I carried him to my bedroom and placed him on the bed, next to the diaper. His face flushed.

"You're still on punishment," I said. "I told you I didn't want to hear another word about Nathan. So you don't get to use the toilet at all tonight. You'll have to wear your diaper."

"And use it?" His voice was breathless and tiny with excitement.

"What's the sense of a diaper if you're not going to use it?"

"I've never been forced to wear diapers as punishment before," he replied. "I like it, Daddy."

"If you throw a tantrum like a two-year-old, you're wearing a diaper." I got the hang of this Daddy business he liked so much. "When you need changing, you tell Daddy, okay?"

He nodded, then picked up his pacifier and put it in his mouth. He looked completely at bliss as he lay back on the bed with his legs falling apart as I ripped off the towel. I didn't cover his nakedness right away. Our eyes met and held.

I cupped his genitals and stroked his soft cock. He thrust his hips up into my touch, but I chuckled and let him go.

"Strike what I said about being Daddy's little angel. You're really Daddy's bad apple, aren't you?"

He shook his head, but I wouldn't be so easily fooled this time. Maybe he hadn't always been this way. Maybe the years he'd been away from under my watchful eye had shaped him into the person he was today, but whatever the reason, we could put the past behind us. He could be the good boy I always knew, and he wouldn't have to do what he did in the past to survive.

"I think the correct answer is yes," I told him and leaned forward. "But Daddy wants to take a bite out of you just the same." I bit his tummy playfully, and he squealed and giggled. By god, it was the sweetest sound I ever heard. I wanted to catch it and bottle it up to carry with me everywhere I went.

I'd forgotten to bring his clothes with me, but I didn't bother to return to his room. I took one of my shirts out of my closet. Ari was jumping all over the bed. I stifled my smile.

"You have five seconds to put this on or no playtime," I said.

He dropped onto his ass on the bed. I pulled the shirt over his head and guided his arms into the holes, then smoothed the shirt down his body. It almost came down to his knees. Ari spat out the pacifier and stuck his thumb into his mouth while grabbing the end of the shirt. He rubbed the material between his thumb and forefinger, giving me a peek of his diaper.

"I'm going to put you on the sofa to watch some cartoons for a little while. In the meantime, I'll clean up your room. Is that okay?"

He nodded and held out his arms to me. Of course I lifted him. He placed his head on my shoulder and wrapped his legs around my waist. He was the perfect picture of calm as we descended the stairs. I was only happy to get his mind off his ill intent toward Judd.

Nothing good could come out of that confrontation.

Eighteen

Ari

JUDD O'CONNOR WORKED AS a carpenter, was forty-two years old, weighed two hundred and sixty pounds, and was fucking his son's best friend, although nobody knew. He ate the same thing for lunch every day — a tuna sandwich — and followed the same routine. He was out of his house by seven a.m. to get to the construction site for the new library. The old building burned down several months ago.

It took me roughly two weeks to find out Judd wasn't an innocent man who just happened to work on the new library. He and a few of his men who'd been strapped for work deliberately set the building on fire so they could pitch an offer to build a new one. They hadn't known the librarian was living in the basement, and the woman died. They proposed the library be named after her.

Most of what I found on Judd at first was gossip, but if there was one thing my old man had taught me, it was that where there was smoke, there was often fire. And Judd was so knee deep in the flames he should have been burning.

Shaw, of course, had no idea what I was up to. I promised him not to go after Judd, and I hadn't broken my promise. I hadn't made a move toward Judd; I just dug up as much dirt as possible about him.

Thank god, I was small. My slender frame got me into places without being seen. I flashed a smile, giggled a little, and they all thought me harmless and let their guard down around me. That was how I followed his closest friend, Bryan, from the construction site one day to the bar where he often had a drink in the afternoon.

I discovered he and Judd were occasional fuck buddies, but they weren't too chummy with each other since Judd started fucking the kid from the high school. Bryan was jealous and mad enough to mouth off to a harmless boy about standing by Judd and them getting that contract after the place had gone up in flames. He spoke in euphemisms, but I was no dummy. He and Judd torched that place and let that woman die.

My relationship with Shaw progressed beautifully, and I was happy, though at times he was distracted. I finally dragged the truth out of him that Judd's kid had been kicked out of school. Shaw wanted me to stay put in the house, never leaving nor opening the door to strangers unless he was home. I placated him with smiles, but he eyed me with unease. Like he found it difficult to believe a word I'd said to him.

Night times were my favorites. We fucked. My god, did we fuck, and then I fell asleep, sucking his dick. Sometimes he stroked my hair. Other times he wanted me up in bed next to him, my back against his front as his arms lay heavily over me. Shaw sweated like a pig during the night, but I didn't mind.

For the two weeks since Shaw sprinkled me with his pee, I'd been stalking Judd and learning as much about him as I could without him or Shaw noticing. I'd used the excuse of jogging in the morning, which Shaw hated. No way was he going to run with me, so he had no choice but to allow me to go out.

I told Shaw I went to the park, which was safer, but I would park my car down the road from Judd's house, then follow him to where he worked. A couple of times, I doubled back to his house and searched through his stuff. He had a pile of unpaid bills, his house was messy, with meth in the drawer, and lewd pictures. The guy was apparently not too smart.

He kept pictures of his misdeeds. Pictures of his son's friend sucking his dick, of his son's bruised back — which I would have bet he caused — and of the library and other buildings he'd burned down. Those pictures, plus what his drunken fuck buddy had said, left no doubt they'd burned down the library, killing that innocent woman. I took shots of the photographs with my camera, then almost got caught when his son came home drunk with some girl who was already half-naked. I escaped through the backdoor.

At first, I got all the evidence I needed about Judd in case he tried any funny business with Daddy, but I never intended to use it. Until last night, when the phone rang and I answered it.

"Hey, this is Daddy's phone."

From the kitchen, Daddy's laugh carried to me. "Ari, that's not how you answer the phone."

"Is that what he makes you call him when he's fucking you?" Judd.

My light and happy mood from showing Daddy how to bake banana bread evaporated.

"Please don't call this phone anymore," I said politely and hung up.

He called back promptly, and I answered. "I said—"

"I know what you said, but now you better hear what I have to say. Tell Shaw he's screwed. I'm gonna make *you* call me Daddy while I fuck you up so much he doesn't want you anymore."

I sucked in a deep breath and turned to Shaw, who'd entered the living room.

"Who is it?" he asked.

I put down the phone. "Just an insurance salesman." What Shaw didn't know couldn't hurt him.

But then the damn phone rang again, and when Shaw stretched his hand out, I gave him the phone. I'd been behaving for him and I didn't want to ruin our night any more than this stupid bastard was about to do.

"This is Shaw," he answered the phone. "Who's this?"

If only I could hear what Judd said, but I could guess enough from Daddy's stony expression. He placed a hand around my waist and pulled me possessively against his side, holding me so tightly he crushed my ribs.

"You touch a hair on his head, Judd, and that's the last thing you'll do," he growled into the phone, then hung up.

"Too tight," I said, and he eased his hold on me.

"You lied to me. Didn't I tell you no more lies?"

"This is different. I didn't want you to be upset."

"Go stand in the corner, facing the wall."

My hackles rose, and my whole ambition of being good disintegrated. "What? Why are you mad at me? You should be mad at him."

"I *am* pissed off at him, but I'm disappointed in you," he said. "No more lies. That's what I told you. How can I trust you if you keep lying to me, Ari? What else have you been doing while I am at work?"

"Nothing."

"And you expect me to believe that after the lie you just told me?"

"I swear I did nothing. I stayed put like you asked me to."

"Then go face the wall and don't move until I tell you to."

Eyes blurring, I did what he said. Angry tears slipped down my cheeks, and with every streak, I swore again that I would kill him. I'd kill Judd, and there wasn't a damn thing Daddy could do to stop me. He was the reason Daddy was mad at me. He had to pay.

The next day, Daddy and I were on speaking terms again. I got up early to make him breakfast, but he barely ate it. He was worried about me staying at home while he was at work.

"I'll be fine. Promise." I went up on the tips of my toes and kissed his cheek. He grabbed me by the butt, pressed me against his car, and devoured my lips, then set me back on shaky feet. I touched my lips with my fingertips, a smile on my face when he drove off.

I gave it two hours, and just as I expected, Daddy called me on the house phone. No doubt checking I stayed put like I said I would. I waited until it was near noon, then hopped into my car and drove to Judd's house. He always ate his lunch at home, for which his coworkers called him a stingy bastard

It gave me great pleasure to see the fear on his face when he walked into the kitchen and saw me sitting at the table waiting for him.

"Fucking hell, how did you get in here?"

I shrugged. "It doesn't matter. I'm here to see you."

"Yeah?" He grinned. "Knew you'd come around once you saw how much better you could do than that—"

"Be very careful what you say about Shaw," I said softly. "I'm approaching you nicely because of him, so you should be grateful."

Instead of looking threatened, his grin widened. "Well, fuck me, you're a spirited little thing, aren't you?" He walked over to me. "Pretty stupid of you to aim a gun at me the other day. I don't take too kindly to that. How did you get into my house? What am I supposed to think except that you're really begging for it?"

"Well, you're wrong. I'm not begging for anything. I'm warning you to stay away from Shaw."

"Or else what?"

"All your dirty secrets get revealed in the local paper."

His grin faded a bit. "I've got no dirt."

"No?" I got to my feet. "Then you have nothing to worry about, but if you've got secrets, Judd, I'd tread lightly if I were you."

I moved past him, but he grasped my shoulder. The knife sliced his arm a second later. He howled and let me go.

"Son of a bitch!" He swiped at me with his forearm, knocking me in the face, but before he could grab me, I brandished my knife again. He backed up, holding his injured arm to his chest, blood dripping onto the kitchen floor.

"Consider this your last warning, Judd." I turned the knife over and sniffed the metallic scent. "It's not nearly enough blood until it's all drained out of your body."

While he tried to figure out what I meant, I walked out of his house, making sure not to leave any sign of me behind. His day of reckoning was coming, and when it did, there shouldn't be anything to link back to me.

Nineteen

Shaw

"I'M SORRY, BUT YOU can't go in there. Sir, no, you can't—"

That was my secretary, Julieta. Alarm speared through me. Judd. Had he come to make good on his threat? The bastard wouldn't actually confront me on school premises, would he? I never pegged him to be that dumb and provoke a fight where everyone would be able to see it.

The door to my office opened, and Ari strode in, Julieta following him.

"I'm so sorry, Mr. Wheeler. He just barged right in."

"Actually, I told you I needed to speak to Daddy, and you tried to stop me." Ari pointed a finger at my secretary.

What happened to his face? The right side was all bruised and discolored.

"You need to make an appointment," Julieta replied, but it only served to aggravate Ari more than he already was.

"I told you I'm his son," Ari said.

"It's fine, Julieta." I walked around my desk. Usually, Ari was friendly to people. Why was he behaving so badly toward her? "Ari's my stepson." Boy, I really needed to work on that if people started suspecting a relationship between us.

"See, I told you." Ari glared at her. "Aristotle. You know me. You worked here while I went to this school."

She widened her eyes, and her face turned a bright pink. "I-I'm so sorry. I didn't recognize you."

Did she really not recognize him? Sure, he'd grown into his features, but he didn't look that much different from when he was a student here.

"I thought he was a student trying to play a prank on me," Julieta said.

I took her shoulder and gently steered her toward the door. "That's okay, Julieta. We all make mistakes. No harm, no foul."

"I'm really sorry," she said again. I closed the door after her and turned to Ari. "Are you insane? What are you doing here?"

"She's lying, the bitch!" Ari snorted. "She knew damn well who I was. She's always been that way to me when I needed to see you."

I frowned at him. "Ari, you'll treat her respectfully. She's a valuable secretary."

"One who never liked how often I hung out in your office."

I shook my head. "Where's all this coming from?"

"You weren't here once when I stopped by to avoid Rich, and she was nasty to me. Told me I couldn't stay in your office until you got back. Then she proceeded to tell me I shouldn't come to your office so much and how weird it is."

"She said that?" She'd never told me.

"Yeah, but the reason I hate her is that I think she is jealous of the attention you give me. Her eyes follow you, you know."

Ah, now that made sense. "That's why you dislike her?" I could barely contain my amusement.

"That's reason enough."

"You're being extra bratty today." I approached him, took his face in my hand, and turned his cheek. "What happened?"

"I ran into a door?"

"The truth, please."

He pulled a small Ziploc bag with a bloody knife from the inside of his coat.

"Jesus, Ari? What'd you do?"

"I'm going to kill him, Shaw. I swear I'm gonna."

Ari's voice reverberated in my head, confident and angry.

I took the bag out of his hand, dropped it into my desk drawer, and slammed it shut. What if anyone walked in, saw it, and asked questions.

"I didn't kill him," he said. I lifted my eyebrows. "What? I swear I didn't kill him."

"Then whose blood is this?" I demanded.

"Judd's, but it was hardly a scratch."

Goddammit, why didn't the boy ever do as he was told? I stalked to him and gripped his shoulders. Hard. "I told you to leave Judd alone," I rasped in a low voice.

"And I did, but then you told me if he messed with you, I could go after him. That's all I did."

"I didn't say anything like that."

"Yes, you did. But he's fine, and hopefully he learned his lesson and will leave you alone."

I turned his face and inspected the bruise forming there. "He struck you?"

"I was stupid and got distracted."

I tightened my hand on his chin and I had to let go before I caused another bruise. "You don't listen. You don't obey me," I growled. "You do whatever you want. What am I going to do with you, Ari?"

"Punish me. And then love me."

He was so matter-of-fact about it. I grabbed his shoulder and pulled him toward the desk. "You want me to punish you, Ari?"

"Yes, but you'll make it better after, right?"

I ignored his question, found the string knotted at the front of his cargo pants and undid it. I tugged them down and almost lost focus when I saw the pink lace thong he had on beneath. My mind was spinning. Did I want to punish or fuck him? I fisted his hoodie at the back and bent him over my desk.

I swiped up the wooden ruler from my desk — being old fashioned came in handy now — and aimed the first smack at his ass. When he squirmed too much, I yanked off my tie and knotted his hands behind his back, then smacked his ass cheeks again.

Crack. The sound of the wood meeting flesh rang out in the room.

"I swear you disobey me just to be punished," I whispered fiercely as I landed another blow on him. I hit him over and over, never the same place twice in a row. Soon his sobs came out muffled, and his shoulders had long since stopped supporting his weight. His torso collapsed onto my desk.

When his ass was a healthy pink, I dropped the ruler on the desk and kneeled behind him. He hissed softly when I pressed his cheeks apart, but it turned into a moan when my tongue pierced his hole.

"You make any sound, and I stop," I warned him, then delved between his cheeks again. I alternated between sucking and tongue fucking his ready hole. His muscles clenched, and his hands clutched at the tie as he blew hard, unable to moan or cry out the way he usually did when we were at home.

I reached between his legs and rubbed his dick, stroking him while I wiggled my tongue deeply inside him. His whispered "oh my god, oh my god" filled the room, and I pulled back just as I promised I would.

"Please, Daddy. Don't stop."

I jerked him to his knees on top of the desk, bringing his back up against my chest. He turned his head, and I kissed him, sucking his tongue into my mouth.

"Do you have those packets of lube?" I asked, biting his cheekbone.

"In my jacket."

I dipped inside his jacket and came up with a small bottle of lube and not the packet he usually carried with him. He said he always wanted to be prepared, but this time, he'd come here with the intention to be fucked.

I didn't take off my pants. Just unzipped them and fished inside for my dick. I rubbed the lube over the head of my cock and slicked it down to the base, then smeared the excess over his hole and a bit inside. With two fingers, I worked him loose, but given we'd fucked last night, it didn't take me long before I held his hips and guided my cock inside him.

A shiver ran through his body. I pulled out, beat my dick against his hole, and pushed back in. Fuck, I couldn't get enough of him. Now I was the one struggling to stay silent as his hole gripped me and threatened to send me over the edge. I couldn't pound him as I wanted, sure the noise would carry all the way over to the front desk, but I thrust so deep inside his body the only thing left to stuff inside him were my balls.

The desk rattled beneath him. I tugged him upward, wrapped him in my arms, and walked us to my private bathroom. I shoved the door shut louder than necessary, then spun him around and set him on top of the vanity, arms still tied behind his back.

"Yes, Daddy," he said softly, drawing my attention to his face. And the bruise.

I yanked his hips lower to the edge of the vanity and, this time, held nothing back as I bore down all my girth and force inside him. Ari gasped, his mouth flying open, and a shiver raced through him. I didn't give him a chance to breathe, pulling out only to slam inside him again. From the way his eyes widened, I was hitting his prostate. I concentrated on that same spot, gritting my teeth to keep my climax at bay.

"If you want to come, you're going to have to do it hands-free," I grunted.

"I-I can't," he sobbed. "Please touch me, Daddy. Please. So good. Oh god, that's so good. I don't want it to stop. Please don't make it stop."

But all good things eventually came to an end. As I snapped my hips forward over and over, Ari dropped his head back against the wall, his face scrunched up in a silent scream as he shot his load. Now. Now I let go, giving in to the burgeoning crush of emotions rolling inside me, the chief of which was an incredible love.

I fell forward, pressing my face to Ari's chest. His heart was firing off in his chest, the beat wild and erratic, not following any particular rhythm.

"I love you," I said the simple words that would bind me to him in heroics and misdeeds. I raised my head. "I love you, Aristotle. Please don't do anything to ruin that."

He looked pained like he was struggling internally. "I love you too," he then said. "I think I always have, long before it was possible to be with you. You're an honorable man, Shaw Wheeler, and I just want to deserve you."

I chuckled. "I don't feel so honorable right now. You're so young. You have your whole life ahead of you. You shouldn't be stuck with a fat old man. It doesn't get any better for me, Ari."

"If you would only see you the way I see you, Shaw." His face was serious, more serious than I'd ever seen. "You're the flicker of flame that my darkness can't ever snuff out. I-I need that, or I would be lost." He lowered his head so his chin rested on his chest. "For four years, I didn't have that, and look what I have become."

I brushed his hair. "You mean beautiful and protective to a fault."

Yes, maybe I was reducing all the bad qualities to just those two, but we needed this. A few lies to make this okay. Because in all honesty, he and I had no future together, but maybe if we believed the lies, they could become our truths.

I touched his jaw, stroking the bruise. "Does it hurt?"

"No, but my arms are going to be sore if you don't untie me soon."

I helped him down from the vanity and smiled at his disheveled state. "I think I like you like this. Trussed up and out of trouble."

"Trouble finds me," he said with a smirk. "It's only a matter of time before it finds me here."

"As long as you're not the one starting it." I turned him around and untied him. The tie was ruined. It seemed Ari had pulled threads out, leaving it mangled like something a dog had chewed on.

"Do you want to stay here?" I helped him clean up, and we fixed our clothes.

"Here where?"

"With me in the office. We could do with an intern. It wouldn't be a paid job, of course, but it'll keep you out of trouble. I can't trust you at home alone."

"But I don't want to be an intern." He wrinkled his nose. "Sounds like a boring job."

"But guess who gets to hide under Daddy's desk and keep his cock all snug and warm?"

A spark of interest flashed in his eyes. Just like I hoped it would.

TWENTY

SHAW

THERE WAS NO WAY I was letting Ari out of my sight after he confronted Judd, so despite the unprofessional nature of my actions, I put him to work in my office. If anyone asked, he was interning while deciding what he wanted to do with his life.

Mostly he sat on one of the couches in a corner with a stack of papers and a pencil. Seeing him there was reassuring. He'd done this before when he was a student here, waiting for me to give him a ride home. He would sit in that corner and do his homework while I tried to get everything done so I didn't have to bring him home late.

Our relationship had been so different back then. So simple. He glanced up, seeming startled when he saw me watching him, but then he smiled and returned to his work. When he was like this, it was so easy to pretend he wasn't what I knew him to be—a killer. But would I want him to go back to being the Ari I knew with the soft voice, bright smile, and bubbly personality? He was still that boy, but now I saw sides of him I shouldn't want to protect, and found myself doing it anyway.

It was easier to focus on Ari than to examine myself. To avoid how much I'd changed since he came back to town. To analyze why I derived such pleasure from hurting him and loving him at the same time.

I walked over to him and kissed the top of his head. Everything was already so much calmer in my head with him here. I was able to focus on my work, since I wasn't so consumed with thoughts of him and hoping he wouldn't talk with random men who tried to lure him away from me.

I picked up one of the papers next to him but paused when he stilled.

"May I?"

He nodded, and I turned it over and studied the dress he'd designed. It was a ballroom gown with a demure neckline, but the cut in the bodice showcasing the skin and the hip-high slits made it sexy.

"This is impressive," I said.

"You like it?" His voice was hungry for approval.

"I love it." I stared at the sketch.

"You don't really like it." He took the paper from my hand. "I'll do it over."

"No, don't alter it. I'm just thinking how much Anne ruined your life."

He snorted. "You have no idea."

"I would have insisted you go to college, pursue your dreams. Don't you want to go to college?"

"I wasn't too good at school, Shaw."

"But there are different types, and you're so talented. This can be very productive."

"And we need me to be productive so I don't hurt anyone else?" He gave me an amused smile.

"Wouldn't you like to have a job someday?"

"Honestly, no. I can't see me in an office working nine to five. I'd rather eat this paper."

"Don't tempt me," I said. "But think about it. If it's something you really want to do, I'll help you figure it out."

He didn't say anything for a while. Just sat there looking at me. Then big fat tears rolled down his cheeks. Alarmed, I pushed the papers aside and sat beside him, reaching for him.

"What did I say?"

He shook his head.

"Ari, tell me."

"You've always believed in me," he finally replied. "Always saw the good in me when no one else did."

"Because you *are* good."

"You wouldn't say that if you knew what I've done."

The air was sucked out of my lungs. I should have asked him what he'd done, but I didn't want to know.

"Whatever it is lies in the past. We move forward and make better decisions."

I kissed his forehead, then returned to my desk and my work. After our conversation, Ari seemed a bit distracted and lost, and the last thing I wanted him to do was go to the dark places inside his head.

"Baby," I called. "Daddy needs you." That would get his mind off whatever he was thinking.

It was definitely not the time or the place to do this, but nobody would know. He sprang to his feet.

"Yes, Daddy?" He was so eager to please.

"Get under the desk."

Wide-eyed, he stared at me. "You want me under the desk?"

"Yes."

He didn't ask why or even for how long. He got down on his knees and snuck into the empty space between the drawers. He was just small enough to fit.

"Unzip Daddy's pants."

His fingers shook as he found my zipper and slowly pulled it down.

"Take Daddy's cock out. Good boy. Now put it in your mouth and stay right there."

"Yes, Daddy." His mouth wrapped around my cock, and I patted his head.

"Good boy, listening to his Daddy."

I was beginning to see that Ari loved to please me. Perhaps I could use this to control his destructive tendencies.

I returned to my computer while he remained in position. Not even fifteen minutes later, someone knocked on the door.

"Come in."

Her confused gaze met mine.

"Your stepson left? I didn't see him go past me."

"In the bathroom," I lied, and Ari sucked harder on my cock.

"Oh, okay."

"I have the quotes you requested from the two companies about the buses you wanted to buy."

"Thank you." I took the file from her. "This is perfect."

"You're welcome." Yet she hesitated like she wanted to say something else.

"Yes?"

"I'm really sorry about earlier," she said, lowering her voice as if she didn't want Ari, who was in the "bathroom," to overhear her. "I wasn't paying attention and forgot you had a stepson."

"Out of curiosity, Julieta, did you really tell him to stop coming around the office so often when he was a student here?"

Her face turned red, and she didn't even need to answer. "I'm sorry. I was trying to protect you."

Ari's hand tightened on my leg, and I prayed like hell he wouldn't be irrational now and pop up to confront my secretary. It would be hard to explain what he was doing under my desk, especially after telling her he was in the bathroom.

"Protect me from what?"

"The gossip. People were saying things."

I narrowed my eyes. "What things?"

She shrugged and looked away. "Just that your relationship with him made them uncomfortable. You were too close and…"

"And what?"

She glanced at me. Then her gaze flitted away again. "He had a crush on you that everyone seemed to see except for you. Some people thought you were encouraging him, but I never believed that. Not after working with you. You'd never have touched that boy."

"He was a child. Of course I wouldn't have touched him."

"That's what I said, but you know people. They like to speculate." She hesitated enough for me to know what she was about to say wasn't something I'd like to hear.

"What is it?"

"There was the notebook." She inhaled deeply. "One evening, he forgot his notebook. He wrote all sorts of things in it about you and him and your ex-wife. It was disturbing. There were pictures too."

My dick slipped out of Ari's mouth. I tried desperately not to show my alarm. "I've never heard about this book before. What did you do with it?"

"I-it's been a long time. I don't know."

I didn't believe her one bit, especially because she wouldn't meet my eyes, but I didn't want to make a big deal about something that had happened a long time ago. I nodded and even smiled at her.

"Thanks for letting me know. You may go."

She let out an audible sigh and walked out, closing the door behind her. The door was barely shut when Ari pushed back my chair and crept out from under the desk. His face was red, his eyes flashing with what I knew now to be a sign of his anger.

"The bitch stole my book!"

"What were you thinking?"

"You're mad at me," he said simply.

"No, I'm mad she tried to prevent you from coming to see me while you were a student here. I'm worried about what she did with your notebook. What was in it?"

He shrugged and stared down at the carpet. "Things."

"What things?"

"Silly things. It's not important. We need to get the book back."

"No, you heard her. It's gone."

He snorted. "You don't believe her any more than I do."

He was right, but pursuing this would only lead to trouble. "What else do you have about us?" I asked. "You need to destroy everything. I can't have people thinking I was sleeping with you when you were a minor. That'll ruin me."

"I don't know what you're talking about."

I caught his wrist before he could walk away. "You know what I'm talking about. Your mother told me."

His face went pale. "The bitch," he spat. "I did what she told me to do, and now she doesn't keep her end of the bargain."

He tried to pry loose, but I held him firmly. "What do you mean?"

"You want to know the truth?" he said. "Yes, it's true. I was obsessed with you when I was living with you and Mom. I scribbled Mr. Ari Wheeler in my book over and over again. Harlan saw it but just thought I meant I wanted you to officially adopt me until he saw the hearts. Then he knew what I was talking about." He inhaled deeply, his chest expanding. "I cut out pictures of us and created a scrapbook, removing Mom from every single one of our pictures. I had pages of what our wedding would be like, our honeymoon, of everything I would do for the first time we had sex. The first time I had sex. With you. But she ruined that. She threatened to show my scrapbooks to you and convinced me you would be disgusted and hate me. She bought me a plane ticket and told me to make a choice. Leave or stay and face your disgust." His eyes welled with tears. "I didn't want you to look at me in disgust."

Anne had been right. More than likely, I would not have felt comfortable in the same house with him had I seen all those things then. He'd been jailbait, someone I had no desire to be with sexually. Still, she was a manipulating bitch to threaten her own son to get him out of our lives instead of seeking professional help for him. Maybe if she had, he would have turned out different. He would have found a healthier way to handle his anger and frustration.

"My first time was supposed to be with you," he said in a trembling voice. "Instead-instead it was with a man who I despised."

"Who?"

Before Ari could answer, the phone on my desk rang. I held up a finger to tell him to hold that thought.

"Yes, Julieta?"

"I just got a call from someone who lives in your neighborhood, Mr. Wheeler," she said. "Your house is on fire. The fire department is there now trying to put out the flames."

"What?"

"She says it's bad. Real bad."

"Damn. I'm on my way."

"Is there anything I can do?"

"Let Vice Principal Miller know why I'm not in the office."

I slammed down the phone and grabbed my car keys from the desk.

"What's wrong?" Ari ran after me.

"The house is on fire." Saying it sounded so trivial. It was just a house, but it wasn't. It was years of savings and mortgage and love that went into making it not just a house but a home. Growing up, I'd never had a loving home, so I had done my utmost to create one as an adult.

I sprinted to the parking lot, Ari at my heels. Double damn. He would lose everything too.

"My sketchpad." He slipped into my car beside me. "My computer. I can't lose them."

"Let's hope it's not so bad." What else could I say to reassure us?

"You don't understand, Shaw. All my designs are on it. Designs I sell to an agent."

"What are you saying, Ari?"

"My sketches aren't just doodles. I sell them. And they pay good money for the designs. It might seem like I'm not working, but I'm not hurting for money. I can't lose my stuff."

I clasped his hand in mine and held on to it. "Whatever happens, we're in this together."

Twenty minutes later, I pulled up in my street, and it was as if we had landed in a real-life movie. A fire truck was parked before the house. Men in light brown suits and masks carrying hoses tried to contain the flames. An explosion from the side shattered the window to Ari's room, and flames poured out, licking at the walls of the building. It was all gone. Everything.

"Oh, my god!" I jumped out of the car. Ari wasn't far behind, his hand fisting the back of my shirt. That touch was possibly the only thing that grounded me as I stared at the rubble of everything I worked so hard for to accomplish.

"It's Judd," Ari said in a whisper. "It has to be Judd."

"Because you interfered. You caused all this. I told you to leave it alone, and now look...look what you have done."

"I'm sorry. I—"

"You're always sorry after the fact, Ari. Always. But that's not going to put a roof over our heads."

"I'll make him pay," he whispered, even as my whole world burned to the ground.

"Stay out of it," I snapped. "For god's sake, just stay out of it and let me handle this."

I stalked over to a large guy who was barking orders. He must be the man in charge.

"Sir, you need to step back."

"That's my house."

"And I'm sorry you have to witness this, but until my men get the flames under control, no one's going close to that building."

"How did this happen?"

"We'll try to determine that after the flames are put out and my men are all out safe. Now please step back." His tone softened, his face full of empathy. "Again, I'm sorry about everything, but we'll see what we can save."

What could they save? He was just being nice, wasn't he? How could anything be saved in this inferno?

"Ari?" I turned, but he was no longer behind me. "Ari?"

He was nowhere to be seen. I turned into a wide circle, trying to spot him among the people milling the streets. Some had their phones out, snapping pictures and making photos for another shot at insta fame. I couldn't even summon the urge to yell at them if they had nothing better to do.

He was gone.

The harsh words I'd thrown at him echoed in my mind. Good god, had I blamed him for something someone else had done? I wanted to go after him, and I had a pretty good idea where he would be heading, but I couldn't leave. It would be too suspect not to stay put.

I dug into my pocket for my cell phone and pressed his number. "Pick up the damn phone, Ari," I growled into the voice mail. "Don't do anything stupid. You promised me. You promised us. Please. I'm sorry. I shouldn't have said what I did. This isn't your fault. I was just lashing out from shock. I'm sorry. Just don't do it."

Please don't kill Judd.

The automatic voice came on, asking if I wanted to send the message or delete and record again. I stared at our home, the place that held most of our memories.

TWENTY-ONE

ARI

"BECAUSE YOU INTERFERED. YOU caused all this."

Shaw's voice echoed in my head as I ran. Ran away from the scene. From our house burning. But more than anything else, I was running away from the contempt on Shaw's face. For years, Shaw had been my safe place. When everyone else hurt me, destroyed me with their words, he'd been my champion, but all that had changed.

Because of Judd.

He had to pay.

Tears pricked my eyes, but I blinked them away as I rushed in the opposite direction of the people moving toward the devastation behind me. Our street was a safe street. Nothing ever happened here, and everyone seemed excited, with their phones out, taking pictures that would never let us forget about this horrible day.

The day Shaw didn't look at me with love and tenderness in his eyes. The day he blamed me for our demise. Not Judd. Me.

I skidded to a halt, my body jerking forward, and I fell. My right knee banged into the sidewalk, and my palms scraped on the rough concrete. The pain felt good. Distracted me from how much it hurt on the inside. I slowly picked myself up from the ground and stared at my knee. It felt worse than it looked. My jeans were torn, but the skin had only a few scratches. It didn't even bleed.

I bent my knee back and forth, wriggling it, then took a tentative step. Each step hurt, but I would live. Unlike Judd. I had to take him out. All bets I'd made with Shaw were off the table. He said if Judd made a play for either of us, then I could kill the son of a bitch. Judd made a bold move when he decided burning down our house was a good idea. That bastard was the culprit. He could have an alibi from here until Sunday, but I'd make him confess to what he did. And then I would end him the way I wanted to do all along, but which Shaw wouldn't allow.

I stared at the plume of smoke and the flames in the distance. It reminded me of when my mother had given me the ultimatum of leaving or having Shaw learn the truth about me. I'd been ecstatic that day because I made dinner with Shaw, and in the blink of an eye, everything changed. A one-way ticket out of town had been placed on my bed with the threat to get the hell out or else.

It was funny I'd gone ahead with my mother's plan to avoid the contempt I expected to see if Shaw found out half the shit I'd done during those years. Of all the fantasies I harbored in my head. Of the headless pictures of my mom replaced by my own in photos with him. Yet here I was in that same position.

"You're always sorry after the fact, Ari. Always. But that's not going to put a roof over our heads."

Shaw had never been that angry with me before. Not even when I'd been a huge brat and he made me pee my pants. Or the time I drugged him.

I turned my back to the fire and limped on. I lost track of how long I'd walked. Without looking, only the thought that Judd had to die reverberating, I crossed the road. Tires screeched, a horn honked, and my heart leaped in my throat as I swiveled my head around. For a moment, I wanted the car to hit me. To take me out of Shaw's life so I couldn't hurt him anymore. I didn't deserve him. I didn't protect him when I should have, and now he was hurting because of me.

The car jerked to a stop a few inches away from me. I cringed at the squeal of the wheels and the acrid odor of burnt rubber on asphalt. For a few seconds, everything went still, and then the door at the driver's side jerked open, and a man stepped out, slamming the door closed behind him.

"Are you fucking crazy?" he shouted at me. "I could have killed you."

I shrugged. "You probably should have."

His mouth bobbed open and shut. "I know you! You're that guy from the school."

"You don't…" Shit, it was the cab driver. The one who'd taken me to the school the first time I made out with Shaw.

He scowled at me. "I almost ran you over. Last time I saw you, you were in a much better mood than this."

I gave him a lazy grin. "The man who I was cheating with dumped me."

"Somehow I don't think that's it. I never believed you that night." He gestured to his car. "Can I take you somewhere?"

"I'm not supposed to ride with strangers."

He gave me a blank stare. "You've driven with me before."

"When I paid you for your service, it was different."

He shook his head. "You're weird, you know that?"

"And that's going to make me get into the car with you faster?"

"Seriously, I can't drive away knowing you would have been happy for me to run you over. Get in the car."

I inhaled deeply. "Are you going to kidnap me, then?"

"If you want me to."

He walked over to the car and opened the door for me. He didn't say anything. Just left the decision up to me, and I made it. My shoulders slumped, I shuffled toward him. I ignored the smile on his lips, but it was a relief to rest my aching feet. He closed the door and got in.

"Do you want me to take you home?" he asked as he pulled out.

The memories crashed down on me like a flood. I wrapped my arms around myself and stared out the window.

"I don't have a home."

"What? That's not…" His silence was telling, but I didn't want to look at him and see the pity on his face. He seemed like a nice guy, like someone I should be all over instead of my stepdad, but my heart was already set on Shaw.

"That's your house I passed back there," he said in a low voice. "I didn't put two and two together. I'm so sorry. Now everything makes sense."

"Yeah."

"But that's not a good enough reason to want to die. You have so much going for you."

I finally turned to him. "You don't understand. I think I just lost everything that's ever mattered to me." My art. How far I'd come with Shaw.

"But you're alive, which means things can get better. The only time they can't is when there's no life."

"Usually, I'd agree with you, but I don't know if I can make this one better. Not when the man I love blames me for everything that happened."

"Well, did you burn the house down?"

"No."

"Then he's talking shit."

"Please don't talk about him."

"Well, if you didn't and he—"

"Seriously, if I'm going to stay in this car with you, don't talk about him. Pretend I said nothing."

No one could badmouth Shaw. He was a good man. *I* was the evil monster. The one who destroyed everything I touched.

"Is there somewhere you want me to take you?"

Anywhere Judd was. I needed to see him, to tell him I knew what he had done and he was going to regret it. I reached for the comfort of my knife. Fuck. I'd given it to Shaw, and he'd placed it in his desk in his office. If that nosy bitch Julieta searched his desk, and I didn't put it past her, then she would find it and hand it over to the police. If that happened, Shaw would be in real trouble, and then he would hate me even more.

"Take me to the school," I told him.

"What? Are you sure?"

"Yes. There's something I need to do." I placed a hand on his thigh, which hardened under my touch. "You don't have anywhere urgent to be, right?"

"Uh-um, no, not right now, but I was thinking of getting something to eat. Maybe you'd like to join me?"

"How about after you take me to the school? I just need to collect something real quick, I promise."

He glanced over at me, and I smiled. His face turned red, and he looked away, coughing. "All right. A quick stop."

"Thank you. You're a nice guy."

I always had a thing for nice guys, but he wouldn't begin to know how to handle me. Not the way Shaw did. He was the perfect blend of nice but also naughty as fuck. Even I hadn't known how perfect he was going to turn out to be. Nor how intense it would be in bed when we fucked. He was the perfect Daddy, and I would deserve to call him that again by righting all these wrongs. The next time he saw me, I would have taken care of Judd.

"By the way, I'm Howard," the driver said as he pulled up at the school. "What's your name?"

"Ari," I replied truthfully, and because he had been nice and concerned, I'd tell him the truth. "I'm going to be honest with you. I'm deeply in love with someone else and I would never fuck around with another guy. I can sense you're interested, and I want you to know that nothing's ever going to happen between us. You don't have to stick around hoping I'll change my mind. I won't, but I could use a friend."

Before he could reply, I got out of the car. By the time I returned, he would be long gone. I used Shaw's name to get access to the administrative offices. Julieta eyed me warily but said nothing.

Without a word to her, I walked into Shaw's office. She did nothing to stop me. I closed the door behind me and spun the lock. I pulled the drawer of Shaw's desk open. The knife was in the same position where Shaw left it. Unlike my notebook, which I was convinced Julieta still had. I hid the knife into my waistband but didn't leave. I sat in Shaw's chair instead.

We'd been so happy here. I ran my hand over the desk, where he'd bent me over and spanked me with the ruler. He'd fucked me right here in his office. He'd had me under his table, his cock in my mouth while he worked. A tiny smile tugged at my lips and made me feel better. He would always think about me while he was here. I was positive about it.

With a happy sigh, I got out of the chair, pushed it back beneath the desk, and left.

"How is everything with the house?" she asked. "I called Shaw, but he wouldn't answer."

"It's all gone," I replied.

"Oh, no."

"We lost everything." I paused at her desk and leaned forward. "Can I ask you something, Julieta?"

She swallowed and fidgeted with some papers on her desk. "Sure."

"Do I make you uncomfortable?"

"I-I'm n-not sure I understand exactly what you're asking."

"Very simple, really. Do I make you uncomfortable? Like at this moment, are you?"

"This conversation makes me uncomfortable, yes."

I leaned even closer and lowered my voice. "Does it also make you uncomfortable when you're thinking of Shaw fucking you, instead of me?"

Her eyes widened and her mouth fell open. Red suffused her cheeks. Busted. "I d-d-don't—" she spluttered.

"Oh, come on." I rolled my eyes. "I can admit that you're not wrong. I've always wanted Shaw. Why can't you admit the same?"

"Be-because I don't. We-we have a purely professional relationship."

"And he and I have a purely father-son relationship." I gave her a blank stare. "You and I both know that's not the truth, but let's settle something now. Shaw will never want you. He's into me. Me!" I took up the letter opener from her desk. "And another thing, you might want to return my notebook. It's only the right thing to do after all. It's not your property." I twirled the letter opener around my fingers.

"I don't have your notebook."

"Don't insult me, Julieta. I may act like it, but I'm not stupid." I replaced the opener on her desk and winked. "Unless it comes to math and science. Yeah, I'm not too bright when it comes to those subjects. See you around, Julieta."

I sauntered out of the office, humming in the back of my throat. I was already feeling better about everything that had happened. Knife. Check. Scare the crap out of Julieta. Check. Now for the next item on my list.

Outside, I trudged past a couple of high school kids smelling of weed. Things never changed. Shaking my head, I fished my phone out of my jeans pocket. A car horn blasted, and a cab backed out of its parking spot and crawled toward me.

How about that? Howard hadn't left despite me telling him I wouldn't sleep with him.

"Need a ride?" he asked, leaning over to the open passenger window.

With a smile, I nodded and got into the car. Maybe this wouldn't turn out to be the shittiest day after all. Shaw's house might have burned to the ground. All my designs might be gone. He might have yelled at me, but I would fix this, and we would get through it together.

Maybe this was a whole new beginning.

Twenty-Two

Shaw

"THE BEDROOMS ARE UP the stairs. Follow me and I'll show you to your room."

Exhausted after the day's turn of events, I merely nodded and trudged after Jackson Miller, the vice principal. Several people had expressed their sympathies, but he was the only one who'd helped me. He'd offered up his guest room to stay for as long as I needed until I worked out my insurance claims and everything else. He was a nice guy. Why had I never taken the time to get to know him better? We had a professional relationship. We met at parties, but they were work related, and the conversations always were about the students and the school district's regulations.

"While you're here, I want you to make yourself at home," Jackson said. "I mean, it will never be home, but we have to make the best of what we have, right?"

"I truly appreciate this, Jackson." Had I said that to him before? I couldn't remember. I'd been numb since I watched my home and everything inside get destroyed. After the fire had been put out and the excitement had gone with it, as well as all the sensation seekers, I walked through what remained of my house. I stuck to the ground floor, as the fire marshal had declared the building unsafe.

"Don't mention it," Jackson said. "It's the least I can do. I'm pretty sure you would have done the same for Tam and me."

Would I have, though? I'd never know until he was in the same situation, which I hoped to hell not. I didn't wish this on my worst enemy. Not quite true. Wasn't that the reason I'd never called Ari to forget his plan to go after Judd? I swallowed hard, dread settling in my stomach. I shouldn't have let him go. Now I had no idea where he was or even if he was okay.

At the top of the stairs, Jackson turned right. To the left, a corridor led to more rooms.

"That's the bathroom." He gestured to the door beside the one where we were standing with his hand on the knob. "Tam and I have our own, so you'll have your privacy."

I followed him inside. On the queen-sized bed in the room lay gray sheets, which matched the walls and curtains with a splash of the same bright green as the cushions on the leather couch against the left wall. Faux plants and frames with inspirational words perched on floating shelves.

"If there's anything you need, don't hesitate to let us know," Jackson said. "I want you to treat this place like your own home. Nowhere's off-limits. Well, except for our bedroom."

I cracked a smile at his attempt at humor. What I needed more than anything was to take a shower and get rid of the scent of smoke and ash, but I didn't even have anything to wear. Shit.

Where the hell are you, Ari?

"Do you have any spare clothes?" I asked Jackson. "I probably should take a shower before I do anything else. Wouldn't want to ruin your bedsheets with the horrible smell."

"Sure thing. Just let me find you a couple of things."

"Just for tonight."

"I'll be right back." He paused at the door. "I'm sorry this happened to you, Shaw, but we're going to help get you through this."

I nodded, a lump forming in the back of my throat. I was so fucking tired. The bed looked inviting, but how was I supposed to sleep tonight after everything? How was I supposed to close my eyes without feeling guilty about the angry words I'd spoken to Ari or for not demanding that he leave Judd alone?

I only had Ari's sketches and colored pencils he'd left behind in my office. I stared at them and, with a groan, dropped them to the bed. I'd hold on to them until he came back. He had to. We were in this together now, and whatever he did or didn't do, I was as much an accomplice. Ari was going after Judd, and by not telling the police before it happened, I was complicit and thereby just as guilty, but I couldn't summon any remorse for what was sure to come.

Could I even stop him now? I doubted it. He'd wanted to kill Judd from the day the son of a bitch had shown up at the house. If I'd let him do it then, I'd have saved us all this heartache.

I dug my phone out of my pocket. Damn, it was dead. I found an outlet beside the bed and plugged my phone into the charger. Next, I opened the closet. The hangers were empty, but on the top shelf lay a pile of linens. I took down one of the big orange towels.

The bedroom door opened, and in walked Jackson's wife, carrying a bundle of clothes in her arms. Tamryn gave me a small smile, her eyes full of concern. She was a pretty, petite woman. Now I remembered why I didn't hang out with Jackson. I'd almost forgotten. Anne hadn't liked Tamryn. She never liked anyone she felt was prettier than her.

"Shaw, it's been a while." She placed the clothes on the bed. "I'm terribly sorry for what happened. I can't imagine what you're going through." She walked to me with her arms outstretched and gave me a comforting hug.

Jackson appeared behind his wife. He merely chuckled and shook his head. "Come on, Tam. Give Shaw some space to breathe." She backed off, and he gave her a quick kiss, then turned his attention to me. "Sorry about that. Tam is a natural hugger. It's her love language. We're going to be downstairs. Feel free to join us for dinner if you want. If not, we'll leave a plate for you, and you can eat anytime you want."

"Thanks."

Jackson waved his hand. "No more thank-yous. We're only doing the one decent thing we can to help a friend. Knowing you're safe is good enough."

When he and Tam left, I powered my phone on, then dialed Ari's number.

"Come on, baby, pick up." But he didn't. "Ari, it's Shaw, your Daddy." I hadn't left him a voicemail the other times I'd called. "I'm sorry for the things I said earlier. This isn't your fault, and I don't blame you at all. I shouldn't have said that. I was angry about the whole situation, and if I'm honest with you, I'm terrified of losing everything. Or so I thought, but I didn't lose everything, Ari. I still have you. At least. I hope so. Please be safe. Call me as soon as you get this. I need to know you're okay. I can't lose you again."

Although I hadn't seen him as a lover when he was younger, I had lost him then, and his absence had left a hole nothing but his reappearance had been able to fill.

Please let him at least listen to the voicemail and hear my apology. I grabbed the change of clothing and towel and headed for the bathroom. After my shower, I checked my phone, but Ari hadn't called back. I called him again without success. What happened? Where was he? I snatched up my car keys and went downstairs. Usually I was ravenous for dinner, but the delicious aroma wafting from the dining room made me nauseous.

"You joining us?" Jackson asked me when I walked in. They had an extra place set at the table. God, I was an asshole for turning down their hospitality. They'd offered up their home to me when they didn't have to.

"I don't feel like eating," I replied honestly. "I need to buy a few things. Toothbrush, underwear, deodorant." Cigarettes, which I hadn't touched in years.

"All right. We'll leave you a plate in case you get hungry and change your mind later."

I started to say thanks, then simply nodded. I checked my watch. Almost time for the local news. "I'll be back soon. Got to catch the eight-o'clock news."

"Same, but I can always record it if you're not back, so take your time."

I took the long route to the mall, slowing down as I drove past the remains of my house. Yeah, I was a glutton for punishment. Just like that, everything was gone. When the police officers had questioned me whether I knew of anyone who would deliberately set the place afire, I lied that I had no idea. As much as I wanted to mention Judd, I didn't have any evidence, and if Ari already had the man killed, I didn't want the crime to be linked back to us.

First, I needed to know what was going on with Ari and what he had planned.

After picking up what I needed from the store, I used the self-checkout, bagged my items, and left. At my car, I lit a cigarette and jammed it between my lips. I inhaled deeply. Goddamn, I needed that.

My eyes closed, I sucked the smoke into my lungs, then blew it out.

"What a surprise seeing you playing with fire after everything, Shaw."

My eyes flew open, and my entire body went stiff. There stood Judd, with his thumbs hooked into the loops at the front of his jeans.

"One fire not enough for you?" He laughed.

I removed the cigarette from my lips. "I know it was you, you bastard. Think you're going to get away with this?"

He gave a mock shudder, then parted his jacket for me to see the gun tucked into his waistband. "You think I'm scared of that boy you have running around town doing your dirty work for you?" He rubbed the bandage on his arm. "If he so much as comes near me again, I'll enjoy hearing him scream."

"You touch him, Judd, you'll regret it." I launched myself at him, but he blocked me with his other arm. I hated that my weight was such a disadvantage when I was up against him.

"I can't promise you that, Shaw. Your boy's got spunk, and it intrigues me. I'm hoping I'll run into your doll again. Give him my best regards."

He marched toward the entrance of the store and disappeared inside. Unless I followed him and caused a scene, which would amount to nothing, there was little I could do about it.

I flicked the cigarette on the ground and crushed it under my feet. That asshole ruined even that guilty pleasure. I unloaded the goods into the trunk, slammed the lid shut, and wheeled the cart to the collection spot outside, then stomped back to my car. I started the ignition and checked the rearview mirror. A blond head popped into view.

"Daddy, it's me."

My heart stopped, then ratcheted up to a thrumming beat. "Ari?" I switched on the overhead light. Was it really him? I turned in my seat and held out my hand. With a cry, he clambered over the seat and hugged me.

"I'm sorry. I'm so sorry," he said, sniffling.

"No, baby, it's my fault." I kissed his face over and over. "I shouldn't have blamed you for what Judd did. I was way out of line and I promise I'll make it up to you."

I took his face between my hands and kissed him, shoving Judd's threat to the back of my mind. "What are you doing here? Where are you staying? I'm with friends, but we can get a motel somewhere until we figure this out."

He stretched forward to kiss me again. "I hated that you were so mad at me. You've never been that angry with me before."

"It was wrong of me to be. Will you forgive me?"

He pulled back a little. "I always will."

I groaned. He so easily gave everything of himself to me. I didn't deserve him.

"How did you know to find me here?"

"I followed Judd," he said.

"And how'd you get into my car? I locked the door."

"I have my ways."

Of course he did. When was I going to learn Ari was far different from the boy I knew? He was dangerous. Exciting, but dangerous.

"Are you mad?" he asked.

"No, I'm not. I'm just glad you're okay. I'm sure Jackson won't mind putting you up for the night too. Tomorrow we can find another place."

"I'm sorry, but I can't. I've got to fix this."

"I'll go to the police."

"With what evidence?"

He got me there. Everything I had was circumstantial.

"Then it doesn't matter. I'm just glad you're safe. We can start over."

"I can't let him get away with this. I can't. I have to make it right."

"Ari, that's not—"

He grabbed me by the head and smacked his lips to mine, his tongue insistent and demanding in my mouth. And despite everything I'd lost today, kissing him reminded me how alive we still were.

"Daddy, I need you."

"Ari."

I couldn't move my body much — I was way too big — but he maneuvered between the seats and slid onto my lap. He found the lever to lower the seat, then leaned forward and kissed me again. Ever since I saw everything I owned burning to the ground, I'd felt dead inside, but now with Ari in my arms, I was living again. I wrapped my arms around Ari's body, down his back, and encountered a pleated skirt and thigh highs. If only I could see him better to admire him in the outfit.

Had he gone shopping since everything happened?

He moaned, rubbing his ass against my crotch, and I lost all train of thought that didn't have to do with the way he was moving against me, hands running from my shoulders down my chest. He found the waistband of the borrowed sweatpants and pulled down the material to expose my hard dick.

"Yes, Daddy. I want it."

I rucked up his shirt front and kissed his chest, licked at his nipples and sucked them into my mouth. We were in a public parking lot, but I didn't even care. I'd plead temporary insanity if anyone caught us. He was the only thing I had left in my life, and I needed to hold on to that.

Clutching him around the waist, I shifted slightly forward and rummaged in the glove compartment for the lube I had there. Impatient, he took it out of my hand and squeezed the liquid gel into his hand. He smoothed it down my dick, his lips finding mine again. He moved against me, rose, and then he sank down onto my cock, his tightness gripping me with such suction that I almost came inside him.

"Give it to me, Daddy!" Ari rode my lap hard, one hand braced against the door. He didn't pause. With his breathing ragged and his voice far from lowered, he took what he wanted, like the first time I penetrated him.

"I need it," he cried out. "Need your cum inside me, Daddy."

I gripped his thong and pulled it to the side while he continued to ride me. I bucked up, and he groaned, head falling forward on my chest while his hand worked on his cock, stroking himself. His body tightened, and I wrapped my arms around him, holding him down against me while I used every muscle to thrust up over and over until I gave him what he wanted. My body stiffened, stomach quivering, as I shot my load inside him.

Moaning, Ari reached behind him, using two fingers to bracket the width of my dick inside him.

"I'm a satisfied boy when you're inside me, Daddy." He sighed, and I tilted his head to kiss him.

"Let's go."

He shifted off me into the passenger seat and fixed his underwear while I worked on my borrowed sweatpants. With Ari in my life, I could do this. I would start over from scratch. The money from the insurance would help us buy another house. I turned to share my plan with him, but Ari jerked the door open and hopped out of the car.

"What are you doing?"

He glanced back at me. "Sorry, Shaw. I need to do this. For you, because I know you won't. He took your home from you, and now I'm going to hurt him the way he hurt you."

"Ari!"

He slammed the door shut. Damn. I pushed my door open and stumbled out of the car. "Ari!"

But he was off, his legs carrying him away from me as he ducked between cars.

TWENTY-THREE

ARI

"YOU KEEP LOOKING AT your phone. Are you expecting a call?"

I tucked my phone back into the pocket of my sweater. Howard sat beside me on the living room couch. I hadn't been checking my phone for a call but the time. I should have been out of the house already, but he was taking his time with his drink tonight when all I wanted was for him to fall unconscious on the couch so I could take care of my business before returning home with him none the wiser.

I didn't drug him every time I went out, which had been every night for the past five days since I accepted his invitation to stay with him. I loved to hit a club or bar, but to go out every single night might be a tad suspicious, so I'd slipped a mild sedative in the can of Coke he religiously drank whenever he was watching television.

"Yeah, I'm looking for an apartment. I was supposed to get a call today, but none came in."

"Isn't it too late to call, though?"

I shrugged. "I'm desperate. I can't live off your hospitality forever."

I held my breath as he picked up the can of Coke. This time he drained it, his Adam's apple bobbing when he swallowed. Howard was an okay guy, who I'd taken a chance on when he offered to put me up for the night. I had been too exhausted and devastated that day to say no. His act of kindness won me over, and now I might actually have a friend. I hadn't had one since Harlan had died.

It was nice to have a friend. Although my lies were necessary, I tried not to do anything that would harm Howard. Not after how kind he'd been to me. Sometimes he watched me a little too much, and I knew he was attracted to me. I appreciated him not making a move on me, though, and I hoped like hell one day he would find someone deserving of his kindness.

"I got something on my face?" he asked. "You're staring."

I shook my head and sank back against the cushions of the couch. "Nope. Let's go back to watching this movie."

A little over half an hour later, he'd fallen asleep. I bounded up the stairs to get a blanket, placed him in a reclining position, and pulled the cover up to his chin. The least I could do was make sure he was comfortable. I turned the volume of the television down low, then swiped the empty can on the table. I never left any evidence behind.

In the guest bedroom, I changed into a black pair of jeans and a hoodie. I wore the same outfit every night, so I didn't have to worry about getting evidence on all my clothes. After the fire, I went shopping. I had raided the women's department for skirts and dresses that would help me feel feminine until I could buy a new sewing machine and fabric.

I took Howard's car, which he'd offered me to use since mine got destroyed in the fire. After five days, I knew the route by heart. I mapped out the different areas I could take to Judd's house and how much time it took me from the apartment. This was the shortest route. I arrived at his house in fifteen minutes and waited in the car across the street, watching to see if anyone was home. There shouldn't be. I didn't want to run into his son, though I noticed the boy was infrequently home.

Satisfied the house looked empty, I pulled my beanie over my hair. It was actually a beanie and a mask in one. I could easily pull it over my face to conceal my features, which I'd done every time I scoped out the house. I cut across the street and into the neighbor's yard, climbed their trellis, and over into Judd's. At the back of his house was a window that didn't close properly. Normally, I would pick the door, but I mapped out my path and practiced entering and leaving undetected.

I removed the glass pane, slipped inside, then settled it back in. The window of Judd's room could serve as another entry point. He never closed it, perhaps because it was high off the ground, but it was conveniently next to a tree.

Once inside the house, I moved silently, checking out that everything was still the same as I found it last night. I climbed the stairs, listening for any sound, but there was none. I was completely alone. I went through all the rooms upstairs, saving Judd's for last.

Rumpled bed sheets trailed to the floor. Judd was a slob. He never made the bed. Two pillows were on the floor, and condom wrappers lay scattered on the nightstand. The same condom wrappers he left there from the night before while he was fucking a woman he brought home with him. I slipped my gloves on and opened the top drawer. I pawed through them, checking he hadn't hidden any weapons.

Next, I walked into his private bathroom and riffled through his trash. I took pictures of a couple of empty pill bottles. Later, I would check out what they were used for. The information might come in handy. I then turned to the cast-iron bathtub. It was the only thing beautiful in this house and perfect for what I had in store for Judd.

I walked back into the bedroom. The handle of the doorknob turned. Shit. No way was I getting out through the window in time.

"Jonas, you sure we can't do this in your bedroom?" a young, feminine voice asked. I made a beeline for the closet and pulled the door closed. Through the slats, I watched the girl enter with Judd's son behind her.

"His bed is bigger." He placed his hands on the girl's neck and kissed her several times. She melted against him, giggling when he hoisted her up and wrapped her legs around his waist.

I closed my eyes and swallowed a groan. I didn't want to hurt these two. They were just like me: young, dumb, and in love. There was nothing to do but wait it out and hope they were too horny to last long.

What I hadn't counted on was Judd's son being a generous lover. He had his girlfriend's legs around his neck while his face was buried between her thighs when the bedroom door flung open, and in stormed Judd.

Shit. Shit.

I slipped out one of my knives. This wasn't how I meant for it to happen, but if I needed to improvise, I would.

"What the fuck do you think you're doing in my bed, boy?" Judd's nasty voice boomed in the room.

Jonas jerked back, his girlfriend screaming and scrambling to fix her clothes.

"Mr. O'Connor, we're so sorry," she said.

"You fucking your dumb bitches in my bed?" Judd asked.

The son seemed paralyzed, his eyes scanning the room as though looking for words or a way to escape.

"I'm sorry, Dad. I shouldn't have. This is the first time, I swear."

I didn't even believe him. Judd pointed at the door. "Get out, you little bitch."

"I'm so sorry." Tears spilled down the girl's cheek as she hurried out of the room.

"Mel!" Jonas ran after his girlfriend, but Judd's meaty fist landed in his face with such force, he keeled over onto the floor, clutching his nose and groaning.

"Where the hell do you think you're going?" Judd demanded. "I'm not through dealing with you yet."

"Just let me take her home," he begged. His words ended in a hoarse cry when Judd kicked him in the side.

I winced. The abusive son of a bitch. I shuffled back as far away as I could to the back, hiding behind clothes should Judd open the door. I covered my ears against the sickening sounds of blows hitting flesh. Bile filled my mouth, and my mind flooded with memories better forgotten.

My heart pounded in my chest at Jonas's grunts and cries of pain. Not too long ago, that had been me and my old man. He'd found every excuse he could to beat me, and I never understood why until the day he'd pulled down my pants and bent me over his knees and hit me with his belt. I could still hear his satisfied grunt as he came in his pants. From that day on, I'd teased him and flirted until I had him in the palm of my hand. His eyes had been so full of surprise when the knife sliced across his face for the first time.

Messy messy. It'd been so messy, but making him bleed was the best kind of revenge.

How much more of this could I listen to? I inhaled deeply and exhaled to prevent me from hyperventilating. If the bastard didn't stop soon, I would have to intervene, and that wasn't part of my plan.

"You fucking disgust me!" Judd shouted. "And you'd better wipe that blood off my floor before I get back home, you dumb shit. Couldn't even stay in school."

A door slammed shut. I peered through the slats. Judd had left. His son huddled on the floor, a bloody, moaning mess. It was now or never. I inched through the closet door, the wood creaking, but he didn't even look up. I took a step toward the window but paused. All that blood splashed onto the floor.

I swallowed the bile down. If not for leaving traces of my DNA behind, I would have spat it out on his floor. Dammit, what was I? A wuss? I went over to the figure on the ground and dropped down on my knees beside him.

"Are you going to be okay?" I asked him softly. "Should I call the ambulance?"

A grunt left him. He raised his head and stared up at me, one of his eyes swollen.

"No ambulance. It's not so bad."

"Don't tell him I was here." Why did I even say that? It didn't matter if Judd knew I'd been here. Then he could stew on how, where, and when we'd meet again.

"Who are you?"

I took a step back from him. Thank god for the mask. "I'm the one who's going to free you from your abuser."

He struggled up to a sitting position, clutching his side with a grimace. "How're you going to do that?"

"Simple. I'm going to kill him."

He looked me up and down. "You don't stand a chance. He's a fucking monster and he will hurt you. I'd stay away from him if I were you."

"Can't." I strode to the window. I'd stayed too long already, and now that I knew he would survive what was possibly not even his worst beating by his father, I had no reason to hang around. "He hurt someone I love and he must pay."

TWENTY-FOUR

SHAW

"I'M TELLING YOU THE truth, Jackson. Do you think I'd make random stuff up?"

"I don't know. Maybe. I told you to lay off the pills for a while."

Cringing at the loud voices coming from the kitchen, I shuffled inside. Jackson was arguing with Tamryn across the island. They both swiveled their heads in my direction. What had I interrupted? This was awkward.

"Sorry, I didn't mean to intrude." I gestured to the coffee maker. "I'll just get a cup of coffee and get out of your way. I hope I'm not the reason behind this quarrel." I'd spent over a week with them now, and every day I felt like I wore out my welcome. Not that they ever said or acted in a way to put that idea in my head. I just wasn't used to living off other people's sympathy.

"Of course not," Jackson said. "Just Tamryn here being paranoid today. Go on. Help yourself."

"I am not being paranoid," his wife said as I sidled by her and took up the new insulated mug I bought. Thank god too. I could pour the coffee and leave them with whatever argument they were having.

"You know how you sometimes get, Tam. That's all I'm saying."

Tamryn's face turned red. "I am not being paranoid. Someone was in our house last night. They were here last week too."

"Why didn't you mention it, then?" Jackson asked.

"Because I-I wasn't sure what it was the first time."

I frowned at her. "Why do you think someone was here?"

"And that's what you should have asked me before thinking I'm crazy." She glared at her husband, then turned her attention back to me. "The first night, it was just a feeling. I always get up at night to-to use the restroom."

"And have a drink," Jackson murmured.

"Yes, Jackson, sometimes I have difficulty sleeping, and a drink helps." She rolled her eyes. "Anyway, last night, I was returning upstairs and I swear someone slipped into your bedroom, Shaw."

"Probably just Shaw going back to his bedroom from taking a piss."

She shook her head. "No, it wasn't. This person was smaller. Like a woman. Did you have a woman in your room?"

"For fuck's sake, Tam. The man just lost everything. He's allowed to have a whole harem if that's what he wants."

"I just don't feel comfortable with it, since we never discussed it."

"Actually, Tamryn, you're mistaken," I said. "That was, in fact, me going back to my bedroom after using the bathroom."

Bullshit. I hadn't woken up once during the night, but if what I suspected was true, Ari might have broken into the house last night. A shiver ran down my spine. He'd slipped into the bedroom without me knowing. If what Tamryn said was true, then it wasn't the first time he had done it either. What did he do when I was asleep? I could easily imagine him crawling into bed with me and jerking off on top of the sheets while listening to me sleep.

My cock twitched, and I angled my body to hide my budding erection.

"See, I knew there was an explanation." Jackson walked around the island, tugged his wife into his arms, and kissed her temple. "You worry too much. How about we spend the day together? Just you and me wherever you want to go?"

"I should go." I backed out of the kitchen, coffee mug in hand. "I have a meeting with my insurance agent today, and hopefully, they'll have some more information for me." How long did they expect me to wait while they carried out their investigations? It could be months before they finally paid me out.

I'd looked for apartments, somewhere cheap for the time being; I wanted to save every penny. Starting over was going to cost me. Even if the insurance company matched what they considered the monetary value of the house, they wouldn't cover the furniture and everything inside. Already, I'd spent quite a lot of money to buy new clothes that were presentable enough for work.

Things didn't go smoothly at the insurance office. Nothing had changed. It was the same tired BS of having to wait for my place in their line for my claim to be processed. They couldn't give me a specific time, but they would get to it as soon as possible, and in the meantime, they were sorry again for my loss. And, did I want a pen?

What a bunch of assholes. I'd gone from owning a home to relying on someone's hospitality and now I had to find somewhere to rent. I couldn't have Ari traipsing through other people's houses at night, and as long as I was there, he would keep coming. He would never face me during the day. Not when he probably knew I would ask him to forget about everything and start over. He meant more to me than anything; and what if Judd hurt him?

I slipped into my car and buckled my seat belt. My phone rang, and I scrambled to fish it out of my pocket. Ari's name flashed on the screen.

"Ari, where are you?"

"I miss you too, Daddy, but it won't be long now."

Jesus, I needed a cigarette. I took one out of the pack I'd hidden in the glove compartment and lit it. "I'm worried about you."

"I'm fine, but I'm worried about you. Are you eating okay?"

"For god's sake, Ari, of course I'm not eating okay. I can't bear to eat while you're out there plotting crazy schemes."

"It's not crazy. In fact, it makes perfect sense."

"What makes perfect sense is you coming back to me."

"Soon, I promise, but now I have a big surprise for you."

I wound down the window and blew out a puff of smoke. "I'm not sure I like surprises anymore."

"You'll like this one, promise."

"You're making an awful lot of promises."

"And I'll make them come true. You'll see."

I slumped against the car seat. "Ari, this isn't right. You shouldn't be the one handling this."

"Why not?" he sounded amused.

"You're so small, Judd will crush you. This is my responsibility."

"And you're my responsibility, just as I'm yours." He made a humming sound at the back of his throat. "I thought you quit smoking when you and Mom got married."

My body shot forward, and I peered through the window, searching for him.

"You're here?"

He chuckled. "I'm everywhere you are. Don't you know that?"

"Hang up and come to me."

"I can't. I have so much to do for tonight."

"Tonight?" My heart leaped in my chest. He was going to make his move on Judd tonight? "Where? Tell me so I can be there. I-I can help."

"I know you, Daddy. You have a soft heart. You'll never be able to go through with this."

"I helped you with Rich," I whispered softly.

"He doesn't count. He was already dead. Hardly anything you could do about it." He laughed.

"What?"

"Rich was supposed to be my safety net, you know."

I ground out the cigarette into the cupholder. "What do you mean?"

"I could have taken care of him all on my own, but I wanted you involved just in case."

"In case what?"

"You have to understand. I didn't know if I could trust you yet."

"What do you mean?"

"I moved the body. I never intended for it to remain in that one place, but I needed you to think that, so if you got cold feet and changed your mind about us and tried to turn me over to the police, you wouldn't because then you would be an accomplice."

I fell silent, completely dumbstruck at his words. It made total sense why he would do that, but it also felt like a betrayal. Here I thought we shared this big secret when he'd been keeping it from me that later he'd gone and dug up the body by himself.

"Are you mad at me?" he asked. "Are you going to punish me when I see you again?"

"Is that what you want? To be punished?"

"Yes, because I should always trust Daddy, but I didn't then. You're the only one I trust now."

"I'll forgive you if you allow me to choose your punishment and you have to bear it."

"Ooh, what is it?"

"You won't know until I see you again."

"That's not fair, but I'll take you up on that."

My phone beeped, and I removed it from my ear. Ari had sent me a text message — an address.

"What's this?"

"Your surprise. Someone will meet you there."

"Ari, what are you up to?"

"Surprise, remember? I really have to go." His voice lowered. "I love you so much, Shaw. Never forget what I'm willing to do for you. For us."

He hung up before I could respond. I sat there, phone in my hand. I scanned my surroundings. Where was he watching me? When I spotted nothing, I checked the address again and drove out of the parking lot. I stopped in front of a modest one-story house. The lawn was neatly trimmed, but the outside could use a fresh coat of paint. Other than that, the house looked to be in great shape.

Was it for rent or sale? Was that the reason Ari told me to come here? It didn't have a sign, though. I parked my car right behind the car sitting in the driveway and got out. I checked out the houses on either side. They were a similar style and seemed well-maintained. The neighborhood looked pretty decent.

I knocked at the front door, but the door was ajar, and I let myself inside.

"Hello?" I called out, my voice echoing in the empty house. The floors were bare, so were the walls. I slowly walked across the hall. "Anyone here?"

A woman walked out a door to the left with a smile on her face and a stack of papers in her arms. Dressed in a gray skirt with a yellow blouse and matching flats, she seemed like a sales agent. A real estate agent.

"Hello there, I'm Jessamyn King of King's Home Solutions."

My face heated up. I knew what was going on here. "Oh gosh, I'm sorry for wasting your time. Did someone tell you I was interested in this house?"

"You're not?"

"It seems great." What little I'd seen of it so far. "But I'm not in a position to make an offer on this house just now. I'm so sorry. I think there's been a misunderstanding."

"Oh, but the house is already paid for."

"Excuse me?"

"Your son wanted this to be a surprise." Her smile was back. "He explained you recently had an unfortunate situation at your last home and he wanted to surprise you. Such a talented young man, and what a lucky father you are to have a son capable of buying a house for you at his age."

Her words took forever to process. Ari bought us a home? But how? When? He hadn't said anything about it.

I have a big surprise for you.

It was big. Huge. I had no idea what I'd done to deserve that precious boy who loved me more than anything and anyone else in the world, but I would never cause him to regret it.

"Are you ready for the tour?" she asked. "I admit there was another we considered, but he insisted on this one because he wanted to work on it with you. I'd say you have some great father-son bonding time in the future."

If only she knew how well we bonded.

TWENTY-FIVE

ARI

PATIENCE WAS A VIRTUE I'd been forced to possess since having to wait until I was old enough to make my move on Shaw. That kind of patience was far greater than the hours I sat in the window of Judd's bedroom, watching his driveway for him to show up. It wasn't as boring as it could have been. I had too much to think about. Once I got rid of Judd, I could pick up my life with Shaw right where we'd left off. In our new home.

I removed my phone from my pocket, my eyes straining to see the low backlit screen, as I didn't want even the flicker of light to alert Judd that I was here. I dialed the number to retrieve my voicemail and waited for Shaw's voice to come over the line.

"Baby, my god, Ari." He went silent as if trying to find the words. That was my favorite part, to hear how pleased he was at what I'd done. I'd used up almost all the money I made from selling my designs, but it was all worth it. I could always make more money. In fact, another fashion house was looking to hire me on a more permanent basis. And I was considering it.

"It's perfect," Shaw finally said. "It needs a little work, yes, but we can handle it, and I swear to you that when my insurance money clears, I'll give you back every dollar you spent on this house."

He was entitled to think that, but I would never take it from him. This was my gift to him. Just another way to show him how much I loved him.

"You can forget about this, Ari," he said. That was the part of the message I didn't like so much. "We can start over together."

I turned off the phone and slipped it back into my pocket. No way would I call off this hit. Then what would happen? What was to stop Judd from trying to take a second home from us? I could never live with myself knowing I could have prevented it but didn't. I didn't take Shaw for a soft man, but he was too decent to do what needed to be done.

Lucky for him, I had nothing emotional to hold me back. Judd simply had to die, even more so after I witnessed how he treated his son. He was a monster, and it was only a matter of time before he killed his son or vice versa. Then Jonas would surely go to prison. Too many people would benefit from Judd being wiped off the face of the earth for me to reconsider my actions.

Lights swept over me. Shit. I had been so lost in thought I missed Judd coming home. My heart leaped in my chest, my body went rigid, and I slowly inched away from the window, not moving the curtain. Although I risked being exposed, I had to check that he was alone. I didn't want to hurt an innocent person.

The bastard stumbled on his feet. My watch told me it was a few minutes past one in the morning. If stalking people had taught me anything, it was how not to become a creature of habit. That was the demise of many. Their everyday routine was so static, with little room for deviating. It made it easy to locate and neutralize my kill.

Like the fact that Judd would be walking into the kitchen right now for a cup of iced tea, something he did every night before he went to bed. Easy enough to put drugs in, then wait until he passed out before I carried out the next phase of my plan.

I scooted beneath Judd's bed. Not too long after, his heavy boots trudged into the bedroom. He burped, and I was so giddy with excitement I had to clamp my hand over my mouth to stifle the giggle. Would Shaw be disappointed in me that I could find something this fucked up to be fun? No one else seemed to understand that it was the most powerful feeling to rid the world of people who did terrible things but would never get caught.

The bed groaned under Judd's weight. This wasn't the first night I'd drugged him. I could have killed him then too, but I needed it to be perfect. That time had been nothing but a trial to make sure my plan was feasible. Not a matter of if it might or might not work. I needed it to be a foolproof plan.

"Fuck." Judd groaned. "So fucking horny."

What the hell was he doing?

His phone rang. A young man's sleepy voice came over the loudspeaker.

"Hello? Judd, that you?"

"Of course it's me. You have anyone else calling you at this time of night?"

"I was asleep, is all."

"I need you," Judd growled. "Sitting on my lap and bouncing on my cock. Come and get it, boy."

Fuck, fuck. If he invited guests over, that would ruin the entire plan. This wasn't supposed to happen.

"I'm sorry, but I can't. I've got this test tomorrow and —"

"Fuck that test. Don't you remember how good I made you feel last time?"

"Actually, it hurt. I told you I wasn't ready yet, but you didn't listen."

"Come on, a little pain is a good thing, right? You exploded in my mouth after, didn't you?"

"Um, yeah, but I still can't. Maybe tomorrow night."

"If you don't show up now, don't bother tomorrow night."

"Judd, don't—"

"Fuck you."

I let out my breath slowly. Thank god that didn't work out like he'd planned. Clothes rustled, the bed dipped, and then I heard what could only be one thing. The sound of Judd jacking off. The bed rocked gently, and soon his grunts filled the room.

"Shit."

The rocking stopped. I stayed put and waited fifteen minutes to make sure he was completely out. When there was no movement, I slowly inched out from under the bed. I straightened to my full height, the tension in my body easing. He was sprawled on the bed, his shirt rustled up to his stomach and his cock hanging out of his jeans.

I touched Judd's body gently at first, then harder. Satisfied he was out for the count, I grabbed him by the armpits and pulled him off the bed. He landed with a thud on the rug, and I held my breath, but he didn't wake up. Holding him by his hands, I dragged him to his bathroom, the rug helping him slide over the floor, then dashed downstairs to the basement, where I had stored what I needed. When I returned to the bathroom, I used a pair of handcuffs to cuff his hands behind him. Chains wound around both ankles and up his legs all the way up to his chest. Then I stood back to admire my handiwork.

Judd weighed a fucking ton, and it took all my strength to roll him into the huge old-fashioned clawfoot bathtub. I couldn't stop his body's momentum from hitting the side of the tub, and a gush of blood splashed against the white interior where he hit his head.

While I waited for Judd to revive, I removed the bathroom curtains and soaked the towels in the sink. I'd set up his own phone on a tripod. It didn't take more than thirty minutes for the propofol to wear off, enough time for me to get everything set up for the grand finale. He squirmed in his chains, his movements becoming more forceful as the drug wore off.

"What the hell?" he grunted. "This isn't funny."

Only then did I get up from the toilet seat. His eyes widened, shifting from me to the blow torch I had in my right hand.

"Hello, Judd. Missed me?"

"You're Shaw's boy. What do you think you're doing? Remove these chains now."

"You're not in charge, Judd. You might want to start begging instead of making demands."

He eyed the torch again. "What are you going to do?"

"It depends." I nodded at the camera. "Maybe I'll let you walk free if you confess to all the things you've done."

"I did nothing, I swear."

I frowned. "Tsk, tsk, I don't like lies, Judd. Maybe you don't appreciate your life, and that's why you're taking this so lightly."

"I am not."

"Then tell the truth. I want you to confess about what you did to the library, what you do to your son and the underage kid you're fucking."

Because no matter how willing that boy was, he was still too young, and Judd was taking advantage. I'd been that young boy once, full of worship of my own idol, but the only difference was that Shaw was no Judd. Shaw never encouraged my attention or used the way I felt about him to engage in an inappropriate relationship with me.

And a good thing too, or I might have grown to resent him.

"Please. I-I'll build back the house," he said, his voice rising. "I swear I will. Just let me go."

"I'm giving you one chance only to get this right." I'd seen him use his phone often enough to know it had face recognition. I held it up to Judd's face to unlock the device, then opened the video. "You have one shot at confessing what you've done wrong and asking for forgiveness."

"Come on, I can—"

"Three."

"We can work something out."

"Two."

"There's nothing he can give you that I can't. I can give you so much more."

"One. Lights, camera, action."

I clicked the Start button, and the red light blinked on the phone. I fell silent, not wanting anything about me to be seen or heard on that video. Tomorrow or whenever his body was discovered, I wanted people to know the horrible, disgusting things this man had done. For them to know he didn't warrant their sympathy after the fires, the life he'd taken, and the innocent ones he'd ruined.

"I-it was me," he finally said softly, staring at the camera. "The library fire wasn't an accident. I deliberately set the building on fire so we'd get the contract to build a new one, but I swear I had no idea anyone was inside. I'm not a killer."

When he paused, I made a half-circle motion with my index finger to encourage him to continue.

"I-I also burned down Lio Bello restaurant and the house on Woodford Street. It's what I do. People piss me off, and I put a torch to their shit." He struggled to get up, but he was trussed up like the chicken he was and he wouldn't be able to get up with his hands tied behind his back.

"And-and I beat my son, and if that's not bad enough, I've been coercing his high school friend to sleep with me."

He swallowed, and I paused the video. "Not bad. You won't win any Academy Awards for that performance, of course, but it'll serve its purpose. But first, I need to hear you acknowledge that you're a monster who destroyed so many lives. I want to hear you beg for forgiveness. Tell them how sorry you are, and mean it."

I set off the torch once, and he flinched. I pressed the button to continue recording.

"There's no excuse for what I've done," he said. "I'm a monster, and I don't deserve your forgiveness, but I'll ask for it anyway. But monsters come in different sizes and shapes." His eyes bored into mine. "And in the end, we're all one and the same."

I ended the video and retrieved his phone. I collapsed the tripod and rested it on the floor out of the way. I wasn't a monster. I was nothing at all like him. For him to even suggest such a thing...

The gag rested on the shower caddy where I'd left it. When he shook his head and shouted, I stuffed it inside his mouth, then brought the straps to the back of his head to secure it.

"There. We wouldn't want to wake the entire neighborhood, now would we?"

Humming beneath my breath, I got the can of gasoline and poured it over his body in the tub. His eyes went wild. He must have figured out what I was about to do to him. He jerked frantically, his legs shuffling but unable to move much. The gasoline only made him even more slippery, so he couldn't find purchase to haul himself out of the tub.

I took up the blow torch and held it at his feet. "I think we'll start at the bottom and make our way to the top. I don't want you to die too quickly. The whole plan is for you to suffer the way you've made others suffer. Get it?"

Twenty-Six

Shaw

THE MORNING AFTER ARI bought us the house, I was in a better mood than I'd ever been since my house burned down. I entered the waiting room of the high school, humming, then came to a halt. Huh, that was odd. Julieta wasn't at her desk. I checked my watch. Was I earlier than I thought? No, I wasn't.

Julieta was never late and she took pride in that. If she was going to be absent, she would call me so I could mentally prepare for a day without her.

"Margaret," I asked the assistant whose desk was a few feet away from Julieta's. "Did Julieta call?"

She glanced up from her computer screen, barely acknowledging me, then lowered her head again. "She was here earlier. Left something in your office for you."

"Okay, thanks."

"Sure thing."

But something else was wrong. I snapped my fingers. That was it. All her personal effects were gone. No photograph from her college days when she'd gone to Mexico with a group of friends. No pictures of her nieces and twin nephews either. And the orchid I bought her last April for Secretary Appreciation Day didn't stand on her desk anymore. It was getting weirder and weirder.

I dug my keys out of my pocket, opened my office door, slipped in, and closed the door behind me. On my desk lay a notebook, on top of which was a brown envelope with my name on it. I picked up the envelope and lifted the flap. Inside was a single sheet of paper.

Dear Shaw,

It has been a great pleasure working with you directly for the past two years. You gave me the confidence to complete my tasks by showing your appreciation for simply doing my daily duties. Every employee would be lucky to work for a superior like you.

Unfortunately, due to unforeseen circumstances, I have to submit my resignation, effective immediately. It is with deep regret that I could not give you more notice. Under ideal situations, I would have been happy to help your new secretary to transition smoothly into the position.

Yours truly,

Julieta

What the hell? I reread the letter two more times, trying to make sense of it. Why would Julieta suddenly resign? She hadn't given me any sign that she would be leaving.

Or had she? I'd been so caught up with my own situation over the past week and a half, I hadn't paid much attention to anyone else. Between worrying about the house and everything I lost, plus Ari's infrequent calls, I'd been doing the bare minimum of work. If anyone noticed, no one said a thing. Jackson even encouraged me to take more time off to deal with my home situation, but I couldn't take him up on that offer. Being around him and his wife and having nothing else to do but wonder what Ari was doing was driving me crazy.

Ari was too reckless for his own good, and I worried about him.

I grabbed my cell phone and pressed Julieta's number. The phone rang off to voicemail. I called again, pacing in front of my desk. She was a damn good secretary, and if there was anything I could do to get her back, I would.

I flipped the notebook on my desk open and froze. It all made sense now. I ended the call and stared at the inside cover. Ari had used colored paper to cut out his name and glue on the inside, with heart stickers dotting the page. Except where his last name should be, it was mine instead. To the right, the first page read *Private and Confidential*.

This would contain exactly what my ex-wife had warned me about and what Julieta had also found alarming about Ari's behavior. I could finally learn exactly what a young teenage Ari had really been thinking about me. Back then, I thought I was sharing special moments with a young man I could mentor.

I itched to turn the page and start reading.

I couldn't.

I closed the book and placed it into my drawer. Would I want to read the accounts of a younger, impressionable Ari? Things had been so difficult for him then. I had been the referee between him and his mother on too many occasions to count.

All day I was distracted, working through all my troubling thoughts. Of a younger Ari. Of the man he was now. Of what he was doing. Of whether Julieta would share what she'd read with anyone else. And I had no doubt she'd read it. For some reason, she returned it and resigned. That bothered me more than anything else. Why did she resign? Why did she bring back the book after all these years? Had something scared her? Someone? Ari?

I stayed behind long after school ended to finish the work I was too distracted to do earlier. Sometime after seven, I left the office. I drove slowly, every now and then glancing in the rearview mirror at the cars in line behind me. Was Ari in one of those vehicles watching me, even now? His stalkerish behavior should have freaked me out, but it was oddly comforting. Like a vicious little guardian angel working overtime to ensure his human was safe.

Since I'd promised Jackson and Tamryn that dinner was on me tonight, I stopped at a Mediterranean restaurant and picked up some food. It was the least I could do before I moved out. I'd taken up enough of their hospitality as it was, and although the house would take some time to completely furnish, I couldn't wait to be back under a roof I could call my own.

I arrived at the house some minutes to eight. Tamryn was having a glass of wine in the kitchen, but Jackson was nowhere to be seen.

"Sorry I'm late." I placed the containers on the table. "I had to put in some overtime, and my secretary quit today without warning."

"Jackson told me," she replied. "That's highly unprofessional of her." She sniffed at the bags. "Oh god, this smells good. Thanks so much for volunteering to grab dinner. I was in no mood to cook after the day I had."

"It was my pleasure. Where's Jackson?"

"Setting up to tape the eight-o'clock news for you. He thought you were going to miss it."

"You guys are the best."

She made a shooing motion with her hands. "Go watch. I'll get the table set up for us to eat after."

"Thanks. If you ever divorce Jackson, you can find me."

"Shaw, I can hear you in there hitting on my wife. Go find your own."

"I don't need a wife." I followed the sound of his laughter to the living room. "I need a husband." A certain paranoid boy who I needed to hold close to me to keep in line. Could I even keep someone like Ari in line?

"What? That means you're…"

"Bisexual." I took the armchair next to the sofa where he was sitting. "That's not a problem, is it?"

"No, of course not. I'm just surprised, that's all." He turned up the volume on the television. "You're right on time for the news."

I gave Jackson a sideways glance. He didn't seem to be dwelling on my news. It'd never been a thing before for me to tell people I was bisexual when I was married to Anne. I hadn't dated anyone after either, so the topic never came up.

"And here we go."

I sat back in my chair as the headlines of the local news came on.

"Shocking discovery of a brutal murder and a video that explains the motive behind the killing. Does Coleyville have its own vigilante? This and more in tonight's news segment."

"What the hell's that all about?" Jackson muted the television as advertisements followed the headlines. "You heard anything?"

"No, I've been locked in the office practically all day. Trying to manage without Julieta."

"A temp agency is supposed to send a secretary over tomorrow," he said.

"Thanks for handling that, by the way."

"No problem."

"Seriously, you've been a big help. I know it couldn't have been easy accommodating me all this time, giving me the time to figure out what to do. You'll no longer have to worry about that, though. I've found a place and I'll be getting out of your hair tomorrow."

"You did? That's great. Though I admit I'm going to miss having another man around the house."

The logo for the local news station flashed on the screen, and Jackson unmuted the television.

"Coleyville has seen its fair share of crimes, but the police are baffled at a murder that took place last night. No one saw it coming," the news anchor said. *"Local contractor Judd O'Connor was found dead in his home this morning by his son. It appears as if the deceased was tortured by fire, an instrument of his own making. We have Laura Todd on that report."*

My heart pounded in my chest, and my hands grew sweaty. Wasn't this why I watched the news religiously every night? To see if he had indeed followed through with his plan? And he had. Common sense said to walk away and not listen to what Ari had done to Judd, but I had to know.

The reporter gave a warning that some of the images contained graphic and possibly disturbing content before walking us through the information she'd gathered at the crime scene and by talking to the police captain.

"The body suffered from burns, which investigators have ruled down to being torched. Wet towels were found on the scene, apparently used to put out the fire in order to prolong the torture. While the police are not saying much, they have confirmed a cellular phone was recovered from

the scene with everything wiped except for a video of the deceased confessing to several crimes. He confessed to arson of at least three buildings, including the library, in which one person died. He also mentioned physically abusing his son and his sexual involvement with at least one teen whose name the police will not release to protect the youngster's identity. While the contents of the video has disgusted the neighborhood, there's a division in whether the perpetrator should be brought to justice or hailed a hero for exposing crimes that went undetected by the police for years."

"Unbelievable," Jackson muttered beside me. "Doesn't his kid go to our school?"

"Not anymore." I forced the words out while my heart hammered hard in my chest. I inhaled deeply and let out the breath slowly.

"You okay? You look a little pale there."

"It's just all so disturbing."

He said Judd would pay, but I didn't imagine he would torture the man. If Ari was capable of doing this, what else could he do? What else had he done in the years he'd been away?

The hairs on my arms rose, and my stomach turned rock hard. For the first time since meeting Ari, I was afraid. Afraid of what I'd encouraged. Not even when he'd drugged me had the fear been so strong. He'd killed Judd because of me, but what was the reason for torturing the man? Had he gotten off on it?

Bile rushed up into my mouth, and I bolted off the couch to find the nearest bathroom.

TWENTY-SEVEN

ARI

WHEN I BROKE INTO the house where Shaw was staying, I didn't expect to find him still up some time after two in the night. Even Shaw had a predictable pattern and he was usually in bed by ten. Eleven the latest if he felt particularly risqué.

The bedside lamp was on, casting a pale light across the room and Shaw's frame sitting up in bed. Like he'd been expecting me. I closed the door silently behind me but hesitated. He'd watched the news. I knew that deep down in my gut and from the way he watched me warily. And what conclusion had he drawn? Did he now think I was crazy? Did he want to lock me up in an asylum?

The urge to flee hit me, but I forced my feet to move closer to the bed. Despite the insecurities in my head, I had to trust Shaw loved me and cared about me. That he would go to the extreme for me as I had done for him. For us. He would never put me away.

At the edge of the bed, I stopped. He still didn't say anything. My hands shook as I reached for the hem of my shirt and tugged it over my head. He blinked rapidly twice. Encouraged by that movement, I kicked off my boots and pushed down my shorts and underwear, then slowly placed one knee on the bed.

"Aren't you going to talk to me?" I asked.

He gave a small shake of his head. "I-I don't know what's there to say, Ari."

I shuffled closer to him and straddled his lap. I nuzzled his neck. "How about a thank-you for the way I take care of you?"

"Do you?"

I drew back and peered up at him with a frown. "What do you mean?"

"When you killed Judd, were you thinking of taking care of me, or were you feeding your need for blood?"

My mouth downturned. "Why can't it be both?"

"It's one thing to kill him because the bastard deserved it, but it's another for you to get off on it."

I tried to keep down the giggle but didn't quite achieve it. When it tumbled out, Shaw's expression went stony. I clamped a hand over my mouth and took a deep breath to stave off more giggles. "I promise you I didn't get off on Judd's body. That's why I'm here. I want to get off with you inside me."

To demonstrate, I shifted my ass over his groin and placed both hands on his shoulders.

"There's a lot we need to say before we think about sex again."

"But I need it. We can talk about everything after."

"I'm serious, Ari."

I kissed him to shut him up. He could act all self-righteous and holier than thou all he wanted, but he wanted me to kill Judd. Now he acted as if I'd done something wrong because I ensured Judd suffered.

Deepening the kiss, I thrust my tongue between his lips, moaning and running my hands down his chest. He wasn't responding. I pulled back, biting into my bottom lip, and my lungs constricted, making it difficult to breathe.

I hit Shaw in the chest. "Are you really going to reject me after everything I've done for us?"

"I am not rejecting you. I want us to talk."

I doubled my fist and smacked him harder. "Go ahead and act all righteous. I told you what I was going to do to Judd, and you never once stopped me. You could have called the cops to warn them, but you never did. You could have warned Judd, but you didn't. You *wanted* him to die, but you didn't have the guts to do it yourself. So I did it for you."

"Ari, stop it."

"No!" I rolled away from him. "I fucking hate you for the way you're looking at me right now. Like I'm someone you're afraid of." I gasped, scrambling off the bed while tears spilled down my cheeks. "Is that it? Are you afraid of me now?" I gave a bitter laugh. "Afraid that when you're sleeping, I'll lose my head and slit your throat, just to watch you bleed out on the bed sheets?"

"That's oddly specific, but I'm not afraid of you."

"Liar!"

"Keep your voice down, or you'll wake everyone."

"What? You don't want your friends to know you're harboring a criminal? Or you don't want them to know you're fucking your stepson?"

"You don't keep your voice down, Ari, and I'll—"

"You'll what? You can't even own the fact that you pissed on me and liked doing it. Why must you see the world in black and white all the time?"

Shaw stumbled out of bed and stalked over to me. "Can't you see I'm trying to do the decent thing?"

"I don't want the decent thing, so who are you trying to impress? Because I think we'd both be happier if you spread me on that bed right now with your cock pounding me so hard it will make me cry."

"You want me to make you cry?"

"You think what I do doesn't affect me? Well, it does. And you can do something about it. Make me do penance. Hurt me. Please, Daddy. I need to feel better after doing what I did."

A few seconds passed in which he said nothing. And then he whispered, "I can't hurt you here without somebody hearing."

"There are woods behind this house."

Shaw licked his lips and swallowed hard, but his eyes gleamed. He didn't fool me one bit. His life would be boring without me. He wouldn't get to do these exciting things and go places I pushed him to.

"We're going to do things my way for a change." He picked my shirt up from the floor and yanked it over my head. "We are going to talk, and that's final."

I bit my bottom lip, itching to argue, but when Shaw became the assertive Daddy, he really got my attention. I nodded, and he pointed at the bed.

"Now be the good boy I know you can be and sit down."

I sat on the bed, pulled my knees up under my chin, and wrapped my arms around them. It meant the shirt rolled back and my lower half was exposed. Shaw's gaze dropped for a brief second. Then he looked away. I hid my smile by burying my face into my knees. At least he still wanted me.

"I don't like you having to go through these extremes to try and protect me or us." He plucked a chair from the corner of the room and placed it before me. He sat and rubbed my toes. "I know you think you're this tough guy who can get away with anything, but" —he touched his chest— "in here, you're the sweet boy who likes to cook and sew and makes the most gorgeous designs. You're the same little guy who looks up at me with so much love and adoration in your eyes, and you're right. We need to start fresh. And to do so, we're going to establish some ground rules and boundaries."

"I hate rules," I grumbled.

"It's a choice, Ari. If you want to be with me and for us to have any semblance of a good and healthy relationship, I have to insist before this gets out of hand."

"What do you mean?"

"Remember you promised I could punish you?"

I nodded, wary at the way he looked so determined.

"When you made that promise to me, I already knew what I wanted you to do as a punishment."

"What?"

"To go see a therapist."

I jerked back as though he had slapped me. "What?"

"But now I see the flaw in that plan. Therapy shouldn't be about punishment. It should be seen as something to make you get better."

"You think I'm defective? That something is wrong with me?"

He released my toes and massaged my ankles instead. "I think there's something wrong with all of us. Like me for example. You were right. I've been holding back all the things I want to do to you because I'm afraid of how people will judge me if they find out."

"But we have nobody in our bed with us. Shouldn't you feel comfortable sharing that with me?"

"I'll try harder to trust you as my partner, but this entire relationship has to be built on trust. Is that clear?"

"Yes."

"I mean it, Ari. No more killing. You will let the law handle these things from now on."

"That's too absolute."

"Ari—"

"What if I promise to kill them without torturing them? Would that be better?"

"No more killing, and that's final. I am your Daddy, and that rule is going to stay in place. It's my hard limit. Do you understand?"

I let out a deep breath. He said I couldn't kill them, but he'd not said anything about hurting them. That would have to do when the situation called for it.

"Yes, Daddy."

"And you will see the therapist?"

I frowned at him. "A therapist would be obligated to report to the police that I've committed all those murders."

"You won't talk about the murders, but you'll find a way to cope with what your relationship with your mom did to you and whatever you experienced when you went to live with your father."

Chewing on my bottom lip, I stared at him. "You think it will help?"

"Yes, I do."

I shrugged. "All right, but only because you asked."

He let out a heavy sigh. "Ari." He dragged out the *i*, and a shiver ran down my spine. "What am I going to do with you?"

"Love me," I said.

"I'm hopelessly in love with you," he said, and I closed my eyes briefly and smiled. Warmth spread through my body, and I relaxed for the first time since entering the bedroom.

"We will be okay, won't we?" I asked him, then whispered, "Because I like myself best when I'm with you. You don't hurt me the way other people do."

Shaw tugged at my legs and pulled me into his arms. He had a half smile on his face. "But I thought you wanted me to hurt you."

Heat filled my cheeks as I stared down at him. "You know what I meant."

"Yeah, but I know what will punish you, Ari, and it's not hurting you the way you want. I'll make love to you slow and sweet and edge you to the point where you break."

Shaw lifted me in his arms and gently placed me in the middle of the bed. He tugged off my shirt, removed his clothes, and joined me. I lay back against the pillows with my legs parted to accommodate him, but he had different ideas. He started with my toes, sucking them into his mouth and licking between them. Kisses trailed the inside of my thighs, and I groaned in disappointment when he jumped over my cock and kissed my upper body instead. His lips touched every part of me, and when they claimed mine, I was shaking and panting beneath him. My nerve endings had nerve endings. My skin prickled under his touch.

"Turn over." Shaw helped me to flip over. I went up on my knees, but he put his hand in the center of my back and pushed me to lie flat on my stomach. Then he lavished my other side with his kisses and caresses until I tingled everywhere except the places where I needed it most.

"Please, Daddy," I begged, turning my head to the side. "I need more."

Shaw took my ass cheeks and parted them. "Is this what you want from me?" His tongue delved into my hole, and I cried out, pushing my face into the mattress to keep it down. Shaw fucked my hole with his tongue and a finger, turning me inside out, but he still made no attempt to touch my cock. I was dying.

"Pl—"

My words came out muffled as he pushed my head back into the pillow. He wasn't joking. He had no desire to be rushed. He licked my hole until I was a weeping mess on the bed. I sobbed, shoulders shaking. I just wanted him inside me already. My hole ached to be filled.

Shaw moved away from me and padded to the closet. He returned with lube, which he slathered down his dick. Finally! But he made me wait, allowing my dick to soften before he came back onto the bed and gently rolled me onto my side. He raised one of my legs and rubbed the head of his dick over and over down my taint without entering me.

"Baby." He licked at my ear lobe. "You've got to be quiet. Shh. Yes, that's it. I won't fuck you until you show

Daddy that you can behave."

I swallowed the next restless groan, closing my eyes and breathing through my nostrils hard.

"See, baby can obey his Daddy, can't he?"

"Yes, Daddy."

"So baby gets what he wants. To be filled with Daddy just like this." He pushed against my hole, and I opened for him. I couldn't swallow the moan as he slid all the way inside me.

"Goddamn, Ari." His groan echoed in the room, and he gripped my ass cheek tight as he stilled.

"You like your boyhole, Daddy?" I whispered.

"Love it. So fucking tight around my cock, and look at that ass, baby." He squeezed the fleshy globe. "You don't come until I'm ready to make you come. Do you hear me?"

"Yes, Daddy."

I almost broke my promise to him a few times. He alternated between moving slow and fast, but he always stopped if I got too into it, allowing me time to wind down before *he* wound me up again. It frustrated me. It excited me. My poor body was confused in what it was supposed to do until all I could do was lie beneath him as he flipped me onto my stomach.

"Please," I murmured.

Shaw jerked my hips so I was on all fours, and this time when he grasped my cock, tears spilled down my cheeks as he pushed his cock inside. So good. The way he stroked me while he fucked my ass. His cock was so big. There was no way I could stop from coming this time, but I tried. Oh fuck, I tried.

"Now come for me."

I had to stuff my head into the pillow as I exploded violently. Shaw's cock was buried deep inside my ass, but he wasn't thrusting. Just filling me. His other hand worked my cock fast, jerking me off until I spilled all I had. I collapsed onto the bed.

He planted a kiss on my back. "That's my good boy."

I was boneless. I couldn't move, my eyes so heavy.

"Need to go," I murmured, but my body wouldn't obey. I couldn't even lift my hand to wipe away the sweat from my forehead.

"You're too tired. I'll wake you up before everyone else wakes." He kissed my shoulder. "Close your eyes and go to sleep, little one."

Little one. I loved that. My eyes fluttered closed, and I smiled, my last thought of how good it felt when Shaw continued thrusting into my sleeping body.

Twenty-Eight

Shaw

ARI'S LOW MOANS WERE caresses in the air as I kept thrusting into his pliant body. Not wanting to jar him as he settled into a drowsy state, I acted with care, slowly sliding into his body. His back relaxed, and his breathing evened out as if my deep strokes were lulling him into sleep. I kissed his shoulder, my breath coming out in quick puffs as I tried to keep it together.

I couldn't. Not for long. My muscles strained, and I clenched my teeth to swallow my groan. I pulled out to the tip to watch my cum spray into his hole. He was going to fucking kill me. I'd been so certain earlier of what I needed to do: to put a stop to our relationship. I'd never turn him over to the police, but he would always think it was his duty to protect me, to remove anyone he thought was a threat. Then he'd entered the bedroom and looked so hurt at whatever he saw on my face, I'd caved in.

It was too late for me now. I was already all the way in, and once I admitted it, the way became clearer. He was a boy looking for guidance, and I would be his compass. It would be okay. It had to be.

My dick slipped out of him along with a trickle of cum. I used my thumb to push the substance back, and because I couldn't resist, I pressed until I was knuckle deep inside him. I let out a sigh and removed my finger. What was it about this dangerously twisted boy that made me unable to stay away from him? Was it because he was so different with me?

I rolled over to my side of the bed. As if seeking my warmth, he followed me. I gathered him to my chest, sucking a deep breath when his lips found my nipple and he sucked the thick bud into his mouth. He sucked on it like a lamb pulling on a teat. Then his jaw went slack, and the pressure eased. His lips didn't fall off, though. It should feel weird having him latched onto me like this, but I liked it. The way he sucked every now and then as if on instinct.

I woke up from sleep with a start. Sunlight streamed in through the window announcing a brand-new day. Damn, I had forgotten to set the alarm.

"Ari." I reached across the bed for the boy, but the space beside me was empty. I rubbed my eyes. Why hadn't he woken me up?

I hadn't gotten quite enough sleep last night, and my body felt heavy. With a groan, I sat up in bed and grabbed my phone. Underneath lay a piece of paper. I unfolded it and read.

I wanted to wake you, but you sleep like the dead, so I decided to leave you be. I have to go out of town for a couple of days to meet with a fashion designer who wants to hire me. *Fingers crossed it goes well for me. Can you get started on the house until I come back?*

I immediately dialed his number. Why had he never mentioned this to me?

"Hey, Daddy, are you just waking up?"

"Yeah, I'm sorry. I should have set the alarm."

"It's okay. I don't need an alarm. And you don't have to worry. I didn't bump into anyone on my way out."

"Good. You weren't so careful a couple of times before, and Tamryn's seen you."

"She has?"

"She didn't recognize you." He might get the crazy idea he had to take the woman out for being able to identify him. "Besides, Jackson thought she was seeing things." I took a deep breath. "Why didn't you tell me about your trip?"

He chuckled. "I planned to, but then we got sidetracked with all that talking and making love. I had a great time, Daddy."

"Me too. You won't get into any trouble on your trip, Ari."

"Of course not. I promised you last night, and I won't break that promise to you."

"Good. When will you be back? I admit I'm still trying to wrap my head around the kind of work you do and how profitable it has been."

"Is that a good thing?"

"Very. I just wish I understood it better."

"Okay, I'll let you in on that part of my life. How about that?"

"Yes. That'll do. I want to know everything there is to know about you."

"Are you sure about that? Even the terrible parts?"

"Even the terrible parts." A flight announcement sounded in the background. "You're at the airport?"

"Yes, I'm flying out to LA, but I'll be back in a few days. Will you miss me?"

"Yes. I feel like we haven't had the chance to settle down since you came back. It's been one thing after another."

"Don't worry. I won't go anywhere else after this. Promise. I'll be around so often and demand so much little time that you'll be sick of me."

"I doubt it."

"Good, because I'll never be sick of you."

"Call me every single day you're away," I told him. "And that's an order from your Daddy."

His sigh came clear across the line. "Yes, Daddy, but I have to go now. Love you."

"I love you too, Ari. Wait!"

"Something wrong?"

"I have something for you. That notebook you lost and Julieta took? She returned it."

Ari went silent.

"Ari?"

"Did you go through it?" He sounded so small all of a sudden.

"Just the inside of the cover page," I admitted. "I didn't want to invade your privacy in case you don't want me to read it."

"Do you want to read it?"

"I-I don't know, to be honest."

Again a long silence and I checked that he was still there. "I don't have to read it. You've grown past that sixteen-year-old boy."

"Except I still feel the same about you. You can read it, but when you do, Shaw, this will be the last thing I have left of myself that I've kept from you. After this, you'll know everything, and I hope you don't hate me after."

"I can't hate you." Or else I would already have.

"We'll see in a few days."

He hung up, and I put down my phone. Now that I had his permission, I itched to get my briefcase where I put the book for safekeeping, but I also knew that once I did, there was no going back. I took a shower, then shaved, taking my time. Did I really want to read his journal?

When I returned to the bedroom, I didn't even bother to put on clothes. I dug out the notebook from my bag, sat on the bed, and flipped to the first page.

October 16

Today I stabbed a boy in my class with a pen. It wasn't my fault, really. He took the sandwich Daddy made me for lunch. I don't know what happened. He was laughing in my face while he ate it, and everything around me turned black. Before I knew it, he was bleeding, a pen pierced in his hand. Mrs. Ramsay, our guidance counselor, says it would help if I start to write about my feelings, so I'm giving it a try because I've been having some bad feelings lately. Feelings I can't talk to anyone about. Well, sometimes I mention a few things to Harlan, but he doesn't get it. At least if I write it down here, it will feel like telling someone and knowing they won't judge me. So let's hope this works.

A

October 22

I hate Rich. He's a bully who forces me to do things to him when the other boys aren't watching. I should just tell everyone in class he's a homo, but I think that will only make it worse. At least now he only does those things to me in private, but if I out him, maybe he'll want to do it all the time, since he won't have a reason to hide. I saw Mrs. Ramsay today, and she feels something is wrong. I almost told her about Rich, but I'm afraid. I don't want to get him into big trouble. Just some trouble. I really just want him to leave me alone.

P.S. The only dick I think of sucking is Daddy's.

A.

November 1

Today was supposed to be a good day. Mom had a night out planned with her girls, which means Daddy and I were home alone. I made plans for us. I would cook, and since Mom wouldn't be around, I would even be able to wear this dress I'd been working on. Mom hates it when I dress up in women's clothes. I think she's jealous Daddy tells me I look beautiful. She always gets angry when Daddy compliments me.

Anyway, Mom's friends canceled on her at the last minute, and she decided to order in pizza, even though I told her I would cook. She wore this smug smile on her face that made me want to smack her, but then Daddy would be upset with me, and I don't want that. I'm his favorite boy ever, and that's the way I want to keep it.

I guess I'll just have to wait on wearing the lingerie set I bought with Mom's credit card until another time Daddy and I are all alone.

A.

November 3

I did something very, very bad. Thank god I wasn't caught. I hid under the bed in my parents' room so I could listen to them fuck. My mom's always so loud, and I get so jealous she's getting to experience everything I want with Daddy. I don't know what possessed me, but I wanted to be closer while they had sex. I wanted to hear Daddy's grunts and imagine him on top of me.

It was exciting. I hated hearing my mom, of course, but I just blocked her out and pictured I was the one riding Daddy. I heard Mom saying over and over how big Daddy's dick is, and now I'm curious. I need to know what it looks like. I always thought being bigger meant it would hurt more, but now I'm changing my mind.

I didn't get to crawl out from beneath the bed until they'd both fallen asleep. That's when I did it. I lowered the sheet and caught sight of Daddy's dick, but he was all soft, so I'm not sure how big is big. Seeing his cock excites me. I wanted to take it into my mouth the way Rich forces me to do his, but I couldn't risk being found out, so I had to leave.

I can't wait for the day I get to feel Daddy's cock inside me. I think Daddy will be so happy when he finds out I saved myself for him. Of course I have to get Mom out of the way first. As long as she's around, Daddy will never give me a second glance.

A.

November 14

I've been studying the routines of both my mother and Daddy. It's the only way I get to have any alone time with Daddy these days. Whenever she's out of the house, I know exactly when to show up. The same for Daddy. I got home from school early today and clogged my shower drain.

Then at the exact time I knew Daddy would be home, I went to use the shower in their bathroom. Mom's in Vegas with her girlfriends, and she'd warned me about playing any tricks while she was gone. She doesn't trust me in the least, and I can't say I blame her.

Anyway, there I am, completely naked and wet in Daddy's shower when he walks in. Whether it was out of shock or if he liked what he saw, I don't know, but he stared at me for a long time. Okay, maybe a few seconds, but he did look especially at my erection. Then he grabbed a towel and wrapped it around me to cover me up. I love Daddy's touch. I just wish he'd taken off his clothes and joined me. I was so horny I nearly came right out and asked him to fuck me, but I know it's not the right time. He doesn't look at me yet the way I want him to. He hasn't stopped apologizing since, but one thing he did say was that we can't ever mention what happened to my mom.

Damn,

A.

I skipped a few pages in which he only had our names scribbled over and over with colored hearts. So much had been taking place in Ari's mind when he was younger. Why hadn't I seen his obsession? His mother had warned me about it over and over, but I thought she was reading into things, being paranoid because she didn't get along with her son. So often, I had been a referee between them, acting like a buffer, that I hadn't had time to contemplate all these little truths Ari revealed in his book.

The pictures came next. Pictures of me I never posed for. Sitting in the living room, cooking dinner, mowing the lawn, and working in the garage. A picture of me in the shower that made me shiver. Pictures of me when I was in bed sleeping. In one, he'd clearly cut out his mother and Photoshopped himself into it.

If I hadn't already decided to send him to see a therapist, this would have definitely done it. I skipped past the pictures and found the next written entry.

December 2

Today I walked in on Daddy and Mom having sex on the kitchen table. I was supposed to be at Harlan's but changed my mind when Harlan called me to let me know Rich was waiting there for me. They didn't notice me at first, and I stood there, watching them. The man I wanted more than anything in this world was fucking her. She didn't even like him that much. I heard her say that to a friend on the phone once. She loved Daddy's dick, she said, but wished he would get rid of the beer gut and take better care of himself to look like Angelina Foster's husband.

Mom saw me first. When she did, she smirked. She wanted me to see that Daddy belonged to her, and that couldn't have come across any clearer when she told Daddy to fuck her harder, all the while looking at me. Daddy started to, but then he stopped abruptly. I must have made a sound. When he saw me, he pulled away from Mom. I ran up the stairs. I heard her trying to convince him that I'm old enough to know that they fuck, but he came after me instead to check that I hadn't be scarred by what I witnessed.

I knew then that my mom would always win the small battles, but eventually I would win the war. He didn't stay with her. He came after me.

A.

December 14,

I'm mad. I'm so mad I can't think straight. All I can think about is grabbing a knife in the kitchen and going after Rich. He'd almost fucked me today, even though I told him no. He had his cock right against my naked ass when someone walked into the locker room. If he'd done that to me, he would have ruined the fact that I've been saving myself for Daddy. I have to find a way to get rid of Rich before he forces himself even more on me. No one at school will believe me anyway. They all think I'm a big flirt and they will probably believe I led Rich on.

I don't want Rich. I only want my Daddy.

A.

December 17

He hadn't written anything, only drawn lots of sad and crying faces. I frowned. What happened on December 17th? And it hit me. It was the day Harlan took his life. The day Rich raped him and the day Ari blamed himself for what happened to his friend because he never spoke out about what Rich had done to him.

A knock on the door startled me.

"Shaw, are you up?" Jackson asked.

"Yeah." I slammed the book shut and pushed it under the pillow. I couldn't have anyone else knowing all these things about Ari's past. Now it made sense Julieta resigned. She knew too much. Did she suspect Ari had anything to do with Rich's disappearance? She must have heard about it.

I shrugged on my robe and opened the door. "What's up?"

"There's someone here to see you. I tried to tell him there was no one here by that name, but he knows you're here. He won't say who he is. He only says that he has to talk to you. I'm one second away from calling the police, but he says calling the police could get you into trouble. What the hell is going on, man? Are you involved in something fishy?"

I held up a hand. "Slow down. Slow down. I don't understand anything you're saying. What man?"

"He won't say his name."

"I'm not involved in anything, Jackson. Let me put some clothes on and see what's going on."

"Yes, please. I don't like the looks of this guy, and I know we shouldn't judge on appearance, but I have a bad feeling about him."

"Just give me a minute, okay?"

"Fine. Thank god Tamryn is gone shopping, or she would have freaked out. I gotta say, man, maybe it's a good thing you've found another place. We don't want any trouble."

My mouth had gone dry. Why would anyone want to talk to me? It wasn't the police. If not them, then who?

I quickly pulled on a pair of sweatpants, and a T-shirt went over my head as I left the room. Barefooted, I headed down the stairs and followed the rumbling of voices to the living room. Jackson stood a few feet away from a man who had his back to me. He had blond hair that was thinning at the top of his head.

"Here he is now," Jackson said.

The man slowly turned. I had never seen him in my life. His face was horribly disfigured with permanent, angry scars like he'd been in a knife fight.

His eyes assessed me from head to toe, and his lips curled in a smile that made my skin crawl. Jackson was right. Whoever this man was, he oozed nastiness.

"You're Shaw?" he asked me in a raspy voice.

"Who wants to know?"

"Of course you are. He's talked a great deal about you. I have to say I expected something better. At least someone in better shape."

"I can say the same." I turned to Jackson, who took everything in. I needed him to be far away before this man said anything I couldn't afford him to hear. "Will you give us a moment, please?"

"Sure, but you need to wrap this up quickly, Shaw." His expression was hard and his posture stiff as he walked out.

"You seem like a smart man," the stranger said, "who's about to get involved in a very stupid thing."

"Why don't you say what you need to and go. Starting with who you are."

"My bad." He smiled and held out his gloved hand. "My name is Ken, and I'm Ari's father."

I shook my head, not taking his proffered hand. "You're lying. Ari's father is dead."

"He thought he killed me." The smile was replaced by a menacing glare. "He didn't manage to complete the act, which is possibly the worst mistake he's ever made. I'm here to teach the little shit a lesson, and you'll do well to stay out of my way. If you think he's bad, you have no idea what you're in for should you come between us."

"Are you threatening me?"

"Just extending courtesy for you to know Ari's only Daddy is back. You don't want to get hurt, so step out of my way."

TWENTY-NINE

ARI

MY CELL PHONE RANG, cutting through the light, gentle, dreamlike quality of Billie Eilish's voice I was dancing to as I packed my suitcase. I had an amazing meeting today and had signed a lucrative contract, which earned me a hefty check for the two pieces I sold. When I flew to LA to meet with two fashion designer labels, I never intended to sell anything, just to use my charm and my art to garner interest in my work.

My trip had gone way better than I could have hoped for.

I dove onto the bed and picked up my phone, smiling at the name that flashed across the screen.

"Hey, Daddy," I purred. "Miss me?"

"Hey, beautiful boy." I melted. "How is everything in LA?"

"Amazing."

"So you're having fun without me?"

I giggled. "Just a little. I'll make it up to you when I come home."

"I'd like that." He fell silent, and my radar went off. Something was wrong.

"Are you okay? Is someone giving you any trouble?"

"Of course not." He gave an exasperated sigh. "You think I can't take care of myself? I'm more than twice your age."

"But you're also my marshmallow Daddy."

"I'm not a marshmallow Daddy." His voice came out harder than I expected.

"I love you the way you are," I said with a sigh. "Did I do something to upset you? You sound off tonight."

"No, you didn't. I'm sorry. I just had a disagreement with someone."

"Who?"

"Ari."

I rolled over onto my back. "You can't tell me who? I'm not going to do anything. I *promised* you."

"Yes, you did, and you better not break that promise."

"I won't. Love you too much."

He sighed. "Good. You're a good boy, Ari."

"The best boy." I checked my watch. I had some time left before I had to go to the airport. "I wish you were here right now."

"When are you coming home?"

"Soon."

He groaned. "Nothing more concrete than that?"

"No. I still have a few errands to run." I had none, but he didn't have to know that.

"All right, then. You let me know when, and I'll pick you up from the airport. Okay?"

"All right, Daddy." I crossed my fingers as I promised him. I didn't want him to pick me up because I wanted it to be a surprise. My work here in LA was done, and I was heading out of the city in the next couple of hours.

"I love you, Ari. I'll talk to you tomorrow."

"I love you too, Daddy."

"And, Ari…"

"Yes, Daddy?"

"Please be good," he whispered.

Even if I had planned to commit murder, after that I would have changed my mind.

"I will."

He hung up, and I lay on the bed long after the call ended. My life had changed so dramatically since Shaw and I got together. In the past, I'd never cared about finding another solution to my problems. If anyone hurt me, I got rid of them, and there had been quite a few people who had hurt me. Now Shaw made me question everything.

He was all the good I needed. Sometimes the darkness in my head was so scary, but the way he loved me unconditionally left me feeling I would be okay. That I wouldn't be consumed by my own darkness.

A knock on my hotel room door startled me. I scrambled to my feet, frowning. I hadn't ordered room service.

I waited, but the person didn't introduce themselves. Alarm bells went off. I scanned my room, but nothing seemed suitable for a weapon. I had to stop sinking back into old habits. Not everyone was out to get me.

"Coming."

Pushing aside my paranoia, I unlocked the door. What was Justin Perrier doing here? Dressed in a trim, dark blue suit without a tie and the top two buttons undone, he was devilishly handsome, and his cocky posture said he knew it. He removed the blue-tinted shades he wore, the rings on his right hand flashing.

"Mr. Perrier." I raised my eyebrows. "I didn't expect you."

"Didn't you now?" His piercing green eyes bored into mine.

"Actually, I didn't. I'm in the middle of packing my stuff to catch my flight."

"Then I came at the right time. Aren't you going to let me in?"

When I presented my work before him today, he had blown me off. What could he want now? I stepped aside. He'd wanted to offer me a lower deal than I was worth, and when I rejected the offer, he dismissed me. I'd taken my designs to another fashion house, Couture Beau, which had been interested. They might not be as big as Trendy

Men, but they were the next best thing, and what they'd offered me was way more than I'd anticipated.

"You really are leaving." Perrier gestured at the carry-on on the bed. "I thought you were joking."

"Why would I joke about that?" I frowned. "And how did you know which room I'm in? I only mentioned my hotel during our meeting earlier."

He puffed out his chest and chuckled. "You really think that information is hard to get for a man like me?"

The hair at the back of my neck stood on end. To put some distance between us, I walked over to the bed and stuffed the last of my things inside.

"I'm surprised you're here at all, Mr. Perrier. You made your decision very clear that you weren't interested in my designs."

"Come now. We both know you were playing hard to get with that ridiculous amount you asked for them. You're a nobody, a designer no one had ever heard of."

"Did my designs look like something a nobody could have made?"

"It doesn't matter. I could only hire you in an entry-level position, but it wouldn't look good for my company if I offered you a higher salary than what other entry-level designers are getting. People would talk, and the fashion industry can be unforgiving. Plus, I didn't think it best that you work for me, considering."

"Considering what?"

"It wouldn't be appropriate for me to sleep with someone who works under me, would it?" He winked at me. "Of course, I can get you a different kind of work. Much more satisfying, and you can earn even more if you're as good as I think you are."

I blinked at this son of a bitch, my hands clenched into fists.

Please be good.

With Shaw's voice reverberating inside my head, I inhaled deeply.

"Let me get this straight. You jeopardized my opportunity at a livelihood because you want to fuck me?"

"We don't have to make it sound that crude, now do we?"

"Excuse me. I meant you jeopardized my opportunity because you want to make love to me. Is that better?"

"Now you're just being sarcastic."

Heat rushed into my face. Goddamn son of a bitch. He was lucky I promised Daddy I would be good. I wanted to do nothing more than wipe that smile off his face with my knife under his nose. Or to make his smile bigger, since he thought it was amusing to fuck with my career like this.

"I have no desire to make money on my back or under you," I said through clenched teeth. "And I'd suggest you get the fuck out of my room right now."

"You're being hasty." He took a step toward me, then stopped. He might have seen the intent in my eyes. "You haven't heard my full proposition yet."

"And I don't need to hear it. Whatever you're selling, I'm not interested in buying."

"If this is about the job, then fine. I'm willing to go twenty percent higher than what the other entry-level designers are making."

"My services are no longer available." I lifted my carry-on and rested it on the floor.

"Why are you being difficult?"

"My services are no longer available, Mr. Perrier," I repeated strongly. "I signed on with another company. One that's more fitting for the kind of working relationship I am interested in having with others. Now for the last time, get out."

"But I can—"

I swung the carry-on with all my might at his knees. A sickening crack was followed by his howl as he went down. The hard-side suitcase cost me a fortune, but it was worth every penny.

"Goddamn it. You fucking broke my kneecap. You fucking psycho!"

I lifted the carry-on and plunked it hard down into his groin, smashing his dick. He howled and tried to push off the luggage.

"You piece of shit," I spat at him. "You're lucky someone believes in how good I am. If you come near me ever again, I'll ruin your empire. Then *you'll* be sleeping under some man for twenty bucks. Fuck you."

I dragged the suitcase over his torso and his face and walked out the door, his screams following me. I probably should feel bad I wasn't so good after all, but compared to what I wanted to do to this prick, I'd bumped St. Francis from most beloved saint.

Daddy would understand.

He would appreciate I hadn't killed the man.

THIRTY

SHAW

"YOU'VE REACHED THE VOICEMAIL of Aristotle…"

"Dammit, Ari, where the hell are you?" I ended the call and clutched the phone in my fist, my body taut with pent-up emotions. I'd been calling Ari to wish him goodnight, as I had done for the past five days he'd been away, but tonight all I got was his voice mail. This wouldn't freak me out so much if I didn't know Ari this well. He would never dismiss my call. Unless something was wrong.

Or maybe he lost his phone.

Damn, since meeting Ari's biological father, I was a mess. My mind was all over the place. Maybe I should have told Ari, but that wasn't the kind of news I wanted to break over the phone, especially not after what the man hinted at before he left. His promise he would see me around town hadn't sounded as if it would be a pleasant rendezvous.

He'd made it clear, without exactly stating it, that he was here because of Ari. What he planned to do with the boy was vague. Whatever it was, it seemed ominous.

I surveyed the mess in the kitchen. I should clean up. Ari always had the kitchen looking spick and span — the counters wiped clean, the dishwasher emptied, garbage taken out. But Ari never burned the pots either, nor had he ever had to throw out an entire meal because it was inedible.

Now that he was away, I'd realized how much he meant to me...how much he did for me. He never once complained about all the household tasks he'd done since he moved back in. I never had to ask for anything, and I never would have either, but he liked taking care of me. He'd taken it so far that he killed for me.

In a trancelike state, I cleaned up the kitchen as Ari would have done. I willed my phone to ring, but the only alert I received was a message from Jackson about me picking up the rest of my stuff I'd left at his place. I was still settling in, but when Ari got back, it would start feeling more than a house. Like home.

Goddammit, but I loved that boy.

I checked all the downstairs doors and windows to make sure they were locked. I couldn't be too careful. Even though I hadn't seen Ken since he confronted me at Jackson's house, I knew he was still in town, lurking... waiting for Ari to show up.

I climbed the stairs, the nervous energy flowing through me making me restless. If I'd been into exercise, I would have gone for a run or something, but I made for the shower instead. I put my phone on the sink just in case. I wouldn't want to miss Ari's call.

The shower helped a lot more than I'd thought it would. The water cascaded over my body, and as I ran the wet cloth over my stomach, I stared at the reflection in the glass. Maybe I should start exercising. I joked for years about losing weight, especially around my middle, but I never got around to do it. Now would be a good time to start before Ari stopped finding me attractive.

He was young and breathtakingly beautiful. He turned heads everywhere he went. His charm only endeared him more to people. Until he deliberately showed his vindictive side.

But he wasn't a psychopath. He felt emotions, sometimes too intensely. His anger could be explosive and his hurt painful to witness. I had to believe the parts of him that were defiant and quick to kill could be healed.

When I was squeaky clean, I turned the shower off. Wiping the water from my face with the back of my hand, I muttered under my breath. I'd forgotten the damn towel. I pushed back the sliding doors open and stepped out of the shower. My heart leaped in my throat at the figure sitting on top of the vanity, his pants down, stroking his erect dick.

"Ari, what the hell? You scared me."

He grinned at me. I placed a hand on my chest as if that would slow down the pounding.

"Hi, Daddy." He swung his feet back and forth. "I missed you."

Damn. He'd come home feeling horny. My dick throbbed. It'd been days since I saw Ari, and using my hand could never compare. My hand couldn't move the way he did or make that slapping sound of his ass connecting with my pelvis.

"Why didn't you call me?" I moved closer to him, not caring I was still wet. "I told you I would pick you up from the airport, and how did you get in here without making a sound?"

"You know how." He picked up a small bottle from the counter beside him. He wiggled out of his jeans but didn't kick them off. Instead, he turned on his side, giving me a perfect view of his ass. Ari shoved away the tiny swatch of fabric from his thong, coated his fingers with the lube, and massaged it into his hole. "We really missed you, Daddy." The way he fingered his ass, there was no mistaking what he meant by *we*.

My cock throbbed painfully between my legs. With a groan, I placed a hand on his cheek and brought his lips to mine. He opened his mouth and greedily sucked on my tongue like he'd been starving without me. I gripped his hips and jerked him closer to the edge, and with my other hand, I guided my cock to his hole. I thrust inside him as far as I could go.

"Oh fuck." He tore his lips away from mine and gripped the edge of the vanity. "Yes, Daddy. I missed that cock ruining me."

I was at a loss for words. I could only grunt as I clasped his hips even harder and thrust. My cock glided in and out of his tight heat, his plump tattooed ass cheeks so tempting I couldn't resist smacking it. His breath hitched in his throat, and his gaze snagged mine, pupils dilated.

"Fuck me," he gasped. "Harder, Daddy. Please."

I couldn't fuck him the way we both wanted with his jeans in the way. I pulled out of him and dragged his jeans and underwear down his legs.

"Please put it back in, Daddy."

"Hush, boy. You rush me, and I might not make you come."

He whimpered but didn't say anything. As soon as his legs were free, he spread them for me, pushing himself all the way down to the edge of the vanity without me having to tell him.

Holding his legs apart, I nudged against his slickness and snapped my hips forward. Ari threw his head back against the wall. I pounded; he got loud. I withdrew; he protested even louder. His enthusiasm, the way he fisted his cock and stroked himself so hard, plus the way he begged me to fuck him harder, did me in. I couldn't help it. With a hoarse shout, I exploded.

"Goddammit, Ari," I groaned, opening my eyes. "Did you come yet?"

He shook his head, his face flushed and eyes disappointed. I couldn't have that.

"On your knees," I said hoarsely. He eagerly got onto his knees in a low crouch.

I snaked my hand under him to his cock and squeezed. He braced his hands on the wall. Leaning forward, I adjusted my height and licked at his hole. He tightened the ring muscles, then relaxed, pushing out the cum I'd just given him. I moaned around the taste of myself directly from his ass. I flicked my tongue over the ring of muscles, then dove in, reaching deep inside him. I stroked him harder and faster as his breathing quickened and his whimpers got louder.

"Close," he whispered. "I'm so close, Daddy."

I twisted two fingers inside his hole and crooked them upward. He shouted, cock pulsing as cum splattered on the counter. Ari's slender back stiffened, and his shoulders tightened for seconds that seemed like hours.

When he slumped forward, I wrapped my arms around his torso and pulled him back to me, kissing the side of his face and his neck.

"Surprise?" He smiled at me, his eyes half-closed. "I really needed that."

"You're satisfied, then?"

"Do you have to ask? You can't tell by the fact that my legs are of no use to me, and you'll now have to carry me to the bedroom? Hint. Hint."

I chuckled. "Let me clean you up first."

I wet a washcloth and cleaned up his body, then washed my sensitive, depleted cock. I scooped him up in my arms — damn my protesting knees — and brought him into our bedroom. When I put him down, he curled up in the bed, hands outstretched. "I need you."

"I should put on some clothes."

"No. Just the way you are, please."

"Not fair. You're still wearing your shirt."

He sat up, tugged his shirt over his head, and threw it across the room. "There. Now we're even."

I shook my head as I stared in open admiration at his body. "Even?" I gestured to my stomach. "I don't think we can ever be even."

"If we were even, I probably wouldn't like you so much." He patted the bed beside him. "Come on, Daddy. Hop in. I haven't slept beside you in forever."

No sooner had I gotten into bed with him than Ari shifted down. He threw an arm around my hip and caught my cock into his mouth. With a sigh, I placed a hand on his head and stroked him. It was so good to have him back.

Thirty-One

Ari

"THAT'S AMAZING, ARI. I'M glad your trip went well."

I sipped my orange juice, then cocked my head to the side and observed Shaw. Something was off about him. I first heard it on our calls when I'd been away, but I shook it off as nothing. After the way he'd fucked me on the vanity last night, I had been sure I had imagined it. But now he'd returned to behaving strangely this morning, barely talking, and I couldn't even tell if he heard anything I said to him.

If all that wasn't a sign something was wrong, the way he picked at his breakfast, pushing the potatoes around on his plate instead of devouring them and complimenting my cooking, as usual, was proof enough.

"Did I do something wrong?" I was almost certain I didn't but I might have without realizing it.

Shaw snapped his head back. "I don't know, did you?"

"No, I didn't." I dropped my gaze to the kitchen table. "He was asking for it."

"Who was asking for what?"

"The asshole who came to my hotel room. Several times I told him to leave, but he wouldn't take no for an answer."

The fork clattered to the plate. "Goddammit, Ari. Did you call hotel security?"

"No."

He closed his eyes tightly, and the prominent vein in his neck protruded. "What did you do?"

"I might have broken his kneecap," I said softly. Daddy looked so upset.

"You promised me you would stop this nonsense." Shaw pushed his chair back and rose to his feet. "We had a deal, Ari. You find another way to cope with this, like calling hotel security and letting them handle it."

"I didn't kill him."

Instead of answering, Shaw walked over to the sink and braced his arms on it with his back to me. Alarm bells rang like crazy in my head. Shaw was acting out of character.

"This isn't about what I did or didn't do to that man, is it?" Dread slowly seeped into my bones. "You're trying to find a reason to be mad at me." It became painful to breathe. "Are you trying to tell me something, Shaw?" That he didn't want to be with me anymore? That he changed his mind about us?

I felt smaller than an ant. If Shaw gave up on me, I might as well die. There was no one else but Shaw for me.

He spun around. "No, I'm not trying to break up with you."

The tension in my chest eased but only a little. "Then what is it? You've been acting differently since I got home."

I scrubbed at his beard. "I-I've got something to tell you. I just don't know how."

"Just tell me already."

Whatever it was, it had to be bad for Shaw to be acting this way. My heart skipped a beat. The police hadn't received any tip that I was responsible for Judd's death, had they? There was always the possibility Judd's son would grow a conscience and snitch on me. Maybe I shouldn't have let him live. After Judd beat him, I just thought he would be relieved I took out the old man for him. Something he would never be able to do himself.

Plus he hadn't seen my face, so how much help could he have been to the police?

"It's your biological father."

Oh. My shoulder sagged. Mom must have told him her suspicions that I'd killed the man, but that happened before I told Shaw I would be good. He couldn't be mad at me for *that*.

"He was a sadistic bastard, Daddy." I frowned. "And one of my most satisfying kills. He deserved it even more than Judd deserved his fate."

"Ari, he's not dead."

I laughed, drumming my fingers on the table. An image flashed through my mind of Ken writhing on the floor, the blood seeping from the wounds I'd inflicted on his face. He'd been trussed up like a pig and barely breathing when I left him there to bleed out in the basement. No way in hell could he have escaped.

"I'm pretty sure he is." I walked over to him. "Is that what you've been worried about? I promise you he's been dead a long time."

"Ari, he's here in town."

I searched his face. This didn't seem like the sort of prank Shaw would pull. In fact, he wasn't the kind of man who pranked anyone. He was the person who got pranked. But what he was saying was impossible.

"He can't be."

"He stopped by Jackson's home the day you left for LA. And he made it clear he's here for you."

I shook my head slowly. "That can't be him. Someone's playing a trick on you."

"It's no trick." He placed his hands on my shoulders. "I saw him with my own eyes. He had scars all over his face. His voice was damaged by what happened to him. By what you did."

The room spun around me, Shaw's arms the only thing that kept me upright.

"Ari, breathe." He squeezed my shoulders. "Breathe, Ari."

I sucked in a gasping breath as Shaw walked me over to the chair and sat me down. He left me alone and returned shortly after with a glass of water. "Drink."

I gulped down the cool liquid, then pushed the glass away. "What did he say?"

Shaw pulled up a chair next to me and sat, holding my hands. "He said you two had a score to settle. That he's here for you and he won't leave until he gets you."

I stuffed a hand to my mouth, but it was too late to stifle my cry. I trembled, my arms shaking. *He can't be alive.*

"No, no, he can't be alive. He can't be. He's going to hurt me, as he did before. Please don't let him hurt me."

Shaw wrapped his arms around me, and I clung to him, flinching at the memory of hands holding me down, fists connecting with my stomach, boot crunching my hand. Oh god, I'd rather die than allow him to get a hold of me.

"I need to leave." I shoved at Shaw. "I can't let him find me here. I need to go somewhere he won't ever find me."

"Or you can stay." Shaw didn't budge. "Stay, and I'll fight this with you. I won't let him hurt you, Ari."

I shook my head, tears filling my eyes. "You don't understand. He did bad stuff to me. Bad stuff. I spent six months planning just how I was going to kill him, and when I got the opportunity, I couldn't waste it. I had to do it for all the bad things he did to me."

"What did he do to you, baby?"

I couldn't say the horrible things. It would all come back, opening a can of worms that would only set me off again.

"Don't make me talk about it, please. I don't want to relive it."

He kissed my forehead, and tears spilled down my cheeks. I was stupid to think this happiness with Shaw would last. It was all too good to be true. I wasn't meant to have a happily ever after.

"It's okay." He thumbed my tears away. "I promise it's going to be okay. We should go to the police and—"

"No!" I pushed away from Shaw. "We can't. I tried to kill him. If I go to the police, I would just land in prison too. And not just for attempted murder, but for all the crimes he made me do with him. He'd make us both go down for them."

"Shit." Shaw shook his head. "I need some time to think about what we can do."

He stood, but I caught his arms and held on to them. "I know what we can do. We can leave and never come back. Find somewhere else he can't track us down."

"He tracked you down here, didn't he?"

"But that's because he knew I would come back to you. If we go somewhere else, he'll never find us. We don't even have to remain in this country. We can pack our bags and take the next flight out somewhere we're both safe."

"That's not a solution, Ari. I'm almost fifty. I can't start over somewhere. What would I do? We've just bought this house to share a life. We're not going to let someone like your father ruin our lives and have us looking over our shoulders for the rest of our lives. We're going to stand our ground."

"But you don't understand. You think I'm evil, but you haven't seen evil yet. I might have been a bad apple all my life, but he created me. He made me the monster I am."

He cupped my face in his hands. "You are *not* a monster. He might have influenced you to do things, but he's no longer controlling you, and you can stop. You have stopped, and we are going to prove it by staying here in town and living productive lives."

"Daddy—"

He stroked his thumb over my bottom lip. "Listen to your Daddy, Ari. We won't run. Have I made myself clear?"

I let out a shaky breath. Were we making the right decision? But what was I supposed to do? I couldn't leave without Shaw. Blackmailing him to leave town with me could work, but that wasn't the kind of relationship I wanted with this man. I wanted his love, admiration, and respect. If I did that to him, he might be in my life, but I would never truly have his loyalty.

"Please don't let him hurt me."

"I promise you I won't," he said. "I have to go to work. You stay here at home and don't leave. Don't answer the door. If anything happens, call me. Just to be on the safe side, I can phone in an anonymous tip that something might be happening on this street so the cops will patrol the area."

I wanted to tell him all that was a temporary fix. If my father wanted to get his hands on me, he would get his hands on me.

"Ari, you're going to be fine." He chucked my chin. "You know why? Because this time, you have me with you to go through this. I won't let anything happen to you."

I nodded. He placed his lips on mine and kissed me. I didn't bother to point out that he did things by the books. That he would never kill anyone, even when he was provoked. And killing was the only way to deal with someone like my father. Like a cockroach, he didn't die easily and he would keep coming back until one of us was dead.

And this time, Shaw would be caught in the crosshairs. If I lost him...

Shaw went upstairs. The moment he left, my skin crawled. It was like my father was already out there somewhere, watching me. I ran up the stairs and darted into the bathroom, where he was brushing his teeth, and sat on the toilet. He raised his eyebrows but didn't mention my weird behavior.

When he was finished, he turned to me. "Daddy has a job for you to do today while I'm away."

"What is it?"

"I want you to make a list of all the things you like to do in little space. All the places you would like to visit one day. The foods you like to eat and add some toys to your shopping cart. Pick out a few movies you want to watch later. When I get home, we're going to have a heck of a night with you in little space. How does that sound?"

Like he was trying to distract me, but it was worth a try. I couldn't spend the day peeking out windows and startling at every tiny sound.

"Okay, Daddy. I like that idea very much."

Thirty-Two

Shaw

I WAS READY WITH an apology for Ari that I had been held up at the office and didn't get home sooner, but the apology wasn't necessary. When I walked into the living room, I didn't find him worried, the way I left him this morning. He didn't seem to have missed me at all. He was in full little mode, dressed in a onesie over his padded butt, a pair of socks, a bib around his neck, and a rattle in his hand. That wouldn't have been bad, except he wasn't alone.

My stomach clenched at the sight of the young man who sat on the couch, only his profile visible to me. Whatever Ari had said to him, he laughed, and spots flashed before my eyes. How could Ari have changed so drastically in a few hours? This morning he'd been terrified of his father being in town, and now it was like none of that mattered. Had it all been one big act?

With Ari, anything was possible. I was so convinced he'd been spooked, and I'd barely been able to keep my head on straight all day. If Ari, the man who'd killed Rich and tortured Judd, was afraid of someone, that meant his father was the most evil piece of shit on the planet. All day, I'd been trying to come up with something to get his father to leave him alone. It took me twice the time needed to finish my work, which was the reason I was home so late.

I'd never expected to find him enjoying himself with someone else.

I cleared my throat, and two heads swiveled in my direction. Ari's face went red. He knew he messed up. I only got angrier. He damn well knew I would be upset to find him with another man. I was his Daddy, for fuck's sake, and not this attractive, younger, probably more interesting young man who looked at Ari like he wanted to be the only one in my boy's orbit.

"Daddy!" Ari ran over to me and wrapped his arms around my middle. "You're finally home."

He pursed his lips for a kiss, but I just frowned at him, then shifted my gaze to the man on the couch who still hadn't taken his cue to leave.

"What's going on here?" I asked.

Ari gulped and stepped back, dropping his gaze as he gestured at the guy. "Umm, this is my friend, Howard. I was explaining ABDL to him, and he wanted to see me dress up as I would for little space."

"Hi." Howard got to his feet and held out a hand. "Ari and I are friends."

I heard Ari the first time. No need for him to repeat that. And what was with the flushed face? It was as if they were both trying to convince me that was all they were.

"Hello." I ignored his handshake. "Ari, I'd like to speak with you in private."

"I was just about to go." Howard scratched the back of his head, giving a nervous laugh. "I didn't mean to stay around this long. The hours just flew by."

I clenched my teeth and leveled an accusatory look in Ari's direction. I called him, just to check up on him that he was fine. He could have told me he had another man in our home, another man he put on a show for.

Why hadn't he?

"Are you sure you don't want to stay for dinner?" Ari asked Howard.

"Maybe some other time."

There won't be another time.

"All right, then, let me walk you to the door."

I wished he wouldn't. The door wasn't that hard to find.

"Nice to meet you, Mr. Wheeler," he said.

I grunted in acknowledgment. Nice to see him out the door. While Ari let out his "friend," I climbed the stairs to our bedroom. I had on a pair of sweats when he walked in. The image of his athletic friend was still fresh in my mind as I yanked on my shirt over my head to cover my stomach.

"He's just a friend," he said.

"I heard you the first time."

"Did you? Because you seem mad at me."

"Why are you dressed like that for a friend?" I gestured at his onesie. "You don't play with anyone else, Ari. That's one of our rules."

"I wasn't playing." He dug his right foot in the carpet. "I'm not even in little mode."

I blinked at him. He was right. He wasn't in little space. If he wasn't playing with his friend, what had all this been about, then?

"Explain, Ari." I rubbed at my temple. "When I left this morning, you were scared and didn't even want me to go to work, and here you are having fun with a friend."

"I'm sorry, but we lost track of the time." He climbed on the bed and sat with his legs crossed. "I didn't want to be alone, so I called Howard, and he came over to keep me company."

"How do you know him?"

"We ran into each other twice, and when Judd burned our house down, he invited me to stay with him."

It was all my fault, then. I should have taken care of him when we lost our home, but I only sought shelter for myself and left him to fend for himself. No wonder he found someone else. Instead of dealing with our loss together, I'd pushed him away, right into the arms of another man.

"Did you…" I couldn't finish the question. I shook my head. "I don't want to know."

"Did I what? Fuck him?" He pursed his lips. "Of course I didn't. I only sleep with you. You always think the worst of me."

"I don't think the worst of you." I sat beside him and took one of his hands in mine. "But we're still trying to figure each other out. If you found someone more suitable to be your Daddy, I—"

He squeezed my hand. "No one's more suitable to be my Daddy than you. It's always going to be you, Shaw. Always."

He straddled my lap and nestled his head under my chin. He clutched the front of my shirt as if daring me to push him away.

"I'm glad." I rubbed his back. "Because now that I've accepted you are mine, Ari, it would be too hard to let you go."

"Good, because you're stuck with me. I'm not going anywhere."

"But you will tell me if I get too boring and you need more from me?"

"Silly, Daddy. When will you get that I love you the way you are? I don't want you to change."

He always knew the right words to say. I kissed the top of his head. "Will you tell me what you're doing dressed up like this, since you're not in little mode?"

"I wanted to get dressed for you," he said. "So that as soon as you got home, we could play. Howard didn't know what a little is, and I wanted to show him before he left. That's all. I promise."

I relaxed my arms around him. "And you trust this Howard guy?"

He nodded. "Yeah, he's a good friend and he helped to keep my mind off my father. I was going crazy sitting in the house all day, feeling like he was everywhere. Howard was a good distraction."

"But just temporary."

"Yeah." A shiver ran through him. "He's still out there, waiting for me."

Oh no, I won't let him slip back into the state I left him in this morning. I got up with him in my arms. Ari wrapped his legs around my waist and his arms around my neck. He clung to me like a koala.

"We're not going to let him ruin our lives," I said. "I promised you some little space tonight, and that's exactly what we're going to do."

I carried him down the stairs to the living room. He'd already taken out his toys. He squealed when he saw them, and laughing, I placed him on the floor.

"Play with me, Daddy!" He grabbed my hand and tugged me down beside him. When I sat, he chose a brightly colored xylophone and banged on it. What he made was nowhere near music. The high-pierced sound grated on my nerves, but he seemed to have forgotten his Daddy. He really had sunk into little mode.

"Your turn!" He handed me the stick.

"Thank you, baby."

Using the little musical talent I had, I played "Twinkle Twinkle Little Star." When I was done, his eyes were wide as saucers, and he clapped loudly.

"Teach me, Daddy!"

I sat him down between my legs and taught him how to play the song. As an adult, he would have picked it up easily, but as he was in little space, it took him a while and lots of concentration to get it right. He laughed when he did, and I hugged him, pulling him into my lap and kissing the side of his face.

"Good boy. That's Daddy's smart little boy."

He flushed and preened under the compliment, then dragged over a big, soft book and begged me to read to him.

"Cookie first!" he demanded.

"I'll get it for you, baby."

He shook his head. "Nuh-uh. I wanna do it."

"But you can't reach the counter, baby."

He nodded rapidly, his eyes full of mischief. "Yes, I can, Daddy."

"No, you can't."

"I use chair!" And he was off on his hands and knees, scrabbling across the floor to the kitchen. I smiled at his wiggling diaper butt in his onesie.

"Daaaaddy!"

"Yes, baby boy?" I called.

"Can't reach."

"I told you. I'm coming."

I grunted as I got to my knees, stretching my back before I took a step. A scream rented the air, causing the hairs on the back of my neck and arms to stand on end.

"Ari!"

I bulldozed my way into the kitchen, where Ari was clutching the table, staring out the window. He turned a pale face to me, tears spilling down his cheeks.

"He's come for me!" he screamed.

As though coming out of a trance, he shuddered, then ran past me. I caught him and held him to me.

"Shh, baby, tell me what happened."

"The window!" he shouted. "He was at the window. His face…"

Shit. No one was at the window, so he was gone. I took a step toward the window, but Ari clung to my shirt, making it difficult for me to move.

"I need to go check it out, Ari."

"I'm scared." He shivered against me. This was none of his games. His father scared him witless. What the hell had the man done to him for him to be this terrified? Ari was my fearless boy. Seeing him like this hurt, and all my protective instincts came out.

"I'm here. I'm here, baby. Just let me check if he's still around."

"No!" he cried. "Please don't go out there. He's evil, and I can't lose you."

"You're not going to lose me."

"Please, Daddy, promise me you won't go out there."

"I promise I won't. But let me double-check that all our locks are engaged."

Ari didn't let me go. He fisted my shirt while I checked that all the windows and doors were closed. He didn't say anything at all.

"There. All done." I led him back to the living room. "And if he disturbs us again tonight, I'll call the police. You're going to be fine, Ari."

"Okay, Daddy."

No protest that I wanted to call the cops. Ari was always dead set against cops being involved in our affairs. He always insisted we could handle it ourselves.

"I want you to sit on the couch," I told him. "I'm going to get you a glass of warm milk and a cookie. How does that sound?"

He shook his head. "No food. Please hug me."

"Hey, come here." I sat on the couch and pulled Ari onto my lap. I couldn't have him being this terrified of his father all the time. Maybe I could speak with him alone and find out what he wanted. Was it money? I would gladly give it to him as long as he left a traumatized Ari alone. I'd never seen him this shaky before.

Ari sobbed softly against my shirt, and my heart broke for him. I couldn't imagine what living with that monster would have been like for him to get this way. And this was all Anne's fault. How could she have sent her son to live with such a vile person? She had to have known what kind of man he was. How could she?

It took a while for the heart-wrenching sobs to subside, but he kept sniffling. I needed to get him a tissue to wipe his nose, but I didn't even dare suggest it with the state he was in. His hand snuck up under my shirt, and he sighed as he played with my nipple, rubbing the peak between his thumb and forefinger. I knew it didn't mean anything sexual to him. He took comfort in it, but I was only a man, and my cock strained against the front of my pants.

"I'm sorry," I murmured, stroking the back of his neck. "It doesn't mean anything."

Ari released my nipple, and I breathed out in relief. Until he reached for the hem of my shirt and tugged up.

"Ari," I protested, my heart beating hard in my chest. I didn't want to have sex with him when he was distraught.

"Please, Daddy." He sniffled again. How could I resist him?

I let him take off my shirt, but instead of unzipping my pants, Ari relaxed in the crook of my arms and latched onto my left nipple. He sucked hard, and my cock jolted. Fuck. He was killing me.

It took everything in me, but I swallowed the curse and allowed him to take liberties that seemed to comfort him. My cock throbbed painfully between my legs, but I ignored it, breathing heavily through my nostrils as he suckled furiously. Seconds ticked by and the frantic tugging motion of his lips dwindled down. His chest rose and fell evenly, and his eyes were closed.

He'd fallen asleep.

Time to put him to bed. Then I could relieve myself in the bathroom. I eased his head back to free myself. Before I could get up, Ari's eyes flew open, wide with panic, and a wounded wail left him that burrowed its way deep inside my heart.

"Shh, it's okay." I brought his head back to my nipple, and he captured it with a satisfied moan.

With a groan, I leaned my head back on the couch and prepared to take the torture just to comfort him.

THIRTY-THREE

ARI

IF I HAD TO spend another day alone in the house while Shaw went to work, I would go out of my mind. The designer label expected the first set of designs next week, and I had nothing. Even though I had the days all to myself, I was too on edge to complete any work. Since his face had popped up in the kitchen window, I hadn't seen my father again, but my skin crawled whenever I heard a sound or saw a shadow. He was still out there, biding his time.

How much longer could I be locked up in the house? Afraid to go out and run into him?

"Ari," Shaw called my name softly as he entered the bedroom.

He walked over to the closet and pulled out his suit for work.

"Yes, Daddy?" I couldn't expect him to stay at home with me when he had a school to run. He already allowed me to be clingy when he was home.

"How about you tag along with me to work today?" He carefully laid the suit on the bed. "Would you like that?"

So much.

"I don't want to get you into trouble." Although he'd come up with the intern excuse, we both knew it wouldn't fly if someone really questioned it.

"Honestly? No, but who's going to say anything if you stay in my office and don't go wandering around the school?"

"Then yes, I'd love to go with you today."

He smiled at me, his eyes full of compassion. He'd been so understanding about this whole nightmare with my father. This wasn't a side of me he was used to. Of course I tried to be my usual tough self for him, but my fissures were widening, and soon I would crack apart if we didn't do something about my father soon.

Maybe he would get tired of the games and leave me alone? As if there was a chance in hell that would happen.

"Go take a shower and get dressed. I don't want to be late."

He wouldn't have to tell me again. I scrambled out of bed and ran to the bathroom. Although I knew he would never leave without me, I breezed through my shower. No need to put him to the test, was there?

The bedroom was empty. I skimmed through my clothes. Thank god the items I'd ordered had arrived last week. But the closet I shared with Shaw was still too empty. We were officially living together in our own house, and as much as I wouldn't have wished what happened to our prior home on anyone, it might have worked out for the better.

No unpleasant memories lingered in this house. It was a fresh start.

Usually, I spent a long time deliberating what to wear when I left the house, but not this time. I didn't have the time nor the clothes. I pulled on black jeans and a stylish dark green sweater with a mock neckline. A pair of black-and-white sneakers complemented my quiet outfit. I grabbed my satchel and raced down the stairs.

"Daddy!"

"I'm here."

I slowed down and let out a sigh as I entered the living room, where he was drinking a cup of coffee and skimming the papers.

"I'm all ready to go."

He peered at me over his glasses. "You look great. Handsome."

I smiled at him, the tension I'd been holding in my shoulders easing. Spending the day with him would do wonders for me.

"Thank you. Are you ready to go?"

"You haven't eaten yet."

"Can I take it to go?" I begged him. I just wanted to get out of the house. The walls were suffocating me, but I didn't dare leave them on my own.

"All right."

Shaw folded the newspaper and got to his feet. He thought I looked great? He was amazing in his professional attire, the jacket stretching across his broad shoulders. I had to resist going over to him just to hug him.

Shaw poured my coffee into an insulated travel mug and dropped sticky buns into a Ziploc bag. He added an apple, one of my Capri Sun, a small bag of animal crackers, and some gummy bear treats to the lunch bag. He was so thoughtful in what he packed, without even having to ask me what I wanted. Everything in that bag was a favorite of mine.

"All right, then, let's go."

"Daddy, I—" I swallowed the words and dropped my gaze to the floor, hating to ask. What if he disliked this clingy side of me? "Never mind."

"No, tell me." Shaw shoved his newspaper beneath his arm so he used his free hand to cup my face. "What's on your mind?"

"It's okay."

"Ari, it's too late for me to effectively punish you for keeping things from me. Now tell me."

"I-I wanted a hug."

"That's it? A hug?"

I never second-guessed myself like this. My father showed up, and now I couldn't trust my emotions or needs.

"I know it was stupid."

"You wanting a hug isn't stupid, Ari. I'm just concerned you thought you couldn't ask me."

He wrapped an arm around my waist and pulled me into his big frame. His arms were my comfort.

"I don't know what I'm doing," I confessed. "I feel so out of place. Everything's a mess since he showed up."

"I know, babe, but he'll get tired and leave us alone soon enough."

I had high doubts about that, but I nodded. I knew my father better than Shaw did.

"And don't ever hide it from me if you need a hug. Understand?"

I nodded.

"Words."

"I promise, Daddy."

He kissed my forehead. "Good boy. Now we really need to go."

We took Shaw's car, and the simple drive to the school, which was closer now to our new home, left me feeling better. Almost like my old self, but not quite.

"Today should be a light day unless we have an incident." He led me toward the entrance of the administrative block. "You'll remain inside my office at all times unless I require privacy to deal with any issue."

"Okay."

I didn't care. As long as I was away from the house.

Spending the day with Shaw wasn't like last time I'd visited him. That had been for fun, but now he was focused on his work. I didn't mind, though, as it gave me the chance to watch him doing his job. He was commanding and firm but also nice. Seeing him in action made me feel like the luckiest boy alive to have a Daddy who was so capable at life.

Seeing Shaw being so productive inspired me, and I opened my laptop to work on the designs that were due. Soon I was so immersed in what I was doing, I lost track of time. Hands on my shoulders startled me, but I recognized them immediately. I glanced up at his smiling face.

"How's it going?"

"Great." I felt better than I had since I got back to town. "I've made progress."

"Can I see?"

I minimized the screen. "Nope. When I'm finished. The mockup is bad, but I know how to refine it for the first design, so it's a great start."

"Okay, that's good." Shaw checked his watch and frowned. "Listen, I have a private meeting in about half an hour. Do you think you could make yourself busy for a few?"

"Sure." I put my laptop to sleep and slid it off my lap onto the couch. "What time is it?"

"A few minutes after one."

I blinked at him. "Are you serious?"

He stroked my cheek and chuckled. "Yes, I'm serious. You've been immersed in your work, which is good."

"I didn't realize how much I needed to get out of the house." I got up and stretched, smiling at the way he watched me, his eyes brimming with heat. I dropped my gaze to the telltale bulge at the front of his trousers and bit my bottom lip. "Anything I can help you with?"

"Not here." He shot me a warning look. "We don't have enough time, but sure, at home, I'll take you up on that offer. You've been too distracted for sex lately."

My cheeks burned. "I'm sorry. I— you do know if you ever want me and I'm not in the mood, you can tell me, right? I'll get in the mood."

"I'm not going to expire if we don't have sex all the times I want to."

"Yeah, but—"

He cupped the back of my neck and pulled me into him. "But nothing, Ari. I value you too much to push sex on you when you're not feeling it. And I need you to value yourself enough to not do anything you don't want to do just to please someone. I want you to know that you count. Your feelings count and shouldn't be pushed aside to please anyone else…even me. Is that clear?"

I nodded. God, how I loved this man. I'd killed for him before and I would do it again because he was worth going to jail for. He was worth protecting.

"How about I go and pick up lunch?" I needed to reclaim some of the power my father had taken from me when he woke from the dead.

"Are you sure?" he asked. "I can order in for us."

"I am. Plus, it will give you time to finish your meeting."

"All right, but don't be too long."

Although I had money, he insisted on me using his card. I stalked off but then turned back, wrapped my arms around his neck, and kissed him hard. When he plunged his tongue into my mouth, I pulled away, chuckling softly.

"Tonight, that's what you said."

He groaned and swatted my ass. "Don't be a tease, and be careful."

I nodded and took his car keys. It was so good to be out again on my own that the drive passed quickly. Way too quickly. I was in Shaw's favorite restaurant when it hit me that I hadn't asked him what he wanted. I pulled up his number but didn't press Call. If he was in a meeting, I didn't want to interrupt him. I sent him a message instead.

"Hello, welcome to Gizmo's," the pretty young hostess greeted me with a big smile, her face flushed. "Are you dining in?"

"I'm actually not. Thanks, though."

The restaurant was a bit busy, so I sat at the bar while they prepared my food. I ordered a club soda, really wanting something stronger, but that would have to wait until I was home with Shaw. It had been a few days since we had sex. Tonight, I'd rectify that and make it extra special for him.

"Is this seat taken?"

That voice. Raspier than I was used to, but the undertones hadn't changed.

The glass slipped out of my hand and landed with a *thud* on the counter, liquid sloshing out. I froze, my chest tightening. The figure moved closer, and everything inside me screamed for me to get away.

"It's about time, don't you think?"

I let my eyes flicker over his features, cataloging the changes. His face was crude with scar tissue that had formed from each stab wound I inflicted on him. One thing hadn't changed. The cold, dead eyes that stared back at me.

"What do you want?" I croaked, trembling.

"Now that's a loaded question."

The bartender came over and wiped up the spilled soda. He glanced from me to my father. Then his gaze landed back on me. "Are you all right, man?"

"Why wouldn't he be all right?" Dad asked with a hoarse laugh. He pointed at his face. "He's not the one looking like Frankenstein, is he?"

"Ugh, if you need anything, just holler." The bartender moved on to another client, but he kept looking back at us.

"What is it about you that makes men want to protect you?" Dad asked. "Even when they know about the monster that you are."

"You made me this way," I said.

"I only showed you your true potential."

"You're my father. You were supposed to protect me, not-not…"

"You seduced me."

"Only to get you to stop beating me." My nostrils flared as the memories rushed in. "It was the only way to get you to stop. But how could you? You're my father. How could you do that to your own son?"

He stretched out his hand, but I snatched my hand away before he could touch my skin. My stomach revolted at the thought of him ever touching me again.

"Maybe because I know you're not my son." This time he grasped my hand. Hard. I tried to pull away, but he was stronger. I could never win with him. "Does that make it all better now?"

"You're lying. You're just saying that to feel better about what you did to me."

"But what if I'm telling the truth? You do want to know the truth, don't you?"

Thirty-Four

Shaw

AFTER MY MEETING WITH the two teachers from the Natural Sciences department, I was looking forward to having a quiet lunch with Ari. Before he arrived, though, I was informed about an incident in the music room that required my attention. With a sigh, I left a note on my desk in case he returned before me, then went to investigate.

Some kid had superglued the mouthpieces of the horns, and I had to deal with two hysterical teens who got stuck to the instruments. EMTs had to be called in, since we didn't want to risk peeling their lips off. While they were being tended to, I had to do the lecturing bit, then have the teacher keep the class together until someone admitted what they did. It was a shit show to handle the issue, and it was almost an hour later before I could return to my office.

"That bad?" Lauren, the new temp, asked when I walked in.

"I swear these kids are going to put me in an early grave."

"But you're so good with them."

I snorted. "If I'm able to reach one, I consider that a success. Will you hold my calls? I'll be having lunch now."

"Sure thing."

"Thank you."

As I entered my office, the scent of delicious food filled my nostrils and made my stomach growl. I hadn't eaten anything since breakfast. Where was Ari? He must have been here, as evidenced by the paper bag on the desk from which the delicious aroma emanated.

"Ari?"

The bathroom was empty. No sign of him at all. Had he gone back out? Why hadn't he called or texted me ?

Frowning, I walked to my desk and stilled. Something wasn't quite right. I cocked my ear and listened, and there it was. A soft humming sound. But where the hell was it coming from? I checked the bathroom again, but the sound faded. As soon as I returned to the desk, it increased.

Typical Ari. He couldn't wait until later. I walked over to the door and locked it. Without acknowledging him, I took my seat and opened the paper bag. Goddamn. How was I supposed to have sex when I was this hungry?

No fingers undid my zipper, though I had expected it. A shiver ran down my spine. Had I gotten it wrong? I pushed back my chair, grunting as I squatted and peered under the desk. Ari was lying in the corner, huddled in a small, tight ball.

"Ari." I pushed the chair farther out of the way, but there was no way I would fit with him, and he didn't move. "Ari, please, baby. Come to me."

I should never have let him go out on his own. He reacted this same way when his father had trespassed and scared him in the kitchen. He'd been fine when he left, which meant only one thing.

No matter how I cajoled, Ari wouldn't leave the comfort of his space. I could wait him out until he snapped out of the mood he was in, but it hurt something awful seeing him like this. Where was the smile he'd had for me before he left? The teasing and sexual desire? It was all gone and what was left in its wake was this shell I didn't know how to relate to.

In the end, I had no choice but to push away the desk. It was heavy and made a god-awful sound scraping over the floor, but the overwhelming need to get to Ari was more important. When I pushed the desk back far enough for me to get to him, I caught him by the armpits and pulled him out. He knocked me over on my ass and climbed into my lap, wrapping his arms around my neck in a viselike grip.

"I saw him," he said with stiff lips. "He followed me."

Just as I'd feared.

"I know he scared you, baby, but remember what I said to you? You're not alone in this. We're going to work through it. Take all the time you need to calm down, and then we're going to talk about this."

I helped him with his breathing until he gradually relaxed against me. I rubbed his arms, warming him up as he felt uncommonly cold to touch.

"He's not my father," Ari murmured.

"You didn't run into your father?"

He took a deep breath. "I ran into him, but he said he wasn't my father."

"I wouldn't consider him one either, given the way he treated you."

"No, Shaw." He clutched the front of my jacket. "He's not my biological father. He told me that when he accosted me at the restaurant."

I frowned at Ari. "That doesn't make any sense. You would have known if he was your father."

He shook his head. "I was too young. I didn't know him. He didn't play any part in my life until Mom sent me to live with him."

My back stiffened. "Maybe he's lying. I know you had your differences with Anne, but she wouldn't have sent her son to live with a stranger."

"He's not a stranger to her. He was a friend of my father's. My real father's dead. And he agreed to let me stay with him and to keep up the facade for her to send him money monthly."

"But still—"

"She didn't want me around you, Shaw. She would have done whatever it took to get me away from you. I never thought she would go so far."

Neither did I. What he was accusing Anne of was unthinkable. She might have been familiar with this man, but how could she have sent an impressionable Ari to live with someone he wasn't related to and trick him about it? I'd tried not to think too much of her as a bad mom, as Ari had been a difficult teen, but this was horrifying.

"Tell me exactly what happened."

"The restaurant was full, so I had to wait a long time for our lunch." He inhaled deeply. "I was waiting at the bar when he showed up. I asked him why he'd done those things to me. How could he have when I was his son? And that's when he told me the truth. That we weren't related at all. The bartender saw how upset I was, so he got him to leave and then walked me to my car after."

"Did he follow you?" I asked him.

He shrugged. "I don't know. He might have, but I couldn't tell. I was so shaken up by what he said I wasn't even sure if I would have gotten here in one piece."

He trembled, and I stroked his arms again. "I shouldn't have sent you out on your own."

"I think I had to," he whispered. "I know you probably don't understand why I'm so terrified of him, but whenever I run into him, it all comes back. The feeling of helplessness as he did things to me I couldn't stop."

Bile rose in my throat. I hadn't wanted to think about what Ari had gone through. It was too difficult to think about, but ignoring it wouldn't help us to handle the situation. I needed to know how far this thing with his "dad" went and find out how the hell we were going to deal with this man.

"Ari, I want to know what he did to you."

His shaking was uncontrollable now. "It's horrible."

"I know, but I think you need to talk about it too. As long as you keep it bottled up inside, the more power he will continue to wield over you."

"He-he was a terrible drunk," he whispered. "He was awful when he was sober, but even worse when he was drunk. He always had friends around the house. Friends who were just like him. I stayed in my room, but then he'd start shit for no reason. I didn't wash the dishes. I didn't vacuum the floors. And then he would punch me. Everywhere. While his friends laughed. They hated how feminine I was. More like they hated how they responded to me, since I was a boy."

I closed my eyes and concentrated on my breathing. "What happened?"

"I lied to you about everything," he said with a sniffle. "I told you I had a Daddy before, but it's not what I made it sound like. He saw how some of his friends looked at me and got this idea to sell me to the one who paid him the most money. It wasn't consensual, but he didn't care." His laugh was bittersweet. "But then he regretted it because he wanted me for himself. The beatings got worse, and then he would have me do other things like steal for him. The first person I killed was because he made me do it. Said he would leave me alone, and I just wanted the hurting to stop. He lied. He didn't leave me alone."

He sighed. "But then I noticed how he watched me, and when he came once when he was hitting me, I knew what I had to do to make the beatings stop. So I became his little bitch. It didn't matter if I was in the mood or not. He would just take whatever he wanted. The beatings stopped, but what he was doing to me filled me with so much hate. He had me kill someone else and then another. And I became numb. Every night after he fell asleep, I would plan out in my head how I was going to kill him one day, and I did. At least I thought I did. I didn't stick around to find out. I ran."

"Oh, my god, Ari."

So much made sense now. The kind of fear he had for his father, which he didn't display for anyone else. The way he killed without even a second thought. Or how he refused to be bullied by someone like Judd but would rather go to the extremes to eliminate them.

And I knew what we had to do. There was only one way to get rid of Ken. The man wouldn't stop harassing Ari until he was completely taken out of the picture. But with Ari incapable of confronting the man, that left only me to handle the situation, and I…couldn't.

I wasn't the killer Ari was. I couldn't take a life, even when it belonged to a man who didn't deserve to live. But maybe…maybe I didn't have to do it myself. Maybe I could get someone else to do it for us.

One thing was for sure. I had to protect Ari from that man at all cost.

Thirty-Five

Ari

SHAW AND I HAD planned to have a movie night together. Every night for the past three days, we'd done something else as a distraction. Fresh out of the shower, I walked into the bedroom, expecting him to be comfy in his usual sweats and T-shirt, but he was dressed in a nice pair of black jeans and a button-down shirt. His belt matched his shoes, and his hair was slicked back. I'd shown him how to use my gel.

"Where are you going?" The ease I'd been feeling ever since he arrived home fled. I couldn't come to the school with him every day. It was unprofessional, so I spent my days at home, safeguarded by the new security system Shaw installed. I felt a little bit safer, not because I believed my dad wouldn't find a way in if he wanted to, but because if he did, he would trip the alarm, and someone would be here in under five minutes to check out the house.

I was convinced I could survive five minutes alone with him. Just as long as they didn't take any longer.

"I'm going out for half an hour," he said. "I promise not to be too long."

"But why? We have plans." This wasn't what we'd talked about, and I didn't like routine changes. It was difficult to figure out what the changes meant. I still feared Shaw would get tired of the babysitting and handholding and go to the police, which I couldn't let happen. If they took in my dad, I would go down with him.

"I know we said we would watch movies tonight, but I'm thinking of something better."

"Is that why you are leaving me?"

"I am not leaving you, Ari."

"That's what it seems like."

He came over to me, took me by the shoulder, and pushed me gently to sit on the bed. He took the towel from my hands and patted my still-wet face.

"I am going out to take care of some business. But then I want us to go out for dinner. I already made a reservation for us at eight, so I promise this won't take long."

I grabbed one end of the towel to still his hands for a moment. "What kind of business? And do you think it's a good idea for us to go out now? What if he follows us?"

"Then let him. He won't do anything to you while I'm with you. Plus, he won't be around for much longer anyway."

"How do you know that?"

Shaw kept silent, and I tilted my head back and stared up at him. My heart skipped a beat at that knowing look in his eyes. What was he going to do? My skin tingled in excitement at the idea that forged its way into my mind. That couldn't be what Shaw was talking about, could it? *Shaw?* I couldn't see him getting his hands dirty.

"Are you going to—"

He placed a hand over my mouth to muffle the rest of my words. "We don't talk about it. We know nothing. Is that clear?"

I widened my eyes, my heart pounding in my chest. He was seriously going to put an end to this. My cock twitched, adrenaline sending exciting thrills through me.

"Is that clear, Ari?"

I nodded, and he removed his hand.

"But how are you going to—"

His hand came back over my mouth. "I said we won't talk about it. Just know that I'm getting it done. Now be a good boy and do exactly what your Daddy says."

I nodded again, so hard now, knowing he was talking about killing a man for me. I would never have thought he had it in him.

"Good boy." He slipped his hand from my mouth and cupped my chin. "As I said, I'll be gone for a few minutes. When I get back, I want you to be dressed and ready to go out for dinner. Wear something fancy."

"We're celebrating?"

"Yes, to us." He brushed his lips lightly over mine. "I haven't taken you out on a real date since you came back, Ari. It's long overdue."

And the perfect alibi for us too if he was going to knock off Ken like I thought he had been hinting at.

"Okay, Daddy."

"Good boy." He tilted my chin higher and trailed his lips over my jaw. "You're going to forget about him and think only about us. We're going to have fun on our date, and no one's going to ruin it for us."

"I like that very much." I was sick of being worried all the time about when Ken would make his move. I knew he was toying with me, biding his time, but now Shaw would catch him unaware. The bastard. I was only sorry I couldn't get a front-row seat to watch and make sure this time that he would stay dead.

"I'll see you soon."

Shaw walked out of the room, leaving me alone in the bedroom. The familiar fear returned, but then I remembered. Shaw was going to take care of it. I would be free of that manipulative asshole and he would never have the chance to hurt me again.

I laughed and dropped onto my back on the bed, hugging myself. I'd never felt as loved as I did at that moment. I had a man who was willing to kill for me, just like I would kill for him. What greater love existed than that? For him to risk everything in his life to make me happy again? I had been so miserable this past week and a half since Ken showed up.

Maybe now we could move on from everything that had happened. We could put everything behind us and live our lives together, burying all the skeletons in the closet and letting them stay there. For Shaw to do this for me, I would do everything for him in return.

I lay there, thinking of our future together, then jolted up. Damn, I needed to hurry. Shaw had told me to be dressed when he returned home. I vaulted off the bed, ran over to the closet, and riffled through my clothes. The elegant rose-pink jumpsuit would be perfect. I plucked the outfit from the rack. Thank god I made a habit to iron all my clothes before I put them away. The material skimming over my body made me already feel ten times better.

How had Shaw known I needed this?

I sat in front of the magnifying mirror. After pinning my hair back, I worked on my makeup—soft and natural with a bronzer, smoky eyes, and a light brown, natural-looking lipstick that made my lips plumper. A touch of false lashes and mascara to add volume to my eyes and my face was perfect. I hadn't gone all out like this for Shaw before, and I wanted to wow him. Every man we passed tonight should envy him whether they were gay, bi, or straight.

Next, I worked on my hair, blowing it out, then curling the short locks to fall perfectly on one side with a few tendrils trailing over my forehead. My hair could do with some highlights, but I didn't have the time. It didn't matter; it still looked amazing. I spritzed all the important places with my most expensive cologne and, closing my eyes, inhaled deeply.

I'd eat me up if I could.

In the bathroom, I took two pills to calm my nerves tonight. The last thing I wanted was my paranoia about Ken to ruin the night Shaw planned for us. I replaced the bottle of Xanax in the medicine cabinet, patted my hair, and walked out of the bathroom. I nearly jumped out of my skin when I saw the figure standing by the bed.

I placed a hand over my heart. "Oh, my god, you almost gave me a heart attack."

"Sorry, I thought you heard me come in." Shaw ran his eyes over me, his face flushed. "Ari, you look…" He shook his head. "Amazing, and that's not quite the word I want to use, but nothing else comes to mind right now. Baby, turn around."

I turned for him. The cut in the back of the jumpsuit was deep and didn't cover up all my tattoos. He made a strangled sound in his throat.

"I don't know if I want you out in public like this," he said. "How am I going to stop every man out there from making a pass at you?"

"But you don't have to. I'm already yours."

In good deeds and bad.

"Your shoes." He gestured at the pair of nude heels I had put at the foot of the bed. "Sit and let me get them on."

"I can do it."

"I want to do it."

Heat traveled from my neck to my cheeks. I shouldn't be shy about letting Shaw do this. He'd helped me put on my shoes before, even when I was a teenager, but this time it was different. He was a Daddy taking care of his boy. He went down on one knee before me and gently lifted my foot.

"Even your feet are beautiful. How did I end up being this lucky?"

My chest swelled. "Are you sure you don't mean unlucky? So many bad things have happened since I returned." I sucked in a deep breath. "Your life would have been so much easier if I hadn't come back."

"Easier, maybe." He secured the strap around my ankle and reached for my next foot. "But definitely not as fun. I wouldn't be anywhere near this happy either." He glanced up at me. "Ari, you're every reason a man needs to both be good and bad at the same time. Because I'll do whatever it takes to take care of you and ensure your well-being."

I blinked the tears away. "Oh, please stop. You're going to make me ruin my mascara, and I'm wearing fake eyelashes."

He laughed, struggling to his feet. "They look nice, but so you know, Ari, I love you just as much plain-faced."

I gasped. "Plain-faced? When am I ever plain?"

"You're right." He pulled me to my feet and into his arms. "My love, there's nothing plain about you. The things you make me do for you, Ari. It's too late to turn back now, and even if it wasn't, I wouldn't do a single thing differently."

THIRTY-SIX

SHAW

ARI SNUCK HIS HAND down to the waistband of my pants, where he found my belt buckle and swiftly loosened it. I swatted at his hand halfheartedly, but inside, I was overjoyed and relieved the light was back in his eyes. The fear, uncertainty, and skittishness of the past ten days had been replaced by the charm and cockiness of the fun-loving boy I knew.

And despite my hesitancy last night, I knew I'd done the right thing in hiring a contract killer to take out that impostor who'd been posing as his dad. Whatever guilt I felt that I was taking someone's life disappeared the moment Ari smiled again.

"Daddy," he whined at my slap.

"You asked to help me to get dressed, not to undress me," I said, injecting enough sternness in my voice. "If I don't leave now, I'm going to be late."

"But it'll be worth it, Daddy." He sat on his knees before me, looking up at me with big, wide eyes. I should have known he was up to something when he insisted on retying my shoelaces, even though they were already tied.

"Are you sure of that?" I asked.

"Yes, so worth it. Last night after dinner, I really wanted to. Wished I hadn't eaten so much, but I already got myself all prepped for you. See?"

Ari scrambled to his feet and climbed up to the edge of the bed on his knees. He unfastened the hooks at the seat of his adult-sized onesie that I'd put him in after our date last night. He didn't stop there. He peeled back the fresh diaper I'd placed on him this morning. The unused material hung from the crotch of his pants, leaving his round bottom bare. Between his cheeks rested a dazzling butt plug.

I sucked in a deep breath. I had to get to the school administrator's conference in an hour, but the sight of my boy's bare bottom with the tattoos fanning over his delicate skin had me hard instantly. We hadn't had sex since the night he returned from LA, and I'd been patient with him the whole time, but now it was hard to tear my eyes away from what he was offering me.

And with that diaper hanging between his legs, it was downright sinful. But so arousing.

"You played with yourself without my permission?" I asked. "You've been a naughty boy."

"Just to make this easier for you, Daddy." He glanced at me over his shoulder. "I didn't want to make you *too* late for your conference."

"Then you're a good boy." I grabbed the end of the butt plug and pulled it out halfway, then pushed it back inside him. It glided easily into his well-lubed hole.

"The best boy, Daddy," he moaned, arching his back. I wrapped an arm around his torso, the material of his fuzzy onesie warm and soft against my skin. "Kiss me."

He gasped, tilted back his head, and offered me his gorgeous, sassy mouth. A mouth for love and lies. I lost the last of my reserve to stay away from him and do the responsible thing by getting to my meeting on time.

"Oh, Daddy."

"Tell me what you want?" I said into his mouth.

"For you to fuck me. I've been so good."

"Yes, you have."

He hadn't been in any trouble lately. I kissed down his neck while I pushed the flaps of my pants aside and pulled my dick out. I was probably getting my clothes crushed, but I had a desperate need to fill Ari. It had been so fucking long since that tight heat enveloped me.

I groaned when my dick was finally free from the confines of my underwear.

"Hold your cheeks apart for me."

"Yes, Daddy."

He didn't hesitate to grab a handful of his generous ass and pull the cheeks apart to bare himself to my eyes. He hissed as I gently pulled the plug out. I couldn't look away from the way his hole opened up, releasing the plug, then slowly contracted again.

"Fuck, baby."

I grasped the base of my cock, shoved the thick head against that hole before it contracted any farther, and thrust. He cried out, and I groaned. Oh god, I'd missed the feel of my cock sliding inside his body. I snapped my hips forward, burying my dick as deep inside him as I could.

"Oh, god, yes, Daddy," he cried out. Thank god he was no longer cowed by his fear of someone else. I was his at this moment, and that was the way I wanted it to be always.

As I thrust over and over into Ari's sweet heat, I acknowledged I hadn't only put that contract out for Ari's sake. I wanted to get rid of anything that took him away from me, and as long as Ken hung around, I would never have his full attention.

Instead of being repulsed by what I'd done, I relished it. Adrenaline pumped wildly, and my nostrils flared as I pushed his hands aside. I gripped his skinny hips and held nothing back as I pounded that tight offering. Ari's moans filled the bedroom, and he placed a hand back on my hip and pulled me more into him. His ass bounced each time it connected with my groin, the movement causing an intricate play of the tattoos that covered his cheeks and lower back.

"Yes, yes, Daddy!" He spat into his hand, brought it between his legs, and stroked his dick. "I deserve that big dick, Daddy. I do."

The diaper rustled between his thighs, which only egged me on. I wanted to yank off my shirt off and throw it to the side, kick my shoes off and mount him on the bed to show him how much Daddy could take care of his boy in every way that mattered.

I was willing to kill for him.

Oh fuck, what has he turned me into?

A man who desperately needed him. All of him. *Need him so much.* This sweet boy, with his alabaster skin and tempting body, had so much vulnerability hidden behind the tough exterior.

Fuck, I didn't want it to end yet. Just a bit more. Everything about him was so perfect. From his loud moans to the slapping sound of his ass each time I thrust into him.

"Say 'thank you, Daddy,' and I'll make you come."

"Oh, please, yes, thank you so much, Daddy! Thank you, Daddy!"

He moaned his gratitude over and over. I grabbed the fleshy part of his ass and angled my hips, nailing his prostate. A shiver ran through Ari, and goose bumps spread across his skin. The slender muscles in his back contracted. I gritted my teeth and held on, but I wouldn't be able to for long.

Ari's hoarse cry was a welcome relief as his body spasmed. Just in time. I clamped my eyes shut, my toes curling in my shoes as I came hard, pumping my cum inside him. Ari collapsed onto the bed, breathing hard, his body shivering. We couldn't have been fucking for long. Certainly not more than ten minutes, and that was stretching it, but that was all we needed.

I leaned forward and kissed the side of his neck, nuzzling him. He tasted salty. Ari giggled.

"That tickles."

"Are you satisfied now, greedy boy?" I ran a hand over his ass cheeks. "Can Daddy go to work?"

He rolled over onto his back and stared up at me. "I wish you would stay."

I scanned his face. "You aren't still afraid, are you?" I should get to the bathroom and clean up, but I couldn't until we got to the bottom of this.

"You said you took care of it," he whispered. "I trust you. I just miss you being home all the time."

"Summer's coming soon. I'll be all yours then." I pressed my lips on his. Ari wrapped his arms around my neck, and I kissed him, slowly fucking his mouth, unlike how I'd just taken him.

I pulled back from Ari's mouth. "I want you to stay in today, okay?"

He pushed himself up onto his elbows as I walked to the bathroom. "Why?" he called after me.

"I haven't received the call yet that it's done." I wet a rag and wiped the cum away, then returned to Ari with the washcloth. He was still on his back, propped up on both arms.

"But it's going to get done, right?" he asked as I cleaned him up.

"Yes." The tapes of his diaper didn't stick anymore, and I pulled the diaper off him. "You want a fresh one?"

He shook his head. "I can't spend today in little space. I need to get some work done."

"All right, then." I fastened back the flap at the seat of his onesie. "The man I hired said he would get it done within twenty-four hours. He'll call me with proof when he's finished the job, and I'll meet him to hand over the rest of the money."

"Did-did it cost a lot?"

I kissed his nose. "Your safety is worth every penny. Just seeing you smile again is well worth it, Ari."

He smiled at me. "Thank you for taking care of me."

I stroked his cheek. "You take care of me all the time. It's now my time to take care of you."

"Like a Daddy's supposed to do?"

"Like the man who loves you."

I dumped the washcloth into the hamper and fixed my clothes. Ari curled up on his side with the pillow clutched to his chest. His eyes followed me around the room as I brushed my hair, then walked over to the night table and snapped my watch on and slipped my phone into my pocket.

"You okay?" I asked.

"Mmm-hmm."

"You seem like you have something on your mind."

He bit his bottom lip.

"Ari, you're not still worried after telling you I took care of this?"

He shook his head. "No, not that. I was just wondering…"

"Well, out with it."

"Can I invite Howard to come over?"

I wasn't too fond of this Howard guy, and the last thing I wanted was for him to hang out with Ari while he was looking so thoroughly fucked. He made a man want to climb back into bed with him and live inside him. No one else could have that with him. Only me.

"You take a shower and get dressed first," I said, brushing aside my jealousy. If I couldn't trust him not to mess around with another man, then our relationship was doomed to fail. "And when Howard gets here, you don't play with him. No Daddy/little stuff. That's reserved for us only."

I held my breath and waited for him to complain about me being too controlling. Ari grinned. "Okay, Daddy. I won't play with Howard."

"I mean it, Ari."

"I know and I promise. Cross my heart."

"Good boy. Now come over here and give Daddy a hug. I really need to get going now."

He scrambled off the bed and threw his arms around me. He felt so good. And although I hired someone to kill a man because of Ari, that wasn't what I was interested in. This was. Loving him and caring for him.

"I love you, Daddy," he whispered. "You know that, right?"

Love? Obsession? The two were rolled into one for Ari, but it wasn't nearly as scary as it had been at first. Now I knew him, what made him tick, and what made him fall apart.

"I know." I kissed his temple. "Remember to keep the doors locked and the alarm activated. I'll call you if I hear anything."

THIRTY-SEVEN

ARI

"HEY, YOU LISTENING TO me?"

Howard's shoulder bumping into mine brought me out of my head as I glanced around the mall, trying to spot a familiar face. Getting out of the house when Shaw hadn't called me yet to tell me it was done had been a stupid idea. After watching a movie together and chatting, Howard suggested we go out for lunch, and after much back-and-forth, with him accusing Shaw of keeping me a prisoner in our home, I'd given in. Just for lunch.

"Sorry, I must have spaced out."

"What's going on with you?" Howard threw an onion ring into his mouth. "You're crazy distracted today. Is it me? Did I do something? I feel like we're sneaking around or something."

"No, not that. Shaw knows we're spending the day together. He didn't have a problem with it as long as I didn't do any Daddy activity with you."

He frowned. "He gets to make that decision for you?"

"Well, he's my Daddy, but we both make the rules."

"And you're okay with that? Not playing with anyone else?"

"I don't want to play with anyone else anyway. See, it's been a long time since I've wanted Shaw to be my Daddy. Since he was married to my mom."

Howard fell quiet, the chewing stopped, and he stared at me. I held my breath and dug my fingernails into the palms of my hands. Stupid. I shouldn't have said anything to him. People who didn't know my history with Shaw would think I was weird for coveting my mother's husband. This was the part where Howard would realize how messed up I was, then leave me. And I would have lost another friend.

I had never been able to keep them for long. Showing them who I really was always ended up with me being left alone. I should be used to it by now, but if Howard did the same, I would be extremely disappointed.

He burst out laughing so hard the people next to us swiveled their heads our way. Why was he laughing? Was it the shock of what I'd just said?

"Dude." Howard wiped at his eyes. "The first night I saw you, I knew you were nothing but trouble. But your mom? Let me guess. Family get-togethers must be fun with you guys."

"You're not horrified?"

"Somehow I don't think that's the most horrifying thing you've done." He slurped at his drink. "So this Shaw guy must be pretty special to land someone who looks like you. You're like, really hot, which I'm sure you already know. And he's not exactly who I would have pictured you with."

"Shaw's always been great to me." I smiled as memories formed. "I know I was too young for him, although at the time, I didn't want to admit it. But he won me this stuffed animal at a carnival. A stranger and he just walked up to me and said to let him try. To be fair, I think I was starved for any form of affection, so the moment he did that for me, I wanted him permanently in my life."

"I can't imagine you starving for attention. I mean, lots of guys out there who would want to spoil you."

"It's easy being with someone as beautiful as me, but it's difficult accepting all my flaws. Shaw does. He knows every single bad thing — well, most of them anyway — I've done, and he still looks at me like I'm the sweetest boy ever. He makes me want to be good, Howard."

My face heated up, and I ducked my head.

"You know what's crazy?" Howard asked. "I look into your eyes and I see all this experience, but I see so much vulnerability too. I guess that's why I helped you that day I almost hit you with my car. I had this weird feeling like I had to protect you or something."

He rubbed the back of his neck, his face a bright cherry red, and he couldn't meet my eyes.

He couldn't hide his feelings, and normally I would have toyed with him and taken advantage of him, but I'd done enough of that when he let me crash at his place.

"You know we can only be friends." I wiped my hands on the napkin. "But in a world where there was no Shaw, you would have been perfect."

He laughed uneasily. "Wouldn't want to put all this awesomeness between you two. We're friends, and I'm good with that. I think you need a friend more anyway."

"I do. I value this friendship, Howard. Very much."

I smiled at him. We got to our feet, cleared the table, and dumped the containers and cups into the trash can. He wanted to buy a pair of jeans. I hesitated, but he promised me we would go straight home after. We shook on it, which made me grin.

Life was great. I had my forever Daddy. Now I had an awesome friend too. And despite the fact that he was attracted to me, I knew he would never act on it. If he did, we couldn't be friends anymore, so I was glad he was a decent guy. Someone I could hang out with and not worry they would want anything more than being friends.

I ended up buying two pairs of jeans too. They were on sale. What else could I have done? After we cashed out, we jumped into his cab and drove back to our house.

"Don't you lose lots of money when you're with me instead of working?" I asked as we got out of the car.

He shrugged. "I don't need the money." He didn't elaborate.

"Are you secretly rich?" I asked him with a giggle as we stomped up the steps. I unlocked the front door, then punched in the code to deactivate the alarm.

"If it's a secret, I can't tell."

I rolled my eyes and locked the front door. He grabbed my wrist and pulled me along with him.

"Man, I need to use the bathroom, or I'm gonna take a leak on your floor."

"I can always give you a diaper."

He gave me a shove, and I laughed, regaining my balance.

"Not my thing, man. Though you looked cute in it the last time."

"Daddy loves me wearing them, which is great because I honestly sometimes can't be bothered to do the adult thing and go to the bathroom."

"You mean you actually use them? I thought they were just for show."

I led him up the stairs to the spare bathroom Shaw used when I hogged the shower.

"Yes, Daddy likes when I pee in them."

I didn't bother to tell him that Daddy liked me peeing my pants overall. I bit my bottom lip. Would he want to pee on me again? I'd felt so owned when he did that.

"You're strange, my friend."

Usually, alarm bells would go off at those words, but he said them without the usual bite and disgust that normally followed them. And I was so grateful for him. He was a perfect friend. I would cherish the friendship.

"I'll drop my stuff in my bedroom," I said. "Meet you downstairs in five."

Howard slipped into the bathroom, and I continued to my bedroom. I hadn't made the bed. Oh, Daddy couldn't find out. Shaw would be upset when he learned I went out today, especially after he'd told me to stay in. Leaving the bedroom messy would only make him madder. He could be stern, which I loved, but I dreaded his anger. I needed him in a good mood tonight, relaxed when I asked him to pee on me again. If he was uptight, he would tell me no.

Or maybe he would do it if I was naughty. The last time he'd done it was when he'd punished me.

No. I didn't want to be bad to get the thing I wanted. Shaw needed to own his kinky side without a flimsy excuse to justify why he peed on me.

It was simple. He did it because he got off on it.

I removed the price tags and put the jeans in the overflowing laundry basket. Time to do a load. I straightened the bedroom to have everything looking immaculate again. Pleased, I grabbed the basket and made my way down the stairs.

"I'll throw some clothes in the washer and be back in a jiffy," I called to Howard.

"O-okay."

The washroom was next to the door to the garage. I loaded the washer, set the basket on the rack next to it, and went to the kitchen, where I grabbed a juice box for me and a can of pop for him.

Howard sat on the couch with the TV on.

"Sorry, but I had to get a load in. I didn't realize how much I've slacked off over the past week. I got you a pop. The day is so fucking hot. You can tell summer's approaching."

I frowned when he didn't respond. "Something wrong?"

The can slipped out of my fingers and exploded on the carpet with a frothy hiss. A scream clawed its way into my throat, but it was trapped there, unable to come out. Howard's unseeing eyes stared right at me, blood still spewing from the slice in his neck. His shirt and the couch were stained red.

"Howard," I croaked his name, tears filling my eyes. "Oh no, Howard."

He was my best bud. A good man. He didn't deserve this.

I stumbled backward, his image blurry. I couldn't stop looking. This... *It's not real. Howard's not dead. He can't be dead.*

"Hello, Ari. It's time."

I spun around to the man who haunted me. How had he gotten in? I trembled as cold dread seeped into my skin.

"I can see you have questions about how I got in." He spun the pocketknife around on its key. "After how careful you and your Daddy have been. Doing everything to protect you from me. You should tell your friends not to open the door to strangers."

"He had nothing to do with this," I whispered. "You killed him for nothing."

"I wouldn't exactly say for nothing. Look at how devastated you are." He clucked his tongue. "You're always getting attached to things I have to kill."

"Leave me alone."

He flashed out the blade of the knife. "Don't worry. I will. Just as soon as I repay you for every scar on my body."

I had to get out of here, but how? He was too big, too crafty.

Ken cornered me against one wall. I held my hands up to ward him off.

"Do you remember how many times you stabbed me, Ari?"

"Please don't."

The knife cut across my lower arm, and I gasped at the burning sensation as my skin opened and blood dripped onto the floor.

"Don't be such a coward. I thought I made a man out of you. Did I beg you once to stop every time you plunged that knife into me? Not once. I deserved it, but so do you."

"Please stop. I'll do anything you want. Just please don't."

I cried out as the knife connected with my flesh again. He didn't plunge the way I'd done to him. Mostly superficial slashes that sliced open my skin.

"I am going to inflict the same pain on you that you did on me that day." He cut through my shirt, leaving a stinging trail. "When I'm through with you, he won't be able to stomach the sight of you. People will turn their heads away when they look at you the same way they do me. We'll both be scorned."

Screaming, I ducked and scrambled away, but he came at me again. I held my hands in front of my face. The blade sliced my palm but thank god not my face. He shoved me, and I lost my balance, falling hard. I tried to crawl away from him, but my bloody hand slipped on the floor. His boot landed on my back, crushing my chest to the floor.

"I'm disappointed in you, Ari. I thought I taught you to be tougher than this. With all those men you killed, and you're afraid to die?"

"I can't breathe," I gasped. "Please, I can't breathe. I don't want to die."

My palm stung, my body was on fire where he'd cut me with the knife, but I didn't want to die. For so long, I was so reckless and didn't care. But Shaw... he made me believe my life was worth living, and I was too young to die, dammit. I had so much to make up for.

I struggled to drag air into my lungs, but his weight on me was too heavy. My vision blurred. Then everything went black.

I woke up from the sting of the knife against my shoulder and the bulk of his body on top of mine. My jeans and underwear were down to my thighs, and he probed his thick cock between my ass cheeks, even as he cut across my back.

Thirty-Eight

Shaw

SINCE I BECAME PRINCIPAL two years ago, I accepted that conferences and workshops were a necessary part of the job. The events usually lasted all day and gave administrators across the district a chance to catch up on new ideas, new regulations, and highlight issues the superintendent had with the current system. There was always something or another that was being introduced, with only a paltry pilot test done before they were implemented in every school.

I had to pay attention, but I was too distracted with everything happening in my life. I couldn't focus if my life depended on it. I'd never hired a contract killer before, and it was a wonder I knew someone at all who was willing to kill someone for money. After working in the school system for decades, I came to the conclusion that students, despite receiving the same education, ended up in all stations of life. Some turned out good, and others turned out bad.

Alex Killian had been one of the rotten apples.

I'd been one of the only ones who had been able to calm him down when he got into trouble at school. Teachers gossiped a lot about their former students, and he had been one of their hot topics. Rumors had it he ran a small gang and wasn't opposed to disposing of someone for money.

Although I knew who he was, he had no idea about my identity. We'd spoken by phone. He'd instructed where to leave the money, and when he was satisfied, he called me, and we made the arrangements.

He could never know who I was. Not only because once he knew my secret, it wouldn't be long before others were aware of it as well, but also because I wouldn't put it past him to blackmail me after. If Ari hadn't been directly involved, I wouldn't have told him anything about it, but I needed him to know I wasn't just a useless Daddy who couldn't take care of him. He went the extra mile to protect me, and we weren't going to get rid of Ken anytime soon until he got to Ari. Or I got to him first.

The things that man did to Ari were sick and twisted. I blamed my ex-wife. I wanted to call her and tell her I knew what she'd done, of the hell she'd put Ari through, but I held back. Every time I thought of her, I saw red. I wanted to hurt her the way she'd hurt her son, and it was too frightening to confront her, not knowing what I might say or do.

My phone vibrated, and I slipped it out of my pocket.

Call me.

It was the same number I'd been in touch with about killing Ken. I excused myself from the table and hurried out of the conference room. In the hallway, I followed the sign to the men's restroom. A quick check told me no one was in the stalls.

I pressed the Call icon with a trembling finger.

"Are you alone?" came the gruff voice.

I cleared my throat. "Yes. Did you get it done?"

"Not so fast. Wouldn't you like to catch up first, Principal Wheeler?"

Blood rushed in my ears, and my legs buckled. I clutched the sink to keep myself steady.

"How did you know?"

"Because guess where I'm standing right now? Across from your house."

Alarm speared through me. Ari.

"What are you doing there?"

"I was trailing your mark. He's been following this rather beautiful boy and his friend all day, so I haven't been able to strike. Imagine my surprise when they entered a house with your name on the mailbox."

Damn. Why had I changed the name?

"Wait a minute. What do you mean they all entered the house?"

"Well, they just let in the mark, which means I can't kill him now, or it'll lead right back to you. I'm just giving you a heads-up that I might need a few more hours."

"They let him in?" My heart raced in my chest. "That man is dangerous. Do you hear me? You need to do it now."

"Sorry, Principal Wheeler. You know I respect you and all, but right now, you're compromised, and if I make my move now, I will be too."

"If anything happens to him…" I hung up the phone and called Ari, but he didn't pick up. I raced out of the restroom and switched to calling the home phone, but it too went unanswered.

The hotel where the conference was taking place was downtown, several miles from where we lived. Even if I broke all the speed records, it would take too long to get to the house, but I had no other option. Ari had begged me not to call the police, and tempted as I was, I couldn't. What if I called the police and it would lead to Ari's demise?

I toed the speed limit. Thank god the lunch hour traffic had dwindled to the occasional car. The traffic lights worked in my favor except for the last one. I gripped the steering wheel and glared at the red light as if I could, by force of will alone, change it to green.

Adrenaline coursed through my veins, hitting its zenith by the time I parked in the driveway. I yanked the glove compartment open and took out my licensed gun. My hands shook as I loaded it. I ran to the garage. The security code tripped me up, and I had to close my eyes and concentrate to remember we'd used a combination of the years Ari and I were born. The garage door opened, and I ducked inside.

I closed the door behind me and tiptoed farther into the house. A scream ripped through the air.

Ari.

I sprinted to the living room and skidded to a halt. My heart stopped beating, then hammered in my chest in triple speed. Ari, lying on the floor, bleeding, with Ken — that fucking monster — slashing the boy's back while trying to poke his cock between Ari's ass cheeks.

My vision turned red at my beautiful boy under this disgusting creature. A hoarse cry tore from my lips.

"You son of a bitch! Get off him!"

Ken jerked back, whipping his head up. He scrambled up, his cock hanging out of his pants. It was the sight of that swollen member that was the last straw. How dare he think he was going to get away with this again?

"It wasn't enough what you did to him before?" I raised the gun and squeezed the trigger. *Boom! Boom!* The impact of the bullets ripping through his chest drove him back. Blood oozed from the wounds, and his cold, hard eyes met mine, then turned glossy as he tumbled to the floor on his side.

Ari whimpered, stopping me from emptying the whole magazine into him. Instead, I turned on the safety and placed the gun on the floor as I kneeled by Ari, who lay facedown on the floor. His shirt was ripped and bloody from the cuts to his back. He covered his head with his hands, and blood seeped from the cuts on his arms. Blood was soaking into his beautiful curls.

"Ari." I struggled to keep the tears at bay. The waistband of his pants and his lace underwear were down under his butt cheeks. I carefully pulled them up and back into place, hoping I'd arrived in time to prevent him from raping the boy.

But what he had done to Ari's body was horrifying enough. How many times had he cut him?

"Baby." I carefully rolled Ari over onto his side. Besides a hiss of pain, he didn't make a sound. His front wasn't bleeding as badly as his back and his arms.

I took in his face. Not the blood but his slack expression and the unresponsive eyes worried me the most. I gently turned him on his belly again.

"Ari, it's Daddy. Please say something."

Silence.

"Oh god, baby, please."

I clamped my eyes tightly closed, then looked at the man who caused all this.

Oh. My. God.

Howard, Ari's friend, sat slumped on the sofa, his shirt and the cushions soaked in the blood from the slit in his throat.

Oh god, what kind of monster did this?

The monster who lay dead for good this time. I'd made sure of it.

I fished out my phone and punched in 9-1-1. I leaned forward and kissed Ari's temple. "Everything's going to be okay."

"9-1-1, this is Charlie. How may I help you?"

The police arrived on the scene quickly, paramedics and the ambulance just a minute behind them. Someone pulled me away from Ari as the paramedics worked on him, trying to stop the bleeding from the most crucial sites. They spoke to him, asked him questions, but he didn't respond. He didn't even move.

"He's in shock," one of the paramedics said to the other, shining a penlight directly into Ari's eyes. Then he turned to me. "Do you know if he's on any medications?"

"He has Xanax in the medicine cabinets with his name on the bottle. He said it helped him to sleep and keep calm," I stammered. I'd never seen him take them, though, so I hadn't questioned him any further about it. Maybe I should have.

A cop pulled a white sheet over Howard's body. The poor kid. He'd befriended Ari, who seemed to enjoy their friendship, and he hadn't deserved to die like this.

"Detective Cooper," the cop said. "You're the one who phoned in about the incident?"

"Yes, that's me."

"And it's your firearm that was recovered from the scene?"

"Yes."

"Can you explain what happened?"

The paramedics were loading Ari onto a stretcher.

"I have to go with them to the hospital," I said.

"I'm afraid we're going to need information first before we let you do that."

"We can talk at the hospital. He needs me."

"And we need you to explain what happened here in as much detail as you can, or we can take you down to the station and question you there."

"I don't know everything that happened."

"That's okay. Just tell us what you saw."

"I came home through the garage and I heard Ari scream. When I came here, I-I saw him slicing that knife into Ari's back while-while—"

"While what?"

"He was trying to rape him." I gulped in a deep breath. "There was so much blood. I shot him."

"You shot him twice."

"I had to make sure he couldn't hurt him anymore."

The cop frowned at me. "And the deceased on the couch?"

"His name's Howard. That's all I know. He was good friends with Ari, and they spent the day together. I don't know what happened. He was already dead when I got here."

"Do you know why Ari was attacked?"

I shrugged. "It's not the first time he's hurt him. Ari lived with him for a while, and he abused him, so he ran away. Ken came back two weeks ago and found him."

"Was any of this reported to substantiate your claim?"

"I don't think so. We didn't think he would do this. I got a security system in the house. I thought we'd be safe."

"What's your relationship to Ari?"

I swallowed hard. "We live together."

"As in roommates?"

"No, he's my boyfriend."

Detective Cooper raised his eyebrow. "Is that all?"

"He's my ex-wife's son. We reconnected when he came back to town a couple of months ago."

He asked me a few more questions, which culminated in taking Anne's number. When he finally allowed me to leave, it was with an ominous warning not to leave town.

During the drive, I trembled so badly it was a wonder I got to the hospital in one piece. I parked as close to the entrance as possible. Thankfully, I hadn't had to lie to any of the questions he'd asked, and I'd just need to urge Ari to tell the truth as well. It didn't matter what else Ari had done wrong. This case was about Howard's death, Ari being wounded, and me killing Ken.

Oh dear god, I killed a man.

I leaned my forehead against the steering wheel and gulped several breaths into my lungs to calm down. Now wasn't the time to freak out. Ari needed me, and Ken hadn't been innocent in all this. No one could blame me for defending Ari as I'd done. I was well within my rights to protect the boy I loved.

When I felt steadier, I climbed out of the car and walked inside. It took me a while to locate Ari, and when I did, the doctor was in with him, so I had to wait. I fought the urge to pace and settled in a chair instead. I laid my hands on my shaking knees.

"Mr. Wheeler."

I snapped my head up and jumped to my feet as a doctor around my age stopped a couple of feet away from me.

"Yes, that's me. How's he doing?"

"I'm Dr. Abrams." He offered me his hand, and I shook it.

"Pleased to meet you."

"I just wanted to give you an update on young Aristotle."

"Please tell me he's going to be okay."

"Physically, he will be. Don't get me wrong. He suffered many lacerations to his body, particularly his back, but for the most part, they are superficial wounds. A few needed stitches, but he's young and should bounce back all right. Now for the psychological aspects. He's in shock and still hasn't spoken or responded to our attempts to stimulate him. It's not uncommon for this type of thing to happen where the brain's incapable of handling the trauma someone goes through."

"How long will he be like this?"

"That we can't say. We may need to bring in a professional to handle that side of his recovery, but I assure you he's in good hands. Do you have any questions?"

"Can I see him?"

"Yes, of course, but I must warn you he's sedated right now. He had a panic attack when they brought him in. We encourage you to speak to him and spend as much time with him as you can. Remind him he has people who care about him."

I thanked the doctor for his advice, then hurried to Ari's room. I took a deep breath and slipped inside, closing the door behind me with a louder thud than I'd meant to. Ari didn't even flinch.

It was as if he was somewhere deep inside his mind.

I tiptoed to his bed. Now that he was all cleaned up, he looked much better. Both hands were bandaged, as was his neck.

"Ari," I said softly.

He didn't acknowledge me.

"Ari, please talk to me, baby. You're scaring me."

He continued staring out the window without any indication of having heard me.

Thirty-Nine

Ari

I LOVE CARNIVALS WITH all the fun and games. Coleyville is usually pretty boring. Nothing exciting ever happens here until the carnival comes to town, transforming the town into a hub of activity. Families come together to enjoy the rides. I've even persuaded my mom, even though our relationship is defective at best.

"Come on, Mom." I frown at the tall, slender woman who'd given birth to me but pretends I don't exist for the most part. "It's just five bucks." As long as she's here, she can make herself useful.

I have some money in my pocket, but I want to use it for the rides. The stuffed sloth sitting on the shelf of the ring toss booth is special, though. It would make a great addition to all the stuffies I already have.

"You're not a child anymore," Mom says, scanning the faces of the people around us. She's pathetic. As if I don't know what she's doing. Picking up men at bars isn't

enough. She's looking for the next hookup to bleed dry. "I'm not giving you my hard-earned money to spend on stuffed toys."

Hard-earned money? That's ironic. She never works. I bite back my retort about what she really does for that money, but the last time I said something like that she slapped my cheek. Now I mutter beneath my breath and never to her face. It doesn't change the way I feel about her. She doesn't care about me. I've learned not to say certain things when she's within earshot.

Reluctantly, I dip into my pocket and pull out the money I've saved up from drawing stuff for the kids at school who couldn't draw to save their lives. It's how I have money at all. I don't get any allowance like most of my classmates.

I hand over the money to the carny, who gives me five rings. Mom glares at me.

"A waste of money. You know these games are rigged."

"I can do it."

"You can't do shit, Ari. Take back your money and go."

"Sorry, no refunds," the carny said.

"Jesus. And I thought you were getting smarter."

She slaps me upside the head. The carny gives me a pitying look.

"Tell you what," he said. "Normally, you have to land five rings to win a prize, but I'll let you pick if you can get three rings."

I beam a smile at the man. "Thank you. That's very kind of you."

Mom snorts. "*And of course your pretty face gets you what you want again.*"

She's always saying shit like that whenever people give me what I ask for or bend the rules a little bit for me. Contrary to what she says, I'm not stupid. I can see I'm a bit more than average in looks, but there are all kinds of beautiful people around. She's not hard to look at either, which I guess is the reason she finds guys so easily. Too bad she could never get them to stick around for long.

Biting my bottom lip, I focus on the bottles and toss my first ring. Mom jostles me, and the ring goes askew, missing the bottles altogether.

"*Hey, you did that on purpose.*"

She laughs, the sound cruel.

"*I'm just pulling your chain. You have four more rings.*"

But the damage is done. With the tension running through me, I only get one ring around a bottle.

"*Sorry, kid,*" *the carny says.*

"*Wait, I'm trying again.*"

"*This is boring. I'm going for a walk-around.*"

Thank fuck.

"*Jeez, kid, I feel sorry for you,*" *the carny says.*

"*Does that mean you'll let me choose a prize, even if I don't get the three rings?*"

"*Sorry. Three rings is the best I can do for you.*"

Shucks. But with Mom out of the way, maybe I can do it this time. I have to. I don't have any money left.

I fail.

My shoulders slump, and I stare longingly at the sloth. I've never seen a sloth stuffie, and I want it so badly.

"Hey, what prize are you trying to get?"

I stare up at the man who has sidled up beside me. He's around Mom's age, with a stocky frame. And he's the vice principal at my school. It's funny seeing him here out of his usual suit and tie. Today he's dressed down in jeans and a short-sleeved shirt.

Does he recognize me? Why would he? The school has hundreds of students.

"That sloth." *I gesture at the shelf.* "It's so cool, and I can add it to my stuffie collection."

He laughs, but the sound is more amused than mocking like Mom's. "Aren't you a little too old for a stuffie collection?"

Maybe.

"No."

"Tell you what. I'll play one game, and if I win, you can claim my prize as yours."

"Really?" *The probability of him winning is slim, I know, but it's his offer that counts. Does anyone else know how kind our vice principal is? Everyone's always afraid of being sent to his office.*

"Yup, why not?" *He pays for his five rings.* "Don't think anything of it. I do this every year the carnival comes to town. Play random games and give the prizes away. I have no use for this stuff, but the carnival brings back memories."

"What memories?" I ask.

"My parents were carnies, so I grew up around the carnival scene." He winks at me with a grin. "I know all the tricks."

And he demonstrates it by getting all the rings around the necks of the bottles.

"I can't believe you actually did it!" I clap my hands and laugh. "That was amazing. Will you teach me how to?"

"Sure, but first, your prize."

He collects the sloth from the carny and hands it to me. I clutch the stuffie to my chest. It's as soft as it looks. It's just become my favorite stuffie.

"Thank—"

"Ari!"

Mom pops up before I can fully get the words out. She glances from me to Vice Principal Wheeler, and my stomach sinks at the smile on her face.

"Who's your friend?" she asks.

I remain mute, not wanting to introduce them. If I do, I know where this is going to end, and he's too nice for her. She'll ruin him.

"Hello, I'm Shaw Wheeler." A few people approach the booth, and we're forced to move out of the way. Vice Principal Wheeler's attention is on my mom. I can't blame him. She's doing that thing where she blinks up at him slowly, flirting with him.

"I'm Anne." She holds her hand out for a handshake that lasts longer than it should have.

"He's my vice principal," I blurt out, so she's aware he's not her regular kind of guy she usually brings home.

He looks at me in surprise. "I am?"

"Yes." Disappointment sinks in my chest. He doesn't know me from school, then. Just as I figured.

"And you won my son a stuffed toy," she says. "That's quite sweet of you."

"It was nothing. Gave me a chance to practice my ring toss."

But it wasn't nothing. They laugh at something Mom says about me and my obsession with stuffed toys. They completely ignore me as they launch into conversation.

When they start to talk of dinner plans, I inch away from them. They won't notice me anyway. He's so wrapped up in whatever she's saying.

"Hey, Ari."

I look back over my shoulder. Vice Principal Wheeler is smiling at me.

"Yes?"

"Why don't you join your mom and me for dinner?"

Mom shakes her head, giving me the signal. She doesn't want me intruding on their date.

"Dinner sounds good."

I'll pay for it when I get home, but for now, the only thing that eclipses the rage on Mom's face is the invitation *itself. He asked me to go with them, which none of Mom's past lovers had ever done.*

I hug the stuffie to my chest and smile widely at him.

FORTY

SHAW

IT TOOK HOURS OF rushed paperwork, several phone calls, each pleading my circumstance, but I'd done it. I'd secured four weeks of paid vacation leave to handle the emotional turmoil of the past month. After all that took place, losing my home due to a fire, involuntarily killing someone in self-defense, and my "stepson" in the hospital, they hadn't given me any crap about taking time off.

If anything, they seemed relieved, as the case was still under investigation. I'd been by the police station once in the past three days since the incident to be interviewed again. They were at a standstill as we all waited for Ari to be responsive so he could corroborate my story of what had happened.

Now I would focus on nothing else but getting Ari well. I stopped at the school to pick up my belongings, dropped everything off in my home office, and went up to take a shower. It'd been hell trying to sleep at night without him, but the days were even worse — sitting with him at the hospital, talking to him, and not getting any reaction. The hospital psychiatrist had me sit in with her while she spoke to Ari, but nothing worked. He didn't respond to her either.

Once I'd freshened up, I walked into Ari's room. What would he like to have with him in the hospital? Nothing stood out. Everything was still so new. All his stuffed animals and toys he would have been familiar with were gone.

The sloth I'd given him.

I took up one of his sketch pads and his pencil case and made my way downstairs back to my office. I spent the next half an hour searching for a sloth stuffie like the one I'd won him. It took me forever, but finally I found one on eBay. Instead of bidding, I sent the seller an offer they couldn't refuse. I was buckling my seat belt when my phone alerted me that my offer had been accepted. The delivery date was three to five business days, which was way too long, but there was nothing I could do about that.

On my way to the hospital, I bought him another stuffed toy — a big silky-soft koala. I clutched it under my arm as I headed for his room, saying a quick prayer that he was doing better today. The hospital hadn't called me, so I didn't anticipate him being any worse. If only he would talk to me. Then I would know what he needed me to do to make it better. Did he even understand that Ken was dead and could no longer hurt him?

The nurse smiled when she saw me. By now, most of the staff who worked the floor were familiar with me being here. It also helped that they'd completely fallen in love with the boy.

"Hello, Emma, how is he today?" I greeted her.

Her smile faded. "He had visitors. The police stopped by, but he still won't communicate with them. Then after his other visitor, he got agitated and had a panic attack. I'm sorry, but he's probably still sedated right now."

Concern spiked through me, but as much as I wanted to barge into Ari's room, he couldn't tell me what was wrong, so I had to rely on the nurse.

"What visitor?" Who would have a reason to visit Ari? His only friend was dead. I was the only one he had.

"I suppose I can tell you, since you're his emergency contact . It was his mother."

Anne was in Coleyville? The police contacted her to ask about her connection with Ken and the kind of relationship Ari had with the man. I hadn't called her to let her know what happened, and she'd never bothered getting in touch with me. I'd assumed she was feeling too guilty about her part in all this and decided to stay away. But now she visited him. The gall of that bitch.

"Thank you."

"You're welcome. He should be glad you're here. He's so much calmer with you."

I doubted she had any idea how much her words meant to me. I'd been convinced Ari hadn't responded to me at all, but she seemed to have found the difference in the boy's mood when I was around. Maybe I should pay closer attention to see what else I missed.

When I entered his room, nothing had changed. Ari lay deathly still, his eyes closed. The beeping of the machines and steady rise and fall of his chest were reassuring, though. He twitched, eyebrows furrowed, then evened out again. What was going through his mind? Did he know Anne visited him? If her visit caused a panic attack, he might have.

Even though a panic attack wasn't a good thing, it was the first time Ari reacted. Could this mean he was coming around?

"Hey, baby, I heard you had a bad day." I leaned over and planted a kiss on his forehead, right between his eyes. Then I kissed his nose and his cheek. *Please feel me, Ari. I'm here.* "But it's okay. I'm here now, and I brought you company."

I tucked the koala next to him in bed and placed his arm around the stuffed animal. "It's a koala. You'll love it. Why don't you open your eyes for me and take a look?"

I held my breath, but nothing. My shoulders slumped. I drew the chair closer to the bed and carefully took his bandaged hand in mine. His fingers twitched. The doctors had been most worried about the slash in his palm, but if he could move his fingers, that was a good sign, right?

Time passed. The psychiatrist encouraged me to chat with him, even if Ari didn't respond. It wasn't easy at first, but once I started, the words flowed. I talked to him about the first time we met and how happy he was when I won him the sloth. In every story I told him, I left out his mother. Few memories I had of her and Ari were good. She'd always been bitter, confrontational, and critical of Ari. Ari, on the other hand, would be mocking, spiteful, and provoking.

At one point, a nurse arrived to administer more medication into the drip line Ari was hooked up to and to empty his catheter bag. After she left, I took a nap. A door opening startled me awake. The doctor on duty entered the room. I kept out of the way as he examined Ari. He has his eyes open now, but I preferred them closed. Then I didn't have to see the deadness in them. No sign of recognition. Absolutely nothing.

"Mr. Wheeler," the doctor said after he'd scribbled down his observations. "Do you mind stepping outside for a few minutes so we can talk?"

"Sure." The word came out confident, but my heart was knocking in my chest, and my limbs had grown heavy. The only reason I could think of for us leaving the room was that he had bad news to tell me. Otherwise, why not just say in in front of Ari?

"What's up, Doctor?"

The man frowned, but it didn't seem directed at me. "Do you know what cyclothymia disorder is?"

"I've never heard of it before."

"But I'm sure you've heard of bipolar disorder?"

Dread sank in as his question started to make sense. "Yes, I have."

"Cyclothymia disorder is sometimes seen as a milder form of bipolar disorder. It's a rare mood disorder that causes emotional ups and downs that's less drastic than those associated with bipolar one and two. I take it you weren't aware Aristotle was being treated for this condition?"

"No, no, I wasn't."

"We asked you to bring in any medication and we were able to trace the doctor who prescribed them. It seems he hasn't been keeping up with his dosage, which might account for the prolonged state of unresponsiveness he's currently in."

What? Why had Ari hidden this from me? He had to have known his diagnosis wouldn't have changed the way I saw him. If him killing and discarding of bodies hadn't changed my mind about him, nothing would.

"I'm not sure what all this means," I said.

"It means that even after Aristotle pulls through this, he's going to need guidance in making sure he takes his medication as prescribed to keep his moods stabilized."

He nodded and walked away. Had I thanked him for the information or said something else appropriate? I really couldn't tell with the buzzing inside my head as memories flashed through my mind like the picture reel in my phone. Moments when he was extremely happy and always on the go, like days he'd cleaned the house from top to bottom.

Then his mood had shifted so dramatically, and he'd thrown a tantrum and earned himself a time-out.

His mother wasn't the only one who failed him.

I must have fallen asleep again. The vibrations of my phone woke me up. I squinted, squeezing my eyes tightly shut, then opening them to check whether Ari was awake. He'd become agitated earlier again, and the nurse sedated him. He was still sleeping, but the koala was still clutched under his arm.

That was a good sign, right?

I let out a yawn, which snapped off at my ex-wife's text on the screen.

Anne: *I'm at the Roseanne hotel. I think we should talk about Ari.*

She added her room number and asked me to meet her. My first instinct was to delete the message and ignore her. We had nothing to say to each other. But that wasn't true. I had a lot that I needed to say to her. Ari couldn't do it.

After kissing his forehead, I held on to his uninjured hand and promised him I would be back soon. A light squeeze wrapped around my fingers. I stilled and stared from our joined hands to Ari's face. Had he intentionally squeezed my hand, or had it been one of those involuntarily twitches?

"Ari? Baby, squeeze my hand again if you can hear me."

But there came no squeeze.

With a sigh, I released his hand. I loathed leaving him, but I couldn't ignore Anne. The Roseanne was only half a mile away from the hospital and I could do with some thinking time, so I walked to the hotel. I was almost there when my phone rang.

Alex Killian.

What did he want? With Ken being dead, our contract was void. I didn't need him anymore.

"Hello."

"Principal Wheeler—"

"Call me Shaw." I huffed a breath. Him calling me by my title sounded weird after what I'd hired him to do. Fuck. How had I gotten to this point where I had hired hitmen and killed bad guys?

"Sounds good."

"Did someone find out?" Why else would he call me?

"Relax. I'm just calling to find out how your boyfriend is."

Oh. I stopped walking. "You are?"

"Yeah, I feel partly responsible, like I should have done something, you know, but you understand I couldn't have interfered. There would have been too many questions."

I understood, but I was still pissed about it. If he had interfered and killed Ken, he wouldn't have hurt Ari.

And all our asses would more than likely have ended up in jail.

"Anyway, I need to return what you gave me," he said. "It's not right for me to keep it, since I didn't do the job."

"That's noble of you."

He chuckled. "I learned some scruples from you, Prin—Shaw." Then his voice dropped an octave. "You were the only one who didn't write me off as a kid."

"Maybe I should have. It didn't seem to help."

"On the contrary, man. On the contrary. Anyway, I hope your little boy gets well soon."

He hung up before I could respond. That was unexpected. And bizarre. As I walked into the hotel, I checked the room number Anne sent me. I made a beeline for the elevator, held it for a woman with a suitcase, and we made the ride in silence. I got out before her.

I knocked, and the door opened. Had she been standing there, waiting for me? I stared at her, emotions slamming me in the gut, but none of them was of the desire I'd felt for her when we'd met. She'd seemed so charming and beautiful then. I'd been so smitten with her, stoked about having a beauty like her in my life.

I'd been such a fool, but I couldn't regret my time with her. Then I wouldn't have met Ari.

"Shaw, you're here. Come on in."

She stepped aside for me to enter, then closed the door. I still didn't say anything to her. The words couldn't come. My mind sorted through the tirade that threatened to spill from my lips.

"We can talk in here."

She'd rented a suite that had a nice sitting room. On the coffee table stood two glasses and a bottle of wine. What was she up to now? I paid attention to her for the first time and did a double take. She was wearing a deep purple silk robe loosely tied around her slender waist. When she turned to me, the slit at the front widened, showing off her long, shapely leg.

Unbelievable.

"Why are you here?" I asked past the knot in my throat.

"Well." She poured the wine and held a glass out to me, but when I didn't take it, she put it back on the coffee table and sat, crossing one leg over the other. The slit showed her leg up to midthigh now. "When the police called me to ask about Ken and Ari, I learned what happened. Why didn't you call me?"

"I thought you didn't care."

"I might not understand the boy, but that doesn't mean I want to see him dead."

"He's not going to die!" The words came out sharp and biting. She startled, and wine splashed onto her robe.

"I suppose he won't, but let's face it, Shaw. The boy belongs in the nuthouse. That's why I wanted to talk to you." She downed her glass and stood. "Now you know I was right all along. You can't ignore it anymore, Shaw. He brought this on himself. He—"

I saw red. Her long fingernails raking down my arm pushed the cloudy haze away and revealed her shocked face, turning red from my hand around her throat, choking her.

I should let her go, but a sense of calm stole over me.

"You cruel, heartless bitch," I spat at her. "You don't care about anyone else but yourself. You never have. Ari didn't bring this on himself. You did." I shook her, and her head lolled around like that of a ragdoll. "You sent him to live with a man who wasn't his father, just to get him out of the picture. Do you have any idea what you subjected him to because of your petty jealousy? You ruined that boy. How can you live with yourself for destroying his life?"

Her face turned a bright shade of red, and her eyes widened. "Sh-aw, pl-ease," she choked out. "Can't breathe."

"Every time he was raped by that son of a bitch, you did it," I said through clenched teeth. "Every bruise on his body, you inflicted. It's all because of you. You're the real monster here."

Just a little longer. If I held on just for a little longer, I would remove her permanently from Ari's life. But to what end? It would be too suspicious if she turned up dead now. It wouldn't help Ari. What he needed right now was stability, love, care, and the guidance and approval he'd always craved from me.

I shoved her away from me, and she fell onto the couch, grasping her throat and half sobbing, half coughing trying to catch her breath.

"You need to get on a plane and go back to wherever the hell you came from," I said. "And I'd be praying that Ari pulls through all right because if he doesn't, Anne, there'll be hell to pay."

She regarded me, her eyes full of fear. "What has he done to you?" she rasped.

"He made me realize that I'll do anything — and I mean *anything* — to protect him."

I turned on my heels.

"You deserve him," she called after me. "I hope he turns your life into a living hell."

I spun around and pinned her with a glower. She pulled her feet up under her body and tried to make herself as small as possible on the sofa.

"That's fine. I'd rather go through hell with him than live without him in it."

Forty-One

Ai

EVERYBODY KEPT TRYING TO talk to me, and I hated it. I just wanted to be left alone, wrapped up in the cocoon of the happy memories of Daddy and me. My favorite time of us was the day we met and he won me that sloth stuffy. I could bask in the way he smiled at me that day forever, and it was exactly what I planned to do. Live forever in the happy memories before all the hurting. Before *he* turned me evil.

I pushed back against the intrusion of the black swirly thoughts about him. I did the same to thoughts and images of my mother. It was only Daddy who was allowed in this world. Daddy who knew the bad things I'd done but still loved me.

I snuggled into my little cocoon of happiness and held on to it, even though they prodded me and poked at me. If I let go, then it would all be real.

This was my reality now.

"Ari, baby, please wake up."

I frowned. The voice sounded like Daddy's, but they couldn't trick me to open my eyes. I was already with Daddy, surrounded by his kind smiles, and his murmurs of "good boy." I'd be his good boy forever.

"Baby, you're beginning to worry me. Just open your eyes for me. Please."

Daddy's image faded. *No! Don't leave. I need you.*

I reached out a hand for him, but he was too far away. Tears streamed down my face.

"Don't leave me. Daddy. Please don't leave me."

"I'm never leaving you. I'm right here, baby. Just open your eyes, and you'll see I'm right here."

Where was he going? Why was he leaving me? The darkness he kept away crept toward me. My heart pounded in my chest as it circled my feet, swallowing me up.

It burned. Oh god, it burned like a million ants crawling up my skin and making a snack out of me.

"No!" I screamed. "Make them stop! Please make them stop hurting me."

I tried to run, but my legs were pinned down. I couldn't move. And Daddy left me.

"I didn't leave you. I'm here. I'm here for you. Just open your eyes. Aristotle!"

My eyes flew open. My full name on Daddy's lips was strange. He never called me Aristotle.

I became aware of everything around me at once. The throbbing hurt in my body, the painful hammering of my heart, the beeping of a machine, and the harshness of the overhead light. Before I could clamp my eyes shut and block out everything again, a familiar sloth appeared in front of me.

"I know it's not the same one you had before," Daddy said softly, "but I tried to find one just like it, minus the torn ear and what not. Do you like it?"

Did I like it? Of course I did. For the second time, Daddy was giving me a sloth.

I nodded and held out my arms. He placed the stuffed animal in them, and I clamped my eyes shut, hugging the soft, plush body against my chest. So soft and nice. I would love it forever.

Daddy's lips pressed against my forehead. My eyes burned, and I sniffled as the memories I'd tried to keep at bay rushed at me. Tears leaked out from behind my eyelids.

"It's okay. I'm here. I swear you're safe. No one's going to hurt you."

A sob tore from my chest. Oh dear god, Howard. Sweet, kind, Howard who never did anything wrong but became friends with me. It was Harlan all over again. Everyone who got close to me ended up hurt and dead.

"Come here, baby." Daddy sat on the bed and carefully pushed my face into his chest. With one hand, I held on tightly to the sloth, and with the other, I clung to Daddy as sobs racked my body.

Daddy whispered words of comfort, stroked, and kissed my hair. My dreams had been nice, but the reality was everything. It felt so good to be able to touch him.

A shudder ran through me, and I let out a sigh. Daddy was so comfy and strong. I popped my thumb into my mouth and suckled. If only I could suck on his nipple instead. That always made me feel better.

"I was so worried about you." He brushed the hair at the back of my neck. "It's been eight days of hell wondering when you were going to wake up.

Eight days? I licked my lips and glanced around. Why was I in a hospital room?

"What happened?" I asked.

"You don't remember?"

I swallowed the lump in my throat and nodded slowly. "I meant after. Did he…?"

I couldn't say the words. In the past, when Ken did that to me, I always fooled myself that I allowed it to happen. That I was using his lust for me against him, but the truth was I'd been scared, and giving in to him was the only way I could get him not to hurt me.

"No, he didn't." Another kiss on my forehead. "I got there in time to stop him. I'm so sorry about Howard."

"I shouldn't have invited him over. If not for me, he would be alive."

"No, this isn't your fault, and I won't have you blame yourself for something he did."

I clung to his shirt even tighter. "But what if he comes back and hurts you? I should disappear again."

"He can't hurt me or you anymore, Ari."

I blinked up at Daddy slowly. "He can't?"

"No, he's dead. The bastard's gone."

"Are you sure?" I'd thought I'd gotten rid of him before too, but he'd emerged again like a scaly-backed cockroach.

"I'm positive. In fact, the police might be here any minute when they learn you're awake so they can take your statement."

"Do I have to?"

"Don't worry. Just be truthful about what happened at the house. I told them everything I could from when I arrived."

"Will you tell me?"

"Are you sure? It doesn't matter now."

"Yeah, I want to know."

Daddy had told me what had happened after I blocked out the world around me. I couldn't believe he shot and killed Ken to protect me. Relief flooded through me.

Before I could ask him anything else, the doctor appeared to check me out. Daddy stepped aside to give the doctor room, but I held on to his hand. If I let him go, he would be gone forever. The doctor took one look at our clasped hands and told Shaw it was okay to stay. He asked me how I was feeling and informed me about my condition over the past eight days. Daddy told me already how long I'd been unresponsive, but hearing it again was surreal.

The doctor was gentle and kind. Gradually I relaxed. Until a nurse announced the police's arrival.

"It will be fine," Daddy said.

My throat was dry as two cops entered the hospital room. The doctor had left, but Daddy stayed right with me.

"Aristotle, I'm Detective Cooper and this is Officer Romano," the taller of the two cops said. "It's good to see you're awake. How are you?"

I squeezed Shaw's hand and sought his help.

"It's okay, Ari. Go ahead and speak to the cops."

Officer Romano frowned at Daddy, and he and his colleague shared a look I couldn't read.

"I'm fine," I said softly.

"We have a few questions we would like to ask you about the incident at your home," Detective Cooper said. "But first, Mr. Wheeler, you need to step outside until we're done here."

"No!" I shifted restlessly in the bed. "Please don't go."

"I'll just be on the other side of the door. I promise." Shaw brushed my hair from my forehead, then leaned in and whispered in my ear, "Be a brave boy for Daddy."

I clasped my hands on my stomach. I would be a brave boy for Daddy.

"Let me remind you that anything you say right now can be used against you in a court of law," the detective said. "We ask that you be truthful."

I nodded.

"What's your relationship with Mr. Wheeler?"

That was their first question?

"He's my Daddy."

"Excuse me?" This from Officer Romano. "Can you explain what that means?"

"He's my partner. He takes care of me."

"As in a romantic relationship?"

"Yes."

"And before that he was your stepdad?"

I squirmed. Why did I feel like Shaw was under trial here?

"He was. We didn't become involved until I returned to town."

"Why did you return?"

"I always missed being here. I missed him."

Silence spanned a few seconds. Then the detective cleared his throat. "Was Mr. Wheeler jealous of your relationship to the deceased?"

"Howard?"

"Sorry for not being clear. I'm talking about Ken."

"No," I said firmly. "Daddy had no reason to be jealous of Ken."

"You can tell us the truth, Aristotle," Officer Romano said. "No one's controlling you now. We can get them to stop."

They thought someone was controlling me?

"No one's controlling me."

He sighed. "You weren't in a relationship with both men that went sour and ended up with one of these men dead?"

I blinked at him, then frowned. "No. I'm only in a relationship with Shaw."

Why had he had to leave the room? He would have confirmed what I was saying.

"So we should believe that Ken flew all the way here to Ohio to find you for the sole purpose of what?"

I inhaled deeply, Daddy's words echoing in my ear to be a brave boy. He'd said to tell the truth.

"Ken Waugh was a monster," I said, my voice shaking. "He raped and pawned me off to others when I lived with him, so I left. I didn't think he would come after me."

The cop had the grace to look ashamed. "Tell us what happened."

"My friend Howard and I went out. Then we got back home. Daddy was at a conference. I went upstairs to put down the stuff I bought, then loaded the machine with laundry. By the time I returned to the living room, Howard was already..." I swallowed hard and licked my dry lips. "He'd already slit Howard's throat. I tried to run, but..." I shook my head. "I thought he was going to kill me."

"But then your partner showed up."

I shrugged, plucking at the sheets. "I don't know what happened after. I hit my head and then I blocked out everything."

"You don't remember anything after he pulled your pants down?"

"No."

They asked me a few more questions that I didn't find relevant at all. Questions about my relationship with Shaw. Eventually, they thanked me and said they would keep in touch. As soon as they left, Daddy came back in. The trembling started then.

"I know, baby. I know."

He wrapped me up in his arms. "I'm not sure they believed me."

"I'm sure it will be fine, but I'll get a lawyer just in case."

Forty-Two

Shaw

A HAND TUGGED AT my shirt, and I raised my head from the computer screen where I'd been reading the email I'd received. Ari kneeled by my chair, the sloth clutched in his arm and a binky in his mouth. Since I'd brought him home from the hospital a week ago, it was like he was stuck permanently in little space. It started when we entered the house. I'd expected him to go through some heavy emotions. I still got the heebie-jeebies whenever I came in. I'd never expected him to fully freak out. He had run back to the car, and the only way I'd gotten him inside was carrying him through the garage.

It was as if he could only cope with being in the house by sinking into little space. Once there, he didn't have to think about anything but playing and having Daddy take care of him. But he couldn't be in little space all the time. It wasn't good for him, which was the reason I'd sent off some job application letters to schools in other states.

We needed to move somewhere far away from here where we could start over. Our skeletons would remain buried here so our life could continue elsewhere.

"Daddy!" He tugged at my shirt again. "Daddy!"

I removed his hand gently from my shirt and swiveled the chair to face him. "Yes, baby?" I lifted him from the floor into my lap, the diaper squishy.

"Diaper full," he said.

"Yes, it is." I checked the time on the computer. "I might as well give you a bath, and then we'll have dinner."

"Nuggets!"

I kissed the top of his head. "Of course. And fries."

"Yeah!"

"But you also have to eat some carrots."

"Boo!"

I chuckled, hitching him on my side as I made for the door. "Yes, carrots."

"I hate carrots."

"I know you do, but they're good for you."

"Only one carrot?"

"Nope."

"Two carrots?"

"Nope."

"Three! Only three!"

He held up three fingers, and I nipped at them. He squealed and pulled them back, and I smiled. I didn't mind him being in little space at all, but I didn't want him to have to rely on it so heavily to cope. His psychiatrist advised me to slowly use activities to pull him out of little space until he was comfortable dealing with the tough emotions of being an adult again.

In our bedroom, I stripped him out of his clothes and the thoroughly soaked diaper. I ran a finger over his damp skin. If he'd peed one more time, the diaper would have started leaking. My breath quickened, and from the way he looked up at me, I knew he did it deliberately. He could have told me at any time that he needed changing, but he'd waited until his diaper was full.

I licked my lips. Hmm, maybe I knew something that would get him to leave little space. We'd had sex while he was a little before. He'd already made it clear he enjoyed sex as a little, and that was fine by me, but this time it was different. He was vulnerable, and little space was a safe place for him right now.

Without a word, I brought him to the bathroom and set him down on the toilet while I filled the tub. When it was the perfect temperature, I added the soap he liked, then had him sit.

I was careful with his bath, but each time I washed him, especially his back, and saw the scars the knife left, I wanted to kill Ken all over again. I traced the outlines of some of the more serious ones, then kissed the back of his neck.

"Stand."

I drained the water, finished rinsing him off, and wrapped him up in a big, fluffy towel. He hummed under his breath and rested his head on my chest. Then he placed his hands over my wet T-shirt, which stuck to my body. He ran a finger over my nipple, and I sucked in a deep breath.

"Daddy," he murmured. "I want."

I kissed his cheek. "You can have when you're an adult again."

"But, Daddy."

"It's not up for discussion, baby." No matter how much I wanted to place him on the bed, push his legs apart, and slide into his body, I couldn't encourage him staying in little space all the time. At some point, he had to face all the emotions he was suppressing as a little.

He pouted as I dressed him, and when I took out a new diaper, he shook his head.

"Are you sure?"

He nodded, and I smiled. If he didn't want a diaper, then he might be ready to be an adult again.

"Okay, then."

I carried him to the kitchen. He wouldn't eat in the formal dining room as we had to pass the living room for that. At the foot of the stairs, his hold on me tightened, but he relaxed again when I walked into the dining room. I placed him on the floor with his tablet to watch cartoons and play with his sloth while I whipped up his dinner. After a week in the kitchen, I was getting better at making him meals.

"Dinner's ready." I helped him up to sit around the table and pulled my chair closer to his. He made grabby hands for his sippy cup, but I kept it out of his reach. "Not just yet. Eat first."

He wasn't too pleased with this, but he opened his mouth and allowed me to feed him the nuggets. I held in my laugh as he made a face each time I spooned carrots into his mouth. He was clearly not a fan in little space, although as an adult he loved them. He drank some juice and kicked his feet.

While he ate, I started on my meal — a microwaved pasta dish. It didn't have much flavor, but cooking for Ari was about all I could manage.

"Full," he announced, and since he was almost finished anyway, I shoved the rest of his nuggets into my mouth. He snagged his sippy cup and stuck the spout between his lips, draining the juice. "More."

"No more juice, but you can have water."

"Please."

He drank two cups of water, and I frowned at him. "You're exceptionally thirsty tonight."

He climbed down from his chair, crawled under the table, and wrapped himself around one of my legs while I ate. I petted his head and finished my dinner. If I hadn't appreciated Ari before, I would have now. House chores were tedious, but he'd always done them without complaint. I loaded the dishwasher and wiped down the counters, then took Ari back upstairs.

"I'm going to take a shower," I said, settling him on the bed. "Be back soon."

"Okay, Daddy."

On the way to the bathroom, I shrugged out of my shirt. Once inside, I closed the door and leaned back against it. The things I wanted to talk to Ari about, but I couldn't while he was like this. My leave wouldn't last forever. We had decisions to make now that the police were off our case about Ken's death. While I'd sent out applications for positions fitting my qualifications out of state, I didn't even know if Ari wanted to leave. But what choice did we have if he couldn't face the living room?

When I stepped back into the bedroom, Ari was no longer on the bed. The door to the hallway stood ajar.

"Ari?"

I hurriedly pulled on a pair of sweats, forgoing underwear.

"Ari?"

Still no answer. Goddammit, what was it now? Where was he?

I checked my office first. That was where he spent most of the day when he wasn't in our bedroom. No Ari. Sniffles drew me to the living room. Ari stood just inside, staring at the empty spot where the couch had been. I'd thrown it out, since I couldn't see either of us relaxing on the sofa where his friend had been murdered.

"Baby?"

He sniffled again. "It's not fair."

His voice no longer had that childlike quality to it as when he was being a little. The tone was broken and sad.

"I know, love."

I approached him carefully and wrapped my arms around his waist from behind, mindful not to hold him too tightly. The cuts on his back were still healing.

"He was a good guy, Shaw. He didn't deserve to die that way."

"No, he didn't. I'm sorry you had to lose another friend."

"Maybe I should be alone. Then I can't hurt anyone else. I can't hurt you."

"Hey." I placed my chin on top of his head. "You need to get that thought out of your head right now because you weaseled your way into my life, and now I need you in it. My life won't be the same without you, Ari."

"But it will be better."

"Never, my love." I kissed his temple. "And all this is moot anyway. As if I could ever let you go."

"You should."

"But I won't."

He sighed and shifted in my arms to face me. He ran a hand along my stubbled cheek. I hadn't bothered to shave.

"You deserve so much better, Shaw Wheeler."

"Then we agree that I deserve what I want, and what I want is you."

I dipped my head to kiss him, but he turned his face. "I have something else to tell you."

"Is it necessary?"

"I want you to know everything. The whole truth. And if you still want me…"

"I'll always want you."

"I killed Murray."

Of all the things I'd expected Ari to say, that sure as hell wasn't it. "That's impossible. He died long before you came back."

"It's the truth."

Which meant…

"You were here before?"

"Yeah, I was here a few times. Mostly in the night. I would sneak in and watch you sleep on and off for almost a year before I showed up in your kitchen that day."

"And you never let me know?"

He plucked at my shirt. "Aren't you mad about Murray?"

"I am shocked you were behind it, but I won't pretend like there was any love lost between us. He was a horrible man, and this is in the past, but no more, Ari. No more killing."

"I know. I don't want to lose you any more than you want to lose me."

"Good."

Ari closed his eyes and placed his head on my chest. "I don't know if I can stay here. Too many memories."

I rubbed his back gently. "Maybe we don't need to stay."

"But your job is here."

"I can get a job somewhere else. In fact, I've sent out a few applications and got a response for an interview. It's in Florida, but—"

"Florida? That sounds great. We could go to the beach."

"Make love on the beach." I tickled his spine, and he smiled. It wasn't as wide as his usual smiles, but it was a start.

"Yes, please."

"But first the interviews. I was thinking we could drive there and spend a week. Then we can decide what we want to do. We both deserve some time away just to be with each other without all the distractions."

"I'd like that. Very much."

"Come on, then. You still have your pills to take, and then we can figure out our trip together."

Forty-Three

Ari

KNOCK. KNOCK. KNOCK.

I rocked back on my heels and waited for Shaw to give me permission to enter his office. A tingle ran down my spine, and I glanced over my shoulder. Of course we didn't have ghosts, but I couldn't shake my unease in the house anymore unless I was with Shaw.

"Come in."

I twisted the doorknob and ducked inside, closing the door behind me.

"Give me a minute," Shaw mouthed but beckoned me over as he spoke into his phone. I was only too happy to be at his side. He patted the desk in front of him for me to sit, and I hopped up. He drew his chair closer and placed a hand on my knee through the folds of my skirt.

I'd tried something different, and instead of my usual dresses, I had on a gingham cherry-print swing skirt with a black quarter-sleeve top. When Shaw and I went shopping for our trip, I found this cute pair of heeled sandals, and I'd been wearing them all morning. Given the way he'd looked at me, I never wanted to take off the outfit. It'd been disappointing when his kiss had been chaste.

As Shaw continued a conversation that seemed to do with our upcoming trip, I lifted his hand off my knee, raised my skirt, and placed his hand between my legs. I wasn't hard yet, but Shaw's hand nudged my cock in the right direction.

"I, uh…" Shaw cleared his throat, staring directly at me. His cheeks were flushed. "Sorry about that. As I was saying…"

I tugged my shirt out of the waistband of the skirt and smiled at Shaw as I slowly rubbed the material against my skin. His hungry gaze followed my every movement. The second the scars on my body came into view, his eyes grew hard.

No, that's not what I want him focusing on right now.

"Thanks for fixing this," Shaw said. "Have a nice day." His tone was strained as he hung up the phone. "What are you doing?"

I tossed my shirt on top of his head and pouted. "You haven't touched me since I've been out of the hospital."

"You've been through a lot."

"We've both been, and you know what will make me feel better? If you screw my brains out right now, Daddy. Can't you feel how much I want you?"

I licked at two of my fingers, then rubbed them over my nipple, hissing as the nub drew tight. My cock throbbed under Daddy's hand.

"I don't want to hurt you," he said.

"Is that why you haven't touched me?"

"I've touched you."

"But not like this." I lifted my skirt to my waist. He homed in on my cock, which he held through my silk underwear.

"Are you sure?"

"Yes." I thrust up against his hand, urging him to do something. I patted my chest right over my heart. "You've made me feel better here." Then pointed at my head. "And here." I widened my legs even more and tilted back as I tapped my ass. "Now make me feel good here. You're the only one who can."

Shaw rose from his chair and fastened his mouth on me in a scorching kiss, thrusting his tongue inside, claiming me. I whimpered at the intensity that burned through him and clutched his shoulders, the only thing that kept me from tumbling onto my back on the desk.

So I wasn't the only one who'd been suffering from our lack of intimacy these past two weeks. He gently cupped my back, as sweet as ever to be mindful not to hurt me. With his free hand, he caressed my torso, flicking his thumb over my nipples, pressing so hard into them I cried out.

He tore his mouth from mine, and there was that look on his face that I loved — pure adoration.

"Too rough?" he asked.

"No, just right. It's been too long, Daddy. If you go slow right now, you'll kill me for sure."

He leaned forward and bit my bottom lip. "Don't. Don't speak so casually about that. Not after how close I came to losing you again."

"You never lost me before. I was always yours."

My head rocked back on my shoulders as he kissed my neck, placing gentle lips on one of the scars on my shoulder, then licking at my right nipple. A shudder ran through me.

"You're a work of art, Ari. So damn beautiful. It's almost a sin to touch you. But I get to touch your beauty. Only me."

"Yes, only you," I gasped as he scraped his teeth over the sensitive nipple.

My stomach trembled beneath his lips, the muscles tightening under his ministrations.

Shaw pulled my ass closer to the edge of the desk and went down on his knees. He tugged my skirt down to cover me.

"What are you doing?" He wasn't thinking of stopping right now, was he?

Instead of answering, he dove under the skirt and ran his tongue over the hard line of my cock. My breath hitched. I wanted to drag the skirts up so I could see what he was doing under there, but it turned out all I needed was to feel.

He tugged down the waistband of the underwear enough for my cock to pop out, and then his lips were right where I'd wanted them to be since I entered the room.

Placing both elbows on the desk, I gave in to the ride, closed my eyes, and enjoyed Shaw's blow job. The way his lips pulled on my cock, his tongue licking the underside up to the tip to circle the plump head.

"Oh, Daddy." Over and over, he sucked up and down my cock, cupping my balls and squeezing them gently.

When I thought I would blow, he released me. I gasped, chest rising and falling hard, as he emerged from beneath my skirt. He leaned over me and took my mouth with his. I moaned, cupping the back of his head and returning the rough thrusts of his tongue and the scrape of his teeth.

"Don't move." He dashed out of the office. I held my position, which wasn't easy. My body was electrified, my skin humming in anticipation. When he returned with the bottle of lube, a sigh of relief escaped me.

"Turn around."

He helped me off the desk and bent me over the top. He flipped my skirt up, and the material pooled up my back. Shaw groaned and fingered the little red-and-black bow at the waistband of my underwear.

"So sexy." He dipped two fingers into the slit at the back. I'd thought that would turn him on. "As pretty as this is, baby, I like to see your naked ass better."

He peeled down the underwear and left them resting between my thighs. "There, that's much better. You've got such a perfect ass. And those tattoos, did you know I hated them until I saw yours?"

"I wasn't sure you would like them."

He pried my cheeks apart. "I love everything about you."

He must have squeezed lube onto his fingers. A wet finger probed between my cheeks and sank into my hole. He kissed my neck and bit my earlobe. "Even the dangerous parts."

A shiver ran down my spine. Shaw twisted his finger and shoved another one inside me. He pushed one cheek apart, hissing a breath as he fingered me slowly at first, then thrust deep and hard over and over.

"Daddy," I moaned.

"Tell me what you want, angel."

"I want your cock inside me. Too long. Please, please."

"Oh god, I love when you beg."

He poked harder, fingers plundering my hole roughly. I tightened around him, my cock just about ready to explode.

And then his fingers were gone. I panted, squirming to feel…something. I needed to come.

"Please, Daddy. I need you."

"Only me."

"Yes, only you."

"No one else can have you, Ari. No one else."

"No one else." I would have agreed that the earth was flat to get him to fuck me.

"This belongs to me." The thick head of Shaw's cock pushed against my opening and slid right in. He clutched my hips and plunged in deeper. I cried out, grabbing the edge of the desk. "I know it's not right." Thrust. "But I'm beyond obsessed with you." Thrust. Thrust. Thrust. "Obsessed with the way you feel around my cock."

Shaw rocked faster into me, panting from his almost deranged speech. "You in these fancy clothes."

He was really pounding into me now, bruising my hole, and my nerve endings were here for it. I threw my ass back into his thrusts, timing his rhythm, but then I didn't need to keep track. We were in sync, desperate for more of each other.

"My sweet, sweet boy." He fisted his hand around my cock and stroked me just as fast as he moved inside my ass. "I love you, Ari."

The words to respond in kind were trapped in my throat. A shudder rocked my body and traveled down my arms to the tingling tips of my fingers. Crying out, I let go as I was swept under the waves of Shaw's lovemaking.

Shaw shouted hoarsely, his grip tightening on my hips. He filled my channel with his seed, grinding against my ass, giving me every single inch of himself. I whimpered at the stinging pleasure-pain around the tight stretch. I'd be sore for sure, but it was worth it.

Shaw slowly pulled out of me, and I clenched my ass. My arms were about to fail me when Shaw scooped me up off the desk. I wrapped my arms and legs around him, finding his lips with mine and kissing him.

"I love you too." I smiled against his lips. "And I think you already know how obsessed I am with you."

He placed his forehead on mine and kissed me again. His hand slipped down to my ass, and he rubbed the pad of his fingers against my hole. I moaned at the sensitive area he probed. His cum oozed out.

Shaw removed his fingers, and then they were at my mouth. I sucked them in greedily, moaning around the two fingers. His nostrils flared, and I grinned at him.

"Yum."

He groaned. "Dirty little boy."

I fluttered my eyelashes. "I thought I was your little angel."

"Maybe a fallen one."

I giggled as he walked to the door with me clinging to him.

FORTY-FOUR

SHAW

"THAT'S EVERYTHING I THINK we need." I turned, but Ari, who had been standing behind me just a minute ago, had disappeared. One day I would have to tie a bell on the boy for how stealthily he moved.

"Ari?" I shut the trunk of the car and walked back to the house. Through the garage door, of course. The front door was still off-limits.

I found him standing in the hall, his hands clutched to his chest, his bottom lip caught between his teeth.

"Penny for your thoughts."

He turned to me and smiled. "That's all you're willing to pay for them?"

"I can go up by a dollar."

"Silly, Daddy. I'm just thinking about our dream. This was supposed to be it."

"Plans change, Ari."

I slipped my arms around him, resting my chin on top of his head. "It doesn't matter where we are. We'll have a home because we have each other. Besides, it's not like we're staying in Florida right away. We're just checking things out, getting through the interview, and seeing how things go. We can make a decision later."

He sighed. "I know you say that, but I think we already know this is the best decision to make for us. To put everything behind us and start someplace fresh."

"Hmm. Maybe."

"When I bought this house, I was so excited for us." He turned into my arms and rubbed the material of my shirt between his fingers. "I saw us living here together forever, being happy, me serving you, you calling me your little angel. I haven't had a steady home for so long, and this was supposed to be it. But I can't even walk through the front door, so I know we have to give up this place, even if we choose not to stay in Florida."

I gently stroked his back. "You know it might take a long time to get this house sold. Many people aren't keen on buying a house where a murder has taken place."

"I know, but at least I can work on my designs from anywhere, so my job won't be affected."

"And I'm sure I'll be able to find something. We have over a month to get everything in order. For now, let's go someplace fun and new where I can finally take you out all the time and show you the love and care you deserve. We've hardly been able to do any of that here."

He nodded, smiling at me. "You're right. Let's go."

I took his hand in mine and led him from the house. Once he was buckled down in the car, I got into the driver's seat and drove off. Ari reached for my hand, and I squeezed it, then placed his hand on my thigh.

"Can we make a stop?" Ari asked. "Two stops, really."

"Sure. Where do you want to go?"

First we went to a flower shop where Ari picked out two bouquets. He didn't even have to tell me where his next stop would be. I took him to the cemetery and cut the engine. Ari had been quiet during the drive.

"I can sit here and wait for you if you want."

"I'd rather you come with me, please."

"Of course."

We had no idea where his friend had been laid to rest, but luckily a caretaker pointed us in the direction of a burial that took place the previous week. Ari had still been too shaken to attend the funeral, and I hadn't pressed him about it.

He slowed down when he neared the headstone with Howard's name. Minutes ticked by, and he did nothing but stand there and stare. He let out a shuddering breath.

"I'm so sorry, Howard," he said softly, wiping his eyes. "You always told me I was trouble, and it turns out you were right. I'm sorry I got you caught up in this mess. I swear I never meant for this to happen."

He stooped and placed one of the bouquets on the grave. I squeezed his shoulders in support, and he smiled at me, his eyes red.

We went to the grave of his other friend, Harlan.

"Your first time coming here?" I asked.

"No, I came here all the time when Mom and I would fight. And when I came back to visit you, I always brought him fresh flowers. His family moved away shortly after he was buried. I always felt they should have stayed, but now I understand. The memories are hard when everything around you reminds you of them."

"Sometimes we have to do what's best for us in order to cope."

"Yeah."

He arranged the flowers, then rose to his feet and nodded at me. "We can go now."

I placed an arm around his shoulders. "You're an amazing person, Ari. You may not always do the right thing, but you love fiercely and are always willing to go the extra mile for those you love."

Even murder.

Our trip to Florida lasted three full days. We decided to make the most of our time by staying in hotels and exploring some cities on our way. It turned out to be the best decision ever as Ari's eyes slowly came alive again. By the time we got to Atlanta, our last stop before hitting Miami, his exuberance and vivacity returned.

Since I did all the driving, I was exhausted when we got to our hotel in Atlanta. I made straight for the bed and fell on it.

Ari jumped onto the bed beside me. "You're not going to nap, are you?"

"I'm afraid so, baby. Daddy needs to rest."

I closed my eyes, but he straddled me and peeled my eyelids back.

"Ari." How could I be mad at him? I was so happy to see the smile back on his face. His cheeks were flushed, and his eyes twinkled with mischief.

"But we need to explore." He checked his watch. "We don't have much daylight left. We can sleep tonight."

How to put it gently to him that I was over twice his age and my endurance and vigor weren't as good as his?

"Baby, why don't you lie down with me and we take a nap? Just a short one. You can set the timer on your phone if you want. Just an hour and we'll go out."

"Promise?"

"Yes, promise."

"Okay."

He set his phone for exactly an hour away, then shuffled over and lay on his side. I spooned him, and he shoved his plump backside into my crotch. Blood rushed down to my cock. I bit back a curse and tried to calm down, but my heart rate was already elevated.

Ari squirmed around, rubbing his sexy ass against me. "Naughty Daddy." He giggled. "I thought you wanted to sleep."

"I do."

"Are you sure?"

When he ground his ass into my cock blatantly this time, I flipped him over onto his stomach and straddled the backs of his thighs. I didn't undress him fully, just pulled his tights down to his knees, pulled my cock out , and used spit. Searching through our luggage for lube would take too much time. He was still stretched from our afternoon stop in a restroom where I'd fucked him earlier.

"Am I hurting you?" I asked when he yelped as the zipper nudged that peachy bum hole.

"No, Daddy. No. So good."

No time to linger on niceties. Fucking him was already taking precious time away from my nap, but I knew my boy. He would continue teasing me for the entire hour if I didn't give him what he wanted. And then I would end up with no sleep.

"Cross your legs," I told him.

He crossed his legs at the back, causing more friction as I pounded him into the mattress. I pulled out and used more spit, keeping his addictive hole moist. I slipped a hand into Ari's mop of curls, tugged his head back, and rode him. He humped into the bed, crying out as his body stiffened beneath me.

"Fuck." I pulled out and stroked my cock fast. Right before I came, I spread his ass cheeks and slid back home, emptying myself into him.

I collapsed onto his back and kissed his neck. "Now go to sleep."

I made no effort to clean us up or to fix our clothes. I spooned him, an arm thrown over his hip, holding him against me.

The next time I woke up, I lay on my back, Ari sprawled on my chest, his mouth snug on my nipple, sucking peacefully. He slept through the alarm, and I had to reach for the phone to turn it off. Apparently, I hadn't been the only one who needed a nap.

Ari stirred and woke me again. He released my nipple and was trying to squirm free of my hold, but I tightened my arm around him.

"Never letting you go," I murmured.

"I just want to pee."

That was a good reason. My bladder was on the edge of bursting too. I released him.

"We should probably take a shower too. We're covered in sweat and cum."

"You know what would make it even better?" He scooted to the edge of the bed and pulled up his tights and underwear.

"What?"

"You peeing on me again."

He disappeared into the bathroom, leaving me dumbstruck. Was that something he really wanted? My breath hitched, and surprise, surprise, my dick was interested in marking Ari too.

As long as it was in the shower...

I trailed him into the bathroom, but he hadn't peed. He'd stripped off his clothes except for his underwear. Damn, I loved his feminine attire. He looked so good in them. He looked damn good in everything.

"What took you so long?" he asked.

"Meaning?"

"I was waiting for your instruction to pee."

My heart skipped a beat, and I hesitated. Ari's accusatory voice echoed in my mind, pointing out my cowardice in not even wanting to admit the dirty things I liked doing to him.

Well, this was a new beginning for us both. No more shame.

"Get in the shower," I said.

He reached for his underwear, but I shook my head. "Keep it on."

His cheeks were flushed, and he licked his lips as he stepped into the glass-enclosed shower stall.

"Now you may pee."

"In my undies?"

"Yes, in your undies."

"But that's dirty, Daddy."

"And you're a dirty little boy, aren't you?"

"Yes."

"Then go ahead. Do it. I want to watch you pee your pants."

Ari dropped his gaze and sucked his bottom lip between his teeth. A wet stream appeared at the front of his underwear, then rushed down his legs. I sucked in a deep breath, allowing myself to feel the wave of heady emotions without questioning my sanity.

We both liked it, and that was all that mattered.

When he was done, Ari clutched his hands to his heaving chest. Both our breathing filled the bathroom.

"What now?"

I pulled down the zipper of my jeans. The button went, and I shoved down the flaps and took my dick out of the denim.

"I'm not going to pee on you like we both want me to," I said. "I know most of your wounds are healing fine, but I won't risk getting them infected. But put your feet together."

He hadn't been stabbed anywhere on his legs and feet, so they were safe.

He shuffled his feet together. I stepped into the shower with him, aimed for his legs, and peed. His breath hitched, and I didn't stop until there was nothing left.

Silence spun around us. Nerve-racking silence that knocked at the back of my skull with doubt. But then Ari grinned at me. "That was so fucking hot. Tell me we'll do it again. Maybe…sometime you could even pee inside me."

I swallowed hard and nodded. "Maybe."

I turned on the faucet and washed away the evidence of what we'd just done. Water cascaded down on us, and Ari moved closer, slipping his hands up my chest.

"I'm so glad you stopped doubting us. It doesn't matter what anyone else thinks about what you do to me. All that matters is that I love it and you clearly enjoy it."

"I do." Admitting it aloud was like a weight lifted from my chest. "I love marking you this way. It makes me feel like I possess you and you're mine."

"Hmm," he growled inside his throat. "And I love when you do it. I'm so glad we got out of Ohio, Shaw. I-I think we'll be fine."

I kissed his forehead and closed my eyes.

It didn't matter if we decided to stick around Florida or go somewhere else. As long as we had each other, we would indeed be fine.

Epilogue

Shaw

I BLINKED IN THE darkness, my heart pounding in my chest, as the mental fog from sleep slowly cleared. For how long had I been asleep? What the hell had woken me up?

I reached a hand out to the other side of the bed to touch Ari, but came up empty. The bed wasn't too cold, so he couldn't have been gone for long.

Damn, was he sleepwalking again?

I reached across to the bedside lamp and turned it on. A pale yellow glow illuminated the room enough for me to find my glasses on the night table. I jammed them on and pulled back the bedsheets. My house slippers were right at the side of the bed where I'd left them. I stifled a yawn and first checked the bathroom by knocking.

"Ari, are you in there?"

Silence.

I cracked the door open and peeked inside in case he was having one of his episodes. Although far less frequent since I ensured he took his meds religiously, there were tough days. Not tough enough for him to slip back into old habits and kill anyone, though, which was the important thing.

Sometimes he had a stroke of creative genius and got up to work in the middle of the night. In two years, he had become one of the most lauded fashion designers of evening gowns.

I descended the stairs and checked his office, which was right next to mine. The door was ajar, but in darkness. I clicked on the light and found our cat, Marigold, asleep on the desk.

Worry gnawed at my gut.

I turned off the light in his office and checked mine just to be sure, but there was no sign of him either.

The last place I could think of to look was the kitchen. On my way, I noticed a draft from the opposite end of the hall. I changed direction and continued down the hall to the open back sliding doors which led out to the patio and huge backyard of the property we'd bought together in California. The job I'd applied for in Florida hadn't panned out, but I received a better opportunity working at a community college in San Francisco, where for the past two and a half years I acted as dean.

"Ari?" I stepped out onto the patio, frowning at the rhythmic sound of something hitting the ground over and over.

What the hell was he doing?

I hurried down the steps, which gave me a better view of him to the right, patting freshly dug up earth with a shovel. If after nearly three years of being good that boy had buried somebody on our property, I'd spank his ass so hard he wouldn't be able to sit for a week!

This was our fresh start, with no reminders of our past.

But the hole he'd dug wasn't human sized.

Whoosh.

I'd resigned myself to loving this boy through anything, but it sure helped that he was at peace with the world.

"Hey, Daddy." He turned to face me with a huge smile. For after midnight, his eyes were bright and full of energy.

That explained it. He was going through one of his high moments. I worried about how much he cleaned and puttered around the house during these episodes, but his psychiatrist assured me as long as he was being productive, he was fine.

"What are you doing?" I asked him gently.

"I couldn't sleep," he said. "There was just too much to do. I finished those designs Couture Beau wanted and then I started spring cleaning."

"And?" I gestured at the shovel.

He giggled. "Don't worry. I swear it's not a body. Did you think it was?"

I groaned. "You're a good boy. You know hiding bodies on our property would be a bad thing to do."

He dropped the shovel, and with dirty hands and all threw his arms around me. "Really? I've been a good boy?"

"You know you have. What were you burying?"

"The journal. I should have destroyed it a long time ago."

"I'd say it's the right time when you feel you're ready to let go."

"I am. It's been so great out here. I don't think I need to hold on to that part of me anymore. You're all mine now."

I lowered my head to press our foreheads together. "And you're all mine. Are you ready to go back to bed?"

"I think I should wash up first."

"Need any help?"

He released me and tugged at my hand. "You bet I do. I have important bits that I can't reach. My arms are too short."

"Yeah, but how did dirt get there? Weren't you just digging? You don't look like you rolled around in the dirt naked."

He grinned at me. "But I might have gotten an itch and scratched my balls. Better to be certain. You wouldn't want your little boy to get sick from bad germs, do you?"

He dropped my hand and entered the house ahead of me. I closed the door and pulled the curtains in place before turning around. To find Ari completely naked and smiling cheekily at me.

What little desire for sleep remained vanished.

"Will you wash me, Daddy?" he asked.

"I'll do more than wash you. I'll lick you and make love to you the way you like."

"Ooh, I like the sound of that. Hurry! Hurry!"

He dashed toward the stairs with me after him. I'd never get ripped, but Ari and I went for walks in the evenings. It was one of the many things we did together, and after two years, I was happy with the results. For one, my improved stamina in bed made it worth it.

Ari was already in the shower when I entered the bathroom. I'd stopped to get the lube from the night table. I shrugged off my pajamas and entered the shower.

"Give me your hands." I took his hands and washed the dirt off them with soap. Then I did the same to his body. My hands glided over his taut skin, his chest, stomach, and down the length of his cock. I washed his balls and his feet before I turned him around and started on his back.

"You promised to lick me," Ari gasped.

I licked down his spine. "Like that?"

"Daddy, don't be a tease."

I grinned and dragged my tongue down his spine. I grasped his ass cheeks and licked first the left, then the right. "How about that?"

"Getting closer."

He reached behind him, swatting my hands away, and pulled his cheeks apart. "Right there. Right there, Daddy. Lick my hole like you promised."

"So impatient."

I went down on my knees behind him and circled his spot with my tongue. Ari hummed in the back of his throat as I made good on my promise and played with his ass the way he loved. He was a moaning mess by the time I rose to my feet and reached for the lube. I slathered the liquid down my dick, then grasped his hips and pushed into his body.

"Hnnng." A shiver running through his body.

I caught his right leg and lifted it, shifting until we were properly positioned for me to pump into him. Ari braced his hands on the wall, his cries of abandon bouncing off the walls.

"Fuck, yes, yes."

"You love that, don't you? You've wanted it for so long, and now it's all yours."

Ari dropped a hand to grasp his cock, his arm jerking fast with each stroke. I pegged his prostate, hitting that same spot over and over. It'd been two whole years of this, and I still couldn't get enough of this boy.

"Ari," I groaned his name, unable to keep the torrential downpour away any longer.

So much for improved stamina.

Ari grunted, stiffening, and his hole tightened around my girth. I surged deep inside him, grinding my pelvis against his ass as I nutted inside him. I allowed him to lower his leg and pulled out of him.

"You could give sex lessons, you know." He swayed against me as I passed the washcloth over his sensitive cock, then his ass.

I chuckled and kissed the spot behind his left ear. "You're biased because you love me. Come on, let's get out of the shower."

"I totally mean it." I helped him out of the shower and reached for a towel to dry him off. "You read me so well. You always know when I'm aching for a sweet love making and when I want you to pound me so hard my ass is sore."

"That's all on you. You become a brat when you want to be fucked hard."

He giggled. "I suppose I do."

In the bedroom, I dressed him before I put on a fresh pair of pajamas. I returned to the bathroom to hang the towels and re-entered the bedroom.

"If you can't—" I stopped and stared at Ari, who was down on one knee in front of the bed. He had a black velvet box with the top pulled back to reveal an engagement ring.

"Ari."

"Hear me out," he said. "At first I thought I'd wait for you to propose, then it got me thinking. I didn't wait for you to love me back. I fought for our love, and now I'm willing to fight for forever with you. Please marry me, Shaw. You're good for me. I know I've done a lot and I'm still learning about me, how to solve conflicts — Shaw, you're not answering!"

"Because you won't stop talking." In a couple of steps, I closed the distance between us. "I love you, and you never have to fight for me. I'm yours. Of course I'll marry you."

"Yes!"

His hand shook slightly as he slipped the ring onto my finger. He was nervous about this. I caught him by the waist and pulled him into me.

"Did you think I was going to say no?"

"I couldn't tell. I've been wanting to do that all day. It might be the reason I couldn't sleep."

"There's only a yes with you, baby boy."

I cupped his face with my hands and kissed him. It didn't matter what he did, he would always be a yes for me.

Thanks for reading Daddy's Stepstalker. If you enjoyed this book, I'd be grateful if you would consider leaving a review on Amazon. You can also preorder the next book in the series, Daddy's Adorable Assassin.

Acknowledgments

Thank you so much dear reader for reading my book, and I truly hope you enjoyed it. I could not have completed this book without the love of my patrons. This story was originally written because they expressed a burning interest in this story of my little deviant boy and the man who captures his heart.

Thanks to Irish T Hill who originally beta-read this story when it was written in episodes. Thanks also to author Ashlynn Mills who encouraged me to let my freak flag fly and keep the kinks in which these characters expressed an interest.

My final beta-readers, Lori Martini, Janet Hunt, Porsha Johnson, and Julie Braley, thanks for the extra eyes on this manuscript. I truly appreciate your efforts.

Gianni

BECOME A GEM

I HAVE A VIBRANT Facebook group that all readers are welcomed to join. I share lots of teasers, book covers, and author friends stop by for giveaways and parties. Looking forward to having you join us at Gianni's Gems.

Also By

Standalone

Ginger Kisses

The Love Permit Series

Let Me Love You

Let Me Hate You

Let Me Remind You

Taking Care Series (Daddy Kink)

Take Care of You

Take Care of Me

Take Care of Us

Mother's Day Special

Father's Day Special

Secrets & Scandal